Pressing her cheek to his lips, Raina inhaled the lingering scent of his aftershave, seconds before hungrily capturing his seeking lips. Several minutes passed and still they stood there kissing passionately, rooted to the spot near the window. There, Nick and Raina started down a path of no return. No more watching the other walk away unfulfilled and unsatisfied; no more longing, craving, and yearning to touch and be touched by the other. This was it. This was now and there was no turning back.

"Nick, I'm warning you. Don't you get me all hot and bothered and even think about leaving me hanging. I don't think I can let you walk out of here tonight." And she wouldn't just let him walk out either. Not when the line had been crossed again and definitely not when her dress lay on the floor . . .

CROSSING THE LINE

BERNICE LAYTON

Genesis Press, Inc.

INDIGO LOVE SPECTRUM

An imprint of Genesis Press, Inc.
Publishing Company

Genesis Press, Inc.
P.O. Box 101
Columbus, MS 39703

All characters in this book have no existence outside the imagination of the author and have no relation whatsoever to anyone bearing the same name or names. They are not even distantly inspired by any individual known or unknown to the author and all incidents are pure invention.

ISBN: 13 DIGIT : 978-1-58571-412-4
ISBN: 10 DIGIT : 1-58571-412-7
Manufactured in the United States of America

First Edition

Visit us at www.genesis-press.com
or call at 1-888-Indigo-1-4-0

DEDICATION

To my husband, Derrick and my daughter, NaTiki, thank you for your ever-present love and encouragement. It is with your constant support and guidance that this book has come forth. Your steadfast belief has been the basis that convinced me to pursue writing. I'm so fortunate and Blessed to have you in my life.

I also dedicate this book to the men and women of the Police Departments all over this country. You bravely put on a uniform to serve and protect us, and I thank you.

With warmest regards,
Bernice Layton

ACKNOWLEDGMENTS

As always, thanks go out to my family and friends. I thank you for your love, support and feedback. Your encouraging words, cards, calls and emails have been wonderful. I cherish you all in my heart.

Special thanks to my mom, Susie. She inspired all of her children to pick up a book and read. She still has plenty to read herself. So, Mom, just add this one to your "to be read" stack.

To Danise (Lu) . . . thank you so much. We made such a great team on this project. Your honest and funny review has made this book happen. I will always remember (and keep) those bright pink pages! Thanks to you, *Raina* stopped those darn tears—well, most of them! I'm still LOL about that and I can't wait for you to review the next draft, and the one after that. I can truly see you in the literary field, "Auntie."

To Angie and the "Nurses," what can I say? You guys have been so supportive and true "fans" every step of the way. I hope you like this book as much as you've continually expressed how happy you were with *Promises Made*. I am truly honored.

To Wenda Royster goes a special thank you. You put my voice on the radio and gave me wonderful advice.

To Deborah Schumaker, Executive Editor, and the rest of the staff at Genesis Press, Inc., thank you so much for your guidance and expertise. To Mavis Allen, thank you for your review and edits. Hope you like the finished product even better! If I have forgotten anyone, please know that I thank you, too!

CHAPTER 1

Raina sat back in disbelief.

No way did Leon just dump me.

But that's exactly what happened just five minutes earlier. Raina stared down at the $100 bill Leon had placed on the table to pay for the check. They had only ordered wine and he had eaten a few breadsticks before she had arrived. But his message was clear—they were finished. Still, she couldn't believe how it happened. Mainly because it was her intention to tell him tonight that it was best they go their own ways before wasting another week in their seven-week friendship.

But Leon had beaten Raina to the punch. She looked down at her freshly manicured nails, wondering why she had even bothered to dress up for the date—that wasn't a date at all. It was Raina who usually did the breaking up, not the other way around. In any case, she was glad she would no longer have to feign work, a headache or whatever she came up with to get out of a date with Leon. Still, she couldn't believe he had broken things off with her first.

Glancing around the small Italian restaurant, Raina saw only two other customers. She recognized them both. Mr. Coates, an attorney who worked on the fifth floor of the building where she worked, and his date, Rachel, the flirty receptionist from the lobby.

Raina wasn't surprised to see that Rachel had latched onto another man in a suit. She didn't really dislike Rachel. She just didn't like her flirtatious, up-in-your face ways. Just look at that dress, she thought, eyeing the crinkle fabric with distaste.

Raina caught hold of her judgmental thoughts and looked down at her own short, form-fitting sheath dress. But she knew exactly why she had worn it tonight, along with her new designer shoes. She also knew why she had spent an hour getting a manicure and pedicure at her favorite salon. She wanted to show "Leon the Loser" exactly what he was not ever going to get. She recalled his bulging eyes when she'd purposely arrived late at the restaurant for their date tonight. Raina had never dressed to impress, or worn runway-worthy makeup for her casual dates with Leon before.

As Raina drummed her manicured fingernails on the red and white checkerboard tablecloth, she realized she had wasted her time . . . and on a weeknight, at that. Yeah, sure she wanted Leon to see her dressed to the nines, and then some. That's why she had stopped at the hairdresser's to get her shoulder-length brown hair styled into wavy ringlets that bounced when she walked, or rather strutted, and that's exactly what she did upon entering the little restaurant. Her satisfaction was the look on his face. Grinning now, Raina recalled how Leon almost tripped over his big feet when he stood up and held out a chair for her. "Yes, he did that, but then to turn around and flipped the script." Raina realized all was not lost. She'd gotten a chance to wear her brand-new stiletto sandals—complete with black and purple polished stones and beads, including the straps, circling her shapely ankles. Raina loved them.

A shadow fell on her table, causing her to put an end to her musings. Raina smiled when the restaurant owner presented her with a warm smile of his own. "Hi, Mr. Antionelli."

"Ms. Raina, did your boyfriend leave?" the little man asked in a soft, Italian-accented voice. Actually, he had seen the man leave.

"What? Boyfriend? Who, him—Leon the Loser?" Raina waved her hand toward the door. "Oh, please, Mr. Antionelli, he was just an acquaintance. That's all he was."

"I see." The small man wasn't fooled. He'd been in the restaurant business for over thirty years and he'd seen a lot of things. Some celebrations, some resolutions, and he had also seen some breakups. He knew this was the case. "Well, Ms. Raina, I'm glad Mr. Loser was nothing more than an acquaintance. His loss, I say." His eyes brightened. "But you look much too pretty to just sit there with breadsticks. Tell you what, you just relax and I'll bring you a treat from my kitchen."

Raina knew she hadn't fooled him. He knew exactly what happened at her table tonight. "A treat, huh?" She picked up the $100 bill from the table and handed it to him.

"Oh no, Ms. Raina, Mr. Loser only ordered house wine and breadsticks, only $10." But when Raina refused to take the money back, he beamed. "Well, okay then, I'll just go fix you up a wonderful dessert of my choosing." He spread his hands wide. "As you can see, it's not busy at all, and you'll give me something to keep me busy for a few minutes. How 'bout that?"

"That would be wonderful, Mr. Antionelli, and please, add chocolate to whatever you fix for me, even if it is pasta. But I'm going to the ladies' room and I'll be right back." Raina stood up when he held her chair out. Then she surprised Mr. Antionelli by hugging him to her small frame, whispering, "Thank you for being so kind."

Mr. Antionelli was touched. "Yes, yes, I'll add lots of chocolate just for you, Ms. Raina, but not to pasta. I think cake," he said, scrambling off to the kitchen.

When Raina neared the table where Mr. Coates and Rachel were dining, she gave a curt nod and would have continued on her way, had Rachel's loud squeal not stopped her.

"Raina! Oh, I just love those shoes." Forgetting all about her date, Rachel stood up to get a better look at Raina's shoes. "And they look expensive, too."

To Raina's dismay, Rachel wasn't letting the issue drop. "Thanks." Raina didn't want Rachel to go on about the shoes or, for that matter, how much they cost. She was somewhat embarrassed by how she was dressed, thinking her flashy dress was no different from Rachel's. "I was on my way to the ladies' room, if you'll excuse me . . ." Raina said, stepping around Rachel.

Rachel glanced at her date, Bill Coates, then grabbed hold of Raina's arm. "He's making a call on his cell phone. I'll just go to the ladies' room with you and maybe you'll let me try those fabulous shoes on. Girl, they look comfortable, too."

CHAPTER 2

Nick Laprelli was an eleven-year veteran police detective with the Pittsburgh Police Department. In those eleven years, he had seen it all and had heard it all. But lately, he'd heard the ass-chewing he was currently getting from his sergeant and lieutenant far too many times.

Damn. I really screwed up, he thought. He had messed up a six-month investigation . . . all because he'd gotten distracted by the hot babe with the mini leather skirt that laced up the back. Absently, Nick wondered if it really was a bootlace like she had told him. Unfortunately, that hot babe was the reason he had become distracted at his post, and now the very reason his superiors were still raking him over the hot coals—forty minutes later.

"Laprelli, are you listening to me?" Lt. Brown's voice blew over Nick like a bullhorn.

Cringing, Nick thought the man didn't know the meaning of "inside voice." Everything Lieutenant Lyle Brown said was a loud, disruptive order to one's ears. Nick even thought the man purposely drew his voice up from his enormous chest, just because he could.

Sitting up in the chair, Nick coughed. "Yes, sir. I'm listening, and like I said, I'm sorry about this mess-up. But, that woman . . . um, what's her name, Sergeant?"

Nick looked imploring at his sergeant and friend, Dennis Walker, for assistance.

Sgt. Walker stood several inches to the left of Lt. Brown and forced a blank expression onto his face. It was his usual expression, calm. He ignored the pleading look Nick sent him. But after a couple seconds, he flipped open the file in his hand. "Ah, yes, her name is listed as Miss Mandy Sweets, or Cheeks, or something like that." Dennis now fought hard not to laugh at the pained expressions crossing both Lt. Brown and Nick Laprelli's face. "Possible typo in the report," he said, then added, "Happens sometimes."

Exhaling audibly, Lt. Brown's eyes rounded on Nick again. "Right. Miss Mandy Sweets," he said, rolling his eyes at the sergeant before boring into Nick again. "Tell me, Laprelli, was that her regular beat, or is she new to work that block?"

Nick swallowed, and for some reason, he couldn't stop thinking about that damned laced-up leather skirt. "Sir, I honestly don't know. I've never seen Miss Cheeks, I mean, Sweets, before tonight." Sweat began to collect under his shirt. For sure, he was going to be fired tonight, and if that happened . . . well, that would be a damned shame. The only bright side if that did happen, he thought, would be his free ticket to kick Dennis's ass without suffering the repercussions for striking a superior officer. The look he sent Dennis said exactly that.

Lt. Brown saw the look. "Laprelli, stay focused! Could this Miss Sweets have been a plant sent there for the purpose of distracting you from your post tonight?

You remember, you were positioned there to apprehend that weasel, Ryan, making the transfer of the drugs for cash. You know—the drugs your snitch said he cooked up in his mama's kitchen? Tell me, Laprelli, did you see anything, anything . . ." Lt. Brown's voice bellowed again over Nick, louder, ". . . other than Little Miss Mandy Sweets . . . Cheeks, ass, whatever it is?" Catching himself and reining in his anger, Lt. Brown snatched the file dangling from Dennis's hand.

Nick winced. Had it not been for the fire-spitting red eyes of Lt. Brown slicing into him, he would have laughed at what the man had said. Nick would have sworn the man's usual pale blue eyes turned black for a few seconds as he glared down at him. He had no answers. He was tired and hungry, and knew with certainty the night was far from over. Still, he had no excuse whatsoever for his lapse in judgment. He screwed up . . . plain and simple. Now his job . . . his reason for getting through each day, could be stripped from him. *Damn.* His light gray eyes jerked over to the lieutenant's ringing telephone.

Three rings . . . Lt. Brown continued to glower down at Nick before finally snatching up the handset and barking into it. "What?"

Nick watched a tightening of Lt. Brown's lips and the vein in his neck started to relax. Nick sensed the call was the order to terminate him, right there on the spot.

Lyle Brown didn't break eye contact with the detective as he listened to the caller. His focus was more on Nick Laprelli than the caller after the first few seconds.

Nick was one of his best detectives, but lately, he had tested his patience with his screwups. But Lyle also knew that Nick was still grieving the loss of his partner of five years. What was originally believed to have been a boating accident was later discovered to be a homicide. Lyle knew Nick blamed himself, but he was also aware that Nick was slipping in his game. The man had lost his focus.

Suddenly, Lyle returned his attention to the caller. "Yeah, get on it. Thanks." Hanging up the phone, he watched Dennis cross the room to stand next to Nick's chair. He guessed Dennis assumed the call was the order from downtown HQ to suspend Nick Laprelli.

That's exactly what Nick read in Lt. Brown's expression and stance. He, too, didn't miss Dennis's move. Nick could only rub his hands on his jean-clad thighs. He would bet that last six-pack in his fridge he was being fired tonight. "Lieutenant, listen . . ." Nick stood up.

Lt. Brown cut him off mid-sentence. "Shut up and sit down, Laprelli," he said, pointing to the phone. "That was a sergeant over in the Third Sector. His guys happened to see Ryan heading up Lister Avenue with a black duffle bag thirty minutes ago. The same black bag you didn't see in the transfer that occurred during your unfortunate distraction. They have a fix on him." Lt. Brown crossed his arms across his chest, watching a smile slide across Nick's face.

Nick did smile, and clapped his hands. "Okay, so we're back in business, right?" Nick was jubilant, looking from Lt. Brown to Sgt. Walker.

"No!" both men bellowed at Nick.

Nick frowned. "What do you mean, no? Come on, let me go back out there and finish this investigation. Ryan's at his homeboy's place on Lister Avenue. They're splitting everything up right now. Sir, I've put six months of legwork into this case, please let me finish it and lock up his stupid ass." Nick grinned. "I'll even throw in his mama for aiding and abetting. After all, she let Ryan cook up his drugs in her kitchen, and on her new stove."

Ignoring Nick's plea, Lyle picked up the case file from his desk and tossed it at Nick. "You're off the case. But what I do want from you right now, Laprelli, is a full accounting of your screwup tonight," he said, pointing at the file now in Nick's hands.

Nick experienced an odd sense of reprieve. He wasn't being fired. "Lt. Brown, I don't have a problem with doing a report on, well, what didn't happen tonight, but the case isn't finished yet. Sir, let me stay on the case until Ryan makes his next contact." Nick knew he was pushing it, but didn't want off the case.

Pursing his lips, Lyle sat on the edge of his desk, and when he spoke, he didn't holler. "If you've misunderstood the word no, Detective, then let me make this perfectly clear—you are off the case and, trust me Nick, you go anywhere near Lister Avenue or Ryan's mama's house, and I'll personally bust your butt down to a traffic cop . . . downtown, during rush hour." He stood up from his desk and walked to stand just twelve inches in front of Nick. "You understand me, Nick? You listen up. You seriously compromised this case because you've spent far too much time working around the clock. That won't bring your partner back. Look, we all miss Scott, and understandably, you're still grieving the death of your partner and friend. Because of that, your focus is off. So much so, you let Little Miss Mandy get in your space and blindside you. I'm not risking that again."

Nick knew there was no point arguing. It was a done deal. The file dangled in his hand. Yes, he was still grieving the death of his best friend, but why did Lt. Brown have to mention it? Why did anybody? With nothing more he could say at that point, he turned toward the door, which he now realized had been open the whole time. That meant everyone in the outer offices heard him getting chewed out again. Not cool . . . not cool at all. He turned back to Lt. Brown. "Thank you for not firing me, sir. I do know that was an option for you."

Lyle was now sitting behind his desk. A sardonic smile etched onto his face. "And it still is, Detective." He pointed to the file in Nick's hand. "I want it thorough, Laprelli. Leave nothing out of that report, not even Miss Mandy's cheeks, or your obvious fixation with them."

Nick sauntered over to his desk in the area assigned to detectives and investigators. His eyes briefly strayed to Scott Morgan's empty desk. Sitting down at his own desk, he rubbed his tired, gritty eyes. On some level, he was thankful for not getting fired tonight. Otherwise, he would go crazy for sure. He would have even more time to dwell on the circumstances surrounding Scott's death. Nick pushed the thoughts from his mind as someone cautiously slid a cup of hot coffee and a box of donuts onto the edge of his desk before slowly backing away. That confirmed it. They all heard what went down in the lieutenant's office. Nick looked up to see Detective Len Stubbs's wide grin.

"Hey, Nick, tough break, and yes, we heard," he said, nodding toward the group of officers over his shoulder. "You'd better get to that report, it's going to be busy in here tonight."

"What's on schedule, Len?" Nick asked.

Len hitched his thumb in the area where two large benches lined the back wall of the unit. "Ladies of the night are going to get some rest," he said, grinning at Nick's groan.

Nick understood. The Vice Squad was in the midst of a sting, and that meant the station house would be fired up tonight. As part of investigations, new and old, the vice officers often went out and picked up the prostitutes and brought them into the station for questioning. For the most part, it was just to see what, if anything, they knew about anything going on out in the streets. Nick knew Len was right. It was going to be a busy night. And before long, those now-empty benches along the back wall would be crammed with ladies as they sat handcuffed to each other, complaining and whining. Wincing, he prayed Mandy Sweets wasn't one of them.

Flipping open the file he had slapped down on his desk, Nick heard snickers and looked up to see Len walking over to his own desk . . . everyone patting him on the back. Nick realized that Len Stubbs had pulled the short stick. He also noticed that everybody was still watching him above their computer monitors and partition walls. He knew they were all wondering if he was going to verbally explode or break another keyboard, both of which he had been known to do. Tonight, he did neither. Instead, he just lifted his coffee cup, nodded his thanks, and turned to his computer.

Raina left the ladies' room while Rachel was still inside fussing with her hair. She would have headed back to her table, but her attention was drawn to a private dining area beyond the main dining room of the restaurant. She had never been beyond the ladies' room, so the back wall of the private dining room, where several paintings hung on walls, immediately captured her attention. She wondered if the paintings were of Mr. Antionelli's hometown in Italy. She recalled him telling her about his village at one time or another.

Raina wasn't aware of how much time she had spent admiring the paintings. Truth be told, she was delaying going back to her table. Shrugging her shoulders, Raina turned to leave the private dining room when she heard a sound.

Zip. Zip.

Hearing the muffled popping sounds, she stopped in her tracks. Startled, and thinking something was happening out in the main dining area of the restaurant, she hurried her steps across the small dining area. But, seconds before her hand pulled on the door handle to fully open it, she glanced through the bubble window at the top of the door. Raina's eyes zoomed in on a tall man in the main dining room. He was standing just a few feet in front of Mr. Coates's table.

Raina couldn't really make out what he was saying, but her instincts warned her not to leave the safety of that private dining room. Next, she watched the man lift a gun with a silencer and aim it at Mr. Coates. *Zip. Zip.* Two quick shots were fired, one to the man's forehead and the other to his chest. The blood dripped from the hole in his forehead and ran down his shocked face, onto his shirt. There, the bloodstains grew larger with each passing second.

With her breath caught in her throat, fear had paralyzed Raina absolutely still. Then instinctively she dropped down to her knees to crouch just behind the partially opened door. She didn't dare attempt to close it, fearing the shooter would turn and come her way.

That's when she heard another commotion. It was Rachel finally exiting the ladies' room, complaining and asking loudly what all the noise was about.

Raina stole a glance just as Rachel breezed down the short hallway heading toward the restaurant's dining room. At that exact moment, the well-dressed shooter walked toward Rachel.

Oh, God . . . No, Rachel, don't! Raina could do absolutely nothing to warn Rachel. She had to force her hand over her mouth to stop from crying out when the man extended a gloved hand to Rachel. He then tugged on her hand, bringing her further into the dining area. He was smiling.

At first, Rachel sent the man a flirtatious smile, but then she turned and stared in shock at a dead Bill Coates. Next, her wide eyes flew to a figure lying on the floor, near the kitchen.

Raina's wide eyes followed Rachel's. It was then she spotted Mr. Antionelli dead on the floor. He was clutching a plate of chocolate cake to his chest. Raina realized the first two muffled shots she had heard must have been when the shooter killed Mr. Antionelli.

Much too late, Rachel realized the situation. Her sudden piercing scream lasted only a second before she too fell to the floor. In horror, Raina had watched the man raise his gun to Rachel's temple and pull the trigger, sending blood sprays across the front wall and curtains.

Watching the horrific scene play out in the restaurant, Raina cried silently, fear clutching her. Swallowing hot tears caused a burning sensation that forced her into action. From her crouched position behind the door, Raina's eyes frantically scanned the private dining room.

Looking back at the wall of paintings, Raina remembered there was a side door . . . probably used for deliveries to the restaurant from the back alley. With one last look back into the dining room, she watched the man drag Rachel's lifeless body and lift her to a chair. Then she watched as he pulled out a digital camera and took a picture of the couple—sitting in their seats, at their dinner table, dead.

Oh, my God, he's a psycho killer.

Without delaying another second, Raina put the strap of her small purse in her mouth and crawled on her hands and knees to the door, all the while praying that it led outside to the alley. Craning her neck up, she saw the door was unlatched from the inside. All she had to do was turn the knob. Part crawling, part crouched to the floor, she did just that and, to her amazement, the door was unlocked. Turning the knob and opening the door slowly, Raina felt the warm June night air hit her face. Glancing back for half a second through the partially opened door, she could see the man looking in the direction of the private dining area. Realizing he must have heard her, Raina wasted no more time crawling out the door and into the alley. There, she slowly and quietly eased the door closed behind her.

She was out—out into the dark, silent and deserted alley. Standing up, she removed her purse strap from her mouth and flattened her back against the metal door. Perspiration covered her forehead and ran down the sides of her face. Fear cloaked her. Deciding it was okay to breathe, her breath came out in gasps and, for several heart-stopping seconds, she was too afraid to do anything else.

Frantically looking around to get her bearings, Raina spotted a metal chair and a grease can to her right, and guessed that's where the employees took their smoke breaks. One look into the grease can, and Raina was disgusted. The can contained hundreds of cigarette butts. The stench from it alone was enough to make her gag. It was then she heard a noise from within the restaurant, and an idea quickly formed in her head. The only question was whether or not she could pull it off.

Raina quietly lifted the metal chair and eased it under the door knob. That should hold for a few minutes, she thought. Then she looked at the chair, doubtful now. *Well, it works on TV.*

Her eyes went back to the grease can containing the cigarette butts, then up at the door again. There was an encased light fixture above the door. Raina's plan was, if she could lift the grease can up to that box, and the killer came out into the alley, it would fall down on him. Hopefully, the sand and ash would spill into his eyes, and she would be long gone . . . that is, once she made it out of the long alleyway. It was a chance she had to take.

Dropping her tiny handbag to the ground, Raina picked up a wooden crate and placed it on the seat of the metal chair. Then using her upper-body strength, she was able to lift the grease can and stand up on the wooden crate. It was then she heard movement behind the door, instantly stilling her movements. Holding her breath, she stared down at the door, praying for it not to open. When she heard the movement again, she realized it was further away from the door, and probably in the dining room. Raina heaved the grease can up to the edge of the box, all the while being careful not to catch the heels of her shoes in the openings of the wooden crate, then she eased her feet down to the metal chair, and finally down to the ground.

With sweat covering her face, she crouched on the ground to pick up the few items that spilled from her purse when she'd tossed it to the ground. Suddenly, her eyes flew to the doorknob. Ever so slightly it moved, just a fraction of an inch, but Raina saw it. She knew at that moment, the killer was on the opposite side of the door. Her eyes trailed up the metal door. She could almost sense the anger from the well-dressed killer on the other side.

Raina kept her eyes on the doorknob as she grabbed up her purse, then took off running down the alley. She ran on the balls of her feet, ever mindful to keep the noise of her shoes to a minimum. *Darn beads.* Maybe it was the stillness of the night or her absolute fear, but to Raina, all those beautiful beads and gems that embellished her designer shoes seemed to echo loudly in the quiet alley. In any case, she ran harder and faster to get farther away from that metal door.

She never heard footsteps behind her. She could only pray that the man did not follow her as she exited the alley and stepped up onto the curb. Her next dilemma was how to get to her car. It was parked one block down from the restaurant.

Raina knew the area well; with her back against a brick wall, her eyes panned around. The quaint and quirky little shops that sold everything from beauty supplies to clothing, eateries and antiques shops, were all closed. Raina glanced at her watch. It was eleven forty-five, almost midnight. Not a safe time for a woman alone on the streets.

But Raina was no fool. She knew she had to get out of the area. She didn't think for one minute that psycho killer wouldn't get in his car and drive up and down the alley or the main road for the sole purpose of looking for someone who might have seen what he had done. The vision of Rachel being shot clouded her eyes, forcing Raina's feet to move faster toward her car.

Walking at a fast clip, her eyes darted all around her. The beads and stones on her shoes were still awfully loud. *No, that is just my imagination.* When she heard a loud clank somewhere behind her, Raina shrieked and dared a quick glance back to see a business owner pulling down a gate over his shop window. The humid night reminded her of those scary movies she'd dared to watch on occasion from under a blanket. At any second, she expected a swirl of thick fog to circle her ankles.

Finally, she made it to her BMW. In one swift move she had unlocked the door with the automatic key lock and slid behind the wheel. She cringed when the alarm beeped to unlock the door. That, too, seemed loud on the quiet, desolate street. She wasted no time in relocking the door and inched her body very low in her seat. Reaching up, she tilted the rearview mirror to look back at the Italian restaurant. The place looked closed if anyone walked by. The heavy wooden blinds had been drawn, and the sign hanging on the door, now read "Closed." To any passerby, that wouldn't be an unusual sight to see, because the restaurant normally closed at midnight. Only Raina knew that the killer had turned that sign over to show it was closed, and he must have closed the blinds as well.

Barely able to see over the steering wheel, she eased her car from the curb. She didn't even turn on her headlights, fearing the killer was perhaps looking out the restaurant's window. Easing her car around the first corner, Raina drove on for three blocks before she felt safe enough to sit up, or even turn her headlights on. Only then did the enormity of what she had witnessed hit her.

"Oh, my God." Raina's entire body began to shake uncontrollably. She had no idea where she was driving to. Tears blurred her vision, but she could still see the dead bodies of those three people, whom she realized she would never see again. Hot tears fell to her cheeks, as silently as she drove her car further away from the area, and away from the horrific scene she had witnessed.

CHAPTER 3

He never carried out a job he didn't finish completely, and he never left a witness. He prided himself on being swift and efficient. Everything had been planned right down to the time of execution. So what had happened tonight, he wondered, pursing his lips in agitation.

Standing in the alley, only his eyes moved. He saw nothing other than a stray cat searching in a nearby trash can. Brushing at the cigarette ash clinging to the sleeve of his suit jacket, his dark eyes took in the mess of spilled cigarette butts, ash and sand laying at his feet, and the chair that had been wedged under the knob. Someone had rigged that up. He expelled a breath. Someone had been in that back room, and instead of running out in fear, that person took the time to rig up a contraption to come crashing down on him. Clever, he thought.

If he was not so pressed for time, he would have laughed at the ingenuity of the person who did that. By always thinking ahead, he'd missed that grease can from crashing down on his head. But it did catch his right shoulder. Still, he'd been distracted by having to take out two other witnesses. An unexpected event . . . first, Bill Coates should have been dining alone. It was something he did every Monday night. It was the least busy night at the restaurant, and second, the restaurant owner should have been in the back, busy stocking the shelves from that afternoon's delivery. The two waiters left at eight, and the daughter wasn't expected to return until twelve-fifteen to help her father close up.

Time was of the essence. He pulled a handkerchief from his breast pocket and swiped at his soiled shoes. Spotting a card on the ground, he bent down and picked it up. A library card. Aside from the ash sprinkled on the card, it was clean. There was no dirt or smudges, as if it had been recently dropped to the ground. It contained only a bar code, no name. Someone else had been inside the restaurant in that back room, and with a certainty he knew that person had witnessed what he had done.

Slipping the library card into his jacket pocket, he went back inside the restaurant. He always took a piece of the victim — one pinky finger — which he kept for his collection. Within three minutes, he had slipped back out of the restaurant the same way he came in . . . quietly, unseen and through the side kitchen door.

Raina didn't even realize where she was until she pulled up at the curb of the familiar building. Numbly, she stared up at the police station, about two miles from the restaurant. Frowning, she wondered how her unconscious mind brought her there. In her haste to get away from the restaurant, she'd not even thought to contact the police initially. After pulling her car onto the parking lot designated for visitors, she stepped from her car on shaky legs.

Raina looked around as officers came and went for the midnight shift change. Smoothing down her short dress, now wrinkled and smudged, she then ran a trembling hand over her hair as she climbed the stairs, taking her inside the station house.

It had been a long time since she had been to this, or any other, police station. For a few minutes, Raina did nothing more than just stand there, taking in the familiar sights and sounds. Her eyes followed several officers passing her, but she didn't recognize any of them. But then, why would she, she thought, not having been in this particular station since she was a teenager.

Pulling in several nervous breaths, she walked the few feet to stand in line at the service desk, and ran a trembling hand over a mop of brown hair. Her earlier bouncy waves and ringlets were long gone, stolen by perspiration, tears and humidity. Her stomach tightened as she watched the hub of activity of shift change. The midnight shift began ten minutes ago.

"Next," the desk sergeant called out to the young lady next in line. "Miss, step forward, please," he said, in a deep, commanding voice.

Raina looked up over the five-foot-high desk, instantly recognizing the sergeant calling out to her. To her surprise, he smiled broadly, recognizing her.

"Raina . . . Raina Wade, is that you? Come on over here, young lady." The desk sergeant's authoritative voice dropped immediately to a friendly one upon recognizing her.

Raina quickly stepped up to the desk. It was Sgt. Fisher. He had worked under her father, former Chief of Police Michael Wade, until he retired ten years ago. Raina was so delighted to see Sgt. Fisher that she reached up to grasp the hands he extended over the five-foot counter. "Officer Fisher, it—it's so nice to see you. How are you?"

Sgt. Fisher had seen Raina come into the police station many times before as a teenager. He could recall many times when she, along with a couple of classmates, would make a beeline to the station to see her father after school. But tonight, this all-grown-up Raina, despite her greeting and dress, looked downright scared to death. "Well, I'm fine, Raina. What's wrong?" he asked, standing up and leaning over the high desk, noticing her hands trembling within his.

With renewed tears sliding down her caramel cheeks, the scene back at the restaurant materialized behind her eyes again. Before Sgt. Fisher could round the counter as he had intended to do, Raina blurted out, "Officer Fisher, please help. I—I just saw a crazy man k–kill three people, execution style. In a matter of minutes . . . they're all dead." Raina's body sagged against the counter, weakened from having to say aloud what she had seen. She was mildly aware that Sgt. Fisher had let go of her hands, yet she wasn't aware that her words or sobs had drawn the attention of several police personnel who were behind the desk with the sergeant.

Lt. Lyle Brown and Sgt. Dennis Walker had been two of the people behind the desk, and now their attention was fully focused on the young woman. Both looked on as the desk sergeant left his post . . . but they, too, heard what she'd said and so followed him.

After pumping water from the watercooler, Lt. Brown passed it to the young woman and then suggested they all go into one of the front offices.

Raina gladly went with the men, fearing her legs could no longer hold her body upright, despite Sgt. Fisher's comforting hand on her elbow.

Once she was sitting in the office, Sgt. Fisher introduced Lt. Brown and Sgt. Walker to Raina. When he told them she was the daughter of former Chief Michael Wade, both men stared at Raina for several seconds. Each was well acquainted with her father, who remained a respected and well-liked former official.

Sitting across from Raina, Lt. Brown asked her to tell them what happened.

Raina left nothing out. She told them in exact detail and then gave them the address. She glanced up at Sgt. Fisher, keying up his police radio and dispatching police to that location. When each of the senior officers fired off question after question, Raina answered each in as much detail as she could.

In a span of only two minutes, the call came back on Sgt. Walker's radio confirming there was indeed a triple murder scene at the restaurant. Raina heard several patrol officers responding, mentioning something about the posed victims and a missing finger of the obvious male target. She knew what all the police call codes meant, and she didn't miss their anxious exchange of glances.

A civilian employee, a female, walked into the office carrying a laptop and began setting it up on the desk. Police radios began transmitting and exchanging urgent dialogue. Police sirens echoed in the backgrounds of those exchanges, reminding her of her father, years ago. When Lt. Brown asked her to describe the man, Raina left nothing out.

Closing her eyes for several seconds, she recalled what she could about the killer before she spoke. "I only saw him in profile, from his right side. He was white, with a square jaw. His hair was dark black and very neatly trimmed and was combed to the left, slightly crossing his forehead. He was attractive with sharp features . . . narrow nose, high cheekbones and thin lips. He looked tanned. He was tall, maybe around five-eleven, but his build was slim, but solid. His upper body looked muscular, like he worked out. From what I could see, I think he had a very thin mustache." Raina ran a finger across her own upper lip. "He wore a tailored black suit, which he wore well, like that's how he usually dresses. The lengths of his pants and jacket sleeves were expertly tailored for him. He had on a white dress shirt with French cuffs, and he wore gold cufflinks, with intricate designs on them. Not initials, but oh, maybe an insignia. His shoes were expensive, and his heels were even, so that his body weight was even, as was his stance. He wore black leather gloves and they were new." Raina looked up at the three men again, noticing their perplexed expressions at her detailed and precise description, and explained that she worked in the clothing business. "I'm certain his suit was tailored and I'm positive his leather gloves were brand new. There were no worn patterns on them from repeated wear, and he flexed his hands a few times, to loosen them a bit. He fired the gun with his right hand and he used a silencer." She looked up again at the men. "Afterwards, he pulled his glove back to look at his watch, perhaps designer, as well." Suddenly feeling uneasy, almost lightheaded, Raina pulled in a slow breath. Something about the man was tugging at her memory. "Something else about him captured my attention. I'm not sure what or why, but it somehow makes my stomach tighten." Drawing in a breath, Raina was uncomfortable recalling the killer's actions. "I–I can probably pick him out of a sideways lineup or give a description to a sketch artist," she said.

Seeing her trembling return, Sgt. Walker left the office, returning seconds later with another cup of water for Raina.

Lt. Brown turned to the female civilian, the sketch artist who had been drawing on the laptop as Raina was describing the killer. She handed him a document from the printer she had connected to her laptop.

Lyle Brown looked down at the picture. His blue eyes met Raina's chocolate-brown ones. "Ms. Wade, is this the man who killed those people tonight?" He turned the profile sketch around and held it before her widened eyes.

Her answer was severe.

Raina took one look at the picture, leaned forward and gagged—throwing up nothing but water and breadsticks onto the floor. Profoundly embarrassed, she accepted several tissues from the men. "I'm so sorry." Raina was beyond words as fresh tears pooled in her eyes. "Oh, God. Yes, that's him."

Lt. Brown took Raina's hand. "It's okay, Ms. Wade. I believe you witnessed a hit man at work, and this man is not new to the PPD. What is new to us is that we've never had a witness who could describe him as you have," he said, passing the picture to the sergeant.

Raina knew exactly what he was saying. With renewed fear, she flopped back against the chair. "What you mean, Lt. Brown, is that he has never left a witness. At least, not one who could describe him. In fact, what you are about to say is that now my life is in danger. Is that fair to say, Lt. Brown?" Raina refused to cry again despite the enormity of the situation.

Lyle had to remember that she wasn't just any witness. She was the daughter of a former police chief. And only he knew also that Raina Wade's uncle, Max Coleman, was the current chief of detectives. He was Michael Wade's stepbrother, and both had obviously taught her well, familiarizing her with police procedures. "I won't lie to you, but yes, that's fair to say. But, Ms. Wade, we are here to protect you. Please trust that." He watched as Sgt. Fisher crossed to her, holding her in his arms.

"I do trust that, Lt. Brown, but I know if a hit man wants to knock off a witness, he can do it . . . with or without police protection," Raina said firmly, meeting his unwavering blue eyes.

Lyle watched this young woman in a new light. She was smart. "As I said, I won't lie to you. But I'll be back.

You stay here and relax." He turned to the female civilian, Jackie, and asked her to get Raina a cup of tea from the administration office off the lobby.

Before leaving, he asked the two sergeants to join him. Raina didn't miss their worried glances before they left. She knew more was going on than what they had told her, but at that moment she couldn't concentrate on anything, as fatigue was claiming her limbs.

A few minutes later, Raina accepted the cup of tea from Jackie and smiled weakly at the janitor cleaning the floor before her. With her nerves as raw and as tight as her aching stomach, Raina allowed her mind to drift back on the scene at the restaurant and, once again, her heart ached for poor Mr. Antionelli. She knew his wife and daughter were going to be distraught, and poor Mr. Coates, and Rachel, she would never see again. That was the one and only time Raina could ever recall talking to Rachel for any length of time. And why was that, she wondered?

But she knew why. She didn't allow herself time to get to know people . . . she didn't have the time. In her role as a mentor and part-time drawing instructor, Raina was introverted and reserved. But Raina also worked full-time as an associate manager for a clothing designer/distributor. Actually, she was more than that. She handled most of the business's administrative work, much to the appreciation of her boss, Mimi. At work, she was so busy she had little time to socialize.

She thought about how she had dressed tonight in the short, flashy dress. It wasn't her habit to dress like that, and the makeup she'd painted on her face was definitely not her, either. But the shoes, well, she had a thing for cute shoes. Looking down at the beaded stilettos now, Raina didn't think she would ever wear them again. Gulping down the now lukewarm tea, she shivered. What her body needed was more cold water.

Raina left the office and spotted the watercooler in the corner. There, she pumped water into her cup several times, draining each cup. Intense grief and sadness engulfed her. Reaching into her purse for her cell phone, she decided to call her Uncle Max. "Oh, I don't believe this," she murmured, seeing that her cell phone battery was dead. Not one bar on the small screen showed life. Looking around beyond the reception counter, she spotted the sectioned-off area where the detectives, investigators and vice unit officers were located.

Somebody over there had to have a cell phone charger. Before she could head that way, Sgt. Fisher came over to her, so she dropped her cell phone back into her purse.

"Raina, we called your father, and of course, he is concerned and worried about you. Now, I have assured him that you are safe," he said, patting her forearm. "Raina, I also want to tell you that just before the police arrived, the owner's daughter had returned and the killer had already left. The daughter was dialing 9-1-1 as the officers entered. She reported she'd just arrived to help him lock up, and she found that awful scene." Sgt. Fisher shook his head sadly, as did Raina. "Listen, dear, as you told Lt. Brown yourself, your safety is in danger now. Please be very careful of everything and everybody,

Raina," he whispered, grasping her hand. "Come into Lt. Brown's office and call your father."

Raina touched his hand. "Okay, but I would prefer to call him out here, if you don't mind." Watching Sgt. Fisher walk back into Lt. Brown's office, Raina dug into her purse for her cell phone again. "Of all the times for my battery to die, why now? I just don't believe this night." Getting up and crossing over into the sectioned-off area she'd spotted previously, Raina became aware of how busy that part of the station was. But it was all familiar to her. Wincing inwardly, she spotted the prostitutes sitting together on the benches along the back wall. She guessed the police still went out and picked up the prostitutes for questioning. But Raina was thrown for a loop when she recognized one young woman in particular and immediately walked over to her. "Julie . . . wh—what are you doing here?" she gasped, sitting down on the bench beside the young woman.

Julie Webster was the 22-year-old sister of Janey Webster, the 15-year-old student Raina was currently mentoring. Julie frowned up at Raina. "Me? What are you doing here, Raina?" It didn't escape her notice how Raina was dressed or her glittery eye shadow and fading ruby red lips and cheeks. "I, um . . . well, I don't think we're here for the same reasons, Raina," she said, lifting her wrist, handcuffed to the woman on her left.

Realization hit Raina like a splash of cold water. "Julie, oh my God, you're hooking. Honey, why are you doing this to yourself? What about your sister, Janey?" Raina was grasping Julie's hands.

"Raina, I'm doing this for Janey. I'm her only provider, and your little mentoring program down at the church doesn't pay the rent to stay in our apartment, keep the lights on, or buy us food." Julie attempted to pull her hand away, but Raina was holding firm.

"Julie, that's no excuse to do this. You should have told me that things were tight at home. That mentoring program has grants to help out, and you know the church helps everyone in need. You know this because the church has helped your family before." Raina recalled the church members rallying around the two sisters when their mother, a long-time church member, became terminally ill and died over a year ago. That's when Raina immersed herself in the church's mentoring program and, for eight months now, she had been a mentor to Julie's younger sister, Janey. Shaking her head sadly, Raina could only mumble, "I wish you had talked to me, Julie. What you're doing is dangerous, you must know that."

Julie did like Raina. It was because of her that Janey was doing so well in school. "I'm sorry, Raina, but I couldn't. Things just got tight after Mom died, and, when the insurance ran out, more bills kept coming in. I did what I had to do, but I'm very careful and Janey is doing okay."

"Oh, my God. Where is Janey now? Does she know about what you're doing?"

"Raina, you just saw her on Saturday, remember? She's spending the night with Jasmine and Dawn, studying for that math quiz. She knows I'm dancing down at the club after work, and, Raina, that's all I'm really doing, nothing more." Julie was unable to say anymore because a vice detective came over and escorted her and the woman to whom she was handcuffed to an interrogation room in the back. Julie shouted back that she would call Raina tomorrow.

In a state of shock over what Julie had been doing, Raina gave no thought to her own situation . . . the psycho killer in that restaurant. That thought forced her to look down at the cell phone still in her hand, reminding her that she needed a charge to call her father or uncle.

Raina looked over to the designated unit again and spotted several plainclothes officers working. Her eyes zoned in on the desk of one detective. His cell phone sat on his desk and looked similar to hers. *I'll just ask him for a five-minute charge.* Raina walked over to his desk and waited patiently for him to finish reading a document.

Nick Laprelli had spent an hour on his report. He was more than a little distracted by the ruckus the women on the bench made. His eyes had flitted over one woman in particular while she chatted away, holding hands with another. Of all the other hookers, she stood out, although Nick couldn't say why, but he'd glanced up more than once to look at her.

He was just about to sign the report when his eyes dropped to the floor and saw a pair of beaded stilettos strapped to sexy feet. He thought they looked like the shoes the hooker he'd been looking at had had on.

Nick tried to concentrate on reading the last line of his report. It was the line in which he again apologized for compromising the investigation. He mumbled without looking up, "Forget it, sweetheart, go peddle it someplace else. I'm busy and I'm broke, but I like the shoes."

Raina was astounded. She went through several emotions, outrage being the first to come to mind over the detective's crude words. "Excuse you! What the hell did you say to me?" she finally shrieked, then sputtered in indignation. And still he had yet to look up at who he had addressed so offensively. "How dare you say something like that to me? Hey, you jackass, I'm talking to you!" With eyes blazing, Raina was spitting fire. If she'd had a bat, she would've cracked him on top of his arrogant, oversized head with it. And that's when she advanced on him. "Who do you think you are, talking to me like that, you idiot!"

Only when he felt her move threateningly toward him did Nick finally look up into the red face of the hooker with striking eyes and sexy body. His first thought was that she was beautiful, and he sat back in his chair looking up into her angry face. His second thought was why wasn't she sitting on the bench, handcuffed like the rest of the hookers? Shaking his head slightly, he slowly enunciated, "Well, I said I was not interested in purchasing any of your services. Is that better, sweetheart?" Nick spoke as he stood up, aware that others were watching him and the hooker. He turned back to pick up his report and mumbled, "Oh, yeah, and I also said I was broke and I don't pay for it. But, honey, I do love those shoes, though." Nick said pointing his papers toward her shoes and gave her a sarcastic smile. That was a bad mistake on his part.

Raina was beyond angry. She was fuming mad. Her instinct was to slap the perfect smile from the detective's smug face. And with lightning speed, that's exactly what she did. The sound was extra loud in the absolute quiet of the Detective/Investigators Unit. The sound vibrated with a snap off the walls of the station house, sounding like a firecracker.

When Nick stumbled back in shock, his chair crashed to the floor, and that brought several officers to their feet. Some now stood flanking him, but two patrol officers came forward and physically restrained Raina just as she was about to pounce on the detective again. It didn't help matters that the prostitutes were in an uproar, cheering, stomping their feet and egging Raina on, chanting, "Pop him again, girlfriend," and "Yeah, drop-kick his butt."

Just seconds before, a meeting was taking place inside Lyle Brown's office. Amongst the assembled group, a district major, Sgt. Fisher, an administrative lieutenant, Lt. Brown, and none other than current Chief of Detectives Max Coleman. They had just completed a conference call with Raina's father, Michael Wade, in Seattle. Her father had one request, and pulled in a favor after being apprised of the severity of the situation. He knew his daughter's life was in peril if she could identify the renowned hit man the PPD had named Pierce. Michael Wade wanted his daughter out of Pittsburgh and in Seattle, Washington, with him as soon as humanly possible. Max Coleman promised Michael he would do all he could to protect Raina, because, after all, she was his only niece.

"Okay, Lyle, we need to get her out of here. Raina's life expectancy is dropping by the minute if she can positively ID this Pierce character. And we know it's likely him because he left his calling card, Bill Coates's missing pinky finger." Max blew out a breath. "Damn. If he has any idea that she witnessed his hit and can ID him, we all know she'll be dead in a matter of hours." He looked around at the faces that nodded in agreement with him. "And we all owe Michael this favor." Max watched each man nod in agreement again. Yes, they were all thankful for the clean-up work Michael Wade did to bring together a unit of detectives who were well-trained and upheld the law. His weeding out the bad apples and replacing of officers had been a model used for every police district within the PPD. "We have to protect Raina around the clock, and there is no room for a screwup whatsoever." Max set his gaze directly on Lyle Brown. His order was direct, and there was no margin for error. "Lyle, who do you have that can provide protection 24/7 and get her to Seattle?"

Lyle's blue eyes widened, but he didn't get a chance to answer. In that exact moment, the commotion in the outer office caused the men to stand up and look out through the half-glass wall toward Nick Laprelli's desk. There, they saw the detective mouthing back at Raina Wade. Lyle Brown and Dennis Walker exchanged a look, to which Lyle grinned behind the backs of his superiors. "Say, Chief, I've got just the officer we need for this assignment . . . he'll be perfect."

Max Coleman watched the fire coming from his niece, whom he loved dearly. He could only imagine what she was telling the detective. He had not seen her in three months. Not since she stormed from his house following another argument about his estranged relationship with her father. Max shook his head because watching that fire-breathing little thing at that moment reminded him of that argument he'd had with her about the ongoing clash with his brother, Michael. She'd told him that both he and her father were stubborn, pigheaded old fools. Hearing Lyle, Max turned away from watching Raina to see Lyle tilt his head to the outer office toward the commotion.

Max's eyes zeroed in on Nick Laprelli, then back at Lyle. "You have got to be kidding, Lyle. Tell me you don't mean Laprelli out there? He just totally screwed up a six-month investigation. Are you crazy, man?" Max asked incredulously.

Lyle cleared his throat. "Trust me, he's the best detective I have, and despite what happened tonight, or what didn't happen tonight on that drug transfer case, I'll vouch for him. I assure you, Laprelli is the man for this assignment." He ended as they all turned and looked back out through the glass wall, and saw a fighting mad Raina being physically restrained by two uniform officers. Nick was about to slap a pair of handcuffs on her.

In that instant, Max Coleman left the office and stormed across the lobby with the other men in tow. As soon as he reached the sectioned-off unit, he bellowed out across the area. "Take your hands off of her, Laprelli!"

Max wasn't about to see his niece in handcuffs, even if she did just strike an officer . . . she was his baby niece.

Nick came to attention at the command and immediately let go of the woman's wrists.

When Max Coleman sent a threatening look to the uniformed officers, each immediately let go of a no-longer-struggling Raina. Max turned to Raina with open arms. Her fear and anger was etched onto her small features. "Hey, baby."

Raina had stopped her squirming the moment she heard her uncle's bark. Without any hesitation whatsoever, she ran into his outstretched arms and was immediately engulfed in a blanket of security and love. Her hands circled his waist tightly. "Max . . ."

At that point, no one moved. With all officers standing at attention, everybody looked on in astonishment at their chief and the hooker, embracing.

Nick's questioning eyes captured those of Lt. Brown and Sgt. Walker's. Since his superior gave him a direct order, he wasn't about to question it. But it was obvious to everyone the chief had a hot, sexy hooker on the side. Nick's eyes reflected as much.

Lyle sensed what Nick was thinking and suggested they all go back to his office.

Max passed Raina his handkerchief. "I'll be right in. I need to speak to Raina alone." Max kept his arm around her and redirected Raina to a private office near the reception area. He needed to explain the gravity of the situation to her and was already gearing up for her arguments and refusal to leave town. But first, he was going to grill her about her manner of dress, or lack thereof, and the makeup on her face.

Once inside his office, Lyle cut to the chase. "Laprelli, you finished that report?" He watched Nick craning his neck to ogle back to the private office before turning back to him, with wide, unbelieving eyes.

"Report?" Nick let out a laugh, but caught the intense look he got from his lieutenant. "Yes, sir, it's finished. I was just about to sign it when she," he said, hitching his thumb back at the outer private office, "propositioned me. So I called her on it, told her I wasn't interested, then she slapped me." Nick turned, aware that the chief and the hooker were standing in the opened doorway. He waited until they were both inside the office before he finished talking. "Anyway, with that slap, she assaulted an officer and I plan on charging her accordingly, and it shouldn't matter who she is. That's what I think, sir." Nick purposely avoided eye contact with Chief Coleman. Besides, the man seemed only to have eyes for his girlfriend, keeping his arm around her slim body.

Lyle intervened and spoke up before Nick really was fired tonight. "Laprelli, you will rethink that course of action. You see, you incorrectly pinned Ms. Wade here as one of those prostitutes out there, and you were wrong, dead wrong." Lyle turned to Raina. "Ms. Wade, please accept my apology for Detective Laprelli's obvious mistake."

Raina only glared at the arrogant detective, as much as he glared back at her. It had become a staring contest for several seconds, as neither was backing down. That is, until Raina turned her back in an effort to ignore his gray eyes piercing into hers. "Max, I want to leave. Please, can I go home now?"

Nick snorted, rolling his eyes at her back. *Mistake, my ass. No mistake.* His action wasn't missed by his superiors, especially Chief Coleman.

Max's eyes clashed with Lyle's. "Remember your vow, Lieutenant, and I appreciate your discretion. That assignment can begin at 0800 tomorrow morning." He turned to Raina. "I'll take you home, honey."

Lyle nodded. "I'll take care of everything." He walked the chief and Raina to the door, where they were escorted to the garage by Max's personal security officer. Only then did he close his office door and turn to Nick.

Nick had been exchanging glances with Dennis. When Lt. Brown returned to his desk, Nick did laugh. "I can't believe what just happened. Chief Coleman has a hot babe on the side." He snickered. "So much for the secretive Max Coleman," Nick said, grinning until he met Lt. Brown's narrowed gaze. "I'm sorry, sir. I didn't mean any disrespect, but, come on . . . I know you're shocked as well."

Lyle grinned inwardly. "Guess what your next assignment is, Detective Smartass?"

Nick sobered immediately. He was back in. "I'm hoping you've reconsidered your previous position and put me back on the Ryan case." Nick sat in the empty chair by the desk.

Lyle pursed his lip before responding. "Wrong again, Detective Smartass. Your new assignment is to protect, serve and babysit that young lady who smacked the hell out of you out there . . . the one whose hand mark is still imprinted on the right side of your face."

"What?" Nick jumped up, then caught himself and sat back down. "Sir, a babysitting job is for one of those patrol officers out there." He pointed to the outer office. "Besides, Lt. Brown, you know my hands are full. I've got cases backed up, one of which is set to go to trial in a couple of weeks. I'm still prepping for that." Nick had the urge to punch something, someone, especially the two men patiently staring back at him.

"Don't worry about your cases. I'll get them covered, but you're on this case effective 0800 tomorrow morning. But there's more." Lyle got up and walked around to sit on the edge of his desk. He weighed his next words, knowing the impact would be shocking for Nick. "Earlier tonight, Ms. Wade witnessed a triple homicide, and she gave a full and detailed account of what happened. By now all that is confirmed. Nick, the hit was carried out by Pierce."

Nick's body went completely still, but his breathing accelerated measurably. Then, on reflex, he stood up quickly and backed up against the wall. He ran a hand over his close-cropped black hair. The elusive Pierce was suspected in the murder of several people, including Nick's former partner, Scott Morgan. It had become Nick's personal quest to catch the previously unseen hit man. Recovering from his shock, Nick let out the breath he'd been holding. "Are you sure she can ID the man we've pegged as Pierce?"

Lyle nodded. "She not only gave a complete description of his profile, but she filled in some blanks, lots of them. As you can imagine, Ms. Wade's life is seriously in jeopardy and I, along with Chief Coleman, well, we're entrusting her well-being into your hands, Laprelli." Lyle picked up the drawing from his desk and passed it to Nick. "Here's what the sketch artist came up with after we talked to her."

Nick studied the profile sketch. It was detailed and could have been an actual sideways picture and not a sketch artist's rendition. By all accounts, Pierce would be considered a handsome man . . . not the monster he had conjured up in his mind. His eyes zeroed on the picture. "She sure this is him?"

Dennis spoke up then. "She was so sure she upchucked the moment she looked at it."

Nick glanced at the drawing again. "Then she's a walking target. How'd she get away?"

"She told us how she'd rigged a chair under the door and put a cigarette can up over it. That is, after she had managed to sneak out. We don't believe the killer ever saw her." Lyle shared a look with Dennis. "There's more, Nick. We need you to get her to Seattle before anything happens to her."

Nick tore his eyes up from the drawing with a sinking feeling in the pit of his stomach. "Okay. What else?"

"You're going to see that she gets there, unharmed."

"Okay, I'll put her on a flight to Seattle. Not a problem, or is it?" His headache began.

"You're going to escort her there." Lyle watched Nick's eyes darken measurably.

41

"Escort her there?" It suddenly dawned on Nick exactly where Seattle was located on a map. "Wait a minute, you mean Seattle, on the other side of this country, where it rains all the time?" Nick asked incredulously, his lips tightening, causing his bottom lip to pout slightly.

"Ah, yeah, that would be the one," Lyle said, nodding.

"Sir, I–I can't do that. Besides, I have that conference in Las Vegas coming up at the end of the week. I can't miss that, Lieutenant."

"You'll miss it."

"Lieutenant, I–I can't miss it. This conference is important, you know I need these certification hours, not to mention I've already paid out two grand that's nonrefundable." Nick looked pleadingly to Dennis for help. He didn't get it.

"Like I said, you'll miss it. But I'll arrange for someone to go in your place and I'll put in a refund request to reimburse you the two grand. Laprelli, she needs to be out of here and in Seattle as quickly as possible."

Defeated, Nick dropped down heavily into the chair. His fight was over and he knew it. He was fuming mad and couldn't express it. "And what's in Seattle, another official ready to protect his girlfriend?" He bit out in frustration.

His superiors eyed each other levelly. But Dennis cringed, knowing his friend was skating on very thin ice with his insubordination.

"What's in Seattle is former Police Chief Michael Wade . . . Ms. Wade's father. I believe he was the training officer you worked under in the Twelfth Precinct." Lyle watched Nick's mouth slack open. "So, I see you do remember the name. Good. Now get out of my office, bring me that report and then go home. I'll call you on your cell phone with the particulars." He watched Nick get up and walk to the door and then spoke again. "Laprelli, if you screw this case up, then, just like they say on that TV show, you're fired."

Nick met his Lieutenant's stern glare. "As in fired, you mean from this precinct? Just so I'm clear."

"Wrong, Detective Smartass, as in fired from this police department, in this state, and if I have anything to do with it, in this country. Is that clear enough for you?"

"Yes, sir." Nick started to leave again, but stopped. "Oh, who did Pierce hit tonight?"

Both men knew that Nick knew the owner, Antionelli, and each hesitated to answer him.

The sinking feeling hit the bottom of Nick's already knotted stomach. "Who was it?"

Dennis walked over to Nick, and placed a hand on his shoulder and explained what happened at the restaurant. "We know Pierce doesn't leave any witnesses, and that's why it's imperative we protect Raina." He patted Nick soundly on his shoulder. "Go on home and get some sleep, Nick. You've been on duty since five this morning."

Hearing Dennis, Nick nodded. "Did he cut . . . ?"

"Yes."

Without another word, Nick walked out of the office, closing the door behind him.

Lyle held up his hand, stopping Dennis from speaking. He had heard it all before. "Yeah, yeah, I know. He's pissed right now, but, Dennis, you and I both know that Nick is coming apart at the seams. He hasn't dealt with Scott's death, and I think the time away from here will do him some good." Both men watched Nick returning to his desk, looking as if he'd lost his best friend, and they knew he had.

Dennis chuckled. "Did you catch the looks that passed between Nick and Ms. Wade?"

"Whew, did I? She'll either rip him to shreds or have him eating out of her hands by the time they get to Seattle." Lyle looked thoughtful for a moment. "Serves him right for his smart mouth. Also, Dennis, I don't want Nick snooping around now that a picture of Pierce exists."

"But Nick could be back here within a day, so how long are you talking about?"

"I want him gone for about a week while this Pierce thing is hot. If he returns in a couple of days, assign him to the Eighth Precinct for a week or so. They always need help down there. Or send him on some field training somewhere."

"Okay. Another thing, what if Pierce finds out, or already knows, there's a witness? We know with certainty he'll go after Ms. Wade."

Lyle closed his eyes briefly. "I know, but I do trust Nick. He'll be careful, but I'll remind him to take extra precautions when I call him later. I'll also steer him to ask her key questions. Remember she said she couldn't recall something that could be significant to the case. I'll have him nudge her a little to jar her memory." Lyle stretched him arms up and cupped the back of his head, noticing the worry lines creep back onto Dennis's forehead. "Ah, come on, Dennis, stop stressing over Nick. He's going to be okay. I think this assignment will be good for him, trust me."

CHAPTER 4

The following morning, Raina was safe once again in the comfort of her condo, having spent the night with her Uncle Max, his wife, Debra, and their two recently adopted preteens, Troy, age nine, and Kira, age eleven. Raina was desperate to feel secure, and the instant she saw her uncle last night, she knew he would keep her safe. He always did, just as her father had done.

When Max took her to his home, Raina was flooded with memories of times long ago when her uncle and her father were still on speaking terms. The family photos displayed throughout Max and Debra's home showed those happier times. Last night, they treated her like she was fragile, but then that's how Max and Debra always treated her . . . always loving, always kind. She liked Debra a lot and, although she was almost seventeen years younger than Max's 57 years, they were still deeply in love.

The kids were entrusted to the Colemans by Debra's longtime friend, who had died just a few short months earlier. Raina could see the kids were already adjusting well to living with Max and Debra. Between the four of them, they'd protectively watched over Raina throughout the night, especially after she'd awakened sobbing hysterically. She could smile now, remembering waking to find Kira sleeping in the bed with her.

When Max had brought her home to her condo just an hour ago, Raina was more than a little surprised to see one uniformed police officer posted in her lobby and another one outside her condo door. It brought back what he'd told her at his house last night. Her father wanted her in Seattle with him, and he was going to make sure that happened. Max had even called her employer, Mimi Tenner. It was a done deal. When Max spoke to her father, Raina sat by listening to their conversation. It was very police-like, not like concerned brothers at all, and that saddened her.

For the past twenty minutes or so, Raina was on the phone with Mrs. Wilson, the coordinator of the mentoring program at her church. An intervention was planned after Raina explained the situation concerning Julie Webster. That was another reason Raina was so distressed. She saw Janey every week and many times she saw Julie, too. Yet she didn't have a clue that Julie was in such trouble, or had sunk so low that she thought prostitution and club dancing were her only means of financial support. That had to stop immediately, and Raina was going to do everything in her power to make that happen.

Raina was pulled from her musings when her doorbell rang. At any other time, she would have just walked over and opened the door. After all, she lived in a secure building where a concierge was stationed in the lobby. Yes, she felt quite safe there. But then Max's words rang in her head. "You witnessed a professional hit man at work. If he finds out about you, he will come after you with one goal in mind, killing you. You're the daughter and niece of police, and neither I nor your father has ever cloistered you from the harsh reality of this world we live in, so you must be extra careful; watch everybody." He also reminded her that she'd made it out of that restaurant by being resourceful and smart, and then ordered her to stay that way.

Raina shook off the feeling of apprehension and looked through the peephole. The officer smiling back at her was named something Dixon. When she arrived home that morning, he'd told her that if he needed her, or if anybody stopped by, he would ring the doorbell first, then step back so that she could see his face. She smiled looking through the peephole and watched him grinning. Absently, she thought he had cute dimples in his cocoa-brown cheeks. She let him in.

Raina had put a pot of coffee on while Max and Officer Dixon searched her apartment. She had forgotten she'd told him she would bring him a cup when it finished brewing.

"Thank you again, Officer Dixon. The coffee is ready. I'll get you a cup."

"Oh, that's not necessary, ma'am. I just wanted to let you know the second shift officer is here and on his way up, so I'll be leaving shortly," he said.

"Well, I can still get you a cup of coffee to go. I have tons of those travel mugs, and fresh cranberry muffins, too. Actually, I have too many, so you have to accept." Turning, she walked through her large living room, to the kitchen. "Oh, how do you take your coffee?" she called out from the kitchen.

"Cream and sugar . . ."

If Raina thought Officer Dixon's voice sounded different, more nasal, she didn't comment on it as she prepared a travel mug of coffee, then wrapped a muffin in tin foil for him. When Raina walked back into her living room, she pulled up short when she came face-to-face with the sarcastic, smart-mouthed detective she'd had a run-in with last night standing in her living room. He was looking at her like he was angry about something, as if he had any right to be.

"W—what are you doing here?" she hissed hotly.

Nick Laprelli's lips tightened. He could not believe he had to babysit this princess. Lt. Brown had made it perfectly clear that not only was Ms. Wade's life in his hands, but so was his job. And there was no error margin on this assignment. He was being forced to get her to Seattle. Hell, why couldn't her sugar daddy do that? Sourly, he simply stared into her tight, angry face. A beautiful face, he thought absently.

"I asked what you are doing here, Detective?" Raina asked, stretching her arm, presenting Officer Dixon the mug and the muffin. Her eyes never leaving the detective's face.

Henry Dixon avoided as much eye contact with Nick Laprelli as possible. He could tell Nick was not happy. Still, he struggled to keep a straight face, which was hard to do, since Ms. Wade was so much nicer to look at. That is, until she walked out of the kitchen and came face-to-face with Laprelli. "Thanks, ma'am. I appreciate the coffee, since I'm working a double shift today," Henry said, ignoring Nick's smirk.

"I'll see you later then," Raina said.

"No, you won't see him later," Nick mumbled, shifting his eyes to the patrol officer. "You're late for roll call for your next shift, aren't you, Henry?" Nick said sarcastically. He knew that Henry had just come on duty last night and heard him getting chewed out over the bad Ryan bust.

Checking his watch, Dixon said, "You're right. See ya, Nick. You take care, Ms. Wade." He made a hasty retreat to the front door, closing it quickly, just as his laughter rang out and echoed in the hallway.

Raina stared after him. "What do you mean I won't see him later? Why won't I?"

"He told you. Your second shift is here . . . that, unfortunately, would be me, Ms. Wade." Nick thought she was even more beautiful with her hair braided down her back and wearing a T-shirt and jeans. Gone was the skimpy dress and glitzy makeup. In her bare feet, she was shorter than she'd looked when she slapped him the night before. But then she'd had those sexy shoes on. Nick bristled at his thoughts.

Raina huffed and crossed her arms across her chest. "What are you talking about?"

Nick broke eye contact and walked around her, crossing the living room to look out of the fifth floor condo's window. "It's good these front windows don't have ledges. No access to them from the outside."

"Thanks for pointing out the obvious. I also have a private balcony off the bedroom, if you must know. Now back to my question." Raina watched him walk around her living room. She didn't like it, him, or his attitude.

"Ms. Wade, I have been assigned the task of getting you to Seattle. And guess what, there's a flight that leaves at six-thirty tonight." Nick extracted two blue envelopes from his jacket pocket, waving them. "Our tickets. We're already booked."

"The hell we are. You can forget that. I'm not going anywhere with you!" Raina retorted, and, stomping past him, snatched up her cordless phone from the coffee table and dialed her uncle. "I'll make sure of that, Detective." She watched him cross his arms across his chest and just stood there watching her as she spoke into the phone. After being told that Chief Coleman would return her call shortly, Raina clicked the phone off, returning the detective's defiant stare.

Nick grimaced in an effort to control his rising frustration over the situation that forced him to be here. This assignment was just Lt. Brown's way of putting him in his place. Nick wished for the hundredth time he'd kept his big mouth shut.

Raina rolled her eyes at him just as the cordless phone rang in her hand. "Hello. Hi, Max . . ." Turning her back to the arrogant detective, she walked into her bedroom. "Max, please tell me why that detective is here telling me that he has been assigned to take me to Seattle? Please tell me this is a mistake." Raina's voice rose loudly in protest.

Max had expected Raina's call after what he'd seen at the station last night. After telling her that the detective would take care of her, Max also warned that he expected her to be on her best behavior. Hearing her sucking her teeth with exasperation, he reiterated, "You hearing me?"

"Yes, I hear you, but I mean, why him? You know that idiot cop thought I was a hooker trying to proposition his dumb ass last night. Oh, and did I tell you what he said to me?" She was primed to recount, once again, what happened when she approached the detective's desk.

"Yes, you did, two or three times already." Max didn't think he could stand another retelling. "But, in his defense, that dress you had on and those shoes, well . . . they were a bit much, dear. You blended with those hookers, honey. Anyway, give him a chance. He's a little rough around the edges, but then you know how us idiot cops are, right?"

Raina grinned, thinking back when her uncle had asked her why she'd dressed like that for a date with someone she referred to as a loser.

"Okay, but only because you're such a sweetheart, Max. I'll be on my best behavior. Happy now?" She smirked at the phone.

"I am," Nick said. He was leaning against her bedroom doorframe, slurping a cup of coffee.

Raina whirled around in surprise and stared at the detective for several seconds. She couldn't believe he had the nerve to walk back to her bedroom. Her uncle's voice forced her attention back to the phone, but her eyes remained on the detective. He was drinking coffee from her autographed Pittsburgh Steelers mug. "Okay, Max, for you, I'll deal with this arrogant jerk and I'll call you as soon as I get to Seattle. Bye." She clicked the phone off. She was livid that he was practically in her bedroom and had eavesdropped on her phone conversation.

"I'm glad that you feel so comfortable and free in my home to fix yourself a cup of coffee and walk back into my bedroom," she said with a fast wave of her hand in the air.

"I should tell you that I also ate a muffin. I heard you tell Dixon you had way too many of them. Maybe you should freeze them." Nick ignored the evil curl of her lips. Actually, he thought she looked cute, and obviously so did Max Coleman, whom she thought was a sweetheart.

Raina pointed in the direction of the living room. "Take your ignorant ass out of my bedroom before you find this cordless phone embedded in your inconsiderate face!"

"Oh, well, then Ms. Wade, I will charge you with assault, and I don't care who your daddy is." Nick chuckled at her reaction and sipped his coffee. "We need to talk. Put some shoes on and join me in the living room." It wasn't a request.

Raina watched his retreating back and only for a second did she think about throwing the cordless at him. She paced at the foot of her bed. There was no one she could call. Max had made his point clear. *Think, who can I call to get another bodyguard?* Nobody came to mind. No point in calling her father, either, because he would only agree with Max.

Raina plopped down on the edge of her bed and stared at her bare feet absently, remembering the combo manicure/pedicure she had gotten yesterday before her date. She frowned when Leon popped into her mind. Okay, she reasoned, one flight to Seattle could take almost seven hours or longer. That was way too much time to have to spend with that detective, even if he did have nice eyes.

Looking up sharply, Raina wondered where that thought came from. "Oh, no, I'm not even going to get caught in that trap again," Raina mumbled. It was Leon's eyes that captured her attention in the first place. "Once a fool, but twice, just call me stupid," she mumbled.

After making a quick phone call, she left her bedroom.

Nick had returned to the living room and was reviewing documents in a thick file he had brought with him. One document was Ms. Wade's account of what happened at Antionelli's restaurant. He read it again while waiting for her to come out of her bedroom.

Nick glanced around the condo. It reflected an expensive taste. Beautiful furniture and impressive paintings adorned the walls. One picture, mounted above the fireplace captured his immediate attention. Intrigued, he got up from the couch to take a closer look at it.

To his surprise, it was a painting of Mica Antionelli himself. He was sitting at a table in the restaurant with the familiar red and white checkerboard tablecloth. The small man was sitting with two large pots on the table and a large brown paper bag on his lap, frowning. It was a scene Nick had seen so many times. His brow was pulled tightly as he concentrated on his task. Nick knew the man was picking something. It could have been peas or beans or nuts. "No, I'm sure it's peas," Nick said aloud, raising his hand to touch the painting, grief piercing his heart.

"You're right. Mr. Antionelli was picking green peas," Raina said, having returned to the living room to find the detective engrossed in the painting.

Nick turned to her. "How do you know that, Ms. Wade?"

"Because I was there." She saw a shadow cross his face. "Do you know Mr. Antionelli?"

"I knew him," Nick said, stressing the past-tense status with a tilt of his head.

"Oh. He was a nice man. He and I talked last night just before he went to fix me a . . . ah, special dessert. And I'm pretty sure he would have sat down with me and made sure I ate all of it, too." Without the ability to rein in her emotions, tears pooled in Raina's eyes. She couldn't help but remember talking to the old man last night, or that he'd died clutching the chocolate cake to his chest.

Nick turned back to the painting. "Well, it's a nice painting. I don't know much about art, but whoever did this really captured Mica as I'll always remember him."

Dabbing at her eyes, Raina asked, "How did you know him?"

"The area used to be on my beat years ago. I helped out there, and I also dated his daughter," Nick said, running his hand along the ornate frame. It, too, was a work of art.

"Maria . . . do you know that she found him last night, just before the police arrived?"

Returning to the sofa, Nick nodded. "I spent most of the morning with her and her mother." His eyes dropped to her bare feet. "No bunny slippers?" He figured she would probably have a pair of those kind of slippers.

"I'm fine, but I desperately need a cup of coffee," Raina said, walking into the kitchen and fixed a cup of coffee. Was it her imagination, or did his cologne linger in her kitchen? When she returned to the living room, Raina carried the coffeepot with her and refilled his cup. "You like that painting?" Raina asked, sitting down in a comfy chair.

"Yes, I do. Where did you get it?" Nick watched her sit down, tucking her bare feet under her bottom. Again, he thought she was pretty . . . very pretty.

"I painted it about six months ago." She watched his dark eyebrows lift in surprise. "I was having a late lunch and had some time to blow off, so I started sketching. I looked up to see Mr. Antionelli come out of the kitchen with those large pots and a big bag of peas. Next thing I knew, I was done sketching."

"He was probably going to make his pea soup. It's a house special most nights," Nick said, sitting on the couch adjacent to her chair.

"Yes, I know, because later that night I returned to get a large bowl he saved for me." Raina noticed his eyes stray to the painting again, sensing it was special to him. "You can have that painting, if you'd like."

"Oh, no. I don't want to take your picture. It obviously has sentimental value to you."

"I painted two of them from my sketches. I gave the other one to Mr. Antionelli. He told me he loved it and was sending it to his home in Italy." Raina sipped her coffee, then said, "I won't force it on you, but if you change your mind, let me know." She looked up from her cup, thinking it was the least she could do, and found him now studying her.

"Well, you're very talented, and thanks for the offer." Nick had to force himself from looking at her and steer the conversation to more pressing matters . . . the investigation of the hit from last night, and pressing her for more details to jar her memory. Nick already had a copy of the preliminary reports and was anxious to pursue leads. "I wanted to talk to you about last night. I read the report and your statement, but I want to hear it from you. I'm sorry to have to put you through it again, but if you don't mind . . ." Nick's plan was to escort her to Seattle, then return to Pittsburgh and step up his search for Pierce, now that the trail was hot again. Now that they had a sketch of the killer, he expected things to heat up quickly. He resented the delay in having to go to Seattle first.

Raina let out a breath and told him everything she had told his superiors the previous night.

"You were having dinner rather late last night, weren't you?"

Raina toyed with her braid. "I had a dinner date. It ended and Mr. Antionelli came over and we started talking. I really wasn't aware of the time and I hadn't planned on staying long enough to have dinner anyway. So when my date left, I decided to stay." Sensing he wanted her to elaborate, she added, "I was comfortable and I was really looking forward to the dessert that Mr. Antionelli was fixing for me in the kitchen, okay?"

"Your date, a boyfriend?" Nick asked, watching her pull in her bottom lip.

"No, just an acquaintance," she said, frowning. Leon wasn't even that in her mind.

"What's his name?" Nick looked down at a document. "I didn't see it in the report."

Raina snorted, with agitation. "Leon the Loser, and he didn't make it that far to be included in the report, Detective." She wished she had never planned that date last night.

Nick nodded. "He dumped you, huh?" He couldn't imagine any man dumping her.

Raina was thrown off by his assessment of what had happened to her. "No! He would've had to *have* me in order to have dumped me. Actually, Detective, I dumped him, as an acquaintance, if you must know, and if it is any of your business, anyway," she huffed.

"So what's his real name?"

"Why? He was, and still is, insignificant."

"Well, maybe he saw something that *was* significant, Ms. Wade."

"Well, he didn't. He left ten minutes before . . . things started to happen," she said.

Nick could see she was getting upset and backed off. "Okay, Ms. Wade, for the next few hours I need you to trust that I will do everything to protect you, but I need you to . . ."

Raina rubbed her forehead. She knew the speech by heart. "Yes, I know the drill. You want me to be careful and watchful, take no chances, and all of that, right?"

"Right." Nick studied her for several seconds. She was frightened. She had reason to be.

Raina looked at the crystal clock on the mantel above the fireplace. It was nine thirty a.m. "I need to go into the office and finish up a few things there, then stop by my church before I leave. Then I'll come back here and pack some travel clothes."

"Why don't you pack now, then we can head over to your job. My understanding is that Chief Coleman already called your boss, Ms. Tenner, and alerted her to the situation." Nick didn't want any delays in getting her to Seattle. He had work to do, and now that he knew what Pierce partially looked like, he was ready to press the investigation forward, once and for all.

Raina glanced up at the painting as she remembered talking with Mr. Antionelli last night. "Yes, he did that this morning before he left here," she said to the detective.

Nick stared at her profile. "Chief Coleman left here . . . this morning. I see." So the chief stayed over last night to comfort his girlfriend. Nice, he thought not so nicely.

Raina sat her coffee mug down and got up. "I'll go pack and get ready for work then." She went to her bedroom to get dressed. As she did, Raina wondered once again why Max and Lt. Brown insisted that she not tell the detective they were related. Their rationale was that they didn't want the department looking like they were giving her special treatment. She agreed that if everyone knew of the relationship it might cause friction in the department. However, she could only wonder what the detective was thinking when he'd made that comment.

While Raina headed to work escorted by her body-guard, the killer, appropriately dubbed "Pierce" for the pain he inflicted on others, was sitting in his home office expertly working away on his computer. He was extremely proficient at researching and finding whatever information he was looking for. Having a laptop at his fingertips was convenient and saved him time.

Earlier that morning, Pierce entered the Fifth Avenue Library. Picking up a random book from a cart, he glanced at the title. It was a do-it-yourself book on installing hardwood floors. He just needed to find a bar-code reader and he would be gone. Then he spotted one on top of a counter in the periodicals section. As he was about to head that way, a librarian came to the counter to assist him.

Smiling, Pierce stepped forward with the book, and the yellow library card he found in the alley outside the restaurant last night. He handed both to the librarian.

"O-kay, let's get you all checked out."

Pierce kept his head low, out of the visual field of the library's security monitoring system. He hoped the librarian wasn't one of those chatty clerks, attempting to engage him in conversation. He soon realized she was exactly that as she took the yellow card and scanned it.

The librarian looked up from the computer. "Oh, you know what, Mr. Wade, there's another book that's also recommended." She pursed her lips, trying to remember the other book. "Oh, now I can't remember the title, but I know exactly where it is. Would you like me to run and get it for you?"

Smiling tightly as she peered over the rim of her glasses at him, Pierce said, "Yes, please, by all means." He waited for her to swipe her ID card to open the door to the section and scramble off. Within seconds, Pierce quickly turned the monitor around toward him, memorized the information he wanted, and was gone.

"O-kay, here it is, Mr. Wade. It was just where I thought it was and . . ." The librarian glanced around and didn't see the man she'd been helping anywhere in sight. "Hum, guess he must have changed his mind," she said pleasantly to the next customer who had stepped to the counter.

CHAPTER 5

Three hours of continuous typing left Raina agitated . . . she couldn't focus. Her thoughts constantly returned to Julie and Janey Webster. *How could I have not known?* Still, she believed she had done the right thing by having a meeting with Mrs. Wilson later. Although Julie was grown, she was ultimately responsible for her sister, Janey. But Lord, Raina thought, leaving town would jeopardize all of her hard work with the girls.

It also didn't help that the detective sitting outside of her office was laughing it up with the receptionist, Brandy.

Glancing up over her monitor, Raina could see Brandy captivated by whatever the detective was saying and shook her head. She couldn't imagine what the girl saw in the arrogant man, besides the fact that he was white. Whatever it was, she sure didn't see it. Okay, he did have nice eyes. They were the palest shade of gray. She suddenly recalled seeing the black pupils of his eyes and frowned, wondering when she had gotten close enough to him for her to notice them. It was when she slapped that smug, cynical look off his face. Forcing her thoughts back to her work, Raina's eyes would occasionally raise above her monitor. Mimi had allowed her to download her work onto portable drives Raina would take to Seattle so that she would be able to work from there.

At one-thirty that afternoon Raina glanced up, startled to see the detective sitting in her office toying with a paperweight that usually sat on her bookshelf. When had he come into her office? She hadn't heard or seen him enter. "What?" She tried to hide the fact that he'd caught her off guard . . . so much that she didn't hear the question he asked her.

"I asked if you were ready for lunch. I got turkey sandwiches on whole wheat, with potato salad, chips and iced tea," he said. He'd been watching her focus on her computer monitor through cute little wire-rimmed eyeglasses when she looked up and caught him staring.

"Sounds great. Where is all of that?" She watched him point to the bookshelf. "Where did that come from?" Her eyes followed when he unfolded his body from the chair, noticing that he was tall. She'd first realized that when they walked from her condo to the back parking lot where his unmarked sedan was parked. She guessed he was about six feet even, with a solid build. Aware that she was studying him, Raina quickly accepted the sandwich he passed her.

"Brandy invited me to lunch. I had to decline, but I did ask her to pick us up something."

"I feel pretty safe here in my office. You could have just gone to lunch with her, if you wanted to." She took a bite of her sandwich then opened her bag of chips.

"I'm working. Ms. Wade, you know you have to be careful, and you know why, right?"

How could I forget that my life had been turned upside down since last night? And just the thought that she had to run and hide from a killer sent Raina's body into a state of tremors. Knowing the detective was waiting for her response, she simply said, "Right."

Seeing the look on her face, Nick passed her a cup of iced tea. "Ms. Wade, rest assured that I will protect you. That's my job." Nick got up and walked around her office, eating his sandwich in silence. He looked at drawings on the wall and touched pieces of fabric samples laying on a large work table in a corner of her office. Rounding her desk, he looked out the large window, but his attention was drawn to two framed pictures sitting on the credenza behind her desk.

She was in both pictures. In one she was standing beside her father, Michael Wade, whom he recognized. In the other picture she was standing behind a seated Max Coleman. Her arms were around his large shoulders and they were outside, in a park or backyard, perhaps. Realizing she was watching him, Nick returned to his seat. "What?"

"What? I didn't ask you anything," she said.

After a few minutes of eating silently, Nick nodded to her wrapper. "You done?"

Raina wondered what caused the tense look on his face. Looking beyond him, she said, "I see Brandy is looking for you. Thanks for the lunch." With that Raina returned to her keyboard and began typing just as he gathered up their trash and went back to the reception area.

At two o'clock they left her building and walked to the parking garage. Raina was very much aware that he was in full police mode. He walked closely beside her, and his eyes missed nothing. His sharp eyes noticed a fresh wad of gum laying in a vacant parking spot. He propelled her around it. Without his vigilance she probably would have stepped on the gum and would have had a fit trying to clean if off, right there on the spot, in the open . . . despite the possibility of a killer lurking nearby.

From the time they'd had lunch, she'd said nothing. Not that Nick expected her to. He just wondered what he'd said that ticked her off again. Groaning inwardly, he was dreading the long flight ahead. If he was lucky, he would drop her off in Seattle, catch a red-eye back and arrive in time to work tomorrow's evening shift. That should satisfy both his commanders.

Next stop was to Raina's church for a planned meeting. Nick refused to leave the small office at the church during the meeting, forcing Raina to explain to Mrs. Wilson and the pastor's assistants, Mr. Brooks and Mrs. Smith, what occurred last night. Nick watched the trio comforting Ms. Wade. Then, forming a circle, they encouraged him to participate as they held prayer. Nick felt oddly connected.

Although raised Catholic, he rarely attended service. Today, he did feel that these three strangers wanted to include him in their prayer, offering protection and comfort for both himself and Ms. Wade as they traveled.

In the meeting that followed, Nick sat quietly. He was surprised to learn that Ms. Wade was a mentor to a young girl. Her concern was evident for both the girl and her sister. He listened as she outlined an intervention, something she had worked on at work earlier. She seemed confident the church family would pull together to make it happen. Nick was equally surprised to learn how involved she was with the mentoring program. Her heartfelt plea was for Mrs. Wilson and Mr. Brooks to approve an emergency financial grant to cover several months rent and utilities for the Webster girls, as well as additional support for Julie. Not surprisingly, it was all approved. Even Nick thought he couldn't have said no to her unselfish requests. Before the meeting concluded, Nick watched a brief slide show presentation where she outlined a proposal she was writing to secure financial grants for the expansion of the mentoring program. Nick was impressed.

Two hours later, while driving to the airport, Raina tried to tune out familiar police chatter coming from Nick's police radio. He'd said very little after they left her church, and despite her request to drive to Janey's school to say goodbye, he refused, explaining that they didn't have time. Mrs. Wilson didn't think it was such a good idea, either, suggesting Raina call Janey instead.

Raina was struggling with the fact that the closer they got to the airport, the further away she was from her home and her life in Pittsburgh. She didn't want to leave, and she was tired of pretending that she was okay with everything. She wasn't. But she also didn't want to be a sitting duck, either, waiting to be killed at the hands of a psycho killer. She sniffed back the sudden rush of tears stinging her eyes.

Hearing her sniffles as he stopped for a red light, Nick pulled off his sunglasses and searched for some appropriate words he thought might comfort her. "Ms. Wade, I realize how you feel, but . . ."

Hearing that, Raina's fuse blew. She was positive he didn't know anything about what she was feeling. This arrogant, snot-nosed white cop didn't know a damn thing as far as she was concerned. Turning an angry face to him, she let him have a piece of her mind.

"You *don't* know how I feel, Detective, so please spare me that perfunctory crap of saying you do. You have no clue how my life has been turned upside down." She noticed that his eyes darkened as he glared back at her, but her tirade continued.

"You get to go back to your cage and do whatever it is that you do. And whatever the hell that is, you get to do it without having to look over your shoulder to see if some crazed killer is on your heels. Some idiot who's ready to put a bullet in you just because you happen to be in a restaurant at the same time he just so happened to come in and kill three innocent people. So, really, you don't know anything at all!" When she finished, her tears had all dried up, and she turned away from the intensity of his hardened glare to stare, unseeingly out the passenger side window.

Blaring car horns pulled Nick's attention from her stiff shoulders to the green light. Oh, yeah, this was going to be one very long flight, he thought, and put his sunglasses back on.

Nick parked the police sedan in the overnight parking garage and pulled their two bags from the trunk. At the security check-in, Nick showed his badge and spoke to an airline official to alert them that he was traveling with his service revolver. His eyes strayed to his sullen and withdrawn travel companion. "Ms. Wade, we'll be going to Gate C to check in." When he watched her lift her carry-on bag and stomp off in the direction of Gate C, Nick was fuming.

When Nick caught up with her after clearing check-in, he could have strangled her. Instead, he ground out through clenched teeth, "Don't walk away from me again, understand?" He walked beside her silently and then stopped and turned her to him. "In case you haven't thought about it, just remember that my life is on the line here as well. That crazed killer on your heels is also on mine." She looked over his right shoulder and not at him. But he knew she understood what he'd said before snatching her arm from his hand.

When they reached the reservation check-in desk, Nick asked the clerk to call over her supervisor. The supervisor verified Nick's ID and introduced herself as Agent Teresa Swain. After clicking a few keys on the keyboard, her eyes widened.

Nick noticed the alarm look on her face. "What's wrong?"

"Well, it seems that Ms. Wade called in this morning to arrange seating other than what is on these coded tickets." Both Swain and Nick's eyes flew to Raina.

Tilting her head, Raina sent a look to both of them. "It's a long flight and I wanted a different seat," was all she said by way of explanation. She noticed the color drain from his face when he asked when she'd made the change.

"This morning. I believe right around the time you were enjoying your second or third cranberry muffin." Raina thrust her hands on her hips. "So what is that look about, Detective?"

"Jesus." Nick blinked her into view, then immediately his eyes scanned the throngs of people milling about Gate C. He paid particular attention to the many passengers waiting to board the same flight they were. He knew Pierce was reported to use many disguises. He could be any ordinary traveler disguised as an old man or young woman also waiting to board the flight.

"Detective, it's your call how to proceed. I can assist you further," she said, showing Nick her FBI ID card.

Nick said, "I need a private room so that I can speak to Ms. Wade."

She pointed to two closed rooms to the left of the check-in counter.

Nick thought the rooms were too close to the boarding area. There were too many people passing by, but it would have to do. Grabbing Raina's upper arm, the look he gave her dared her to utter one word of protest.

Raina considered a smart remark. She knew that under the circumstances it was prudent to keep her mouth shut. She knew she'd screwed up by changing her seat assignment.

Nick kept their bodies close behind Agent Swain, knowing her service weapon was holstered at her side, whereas his was strapped to his ankle. He asked her to stand by the door.

Once safely inside the conference room, Nick turned disbelieving eyes on Raina. "I don't believe this shit! More importantly, Ms. Wade, I don't believe you could be so careless. I would have thought you, of all people, would have known better!" He stood right in front of her, fuming and pointing his finger at her.

"Get your finger out of my face and don't you dare . . ." Raina was ready to give him another piece of her mind, but he had reached into his bag and held up pictures for her to see, effectively shutting her up. The pictures were crime scene photos from the restaurant. Raina couldn't look at them for more than a second without feeling revulsion and a sharp pain to the front of her head.

"Spare me your bullshit hurt, your crappy attitude and your explanation, Ms. Wade! Look at those people. They're all dead. One could have been you. The man who did this . . ." Nick slapped the pictures on the table, fanning them out and forcing her to turn and look at them again. His hands on her shoulders kept her in place, staring down at the pictures. "This man is a professional hit man. He leaves no witnesses. Do you hear me, lady? This is no fucking joke. If he has any idea who you are, and more importantly, where you are, than you were absolutely correct in what you said in the car—your life, as you know it, is over, and guess what, so is mine. I don't know about you, but I have plans for this life of mine." Nick pushed himself away from her, then pointed to her chest again. "So you tell me right now that you don't give a damn about your life, and I'm out of here." He thrust his hands to his hips, waiting for her to answer, because at that point, he didn't care about the job any longer.

Raina's throat constricted with revulsion and behind her eyes the pictures flashed brightly. Still, she was not going to let this cop disrespect her. "Like I reported, and have said repeatedly, you idiot . . . he didn't see me! How would the killer even know I was there? That's just your assumption and that of your superiors. And for your information, I do care about my life, regardless of what you think. And for real, Detective, what you want or what you think and your opinion means nothing to me!" Sarcasm laced her hot words as she waved a hand in front of his face. Anger had turned her face beet red.

Nick ran a hand through his short, dark hair in frustration. He knew she wasn't as clueless as she sounded. "How long do you think you were in the back room of the restaurant? How about the alley? Several minutes, maybe? Surely, enough minutes to realize he would eventually come out into the alley, right? Enough time for you to rig up that contraption with the cigarette can and the chair." Regrouping, Nick moved away from her, rubbing the knot of tension from the back of his neck, and then turned back. "Listen, I don't know what Chief Coleman told you last night or this morning or whenever . . . in any case, this killer's name is Pierce, and he *did* come out into that alley last night. He came out after you, probably just seconds after you cleared out of it. That's not an assumption, Ms. Wade. He stood out there long enough to leave shoe impressions in the ash from that can. What do you think he was doing?"

Fear crept into Raina's spine as he spoke. "I—I don't know. How could I? According to *your* information, I had cleared the alley, remember, Detective Know-It-All?"

Nick quelled the desire to shake the daylights out of her. "In your statement, you said you might have thumped something and he turned in the direction of that private dining room. He didn't come back there because the female victim had already left the ladies' room. He'd already killed her, remember, Miss Know-It-All? He knows someone was in that room and made it out that back door. From his shoe marks in the sand and ash, he stood out there in the alley, Ms. Wade. He was sniffing the air for your perfume. Although it's light and quite pleasant, I smelled it last night at the station when you approached my desk." Nick was suddenly floored and couldn't for the life of him explain why he'd told her that he had noticed her perfume. "The killer was listening for the distant sounds of those beaded shoes you had on as he stood there and brushed the cigarette ash from his jacket. He knows his stuff, Ms. Wade, and he's thorough. Trust me, if he *knows* you were there, it will become his mission to *find* you and *kill* you. And you know why." Nick's frustration mounted. "Because he doesn't leave witnesses and, right now, you're the only one who can identify him!" Nick stopped his tirade immediately when he heard a tap on the door.

Raina watched him pull his service weapon from his ankle holster, then shield her body with his.

Nick opened the door and stood aside for Agent Swain to enter. "Detective, it's time to board, if you're still taking the flight. Those original tickets are still in the system under the name of Smith, and even if we delete the new reservation Ms. Wade made this morning, it won't do any good, it's still traceable."

Raina met the agent's glare head on, but wisely didn't dare comment.

"Okay, here's the plan, Agent Swain. We'll board the plane, but just before the door is closed, we'll need to get off and leave the terminal as quickly as possible. Can that be done?"

"I'll make it happen. When you two disembark the plane, go out the door marked "Supplies." I'll go unlock it after I leave here. That door will take you down a level and you will come out a side door in baggage. It's marked "Freight," and it's unlocked on the inside. Just go out that door and you'll come out at passenger baggage and the parking lot is . . ." She hesitated briefly. "Wait, if you suspect you were followed here, then you should rethink going back to your car. In fact, give me a description of the car, I'll send someone over there to stand by now."

"Thank you," Nick said and gave her the parking stub and description of the car.

Agent Swain then explained that a meeting of security officials had taken place earlier that morning, and that she was scheduled to accompany them to Seattle as backup. Her eyes strayed to Raina, and didn't hide the fact that she thought Raina had made a stupid move. "Unfortunately, at that meeting we didn't know that Ms. Wade had called in and used her credit card to request a different seat assignment."

Raina stared at a space on the wall.

Turning to her, Nick said, "Ms. Wade, your credit card data is on the grid. Don't use it again." Nick dragged his hand down his face. "Let's board."

"Okay, but if anyone else demands off of that plane before the door is locked, we won't be able to stop them, particularly if they're also seated in first class, which is in the front of the plane. But I want the two of you sitting in the first seats, in that first row on the left, got that?"

"Got it," Nick said, scooping up the pictures from the table in one swipe.

Everything happened so fast. Although Raina heard the plan as it was laid out, she was unprepared for the swiftness of it. Literally a split-second delay and the heel of her shoe would have been caught in the closing door of the plane. She was also unprepared for how fast the detective moved, dragging her along with him. When they ran down the steps leading to passenger baggage, Nick kept his eyes and his feet moving. When they had to walk along a narrow seven-inch-wide platform, all the while avoiding a moving conveyor belt loaded down with tumbling luggage, the look Nick sent Raina dared her to complain. She didn't, and neither did she think she would ever make it outside of the airport. But before she knew what was happening they were standing outside in the muggy night air. Nick's loud piecing whistle hailed a taxi cab almost immediately, and he all but shoved her onto the backseat floor.

Only when they were hunched down in the backseat of a yellow taxi, the airport disappearing behind them, did Raina dare to breathe. She'd been literally holding her breath since they squeezed their bodies and travel bags through the jaws of the closing airplane door. She heard him give the taxi driver directions to her condo, uptown.

Thirty minutes later, after a silent ride, they arrived back at her condo. Entering with his gun drawn, Nick scanned the living room. Seeing nothing out of place, he pulled her from behind him and noticed she was crying.

"Stop that. It doesn't help us now," he said in a gruff voice, his eyes scanning the room.

"Sorry I changed the seating," Raina murmured as she stepped around him.

"You didn't just change the seating. Ms. Wade, you put us on the killer's radar, making it that much easier for him to find you. As the daughter of a police captain, I would have expected you to know better." Nick resisted adding, *and girlfriend of a high-ranking chief.*

"That's former police captain, Detective," she replied, her tone weary.

"I stand corrected." His gray eyes bored into her brown ones for several long seconds before they strayed beyond her shoulder to a fallen vase above the fireplace. Nick remembered touching the painting, but didn't recall knocking the vase over. The painting now sat askew.

Stepping around her, Nick was assessing how he remembered the room when they left that morning. He recalled her insisting on straightening up the living room and washing their coffee cups before leaving that morning while he secured all the doors. Now, something felt off and he didn't know why.

"I need to use the bathroom," Raina said, walking back to her bedroom. As she reached to turn on the light switch, she was grabbed from behind and lifted off her feet. Struggling against the gloved hand clamped over her mouth, she felt a cold metal object at the base of her throat and instinctively let her body go slack with dead weight. When her assailant heaved her body and moved his hand slightly, Raina let out a bloodcurdling scream as she dropped to the floor in the darkened room.

Nick ran in with his gun drawn and ready. He hit the light switch. No lights came on, and he just barely missed trampling over Raina, who was crumbled in a heap on the floor just inside her bedroom. He felt the sudden rush of night air from the hastily opened window . . . someone had just leaped out onto the balcony. Nick pulled out a pen flashlight and took one look and saw that her bedroom had been ransacked. Every drawer had been pulled out and emptied onto the floor. Every piece of clothing had been pulled from the hangers in the walk-in closet, and the tops of her dressers were swiped clear of toiletries, framed pictures and knick-knacks. "Oh, shit. We have to get out of here."

Scrambling to get up, Raina's her eyes took in the state of her bedroom. "Oh, my God." Hampered by her travel bag and purse, she could do little else. With the light now spilling in from the outside, Raina looked at Nick and saw the tension on his face. She also saw his fear, and it reflected her own.

Quickly, but with purpose, Nick pulled Raina and her bags out of the room with little effort. He held onto her as he ran out of the condo, hitting the light switch in the hallway to the living room. He took the back stairs two at a time. Once they cleared the service entrance in the back of the building, he kept them running, glad that he'd remembered the layout of the building itself. Flipping open his cell phone, Nick pressed a single key as they continued running along a dirt path that ran alongside the highway. They crossed into a heavily wooded area where traffic zipped along the expressway, some three feet above their heads.

"The flight was a no-go and it was too risky to go back to the sedan. We encountered an intruder in Ms. Wade's bedroom at the condo, but he jumped out the bedroom window. It was a setup. The room has been ransacked and the lights disabled. I need a car and a destination."

Raina was breathing heavily as she listened to him on the phone. She was too scared to blink, let alone ask him what was next, and despite a stinging sensation on her neck, she just concentrated on keeping up with his fast pace.

"Ten-four, so now we know he knows about her. Damn." Snapping the cell phone shut, Nick was deep in thought for several seconds. He turned to her.

"We need to get away from here."

"Wh-what did your lieutenant say?" Raina asked, climbing a hill behind him.

"Secure a location ASAP. No landline communications and stand by for further details." He turned and noticed her staring at him, then began to explain, "What all that means is . . ."

"I–I know what it all means," Raina said through suddenly chattering teeth, the enormity of their situation beginning to settle in.

"Good." Nick scanned the area, already knowing they would never get a taxi cab from their location. He spotted a couple of cars parked in a motel parking lot across the road. Unfortunately, the motel was way across the road, at least half a mile across, through brush. But first, they would have to cross the busy highway. He knew if he told her the plan, she would probably end up tripping, so he didn't. "We need to borrow somebody's car, come on," Nick said, intently concentrating on the traffic pattern for an opportunity to cross.

Before Raina could even turn to look in the direction he indicated, he grasped her hand and took off running across the four-lane highway. They then slid down an embankment on their backsides, their bags, as well as rocks and brush, assaulting them along the way. Raina was mildly thankful she had decided to wear sensible walking shoes and dress slacks to work.

After running the stretch, Nick pulled up beside a bank of vending machines at the far end of the motel. He pressed her flat against the wall, silently indicating for her to stay put.

With her lungs burning, Raina could only nod as she shrank against the wall. Her eyes followed, as he crawled on his hands and knees toward an older model sedan. She watched him pull something from his pocket and swiftly pick the lock. Raina couldn't believe it when he eased in behind the steering wheel, started the car and silently backed it up to where she was standing. Her mouth dropped open when he pushed the passenger side door open, took the bags and whispered for her to get in. As if by remote, she complied.

Raina sat in shock as they drove backwards for several more feet into an adjacent parking lot. Only then did he turn the headlights on and pull out onto the highway. "You just st—stole a car, you know," Raina stammered. She glanced over and noticed he had put on a pair of black leather gloves; immediately she had to force away the image of the killer flexing his hands in his new leather gloves right after he'd killed Rachel.

"No, I just borrowed somebody's car. They'll have it back by this time tomorrow night." Nick drove out of the city and kept driving north. He was in deep thought, wondering if it was Pierce who broke into her condo, although he was fairly certain it was. The living room was pretty much intact and that possibly was the intent . . . to draw her into her bedroom, where the light switch had been busted. Only now did Nick realize Pierce had been lying in wait to kill her. And that didn't happen because she wasn't alone. And therein was another concern that Nick chided himself about. He hadn't checked her condo when they returned—something he should have done immediately. That was bodyguard 101. Check everything out, and he hadn't.

It might have been an average break-in, but Nick didn't think that was the case. He believed in his gut that it was Pierce who had looked at the painting above the fireplace, maybe recognizing the place of his latest hit . . .

or perhaps, he'd recognized the man he'd killed, in the painting . . . Antionelli.

Raina had fallen asleep during the ride. When she awakened thirty minutes later, the car was stopped and the detective was nowhere in sight. Alarmed, she almost went into panic mode, frantically turning and looking out the windows. Only a dark, wooded area greeted her. When the rear door sprang open suddenly, Raina's scream punctured the stillness.

"It's okay, it's me. Relax. I'm just getting the bags. Come on, get out of the car," Nick said, opening the passenger door for her.

Her eyes having adjusted to the darkness, Raina glanced around. They were at a large, country-type home. Stepping from the car, she cautiously followed the detective up the front steps to the wide porch. "Where are we?" she asked when he held the door open for her, unsure if it was safe to enter.

"We're in Warrendale. This is my place, or my cage, as you called it earlier. Will you go on in, please? You're inviting the bugs in." He watched her step inside tentatively and then followed with their bags.

Raina stood in the wide foyer, not daring to go further. "Why are we here, Detective?"

"I couldn't think of any other place to go," Nick said, turning on lamps in the living room and hallway as he spoke. "I put in another call to my lieutenant and he's calling the chief, so I expect to hear from them soon."

"How long will I have to stay here?" she asked, looking around. From what she could see, it was a very nice and very large house. It was tasteful, not too masculine and very neat.

"I don't know, but I suspect the original order will be unchanged—to get you to Seattle. Listen, sit down and relax. You fell asleep as soon as I got on the highway." He watched her go into the living room, taking a seat on one of the two sofas before turning to go up the steps.

Raina stopped him. "May I use your bathroom?"

"Oh, damn, I forgot you needed to use the bathroom back at your place. Come on up."

Raina followed him upstairs and went into the bathroom he indicated at the end of the hallway. Once inside and alone, her body gave way to the intense weariness and fear she felt. After one look into the full-length mirror on the linen closet door, Raina was horrified to see that she looked as if she'd been dragged through the mud. Dirt clung to her from head to toe. She couldn't remember the last time she'd had dirt under her fingernails . . . yes, she did, she thought . . . last night in that alley.

Nick set her bags on the floor in one of the two guest bedrooms on the second floor, then stood in the hallway waiting for her to come out of the bathroom. Concerned after ten minutes had passed, he knocked on the door. With no answer or movement from the other side, he turned the knob. "Ms. Wade?"

He found her sitting on the edge of the tub, staring into space, tears silently running down her cheeks. Watching her for several seconds, Nick could not find anything appropriate to say.

Noticing movement, Raina looked up, mortified that he had caught her hiding out in the bathroom, crying. She said nothing as she stood up, hung the washcloth on the towel rack and then followed him out into the hallway.

"O-kay," Nick mumbled, then told her which room he had put her bags in.

At the top of the stairs, Raina asked, "I'm spending the night here, with you?"

Catching something in her voice, maybe dislike, Nick turned and said, "I think that would be fair to assume. I was thinking about fixing us something to eat?"

With the detective standing one step down while she remained on the landing, Raina felt an odd sense of vulnerability, looking down into his upturned face. "I–I can help you."

"Great," Nick said. He would take anything over her crying, and suddenly wondered if most guys felt as helpless as he did to see a beautiful woman crying. She was indeed beautiful, especially when she wasn't scowling and throwing her haughty attitude in his face.

Back downstairs, beyond the living room, a wide hallway opened up into a large kitchen. Raina was surprised to find it contemporary, with smooth granite counters and stainless steel appliances. He flipped on a small TV that sat at the end of the center island top, which was covered in the same sand and gray-colored granite. "Nice kitchen," she said, running her hand across the cool material. "Not your typical farmhouse. Warrendale is farmland, isn't it?"

Nick had already finished pulling salad items from the refrigerator. "Yes, it is, and thanks. I'm still renovating. I have the backsplash to do next." Nick hitched his chin to indicate the area behind the sink, and began preparing two bowls of salad greens.

"Oh? What are you going to put up there?" Raina asked crossing the kitchen to the areas already primed to be covered. She was centering her frazzled mind. Home design was one of her areas of expertise, next to fashion design, that is.

"Just some tiles I saw at the home improvement store. They're kind of a mosaic Spanish thing. I have a couple of sample tiles around here somewhere," Nick said, slicing tomatoes onto large chunks of lettuce in the bowls and wiped his hands on a dishtowel. Opening a cabinet, he took out six four-by-four-inch decorative ceramic tiles and handed them to her. "They're on back-order at the store."

"Nice," Raina said, rubbing her hand over the textured tiles and then held them up to the wall. "I think you should stagger them, you know, like pyramids. Then level them off to maybe a single row at the bottom. Your home is beautiful. I apologize for referring to it as a cage." She smiled tentatively, barely. "It's quite neat."

Nick couldn't take his eyes off her. He'd seen a genuine smile . . . a beautiful smile with pretty lips and perfect white teeth. And, Lord help him, she had a nice body, too. "Thanks."

"What I meant is that most guys tend to be kind of slobs, you know."

"I have a local lady who comes in weekly to clean. But I used to be a slob. Well, that is until I had to live with my sister for four years, and, trust me, you don't get to be a slob around Jenny," Nick said absently as he chopped more vegetables and dropped them into the bowls.

"How old is your sister?" Raina asked, picking up a cucumber and beginning to slice it.

Nick looked up. "Let's see, I'm 32, so she should be 36."

"I'm 32, also." He lived with his sister, she reflected. "It's just the two of you?"

"Yes, but she's married with a son," he said, setting out placemats and silverware.

Raina looked beyond his shoulder to a set of double French doors that led outside. It was dark, but she could see neighboring porch lights in the distance. "What's out there?"

Nick walked over to the light switch and turned on the lights to an outside deck. "You want to go outside?" Nick saw the widening of her eyes as she came up beside him. "Not many people who don't live here, come out here and nobody followed us. I made sure of that. I also have a full security system and I also have backup security, my partner. He's around, probably next door visiting his girlfriend," he said, absently turning back to the TV to catch a tennis volley in replay.

"You have a roommate, or is he your partner?"

"Well, yeah, he's both really." Nick let out a loud, piercing whistle, causing Raina to put her fingers in her ears, just as she had done when he hailed the taxi at the airport.

"And he has a girlfriend?" Raina's eyebrows lifted.

"Uh-huh. He'll be here in a second. I'm starved, let's eat." Nick turned, leaving the French doors open and the screen door slightly ajar.

Raina got up on a stool at the center island and noticed the two large salads he'd made. "This is a lot. Do you want to fix another bowl for when your roommate gets here?"

Chewing his food, Nick looked at her oddly and shook his head.

Raina was hungry. She was almost finished eating when she looked down and grinned.

Seeing her turn, Nick dragged his eyes from the tennis match to look down at his dog, Reed, a two-year-old sandy-colored Lab. "It's about time you came home. Reed, say hello to our houseguest, Ms. Wade." Nick looked up to see her covering her face with her napkin. "What's wrong?" he asked.

Raina was on the verge of uncontrollable laughter. She struggled to hold it in as she told him what she really thought he'd meant about his roommate. "I'm sorry, Detective, but, I—I thought . . . well, when you said you had a roommate and a partner. I kind of thought that, your dog, well . . . I thought he was your boyfriend, and you were gay."

Nick's fork dropped from his fingers with a clang onto the granite top. "What? Why the hell would you think that?" He stared at her incredulously.

Recovering, Raina was almost afraid to look at him for fear of more laughter erupting from her. "Oh, come on. Anyway, who cares, and I only thought that because you said that your roommate was your partner. It's an accepted lifestyle."

Nick would have laughed had he not been rethinking their conversation when he had described Reed. "Well, Ms. Wade, trust me, I am not gay. I think my last date can attest to that, and trust me, *she* was female." He got up, retrieved a container of dry dog food from a cabinet and then filled Reed's bowl.

Raina's lips tightened. So he had a date, so what. "Sorry that I misinterpreted what you said." She turned to Reed, who continued to stand beside her stool, watching her. "He's still a puppy. He won't bite me if I rub his head, will he?"

"I don't know. He's a very smart dog with excellent hearing. Maybe he, too, is a little pissed about being misinterpreted."

"Well, I'll just take my chances," she said, and rubbed the dog's head. Reed promptly stood on his hind legs, licked her hand, then laid his head in her lap, loving the attention. "Hello, Reed. It's nice to meet you, boy," Raina cooed, but her eyes followed the detective as he put their bowls in the sink. She thought he looked quite handsome, and she found it hard to pull her eyes away from the movements of his body. Raina was acutely aware of his maleness. The feeling hit her with a jolt. She recalled the strength of his arms lifting her up from the floor in her bedroom. Inching her eyes up to him again, Raina experienced an unsettling feeling stir within her chest. It gave her goosebumps.

Nick kept himself busy. He took out a bottle of beer for himself, and offered her a glass of wine, but only if she stopped smirking.

Raina didn't think he would appreciate an apology, so she let the matter drop. "I'd rather have one of those, if you don't mind," she said, nodding towards his beer.

"Hmm, another surprise," Nick said, studying her.

"What does that mean?" she asked, accepting the bottle but declining the glass he offered.

"It's just that you surprised me. Like earlier, when we were running from your condo, you kept up with me. You didn't fall down, stumble, or trip once, and you drink beer from the bottle." Nick's eyes took in the caramel perfection of her skin. He wondered if her skin felt as soft as it appeared, then swiftly pulled the reins on his thoughts by taking another swig of beer.

"Lots of women drink beer, and why waste a glass? As far as keeping up, I do aerobics."

"O-kay," Nick said slowly. "I'm going into the living room and watch this match." He passed her another beer. "Hey, make yourself at home, Ms. Wade."

"Thanks. I, um, think I'll take a shower or maybe a bath. I feel so dirty."

"Yeah, I feel the same. You'll find linens in that closet in the bathroom upstairs."

"I'll try not to take too long or use all the hot water," she called out, climbing the steps.

"Don't worry about it. I have another bathroom down here I can use," Nick called out. He walked into the living room and turned the TV on, then settled down on a sofa. No sooner had he gotten comfortable, he heard water running for her bath upstairs. Try as he might, Nick could not concentrate on the tennis match. Instead, his mind was drawn to the beautiful woman from the other night, standing before him in a sexy dress. He could envision how she looked under that dress. Today, she'd dressed in a form-fitting frilly blue sweater and black slacks. Yes, he'd noticed her figure, too. But, Nick didn't want to think of her as anything other than a witness who needed his protection and someone he needed to get information from. He had planned on getting her to Seattle and if he was lucky, he would get her there, unharmed and in one piece. That is, if he didn't throttle her first, for her sarcastic smart mouth. *Her sexy mouth*, he thought. "Damn," he mumbled in frustration, pushing himself up off the sofa, and went to take a shower in the bathroom off the kitchen.

Raina settled into a steaming bubble bath. She was glad she had the forethought to pack her favorite bath salts in her toiletries bag. Okay, maybe she shouldn't have spent $60 for an eight-ounce bottle of the stuff, but she liked it. It was a soothing balm for her frazzled nerves, and since last night her nerves were downright drained. Finishing off her beer, she glanced around the large, old-fashioned bathroom. It was standard, complete with a white porcelain tub, sink and toilet and old-fashioned wainscoting around the wall. Raina couldn't help comparing it to her own garden bath in her condo . . . complete with a deep whirlpool bathtub and a steam shower. For several minutes, Raina closed her eyes and thought how her life had changed over the course of two days, but really, she thought, how her life had changed over the past few years.

It all began ten years ago when her father retired and moved away. He had accepted an instructor's position at a classified law enforcement agency in Seattle, Washington. Raina last visited him almost eight months ago, and she realized how much she missed him then. He'd recently met and was dating a woman he described as very sweet and kind. Raina shook her head at the thought of her father having a girlfriend and her mother having a boyfriend. That is not how her parents' love story was supposed to play out, she thought sadly.

But Raina knew several years before her parents' divorce that their relationship just didn't seem to make either of them happy, so their split didn't upset her or her younger brother, Marcus, at all. She just wondered why they stayed together so long when they were obviously so miserable, ultimately making their two children miserable in the process. Her life had changed only marginally when her parents divorced and her brother enlisted in the Navy, but Raina had buried herself in college courses and then work. She started off by graduating from college as an aspiring clothing designer. Like everyone in her class, her dream was to be a famous fashion designer, her creations modeled on runways, but she found out quickly that landing a job in the competitive field was very difficult. So when she found a job as an assistant to a buyer, she discovered that was where her real passion was. Raina loved the challenge of finding just the right fabrics for designs that were only on paper. Her boss, Mimi Tenner, praised her efforts so much that she paid tuition for Raina to attend a year-long, intensive business management course. The result was reflected in her work. After doing fashion designs for six years, Mimi was expanding her business to home designs. Only now, Raina knew she would have to put her dreams on hold because she would have to work from a computer—in Seattle. That is, until the killer was found.

That thought brought her back to her present situation. She blamed herself for being in that restaurant with Leon the Loser, because she suggested meeting him there. And as she had predicted, incorrectly in retrospect, that she would have been the one to drop a few bills on the table, stand up with a flourish, and say adios to Leon. She was to be the one to walk out and leave him sitting there, looking foolish and pitifully alone. But that's exactly how she felt sitting there when Leon had turned the tables.

He dumped you. The detective's words echoed in her head. What did he know, anyway? She frowned. But that's exactly what Leon did, and that was a first. She was always the one to end the relationship. Usually for no other reason than the fact that it was too much of an effort to pretend the friendship was anything more than that, a friendship. It was never what she had hoped and prayed for. It was never that all-consuming love that her friends professed to have found. It was never the kind of love that made one's insides tight with longing at hearing a lover's voice. That is, if such a thing really happens anyway, she thought.

The way Raina saw it, the kind of love that she was looking for really didn't exist, except in the movies and in novels. It certainly didn't exist for her parents. She guessed that must be where she gained such a negative view of how a relationship should be between a man and a woman. If it was, then she was destined to spend her life alone, and that was okay with her. Realizing her bath water had cooled, Raina quickly got out of the tub, toweled off and returned to the guest bedroom adjacent to the bathroom. There, she walked around the comfortable room. Like the bathroom, it was functional, with simple furniture and nondescript bed linens. It was cozy and clean and she felt an odd sense of peace. But then she realized there was nothing like having one's own personal bodyguard to feel that way. As Raina towel-dried her hair, she wondered if the detective was still watching TV. Thinking about him, she couldn't help but snicker at his shocked expression when she told him she'd thought he was gay.

His gray eyes had darkened to the shade of cool steel and she took notice of him, even when she didn't want too. She remembered his presence had filled her living room and her office earlier, and when he sat in on the meeting at her church she fought to block him out when she explained the situation Julie was in. Raina thought, for a white guy, he really was quite handsome. He was tall, with a kind of military look. His dark hair was worn short and his jaw was square and strong. His body was a solid mass of muscle and strength. She recalled feeling that when he'd first pulled her against his side as they ran from the airplane. Raina wasn't at all surprised that he'd had a hot date like he'd said. Why wouldn't he? But, that wasn't her business, she thought and quickly finished drying her hair, tugging hard on the strands for no particular reason at all. When her need for something sweet kicked in, Raina wondered what snacks he might have downstairs. She went to find some dessert.

She met Reed at the bottom of the stairs and together they walked back to the kitchen in her search for sweets. She didn't see the detective, but the TV was still on and guessed he was somewhere in the house. Absently, she remembered he'd said for her to make herself at home, and this was her usual time for a chocolate fix.

As soon as she walked into the kitchen and flipped on the overhead light, the detective rounded the corner coming from what was probably the first-floor bathroom, near the back door. They stood staring at each other for several seconds before self-consciously averting their eyes to other areas of the kitchen. Reed stood near the base cabinet, in anticipation of a treat himself. Nick stood holding a towel around his waist. "Sorry, I didn't know you came downstairs," he mumbled.

Raina tried to act unaffected by his near-nakedness. The towel left nothing to her imagination. His body glistened with water droplets sliding down his face, to his chest, to his taut stomach, and beyond. She thought it funny that men never dried off after a shower, like women did. Uncontrollably, her body reacted with a will of its own. *Good Lord*, she thought, turning away from him. Swallowing hard, she began opening cupboards in search of the . . . what? For the life of her, Raina couldn't remember what she was looking for.

If Nick thought she was sexy in regular clothes, then the short, pale green PJ set she had on took his breath away. For several seconds, he couldn't speak and was glad when she turned around. Her stretching movements as she reached up into the cupboards gave Nick a good view of her backside and bare legs. His reaction was immediate. He moved so that the lower half of his body was covered by the base of the center island.

He cleared his throat of the lump that had formed there. "Are you looking for something in particular, Ms. Wade?" The smell of whatever she had on swirled around him, infusing his senses. *Damn.*

Raina turned. "Huh? Oh, yes," she said quickly, "chocolate, or anything sweet or wet. I mean, um, like ice cream, maybe." She stammered, thinking the kitchen was growing smaller by the second with him standing there like that. He was almost naked, for Christ's sake. She watched Reed go over to his master.

"In that cabinet above the sink there should be some cookies, and there's peach ice cream in the freezer. But if you want chocolate, look in pantry in there," Nick said, tilting his head toward a door to her left. It was becoming an effort to stand there and have a conversation with her and not check out her body.

"Great." For several seconds Raina didn't move, and neither did he.

Nick held onto the knot in the towel with a white-knuckled fist. "I–I better go and . . ."

"Put some clothes on," Raina finished, forcing her eyes up from his stomach.

"Right. Excuse me," Nick said and left the kitchen. Once inside his bedroom, he expelled a shaky breath, letting the towel drop to the floor. Looking down at his body he snorted. "I don't think the proper Ms. Wade would've thought I was gay if she'd seen this earlier." Sobering, Nick quickly donned cotton shorts and a T-shirt with a cartoon drawing on the front of a police officer standing in front of a closed donut shop. When he went back downstairs, he found his houseguest stretched out on the sofa, enjoying a candy bar and watching TV. "I see you found something to satisfy your sweet tooth, huh?"

Raina lifted her head, grinned at his T-shirt and said, "I sure did, thanks."

Nick sat on the opposite sofa, noticing Reed sprawled out beside her with his head resting on her lap. "I see my roommate is a traitor." He met her grin with a glare. He watched her absently run her foot along the dog's back. Imagining it was his back, Nick coughed at his uncomfortable and inappropriate thoughts. Raina got up and crossed over to the steps. "I'm going to turn in. Thank you, Detective. I have been remiss in saying that to you today." She climbed the stairs with Reed at her heels.

At exactly 2:15 in the morning, Raina awakened with a start. Lifting her head from the pillow, she saw the dog standing on his hind legs, looking out the guest bedroom window. He was whining with his tail low. "Reed? What's wrong?" Groggily, she climbed out of bed and looked out the window but didn't see anything out of the ordinary. She patted the dog's head and, just as she was about to fall back into bed, she heard a sound outside. Reed let out a low growl in his throat. Fear trickled though her veins. *Pierce.*

Raina ran from the bedroom and out into the hallway, lit up by two old-fashioned wall sconces. Reed went down the stairs to the first floor, leaving her to look about the hallway, wondering which room was the detective's bedroom. There were three other rooms on the second level, but she noticed a door at the end of the hallway was ajar.

Raina approached the door on tiptoes and peeped inside. It was his bedroom. The detective lay sleeping on his back on top of the covers. With the light spilling in from the hallway, she noticed he had one arm raised above his head on the pillow and the other lay across his naked stomach. Pushing the door opened further, Raina slowly approached his bed. She stared at him for several long seconds. He had dark hair on his chest and legs, and she found that incredibly sexy. She didn't mean to stare so openly at him as he slept, but she couldn't seem to pull her eyes away, despite her reason for coming to his room in the first place. Her eyes trailed up to a tattoo on his bicep, and that's when she heard the dog's growl, putting an abrupt end to her perusal of his sleeping form.

Just as she inched out her hand, about to touch his arm to wake him, Nick quickly grabbed her wrist. Within seconds, she was pushed up against the interior wall, between the windows, with his forearm pressed across her chest. The heat of his body pressed into hers. Raina blinked several times and, when she saw that he had a gun in his other hand, she let out a frightened shriek.

Nick came instantly awake, recognizing who it was he had pinned against the wall. Seeing her fright, he eased back from her and turned the bedside lamp on. "What's wrong?"

At first, Raina couldn't catch her breath. She could only manage to gulp in air. Then, within a span of ten seconds, her body went through several emotions, and that's when she began to tremble violently. "Your dog . . . R-Reed, he woke me with a funny sound. H-he was looking out the window. I-I think Pierce is out there." Her wide eyes flew to the window to her right.

Nick whistled quietly to Reed. As soon as the dog whined back in response, Nick moved away from her and picked up a remote from his nightstand, then aimed it at the monitor sitting on a built-in shelf. He glanced from the flickering screen to Raina Wade, who hadn't moved from the wall. Her hands clutched the front of her night-shirt fearfully. "I'm sorry I went into police mode like that. You okay there, Ms. Wade?" His eyes took in her shaking body, from her heaving breasts under the pale green nightshirt down to her shapely thighs and petite feet.

Raina could only shake her head up quickly. No, she was not okay. How could she be when her heart took a freefall, and was now lodged somewhere in the bottom of her stomach? Then her eyes flew to the monitor at the two men standing on his front porch. "Oh, no," she gasped again.

Nick turned back to the monitor and, recognizing his superiors, he turned to her. "It's my lieutenant and Chief Coleman."

"What? Max? At this hour? Something must be wrong." She swung wide eyes at him. Nick walked out of his bedroom and headed downstairs, while Raina ran to the guestroom for her robe, only then aware she had forgotten to put it on.

After turning off the alarm, Nick invited the men in. "Good morning." Nick followed them into the living room, just as Raina was coming down the stairs. He noticed the robe she'd put on gapped and flapped around her slender legs, and instantly recalled the warmth of her body when he had pinned her to the wall. After letting Reed out for a spell, Nick turned back just as she crossed the hallway to the living room and into the open arms of Max Coleman. There she promptly dissolved into quiet tears, mumbling incoherently about the condo being broken into.

Max cradled Raina in his arms and kissed the top of her head. "I know, and I dispatched crime scene technicians to go there right after I got Laprelli's call. I also called a maid service to go in and clean after the techs finished." Max led her to the sofa and made her sit down.

"Baby, we still need to get you to Seattle, but a flight at this point is not an option."

"Why not?" Both Raina and Nick responded, each asking with a sense of urgency.

"This killer, Pierce, obviously knows you were scheduled for a flight this morning."

"How would he know that, Max?" Raina asked, looking from Max to Nick.

Max decided to treat his niece as he would any other victim who was withholding information. He chose his words carefully. "He knows where you live."

"But I don't understand. How did he find out where I live?"

His eyes searched her face. "Why don't you tell me?" he said, waiting for her to answer. "What fell out of your purse in that alley?"

Raina blinked. "Huh? Oh, just a few things, but I picked them all up," she said quickly, recalling that's how she had gotten dirt under her fingernails.

"Where is the purse now?" Max asked through tight lips.

She thought for several seconds. "It's in my travel bag upstairs. When the detective here told me to pack this morning, I didn't have a chance to think, so I just grabbed a few things and dumped them into my travel bag. Why?"

"If you don't mind, go get it," Max said impatiently.

Raina stood up. "No, I don't mind, Max. I just don't know what you're getting at. Stop talking to me like I'm a child." She brushed past him and ran up the stairs, taking two at a time.

Nick had listened closely as the conversation unfolded. Something was wrong. "Sirs?"

Neither Max or Lyle Brown had a chance to answer because Raina returned, thrusting the small purse at Max. He opened it, noticed the few dirt-smudged items still inside from the other night, and looked up at her. "Where's your library card?"

Raina's chest sunk in. "What? It's in there. I know it is because I returned a book earlier that day." She looked up to see the detective studying her.

"No, you didn't, and it is not in here, *Suraina*." Max's usage of her full first name meant one thing, he was upset with her.

"But it has to be in there," she said feebly, taking her purse from him and searching for herself. "I remember seeing it when I was in the restroom at the restaurant." Not finding the card, Raina looked up at the men. "It's not here," she said after a while.

Lt. Brown spoke up. "Did you go to the library this morning around eight thirty?"

Both Raina and Nick responded, "No." But Raina could not meet their eyes now.

Seeing that Nick was about to ask the pertinent question, Max explained, "I went back to Raina's apartment after you called Lt. Brown informing him about the missed flight and the break-in. The answering machine was flashing, so I checked the messages. A librarian from the Fifth Avenue branch called, asking for *Mr. Wade*. She was concerned that *Mr. Wade* couldn't wait this morning to check out a book on hardwood floors and then rattled off the hours the library was open." Max watched Raina began to shake and eased her down to the sofa. "Raina, you dropped the card in the alley and that man picked it up. He went to the library this morning to have the barcode read and that's how he got your home address. He broke into your condo by way of the balcony, while the police stationed there went on a bathroom break."

"Oh, my God." Raina did look up at the detective then. "You were right. He had to have come out into the alley and must have found my library card." The large tears that had welled up finally spilled from her eyes. "I'm so sorry."

Watching his superior comfort his girlfriend, Nick said, "Chief, maybe we should check out the security cameras in and around the area of the library."

"Already done, but the man we can see on the video purposely kept his face averted from the cameras while he was in the library, and he wore a dress hat. A few minutes later, he's seen getting into a taxicab on Main Street and from the camera mounted on that street, is not conclusive, but he fits the description Raina gave us." Max looked up at Nick. "We have to come up with another way to get her to Seattle."

"Agreed, so how do we do that if flying is not an option?"

"I'll let Lt. Brown explain, but I'd like to talk to Suraina in private, if you don't mind." Why would he mind if the man wanted to talk to his girlfriend in private? Nick thought, waving his hand toward the kitchen.

Raina led Max through the kitchen, and opened the French doors so that they could talk on the back deck. The minute he closed the doors behind her, Raina collapsed in his outstretched arms. "Oh, Uncle Max, how could I have been so stupid? I should have known better."

Max encouraged her to sit in one of the deck chairs and sat down beside her. "You were scared. Now it's just us, but baby, honestly, when did you realize that library card was missing?"

"After you left this morning, I searched everywhere for it and I didn't mention anything because the card only had the bar code on it," she said pulling in a shaky breath. "That detective is putting his life on the line for me. And trust me, he's told me more than once so that I won't forget it, either. But I honestly didn't think about the library card, otherwise I would not have let us go back to my condo."

"I know that. So, how is it dealing with Detective Laprelli? He okay with you?"

"How do you mean?" Raina wiped her eyes with the handkerchief Max gave her.

"I mean he's a man without a shirt on and you are an attractive young lady. You just say the word and I'll find some old fart detective to babysit you to Seattle." He grinned at her exasperated expression.

"Oh, Max, you're awful, but no, he's okay, I guess. He hasn't done or said anything out of line to me, at least nothing that I didn't deserve to hear." Raina didn't think it necessary to complain how the detective forced her to look at those crime scene photos in that room at the airport. "He thinks I'm some kind of pampered princess. He was even shocked to see me drink a beer from the bottle." Raina snorted and rolled her eyes upward. "I got that from you, but I did refrain from the audible belching."

Max laughed. "Oh, if he only knew the real you." His eyes softened; Max knew how scared she was. "I have something for you." He pulled from his jacket pocket a thick envelope and handed it to her.

At that exact moment, Nick had returned to his bedroom to get his cell phone. His attention was immediately drawn to the security monitor, which had remained on. He watched the chief and Raina Wade sitting together on the deck, their hands clasped together. Not sure why he did it, but Nick pressed the remote . . . enlarging that picture, then pressed the volume up to hear their conversation.

Raina's eyes widened at the large amount of cash inside the envelope. "I have money in my checking and saving accounts—I don't need this," she said, holding it out for him to take back.

"Yes, you do. It should cover both of your traveling expenses, but if you need more, just call me—my cellphone is always on. And Raina, do not use your charge cards or your real name, anywhere. Det. Laprelli will go over everything with you later."

"Okay, thanks, Max." She kissed his cheek, then stood up with him.

"I love you with all my heart, Raina." She was indeed his only niece, and Max prayed she would arrive at her father's safely.

"I love you, too, Max. I hope you catch this Pierce guy soon so I can come back home and get back to living my boring life."

Hugging her to him, Max said, "Suraina, I have a feeling your life is going to be an adventure and the journey is just beginning, but just stay smart and you'll stay safe."

Nick saw they were about to come back into the house and flipped the monitor off and went back downstairs. He didn't have to hear them confessing their love for one another because he could see it in their actions and on their faces. Lt. Brown was still waiting to give him several phone numbers to key into his cell phone.

"Took your own sweet time, Laprelli," Lyle said just as Max returned to the living room with Ms. Wade.

"Sorry, pit stop." Nick looked up to see that his witness wore a dejected expression. He guessed she was already missing her lover. Judging by the size of the envelope she clutched, he was her sugar daddy, too.

Max was admiring Nick's living room. "Nice home. Tell me, Detective, have you thought about taking the test for a higher rank?" he asked, coming to stand in front of Nick.

"No, sir."

"Bullshit, all detectives do. But if you do think about it again, let Lt. Brown know. I would concur with you moving in that direction."

"I'll get there on my own merit eventually, sir," Nick said sourly.

"That's the only way you can make it, with integrity, Laprelli."

"I'll think on it, sir." Fat chance now, Nick thought. He was missing out on a conference in Las Vegas that would have given him the equivalent of eighty-plus hours to count toward the certification he needed for sergeant. *I can kiss that goodbye now because of this babysitting job,* he thought.

"You do that." Max turned to leave. "Sorry to have awakened you guys, but it was best that no one knew of this meeting except for a few key individuals for several reasons."

Other than their relationship, Raina sensed there was more. "What *other* reasons, Max?"

He turned back to his niece, but his gaze settled on Nick. "The killer is connected to another case . . . he killed an officer. We want to catch him for that, in addition to many other homicides, including those three people at that restaurant. We don't need cops out there being vigilantes and taking matters into their own hands, you understand?" Max stared above Raina's head into Nick's steely eyes.

Raina shook her head, not missing the look Max shot the detective as he spoke.

"Lt. Brown explained things to Laprelli and he'll fill you in." Max kissed her forehead again before walking to the hallway, where Lyle stood waiting.

When Nick crossed to open the front door, he let out a piercing whistle, calling for Reed.

Rubbing at his ear, Max stopped in the opened doorway.

"You two better behave yourselves. Sorry, Detective, but I'll put my money on her any day. Oh, and try not to let her kill you in the process of getting her to Seattle." Max grinned at the detective's dubious frown.

Reed flew into the house just as Max walked out. Closing the door, Nick suggested they turn in, promising to tell her of the travel plans tomorrow. Waving her to proceed up the stairs before him, Nick discovered another surprise about Ms. Wade. First, her full first name was Suraina, and second, she had a tattoo of a colorful flower with open petals on her right ankle.

He thought she had nice calves, too.

After a fitful sleep, Nick awakened at seven the next morning. His first dream involved his former partner, Scott. They were sitting on his deck, drinking a couple of beers and talking. Then he dreamed of catching Pierce and actually killing him. Nick remembered the feeling of relief welling up inside of him as he watched the last breath leave the man's body. The face Ms. Wade described in profile, and now in print, had turned grotesque. Lastly, he dreamed of Ms. Wade herself. She stepped from her steaming bath and into his arms . . . wet, and totally naked. Her honey golden skin was glistening, beckoning for him to kiss the water droplets from her body. *What the hell . . . ?*

Nick bolted up from bed. He was uncomfortable with the physical and emotional results of that last dream. Trotting down to the kitchen, he put on a pot of coffee and pulled a bowl of eggs and bacon from the fridge.

He wondered if his houseguest was still sleeping—in that mint-green, sexy boxer set. Nick groaned. Needing air, he opened the French doors, then walked out on the deck. Recalling the portion of the conversation he overheard between Raina Wade and Max Coleman, it was obvious to him they loved each other. Nick didn't want to dwell on them any longer than he had to. He wasn't assigned to judge them, just to get her to Seattle. Still feeling the need to burn off some of the frustration he was feeling about the whole situation, Nick walked from the deck, rounded a tree-lined walkway and continued on for several more feet until he stepped onto the tennis court he'd had installed five years earlier. Absently picking up a racket, he began bouncing a tennis ball on the court. He hadn't played tennis in over six months, not since Scott was killed.

Raina awakened to the aroma of coffee. It brought a smile to her face as she stretched her arms above her head, glad she'd remembered to set the automatic timer on her coffeepot. That's when her eyes flew open. Realization hit her like a ton of bricks . . . she hadn't set the timer and she wasn't in her own bed. With clarity, she remembered where she was and why.

Pulling herself from bed, Raina made her way to the bathroom. After dressing in white cotton shorts and matching T-shirt, she headed downstairs expecting to see the detective. Padding back to the kitchen, she saw the breakfast items sitting out on the counter and went about frying the bacon and scrambling the eggs. Finding frozen orange juice in the freezer, she prepared that as well.

To her delight she found a canister of cinnamon rolls in the fridge and popped them into the oven. She wondered where the detective was and walked about the first floor. She admired the large, airy rooms, the rich honey brown hardwood floors, doors and moldings. In the daylight, she saw the house was tastefully decorated and bathed with early morning light that spilled though the windows, bringing with it a delightfully warm breeze. The window curtains moved silently with the breeze as she made her way along the hallway to the living room. Just off the kitchen was an office and spotting some photos on a shelf, Raina went inside for a peek. One picture captured her attention immediately, catching her by surprise. The detective, much younger at the time, was standing beside her father, Michael Wade. Raina squinted and rubbed at her eyes just to make sure she was really seeing her father as he looked twelve years younger. She smiled at her father's stern expression. Only she knew what a teddy bear he really was. The detective had never said he knew her father, but judging from the picture her father was either his training officer or his captain. With sudden emotion bubbling up in her and renewing a sense of uncertainty for her future, Raina put the picture back on the shelf and quickly walked back to the kitchen to take the rolls out of the oven.

She had been downstairs for almost forty minutes and took that time to call Mrs. Wilson at the church to check on how things went with Julie and Janey. To her relief, Mrs. Wilson reported that she was working with Julie directly and the finance officer would be drafting checks for the girls' rent and utilities later that day. With that heavy load off her mind, Raina walked over to the open French doors and stepped out on the deck. She was amazed by what she'd missed in the dark last night. On the covered deck were a table and four chairs. The house itself sat on several acres of property with well-manicured lawns. The trees were large, numerous and quite full for June. Glancing around, she noticed the morning sun bounced off of everything green. The shrubs surrounding the bottom of the deck were healthy and full of fat buds, promising flowers soon. Leaning against the porch column a warm feeling washed over her and, for an instant, Raina realized she wasn't scared. She felt safe there.

Suddenly aware of a constant sound, she stepped down off the deck and began walking in the direction the sound was coming from. Rounding a grouping of trees and more bushes along a stone walkway, she was enjoying what she saw . . . spring in abundance. She longed to take off her tennis shoes and run barefoot through the lush green grass. She knew the area to be rural, mostly farms, but would have never imagined it to be so picturesque. Then she stopped in her tracks and stood in shock. A full tennis court lay ahead, and the detective was hitting neon yellow tennis balls across the empty court.

She nodded when he turned, sensing her approach. Stopping at the open cubie of rackets behind him, Raina picked up one, testing the balance in her hand. She knew he was watching her. "Good morning."

"Good morning, Ms. Wade," Nick said, watching as she walked toward the other end of the court, expertly bouncing a tennis ball with the racket as she went, then turned to face him from the baseline.

"Ah, I'm going to take a stab at this, but I'll bet you want me to hit some balls your way, right?" Nick called out, thankful she was at the opposite end of the court, and couldn't see the comical expression that crossed his face at his choice of words. But then she surprised him by throwing her head back and laughing. The sound pleasantly tickled his ears.

Raina laughed for several seconds. "That was a good one, Detective. You ready?" She had started bouncing the ball with the racket again as she called out to him.

Nick shrugged his shoulders, then gawked when a tennis ball flew past him. Turning back around, he had no time to recover, when she sliced another serve, missing his calf by mere inches.

"Are we playing or what?"

Nick thrust his hands on his hips. "I won't be gentle with you," he said.

"I can deal with what you send my way. So bring it on," Raina said.

After almost an hour of nonstop tennis, Raina was surprised how good it felt to play the game again. A few months ago she had begun showing Janey how to play, but the girl thought it was boring and just plain stupid hitting balls across the court. But not Raina, she liked the sport and missed finding the time to play anymore. The detective kept her running from one end of the court to the other, but she returned almost everything he sent her way, and in turn, she kept him running along the baseline. They were almost at a tie, with her leading by one point.

Nick was surprised by her serves and hard returns. As much as his calves were burning and the sweat was dripping into his eyes, he refused to give in or give up. He decided he would just tell her that he hadn't played that much, which was true. *"Psst."* Nick heard another tennis ace whiz past him. She won the match, and was now walking toward him, grinning.

"Sorry, I won the match," Raina called out, walking back up the court toward him. Nick blew out a breath. "No, I'm glad you did. You're quite good." His eyes took in the golden highlights in her brown hair as the sun beat down her glistening face.

Raina laughed as she put the racket back in the cubie. "I used to play a lot with a couple of friends, but I haven't had much time to do it lately." Being so close to him again, Raina had to force her eyes from the sweat sliding down his neck to his chest. "Hey, I'm starving," she said, walking back the way she'd come. Suddenly she needed distance from him . . . totally aware of his body. *This is stupid, he's just a man.* A sweaty, solid mass of masculinity, she thought, picking up her pace, irritated at herself for noticing him in that way.

Grabbing a towel from the cubie to mop his face, Nick grimaced. She was barely perspiring, whereas he was drenched. Walking several feet behind her, he had to force his mind from the sway of her hips, outlined in cotton shorts. When he stepped through the French doors, Nick stopped in his tracks when the smell of bacon and cinnamon filled his head. "Hey, you did this?" he asked, walking over to see food warming in covered dishes on the stove.

"I hope it was okay. I mean, I saw stuff sitting on the counter." Worry lines creased her forehead. At times, Raina had a tendency to overstep, like being in someone's home and giving her decorating or coloring opinions even when they weren't solicited.

"Yes, it's fine, but I'm supposed to cook for you, or so I was told," Nick said, lifting the paper towel from the tray of rolls and inhaling.

Raina crossed to the sink and washed her hands. "Did your sister tell you that?"

"No actually, I remember my mother telling me that." He studied her for a few seconds more then walked into the first floor bathroom and washed his face. When he returned to the kitchen a few minutes later, he found her fixing their plates.

Raina handed him a mug of coffee. "Cream and sugar. Um, sorry if I got personal."

"Thank you," Nick said, accepting the mug and thinking about what she'd said. "It wasn't a personal question. Ms. Wade, my parents were alcoholics. My sister was left to take care of me from the time I was about ten, perhaps younger. As we got older, we became their caretakers, right up until they left us." Nick realized she was waiting for him to finish. "They were gone for a couple of weeks, taking another traveling drinking binge thing, something they often did, and a week later we got word they had been killed in a car accident. They were both intoxicated." He picked up a roll and bit into it.

Raina had watched him as he talked about his parents. She was at a loss at what to say or even why she felt compelled to say anything at all. He was a stranger. "I'm sorry, that must have been such an awful burden on both of you. You said your sister's name is Jenny, right?"

"Right, but I'm not bitter about how I was raised, and neither is she. We survived a terrible home life with parents who were teenagers when they had us, and they were forced to get married by their parents." He lifted his shoulders. "We were just smart enough not to bring any friends home."

"Still, it must have been rough," Raina said quietly, knowing that many children in the mentoring program came from the type of home he had just described.

Nick guessed she had no idea how rough it really was for him and Jenny. Suddenly uncomfortable, he held out a stool and waited for her to take a seat. His eyes strayed to the back of her neck, where tendrils of her hair rested against the dampness of her neck.

Raina changed the subject. "I didn't sleep well after the visit from your lieutenant."

"And Chief Coleman. He probably just wanted to come and see if my place was suitable enough for you to be here. It's kind of rustic and old fashioned," he said.

"He admired the soundness of your house and he thought the deck was expertly crafted. He said once you finished the step railings, it would be perfect. He notices things like that."

"I guess you would know." Nick mumbled, wondering why he'd said that.

Raina knew exactly what the detective thought . . . that there was something going on with her and Max. Well, she wouldn't break her agreement not to disclose their true relationship. She decided to let him think whatever he wanted to think. She didn't owe this cop any explanation whatsoever. She changed the subject again. "So, are you going tell me how you're going to get me to Seattle?"

Nick was glad to let the matter of Max Coleman drop. "Okay, we're going to drive from here on Saturday at about six in the evening and head west. I'll map it out on GPS here. We'll cut through Chicago and from there we may take a train, or, if it's safe, we'll catch a couple of commuter flights to reach Seattle."

"How long will this trip take?" Today was Wednesday . . . she'd have to stay with him for several days.

"I'll push it and then you won't have to suffer too long with my company." He sipped his coffee to keep from talking.

"That's not why I asked."

"Oh, really?" He raised skeptical eyes at her.

"I asked because I only packed clothes for a couple of days. If you'll remember, Detective, I expected to have been in Seattle by now," she said tightly, ignoring his sarcasm.

"Yes, but then you changed your flight seating so you didn't have to suffer my company on such a long flight." When he saw the narrowing of her eyes, Nick rushed on, "In any case, we can stop and pick some things up."

"Thanks," Raina said, rolling her eyes at him. "Max gave me $5,000. He said it was traveling expenses for the both of us."

"Whoa, then the gas and airline tickets are on you." Having cleaned his plate, Nick got up and put it in the sink. Behind her, his eyes were drawn to her stiff shoulders. "I'm going to take a shower. Leave the dishes and thanks for breakfast."

Raina remained quiet as she watched him refill her coffee mug and then walk out.

Pierce sat in an internet café downtown, searching the web. He was checking flights to Seattle. He knew Raina Wade hadn't boarded the flight yesterday evening. He guessed she would be looking for another flight to get to Seattle.

Several hours after leaving the library, he'd gone to her condo, but didn't have a chance to check it thoroughly before she'd returned. He was just glad he had already disabled the light switch. Still, he'd been caught off guard when she suddenly returned, and had it not been for her male companion, he would have ended her life then and there by cutting her throat. Now, he just needed to make sure she didn't arrive at her destination. From what he could tell, she would be traveling alone, no kids and no husband, and only her name was on the airline reservation. He believed she was at the Italian restaurant alone and maybe she hadn't told the police what she had witnessed.

Studying her motor vehicle picture now appearing on the screen, Pierce smiled. She was pretty and smart. His shoulder still ached from the impact of that cigarette butt can crashing down on him. Rubbing at the sore spot, he thought about how he was going to pay her back for that before he ended her life.

Pierce's fingers swiftly flew over the keyboard. His next assignment was in Chicago. *I haven't been to the windy city in quite a while*, he mused. But for the purpose of eradicating the world of another criminal, he thought the trip was worth it. He printed out a map.

CHAPTER 6

Nick managed to steer clear of his houseguest for most of the rest of the morning. She remained shut away in the guest room until noon. He went up to get her for lunch. After knocking on the door several times, he didn't get a response. "Ms. Wade." Nick turned the knob, easing the door open. He saw that she had fallen asleep in the armchair, clutching a book to her chest, and with music playing softly on the small stereo.

Several seconds ticked by as Nick stood watching her sleep. He remembered her mentioning not sleeping well after their visitors. Nick was at a loss as to what to do. Clearly, he knew she would awaken with a stiff neck if he didn't wake her.

Walking over to her, he plucked the book from her slack fingers and then lifted her reading glasses from her nose, placing both on the dresser. Letting his eyes travel down her body, he would guess she weighed no more than 105 pounds; aware of his train of thought, he pressed his lips together tightly.

"Oh, hell." He expelled a breath and, without waking her, effortlessly lifted her from the chair and carried her to the bed. Her body felt warm and soft against his. Her bare thighs resting on his forearms heated him throughout. The hair on the top of her head touched his nose, and unconsciously Nick lowered his head, inhaling lightly. He thought her hair smelled fruity. Gently, he laid her on the bed and pulled a cover up over her, and still she slept. Nick backed up to the door to leave. Hesitating, he thought she reminded him of a sleeping beauty, because she was certainly that . . . a beauty.

It was two in the afternoon when Raina awakened and finally ventured downstairs. Walking through the first floor to the kitchen, she spotted the detective sitting out on the deck. He was working on his laptop computer. Raina watched his profile as she stood, unseen, in the kitchen. Although she had never given men outside her race any serious consideration, she again thought he was very attractive for a white guy, and wondered why she was so aware of him. Letting her eyes travel up his bare forearms, she couldn't help but recall his body pressed against hers when she awakened him in the early morning hour. Just then he looked up, catching her staring at him, and beckoned her to join him.

Nick knew the moment she stepped into the kitchen. Her light perfume filled his nose when air circulated from the open kitchen windows through the open screen of the French doors. He wondered how long she was going to stand there. When she stepped out on the patio, he sat back in his chair and watched her. "How was your nap?" His eyes took in her natural beauty. Her expressive, chestnut-brown eyes lit up her face.

"Definitely needed." Raina watched him cautiously. She didn't even know how to ask if he'd put her in the bed, but knew she hadn't gotten there on her own. "Did you come upstairs?"

Nick held up his hand to stop her from talking. "I came up to wake you up for lunch. I knocked several times and then let myself in. You were sleeping in that chair, I put you on the bed, and left." He tilted his head back further, watching her.

"Oh, well, I figured as much." Raina broke eye contact with him when Reed came up the deck, circling her bare legs. "Hello, Reed," she said. She bent down and scratched behind the dog's ears.

"And that's all I did, Ms. Wade." Nick clearly enunciated each word to alleviate any misunderstanding. "You're a witness and a guest in my home." Guiltily, Nick recalled letting his eyes roam over her sleeping body and forced his eyes away from her bowed head.

She continued playing with the dog's ears, then glanced up to find him staring at her with those penetrating gray eyes. Immediately she was on the defensive. "What?"

"Nothing," Nick said, dropping his eyes to Reed. "Are you hungry?"

"Yes. You said you fixed lunch, what'd you fix?" she asked, pulling herself out a chair and sitting adjacent to him. She noticed he'd picked up a slight tan from their tennis game.

"Chicken salad. Can I fix you a couple of sandwiches?"

"A couple, no, but one would be fine." She watched him move his papers and bills from in front of her. "What are you doing?"

"Paying some bills I know will come due while I'm gone."

"Oh." Her eyes swept over the stacks of envelopes, address labels and stamps. "You don't pay your bills online, Detective?" She frowned when he shook his head and began flipping through his stack of household and credit card bills. "Don't you know that by the time you write out the checks and mail them and the post office clears them and sends them where they're supposed to go, they'll be late? If you were to pay them online, your bank can clear them in a day or so. It's a much better system, especially for the environment—no wasted paper. I can set it up in no time and have all these bills paid." She patted his stack of bills. "What'd you say? Want to join the new millennium a few years late?"

Nick was interested. He was tired of writing out checks. "You wouldn't mind?"

"No, and next month, you just log on to your bank's website, pull up the list I'm going to create for you, and fill in the amount you want to pay. It's as simple as that. Do you have direct deposit?" When he said he did, Raina smiled, slid his laptop over to her and began typing. "I'll take lettuce and tomato on that chicken salad sandwich."

Nick watched her fingers fly across the keys, then backed into the house.

Within an hour Raina had given him a working knowledge of how to pay his bills and manage his account online. She had also finished her lunch, but was still munching on the carrot sticks he'd served with her sandwich.

"I'm amazed, and I'll be checking to see if you use my credit cards to buy more romance novels." Nick thought she was cute trying to hide what he knew she'd been reading upstairs. "Thank you."

Raina got up and walked over to the deck, where she gazed out across the green lawns. "It's really nice here." She was already regretting having to leave soon.

"Yeah, that's why I stayed on here." Nick got up and went to stand beside her. Raina turned to him. "What do you mean stayed here? This is your home, isn't it?"

"This farm, as well as all the surrounding land, was left to me and my sister by our grandparents. My sister wanted no part of it, so I bought her out and sold off a lot of the outer property to the four neighboring farms. I kept maybe ten or twelve acres."

Raina watched a bird fly by. "How come you didn't tell me you knew my father?"

Nick turned, studying her side profile for seconds. "It wasn't important."

"He was obviously important to you. I saw a picture inside, both of you in full dress uniform. I would guess you were being pinned as an officer. I happen to know my dad only did that with officers he cared about, and those who'd completed their training under him. He was important to you. Why didn't you mention it?" she asked.

Nick was still watching her. "Like I said, it wasn't important to your case."

"You mean you didn't want to let him know that you're the one responsible for babysitting his daughter all the way to Seattle?" She turned to face him then. "I think he would be happy about that, Detective, wouldn't you?"

"Actually, Ms. Wade, I was a thorn in Michael Wade's side, so I'm pretty sure I'll be dropping you off on his front step very quickly before he kicks my ass off of it."

After a few seconds reflecting on what he'd said, Raina nodded. "You liked him."

"Can we change the subject, please?"

Raina looked out beyond a line of trees to the left, about two hundred feet in the distance. "What's out there?"

Nick turned in the direction she was looking, thankful for the change of subject. "That building on the right is an unused barn. It just has old farm equipment in there. To the left, beyond those trees, is a small creek. Great for swimming, and lots of fish. Around that bend . . ." Nick said, pointing out another area.

Raina cut him off. "Can I walk out to the creek and check it out?"

"Ah, sure, but I think I better go with you. There're some rocks up there that are kind of jagged. They get slick when they're wet, so watch your footing." He looked down at her tennis shoes just as she stepped down off the deck. "Hey, can you fish?" Nick doubted she had ever touched a live fish in her life.

"What do you think, Detective Know-It-All?"

Nick was left wondering how to respond, so he simply grabbed a couple of fishing rods and his tackle box from the corner of the deck and hurried to catch up with her.

Walking side by side to the edge of his property line, Nick waved to neighbors and called out greetings. When he whistled in the air for Reed, the dog pounced from under the porch of another neighbor's house and joined them.

Laughing when the dog circled their legs, they soon disappeared through the grouping of trees. And after a few minutes of walking along a worn path of thick ground cover, surrounded by tall, lush trees, they came to a clearing. Nick watched her reaction to the creek—a place he had spent many hours as a teenager, and beyond.

"Wow." Raina inhaled deeply and smiled as she stared out over the glistening, bubbling water as it slowly moved downstream. The early afternoon sun was reflecting off the water. A profusion of colorful and fragrant wild-flowers and flowing bushes covered a lot of the grassy area circling the banks. Above her, birds sang out melodies, and butterflies were hanging out on leaves, showing off their colorful wings. Spring was in full bloom. "It's just beautiful."

"Yeah, I think so, too." He thought she was beautiful, too.

"You know, I think I've seen this same creek on *The Andy Griffith Show*," she said, turning to smile at him. "Actually, I think it's a lake or a pond, definitely bigger than a small creek, Detective."

"Fun-ny," Nick said, inclining his head to the right, where several rounded rocks stuck up from the ground. "I like to fish up at that end."

Raina's gaze drifted past him briefly, and then she took one of the fishing rods from his hand. "Okay," she said, walking ahead of him, testing the line and the reel as she did.

"That's my favorite rod, lady," he said with a shake of his head. "I'm only sharing it with you because you're my houseguest." He set the tackle box on the rock and opened it. When he reached for the rod so he could hook her line, she plucked the fishing lure from his hand.

Knowing he was watching her, she deftly attached the lure to the line and said, "I know how to do this." When he gave her a doubtful expression, she walked forward and expertly cast the line, sending it far out into the water. Turning back, she gave him a triumphant look.

Another surprise, Nick thought. Within seconds, he saw her line jump vigorously. Throwing his rod to the ground, he ran over to her. "I don't believe this." He tried to take the rod from her hands, but she shocked him even more by snatching the line in the water sideways to make sure the hook was set before she slowly began reeling the line in.

"Are you not going to catch your own?" she asked, casting a sideways glance at his rod, which was still laying on the grass.

Nick was intently watching the line, waiting to see the fish she had caught. "Huh?"

"This is my dinner." She grinned when his gray eyes grew wider watching her lift the foot-long fighting and curling fish from the water. "He is gonna be so good all battered up."

Nick laughed hard for several seconds. He couldn't believe she could catch a fish. He watched as she expertly unhooked the fish, fed the nylon rope he handed her through the gill, and hung it on a nearby tree branch.

Raina hooked the line again. "I mean it, you better catch your own fish."

"That sounds like a challenge," Nick said, casting his own line. Within a couple of minutes, he proceeded to catch a fish—a much smaller one than hers.

Biting his lip in frustration, Nick tossed the little fish back into the water. "This is your fault, you know," he said, pointing to her fish dangling from the tree. "You do realize that since you took my favorite fishing rod, that fish really is mine."

"You think so?" Raina wedged the rod down between two rocks, intending to walk toward the tree where the fish was hanging. But just as she turned, her tennis shoe hit upon a wet spot on the rock, and she began to tumble down from the four-foot-high rock.

Seconds before she hit the ground, Nick caught her. Holding her trembling body firmly against his, he became lost gazing into the depths of her brown eyes. With effort, he dragged his eyes down to her ankle. "Your foot . . . can you move it?

Raina swallowed hard. She'd had an immediate reaction to being held in his arms. Her arms had instinctively wrapped themselves around his wide shoulders. Her breasts were plastered against the solid wall of his chest, and she could even feel his heart beating. Shaken by the contact, Raina nodded that she was okay. "I–I'm sorry. I guess I should have paid more attention when you told me to watch my step out here."

Easing her body down and away from him, Nick, too, was stirred by the contact, but managed to encourage her to test her ankle. "It seems okay." He stood back from her. Heat permeated his body with sensual awareness. Not good. "You sure you're okay?"

Because her stomach began to do somersaults, Raina shook her head, yes, and stamped her feet a couple of times. Looking up, her eyes were drawn over his shoulder. Her fishing line was bobbing in the air. "Yes, I'm fine, but, I . . ."

Nick pulled his eyes away from her breasts, now visible through her T-shirt. "What is it?"

Raina pointed to the bouncing fishing rod. "I think I have second helpings of my dinner." She hurried off, careful of her footing, and reeled the fishing line in. But it took several minutes to still her trembling hands . . . and that was not because of the second large fish she was reeling in.

Only Reed's insistent barking pulled Nick's attention from her movements to his own bouncing line. He was astounded by his reaction to his witness . . . who just happened to be another man's woman.

Several hours later, Raina knocked on the door to the den where Nick was working. She pushed the door opened slightly. "Dinner's ready. I cooked the bigger ones." His eyes narrowed at her burst of giggles. "Oh, you're being a spoilsport, Detective. In fairness, you get credit for cleaning them."

Nick stood up and walked out into the hallway. They both had showered after returning from fishing, and whatever fragrance she had on was once again distracting him. He wondered where she'd sprayed it on her body.

In the kitchen Raina had set out fried potatoes and salad to go with the fish. "You know, your kitchen is a vegetarian's paradise. You have tons of fresh veggies, and even your freezer is full of them. I know you're not a vegetarian because you ate bacon and chicken today, so what's up?"

Grinning, Nick explained that his neighbors were all farmers and whatever he needed he always got from them . . . whether he wanted it or not. Sitting on the stool beside her, he said, "It has been a long time since someone cooked for me in my kitchen. And you surprise me, Ms. Wade. I mean you cook and you know how to fish, so now you tell me what's up."

After listening to him and wiping her hand, Raina extended it to him. When he presented a puzzled look, she said, "I'm introducing myself, Detective. I'm Raina." Her eyes searched his. Nick shook her hand slowly. "Nick Laprelli and it's nice to meet you . . . Suraina."

Raina was surprised that he had remembered her uncle calling her by her full first name last night. She liked the way he said it, though, and for several seconds found it hard to pull her eyes away from his, let alone let go of his hand.

Nick resumed eating. "Why don't you use your full name? It's kinda pretty. It's not like your name is Hannah or Eloise, or some other old-fashioned name like that."

"Nobody calls me that anymore, except for Max. You heard him the other night, right?"

"Um-hum," Nick mumbled around a mouthful of perfectly seasoned potatoes.

"I figured that was it, because I only use Raina, and that was on the police report." Raina geared up for another tense discussion about her uncle.

"I think it's a nice name, and Chief Coleman must think so, since he used it." Nick watched her face grow tense and was hard-pressed to find a reason why he even brought the man up at all.

"So, what time are we leaving on Saturday . . . Nick?" Raina thought changing the subject from her uncle Max to something safer was called for.

"We'll leave about six in the evening. That'll put us in the middle of evening traffic. Less chance we would be spotted, that is, if . . ." He turned to her and weighed his words. "Suraina, out here you're safe. Trust me, if my neighbors saw a stranger walking up the road, they'd be on the phone calling each other, then the local sheriff, then me. But when we leave here, it's back to how it was before. Pierce is still out there."

Raina hadn't forgotten about the killer. She only had to close her eyes to see his face and the devastation he caused again. Each time she drifted off to sleep, she saw him walking toward the back of the restaurant where she was hiding. "I know you're right, Nick, and I know I can't stay here hiding out, but I can tell you I feel safe here," she said quietly.

"I know you do, but my job is to get you to Seattle safely," he said, noticing her worried frown. "Raina, um, in your statement you hinted at something about the killer that you couldn't recall then. But I can tell you that over time many witnesses do remember bits or fragments of vital information. Sometimes it's that information that can lead to a capture. As your mind relaxes and processes the event, it will allow you to see other things that may have occurred at the time."

"I've been struggling to see it, or at least remember whatever it was, and so far nothing. When I think about that night . . . it's just so awful, so painful." Raina didn't want to tell him that whenever she drifted off, she saw the killer's profile. "You think he's laying in wait for me, don't you, Nick?" Raina fought against the urge to cry.

He wasn't going to lie to her. "Yes, I do. You saw him kill three people in cold blood, and you're the only one who can link him to crimes. You're the only thing standing between him and a prison sentence, and that's why he broke into your condo. I'm glad you outsmarted him by feigning passing out." Nick recollected her telling him that as they ran from the condo.

"Max said this guy also killed a cop. Did you know him?"

Nick sat back. He was never prepared to talk about his ex-partner, Scott. To talk about him was like picking at the scab of a slowly healing wound. It still hurt like hell. "Scott Morgan was my best friend and my partner." He gave her a direct, unsmiling look. "He'd been on the force for six years." Nick sipped the lemonade Raina had served with dinner. "We didn't know it was a hit until his body was recovered . . . the manner of death was similar to others . . . a severed finger and single gunshot to the head. We're pretty sure this sicko has some sort of collection hidden someplace. It's been six months since Scott was killed."

Raina's heart broke. She hated to see anyone grieve. Realizing that he had lost his friend so recently, she was sure that was the cause of the sadness that she sensed in Nick. She had seen it earlier while they sat on the rocks fishing. She'd asked how often he'd gone fishing, and after a few seconds of quietly staring out into the water, Nick told her that he and his friend used to fish there often, with Scott's two young sons.

"I'm sorry you lost your friend, Nick. That must still hurt a lot." Raina's hand ached to touch him. She found that was very odd, considering he was practically a stranger. She reasoned her empathy for him was no different than what she felt for the kids in the mentoring program. They too were often sad, heartbroken and lonely.

"Everyone has told me time heals," Nick mumbled, absently toying with his glass.

"Yes, that's what they say, but they never say how long it will take. I think it's part of the grieving process that you feel such hurt. Then one day out of the blue, for some reason it just doesn't seem to hurt in here so much anymore," she said pointing to her heart. "And maybe that's when you get comfort from your memories, Nick."

Nick heard her words and he felt her sympathy for what he was feeling. His attention was drawn to her lips, inviting when she spoke. And had he not accidentally tipped his glass over, spilling lemonade and ice cubes, because of his trembling hand, Nick knew without a doubt he would have inched forward and kissed her. In fact, he did lean forward to do so. *Oh, damn!*

Simultaneously, Nick and Raina jumped up and grabbed paper towels from the counter and began quickly wiping up the lemonade from the center island.

Raina's hands brushed his as she swiftly pushed the paper towels around. She couldn't look at him because she felt extremely guilty and embarrassed. Whereas she had thought she only wanted to touch his arm in a comforting gesture over his grief, she desperately wanted to kiss him and that's why she leaned toward him. *Stupid, stupid.* Chastising herself, she went to the sink, wet a sponge and began wiping down the island top. "It didn't spill on our food, did it?" Only then did she dare to raise her eyes to his steely ones, which were staring at her intently.

Shaken to the core, Nick forced his gaze from her. He couldn't explain it. What was he thinking, trying to kiss her like that, he wondered. But then, he could have sworn she leaned forward, too, like maybe she wanted him to kiss her, or knew that he was about to. No, no. It was him, and he needed to get a handle on himself, or he was going to be fired, like those contestants in that game show. *You're fired.* Just then, Lt. Brown's words echoed back in his head. Nick also remembered what Chief Coleman said before he left. *You two had better behave yourselves.* Temptation sucked. But so did inappropriate longing, he realized.

He took the sponge from her hand. "I'll do this, you sit and finish eating."

Returning to her seat, Raina watched him behind her glass. *He's upset. Did he know what I was about to do?* She prayed he didn't. "I think it's all cleaned up now."

Nick retrieved the pitcher of lemonade from the refrigerator and refilled their glasses. "I think I need something a little stronger than lemonade." He sat the pitcher down and reached into the cupboard, pulling out a bottle of vodka. After pouring a shaky splash into his glass he held the bottle up, offering her some.

"Why the hell not? Eat, drink and be merry tonight, for tomorrow we . . . I mean, me . . . may die, right?" Raina's ill attempt at humor failed miserably. "I'm sorry," she said plaintively, remembering his partner's death, and dropped her head in embarrassment.

Nick ruffled her curls and poured vodka into her glass. "No, we are not dying tomorrow, Suraina. We're preparing to go on a road trip in a couple of days and, somewhere between here and Chicago, we'll find a Wal-Mart so you can buy some more clothes." Testing his drink and finding it to his liking, he smiled just as her head popped up.

Having just taken a gulp of the spiked lemonade, Raina caught his smile. The brew barely made it past her windpipe when she sputtered and coughed. "What? Wait a minute . . . Wal-Mart? I–I don't shop for clothes at Wal-Mart, Nick." She watched him drink from his glass, fascinated to watch his Adam's apple bob as he swallowed.

Setting his glass down, Nick leaned down on his elbow so that they were at the same level. "Ah-ha, so now the little princess pops out. What's wrong with Wal-Mart? I shop there all the time."

"Well, of course you do." When she saw his eyebrows lift, she hurried to explain what might be construed as an insult. "What I meant was . . . well, you're a man, and I don't think men really care where they buy their T-shirts, socks and underwear. But I prefer to shop at ladies' apparel stores." She sipped her drink. "Hey, and what do you mean by 'so now the little princess pops out'? What's up with that?"

Nick resumed his seat. "First, there's nothing wrong with Wal-Mart stuff. My T-shirts, socks and underwear hold up just fine, okay, lady?" He saw that her face was turning red and guessed it was because of the vodka she was sipping, and not the indignation of being called a little princess. Or maybe it was what was most pressing on his mind . . . that almost-kiss. "I just meant that's how I expected you to be. Remember, it was my first impression of you."

"Oh, you mean that slap at the police station."

"Hey, I haven't forgotten about that. My face was red for a while." He grinned when she rolled her eyes at him, then began eating again.

She looked up. "It was just dumb of you to say that stuff to me. You were a jerk."

Drinking from his glass, he watched her. "I'm sorry I thought you were a hooker."

Raina was feeling a warming buzz. "I can't believe you insulted me like that." Her lips went tight recalling the incident, and she geared up to give him another piece of her mind. "Oh, was I mad at you. I still cannot believe what you said . . . why, you arrogant, big-headed . . ."

Nick cut her off. "Was mad? That must mean I'm forgiven. The truth is I had gotten chewed out for messing up a case just before you came over to my desk. And I knew that vice had a sting going on to bring in prostitutes, so when I looked down and saw a pair of kick-ass shoes and beautiful legs, well . . ." Nick spread his hands, grinning.

Plopping her chin on her open palm, she said, "I was a mess, but those shoes were fabulous, weren't they?" Within seconds, her faced sobered and she burst into tears. She was immediately embarrassed for coming apart in front of him. Raina didn't even think she could explain what she was feeling, even when he stood up and placed a comforting hand on her back. When she'd managed to control her sobs to a point where she could talk, she lifted her wet face from her equally wet hands. "I–I'm sorry."

"If you're crying about that slap, I've gotten over it." He watched her shake her head. "Is it the fish? After all, you were the one talking to them all the way back to the house." Nick's stomach tightened, holding back a laugh, recalling her telling the fish how she was going to fry them up, nice and golden. She shook her head, no. "Okay, I'm lost. Tell me why you're crying."

"I was thinking about Rachel and the shoes, that's all." Sniffing back more tears at saying the name, Raina managed to explain. "Rachel was in the restaurant with Mr. Coates. She worked in my building, but I didn't really like her that much. On my way to the ladies' room, she stopped me and admired my kick-ass shoes, as you called them. She forgot all about Mr. Coates and went to the ladies' room with me." More tearful sobs came. "I let her try the shoes on." Exhausted, Raina dropped her head into her hands again.

Remembering the female victim's name was Rachel, Nick felt bad for forcing her to relive those awful moments again. Leaning closer, he tried to pry her hands away from her face, but she wouldn't' budge. "So you let Rachel try your shoes on?"

Raina looked up, her eyes settling somewhere beyond Nick's shoulder. She smiled, recalling Rachel's antics in the ladies' room. "Yes, I did. Her feet were a full size larger than mine, but it was okay because they were sandals, you know. She said the shoes made the junk in her trunk bounce." Raina sniffed, and sobs began again.

Frowning, Nick shook his head. "Excuse me, her what, in her what—did what?"

"Rachel was bootylicious," she said casually by way of an explanation.

Nick laughed. "What language are you speaking?"

She looked at him, exasperated. "Rachel was a sister with a really big butt."

"Oh, you mean she drew attention when she walked down the street?"

"She sure did," Raina said with a belch.

Nick held onto the laughter threatening to burst from him. He thought Raina Wade had a pretty nice trunk herself. That sobered him immediately. "So, um, Rachel had a few happy moments before she died. You let her put those shoes on and shake her ah, junk or trunk, whatever it was . . . anyway, you gave them to her, Raina." Nick cringed at the fresh watery pools welling up in her red eyes. But before she dropped her head to her hands again, Nick grasped her hand, encouraging her to stand up. When she did, he folded her within the circle of his arms. Her cheek rested on his chest and her arms eased around his waist, and he felt his heart rate accelerating. And knowing it was wrong to hold her that way, he couldn't stop himself because he wanted to comfort her.

With one hand loosely around her waist, he said, "Here, drink some more of my special lemonade. It is a cure-all." When she lifted her head from his chest, he held the rim of the glass to her lips, trying hard not to focus on her small pink lips or her beautiful face.

Raina definitely wasn't a big drinker, and rarely did she drink hard liquor. It just added to the emotional roller coaster she felt she was riding. She was comforted just by resting her head on his chest, where the rhythmic beating of heart was a soothing balm for her frazzled nerves. When his arms held onto her tighter, Raina inhaled his masculine scent.

A combination so powerful, it sent a pleasurable shock through her body. Seeing he was still waiting for her to drink, she took a sip and dropped her head back onto his chest.

Nick was in deep. The scent and feel of her shot a swift path to the pit of his stomach, and was moving lower. If they stayed that way much longer, he would be in trouble.

"Suraina." He managed to say her name, but just barely.

Raising her eyes up a fraction, to his chin, she said, "I'm such a mess, but honestly I'm scared to death, Nick. You remember at the airport when you said you had a lot you still wanted to do with this life? Well, so do I. But when I go back out there, it'll be open season on me. I would be devastated if I get careless and some innocent person got hurt." Her eyes lifted to his mouth. His lips looked moist, and tempting. Raina wondered how they would feel on hers. She wondered what it would be like to kiss him.

The urge to kiss her was great, and yet he knew it was wrong. Nick raised his hand and touched her cheek with his open palm. Seconds later he lowered his head. His common sense was battling with what he wanted to do . . . what he desired to do. And she wanted him to kiss her. But it was still wrong. He couldn't take advantage of her, and dropped his hand away from her cheek. "Raina," he said. His voice sounded raspy.

His five o'clock shadow grazed against her cheek for a moment, then Raina felt him ease her back from him. Stepping back from him, she knew he was as affected by the brief moment of intimacy as she was. His arm remained around her waist, more loosely now, and when he reached for her chin . . . and the second she was about to go back into arms, her cell phone rang its musical tone, loud, intrusive and timely.

Each was shaken by her seemingly deafening ring-tone, but each knew the ramifications, had her cell phone not rung.

Raina stepped away and picked up her cell phone from the counter, where it sat charging. "Hello." Her breath came out in a rush, "Max, hi. Yes, I–I'm fine." As she spoke, her eyes strayed to Nick. He began putting his leftovers in containers and into the refrigerator.

Nick's heart was hammering in his chest. He had to do something with his hands lest he reach for her, because he wanted to touch her again. He was about to jeopardize yet another important case by becoming distracted. What was wrong with him? Was he so hungry for female companionship that he was ready to pounce on a helpless, frightened woman? A woman who was also a witness? Nick wiped the counters down while she talked quietly to her lover.

Raina didn't want to talk to her uncle. She wanted to talk to the man who, for a few brief moments, made her feel like a woman. A man who'd made her remember long-ago moments of intimacy with a slight touch and a look. Snapping her cell phone shut, Raina turned back to him and found it hard to speak. "That was Max, checking in."

Nick nodded. "Well, I've eaten all of my dinner and you still have plenty left, so, um, I'm going to finish working in my den," he said, walking around her. Her words stopped him in his tracks.

"We're not even going to acknowledge what happened before my cell phone rang?"

At first, he didn't want to acknowledge that anything had happened, but he knew it had, or almost had. He'd almost just done what he wanted to do . . . kiss her. He still wanted to, and that was why he needed distance from her. Turning, he faced her and crossed his arms over his chest. "There's nothing to acknowledge, nothing happened." His eyes searched hers.

"Okay, Nick." Raina sat down on the stool, picked up her fork and began eating. She could act like nothing almost happened just as much as he could.

Nick watched her, immediately recalling her lips on the rim of the glass he held for her. "Raina," he began, taking two steps toward her, but a tap on the open French doors forced his attention away from her.

Raina looked up to see a pretty woman standing on the other side of the screen door.

The woman called out to Nick as she stepped into the kitchen, then immediately stopped when she saw he had company. "Oh, I'm sorry," she mumbled in apology, her gaze on the pretty black woman sitting at the center-island.

"Hey, Marcia." Nick came forward and kissed the woman lightly on her cheek.

"Hi, Nick. I didn't mean to barge in on you," Marcia said, turning curious eyes to his guest and waiting for him to make a proper introduction. He did.

"It smells wonderful in here," Marcia said, handing Nick a large covered plate.

Nick smiled. "Raina was gracious enough to fry the fish we caught earlier. By the way, tell your dad the big fish were biting today." He winked at Raina.

Raina felt she was in the way. "Well, it was nice to meet you, Marcia." Turning to Nick, she said, "I'm going to turn in." Getting up with her plate, Raina dumped the contents into the trash and sat the plate in the sink. She then walked past Nick on her way out of the room and rolled her eyes.

It seemed like hours since they had eaten dinner together, but only two hours had passed. Nick sat alone in his den, having finished his paperwork. When Marcia came right out and asked him why Raina was there, he made a point of telling her they were taking a short road trip together. And that was all he'd said. When he walked Marcia to the screen door an hour later, he didn't miss the look she gave him, but Nick brushed it off. "Hey, is Reed over at your place?"

"No, but I saw him heading under the Loemans' front porch. Guess he's sticking close to Mitzy since she's getting heavy with their puppies. You need to get him neutered, Nick, but you're a male, so we know how that goes, right?" She waved and walked away.

Wincing, Nick thought, yeah, he knew how that went.

The smell of the apple pie drifted from the kitchen to his den. He decided to use the apple pie that Marcia's mother sent over as a peace offering to Raina because he sensed that she was upset with him. But it didn't escape his notice that he cared if she was mad at him or not.

While Nick visited with the woman downstairs, Raina had taken a shower and dressed in a sleeveless cotton shirt and a pair of shorts. She wondered who the woman was. Obviously she was familiar enough with Nick to just walk right into his home. Raina was sitting on the floor sketching on a large pad when she heard him knock and call out. "Come in," she said.

Nick was surprised to see her sitting on the floor. "Hi," he said. "You going somewhere?" he asked noticing her clothes, as well as the empty glass on the nightstand.

Looking up, she frowned at his question. "No. Why?"

"You're dressed like you're going to the store or some-place."

"Oh, I only packed one set of night clothes, so I have to sleep in these."

When he asked if she needed to do laundry, Raina replied that she did. Nick walked over and sat in the chair beside the bed. "Why didn't you say so?"

"Nick, I'm a guest and I've already taken liberties in your home." *And with you.*

Nick rubbed his forehead. "The utility room is off the kitchen. It's that door next to the bathroom. There's a washer and dryer in there. Would you like to do your laundry now?"

She shook her head. "I can do it tomorrow, if you don't mind."

"I don't mind. Are you going to be comfortable sleeping in that tonight? I have tons of those Wal-Mart T-shirts." He looked at her sideways, a smile tugging his lips, picturing her wearing one of his "double X" T-shirts.

She snorted. "I'll pass. Besides, I've slept in much less." When his eyebrows shot up, Raina said, "I mean . . . whatever. I'll be fine."

140

He watched her swiftly running a pencil over a large sketchpad she'd packed in her bag. "What are you drawing there?"

"It'll be a surprise."

"For me?" Nick asked looking doubtful.

"Maybe, but I'll show you the beginning sketch. One day I might paint it." She turned the pad around for him to see and was delighted when he smiled after a few seconds.

Nick studied drawing. "It's the creek, isn't it?"

"You mean that large lake out there beyond the trees, don't you? But yes, that's what it is."

"It's very good," he said as looked down at her. "Really, it's a very good likeness."

"Thanks. What's that I smell?" She glanced at the covered plate he was holding.

Nick had completely forgotten the reason he'd knocked on the door in the first place and looked dumbfounded at the plate in his hand. "Oh, I brought you a piece of apple pie."

She glanced up on him. "Aaww, Marcia baked you a pie. That was sweet," she mumbled.

Her sarcasm wasn't lost on him. "Her mother bakes pies that are sold in some well-known restaurants in this state. She happened to send one over for me, and I thought to share it with you. But since you have attitude, I'll just eat it all by myself." Nick pretended to get up, passing the plate under her nose and lifting the napkin covering the slice of pie.

She surrendered to the aroma of the pie, as well as to his gesture of concern. "Oh, okay. I'm sorry, and I'd love some pie. I'm still hungry." She took the plate from his outstretched hand.

"Why didn't you stay downstairs and finish your dinner?"

"Because you had company and I didn't want to be in the way."

"You wouldn't have been in the way. Let me go heat up some leftovers for you."

"No, this pie is just fine, and it is delicious," she said around a forkful.

Nick sat down on the floor beside her and flipped through some of her sketches as she ate the pie. Putting aside the intimate moment down in the kitchen, as well as now sitting closely beside her, Nick dug deep to find words to say what he wanted her to hear. "Suraina, listen . . . I grew up in a house where there was hardly any food, ever. Many liquor bottles and drunks passed out on our sofa, yes . . . but rarely any food. My parents' only focus was on drinking, partying, screwing and more drinking. They didn't give two thoughts about me or my sister, so we had to fend for ourselves. That often meant begging for handouts, like food. I know what it's like to go to bed hungry and wake up even hungrier. So please, if you're in my house and you're hungry, eat whatever you want, whenever you want, and if you need to do laundry, just do it. I'm not offended by what you call taking liberties . . . I call it hospitality."

Guessing he was reliving a painful situation, she wanted to say something, but didn't.

"I'll let you get back to your sketches. I'm going to grab a shower." As he stood up and handed her her sketchpad, she asked him where Reed was.

Nick laughed and told her that Reed was getting busy with Mitzy down the road.

"Oh." Her eyes lifted to his briefly before dropping them back to the half-eaten pie.

"Good night, Suraina," Nick said, turning and pulling the door closed behind him.

"Good night, Nick." She watched him leave. "So, we're not going to acknowledge what happened earlier . . . that almost kiss," she whispered to herself.

CHAPTER 7

On Thursday, Nick talked Raina into driving to the next county with him to drop off some items for a neighbor who was recovering from a broken arm.

Raina was more than surprised to see that Nick had a motorcycle in his garage. "Nice. It's a touring bike, right?" His surprise wasn't lost on her, prompting him to ask what she knew of motorcycles.

"Not much. I dated a guy who had one a few years ago. It was similar to yours." And when he suggested they ride his bike instead of driving, Nick was hard-pressed to hold back his smile at her delighted grin of approval.

Despite the heavy helmet, Raina loved the ride and the feeling of freedom on the open stretch of road. It was breathtakingly beautiful. She had to force away the erotic visions that filled her head when she climbed onto the back of the motorcycle behind Nick.

Nick, on the other hand, couldn't force that very vision away. It made for an uncomfortable but pleasant ride. They spent the rest of the day coasting the back roads. Later, when they returned to Nick's house, Raina helped him grill hotdogs, which they ate out on the deck for dinner.

On Friday, they spent much of the day packing for the trip.

When they went out into the garage, Raina ventured deeper into the large garage. Only then did she wonder about the car that Nick had stolen from the motel parking lot that first night. Nick explained that Lt. Brown had it towed the night he and Chief Coleman showed up.

What was left in its place was a sleek, top-of-the-line rented SUV. It had all the bells and whistles, and was brand-spanking new, ensuring a comfortable ride.

Later in the day, Raina helped Nick box up a variety of vegetables and fruits he had received from several neighbors. Because it was way too much for him, he decided to give the veggies to his sister, Jenny. Stopping at Jenny's place in Chicago the next day wouldn't take them out of their way. They had separated and cleaned everything out on the deck before packing it all into boxes.

Late Saturday afternoon, as Nick came upon the city of Chicago, he stole a glance over at a sleeping Raina. He shook his head, recalling what a fight that conversation had been.

It all started when he'd told Raina that his sister was going to try to get him to stay in Chicago for a few hours. "We can't do that," he'd said. "We have to keep on schedule. So you have to agree with me that we have to get you to Seattle, to, ah, see your sick father and you're too distraught to drive yourself." Nick liked that explanation. Raina, however, thought otherwise and emphatically told him so.

"Forget it! I'm not saying that my father is sick. Then he'll end up really sick, and it would be your fault! You need to come up with something else, Detective." She stared him down, waiting as he thought up another plausible explanation.

"Okay, then how about you have a job interview in Seattle and have no money for an airline ticket, so I'm driving you there. That sounds great. I would even buy that story myself," Nick had said, smiling to himself.

Rolling her eyes, Raina smirked. "Do I look like I have no money or job, Nick?"

He couldn't help but laugh. "Well, you will once we get you into some Wal-Mart clothes from the sale rack." The look she sent him was priceless. But he hadn't expected her to throw a ripe tomato at him, which had splattered across the front of his T-shirt. He'd been forced to change.

By way of an apology, Raina decided to use the job interview story if his sister asked. Still grinning, Nick recalled what had happened when he returned from changing his shirt.

They were still boxing up some leafy greens, when suddenly Raina shrieked and ran from the deck. A large bug had crawled out from the box. All Nick knew was in one minute she was on the deck explaining the proposal she was writing for the mentoring program and the next she screamed and ran down the steps. By the time he looked up, she'd run halfway to the line of trees leading to the creek. When she finally stopped, she yelled back to him. "Oh, my God! Did you kill that thing? It has to be at least four inches long? Wh–what is it? I've never seen anything like that in my life. It had enormous eyes and eyebrows!"

Nick was still laughing when she refused to come up on the deck again, even after assuring her the bug was long gone. He did threaten to go after her when another bug showed up. Raina ran around to the front of the house to get back inside and then refused to go back out on the deck. She'd even rewashed her clothes and brushed out her hair. Throughout the day, she kept looking around for more bugs. All the while Nick teased her, telling her she was such a girl.

And before she could get settled in the SUV for the ride in the early-morning hour, she made sure he'd wrapped the boxes up in large trash bags—in the event more bugs were living amongst the veggies and wanted out during the ride to Chicago. Glancing in the rearview mirror at the sealed bags, Nick sure hoped not, because he was positive she would jump out of the SUV while it was still moving.

Coming off the expressway, Nick experienced a wave of homesickness and wondered why he missed the place. He hadn't been happy growing up there, and, but for Jenny and her family, he really didn't have many ties there. Sure, he missed old friends, but he didn't keep in touch all that much. If it wasn't for Jenny he wouldn't come back at all.

Darkness had settled over the city, and he thought he could smell pizza from his old hangout where he used to go to after school. That is, until his father came looking for him one night drunk and mad because it was after midnight and Nick hadn't come home from school. Nick knew his father only came looking for him because Jenny threatened to do it herself. Frowning at the memory, Nick reflected he'd had enough of his father shoving him up the street after coming to get him from that pizza hangout. And when Nick tripped over the curb and fell down, he looked back to see his friends laughing at him. Angry and embarrassed, he got up and angrily shoved past his father, deliberately causing him to fall down in the grass. A week later, his mother and father left and never returned.

Raina awakened, stretched and squinted out the window at the downtown skyline. "Is this Chicago already?" She glanced over at Nick, noticing his clinched jaw. "What's wrong?" She turned to look out the back and side windows. "Are we being followed? Oh no, did Pierce . . . ?" Fear etched into her facial features as she turned and stared at him.

"No, relax. I–I had a pain, that's all." It really was a pain, and it never left his heart.

"What?" She mumbled, looking from his face down to his leg. "Did you get a cramp?"

"I'm fine now. Hey, welcome to the Windy City . . . my hometown."

Raina frowned at the swift change in him. "What?" she asked, looking at his profile.

"What?" Nick mimicked, stopping the SUV and facing her.

"I–I thought you were from Pittsburgh."

"I never said that. I was born and raised here." He nodded toward the windshield.

Following his nod, Raina turned back to him. "When did you leave Chicago?"

"I left when I was twenty. I went to Pittsburgh to attend law school."

"Law school? So what happened?" Raina asked, fascinated.

Nick reached behind his seat and took out two bottles of water from the cooler, passing one to her. Only then did he answer her question. "Michael Wade is what happened."

"Michael Wade? My father? How so?"

"He came to the university I was attending for career day. I asked him if he got job satisfaction from locking people up all the time. Then he asked me if I thought I would get job satisfaction from getting people off, people who I believed in my heart to be guilty." Nick gulped down half the bottle of water. "That gave me a lot to think about."

Raina was amazed to hear just how instrumental her father was to this man *before* he joined the police force. "So what happened next?" She listened as he told her about spending two ten-hour work shifts shadowing her father.

"You have no regrets about not becoming a lawyer?"

"Not one." Nick patiently answered her questions. He thought it was better to focus on her questions than her beautiful, sleep-laden eyes or her lips, now glistening with water.

Raina smiled. "So I was right."

"About what?"

"My dad was important to you."

He didn't answer. Instead, Nick pointed to the passenger-side window. "We're here."

Raina captured his forearm and felt him tense. "Nick, you know it's perfectly all right to admit that someone had a positive impact on your life. It is the one thing I tell the kids in the mentoring program all the time, and it's the one thing that I feel I give them every day." She waited him out. "It doesn't matter if you're an adult or a teenager, people want to know they mattered in the shaping of other's lives."

Her words touched him on a deep, personal level, a level he kept reserved to himself. "All right then, yes. Michael Wade had a positive impact on my life. I never had an image of what a real father was supposed to be. All that stuff you mentioned yesterday about mentoring, being supportive, encouraging and caring, all of it, well, he came pretty damn close it for me."

And that's exactly how she would describe her father. "Nick, did you ever tell him that?"

Pulling the key from the ignition, he started to open the door, but her hand tightened on his arm, stopping him. "No, and don't you tell him, either. This conversation was between you and me." He watched her purse her lips defiantly. "I mean it, Suraina."

"Okay, I won't tell him. But at some point, Nick, maybe you'll want to drop him a postcard and say thanks for caring about me. Thanks for all your support and for encouraging me to take the leap to do something that makes me feel good at the end of the day. I know my dad, Nick, and he would be honored and happy that you did."

The reunion of the siblings was emotional. Jenny had long, dark hair and the same intense gray eyes as her brother. "Oh, Nicky, I've missed you, and I'm glad you called and said you were coming home."

"I'm not home, Jennifer. I'm just stopping by." After making introductions, Nick explained he was driving Raina to Seattle, then followed Jenny and Raina into the living room, sitting beside her on the couch.

Jenny opened up with her barrage of questions. "So, how good friends are you two? Are we talking, I'll be a matron of honor?" Jenny asked, excitedly clasping her hands together.

"No!" Nick and Raina said loudly and in perfect unison. Then Raina went on to say they were just acquaintances.

Jenny's face fell as she watched both of them. "It's a long ride to Seattle, you realize."

There was no time for anyone to respond because Jenny's husband, Seth, and their nine-year-old son, Aaron, rushed into the living room and both hugged Nick tightly. Then Seth, a bear of a man, playfully punched Nick in the stomach. When Seth started in on the questions about him and Raina, Nick quickly changed the subject. "Hey, I've got lots of stuff out in the SUV. You know I couldn't come all this way and not bring you fresh veggies and stuff." Sensing he was rambling, Nick quickly walked out the front door, calling over his shoulder for Seth to give him a hand.

Jenny turned to Raina. "Well, Suraina, this is the first time Nicky's ever brought a pretty girl home. He looks nervous, why's that?" Her smiling gray eyes studied her houseguest. But Jenny's face, as did everybody's, fell when Nick returned and told his sister they could not stay, stressing they were on a tight schedule to get to Seattle and that he had to get back to work.

"What do you mean you can't stay? Nick, I haven't seen you, my only brother, in three years, and you're telling me this visit is to drop off some stupid farm food!" She crossed the kitchen to him, now calmer. "Haven't you missed us, Nick?"

He held her in his arms. "Yes, of course I've missed you, all of you, but our timing is too tight for me to swing a visit right now."

Raina took in their faces. Aaron was practically in tears. "You know, Nick, my job interview isn't for a few more days and, hey, I'd love to at least be able to say that I came to Chicago and had some of that famous pizza or a Chicago-style hotdog with the tomatoes and stuff on it . . . you know, some of the stuff that I've heard about that makes this place famous." Raina cringed inwardly as he gawked at her. "And just the other day you told me how much you missed Jenny."

"But, Su-raina," he said, purposefully stretching out her full name. "The interview?" Nick didn't miss the innocent blinking of her eyes.

"Oh, please, Nick, I might not even take the job," Raina said, waving her hand. She didn't wait for him to answer. Instead, she turned to Jenny. "Does that help at all, Jenny?"

Jenny hugged both Raina and Nick tightly. "Oh, you bet it does. This is going to be the best birthday I've had in quite a while."

"Jenny, I forgot." Only now, he remembered her birthday was tomorrow. "I gotta get you a gift."

"You already did, little brother and it's the best gift ever."

After a pizza dinner, Jenny and Seth and Nick and Raina spent the evening talking and playing cards. Raina could see that even though Nick and Jenny had grown up with so little, both were loving, funny and well-adjusted adults. She made a mental note to call her brother Marcus, who was stationed in Hawaii, and her mother, who now lived in Virginia.

Raina closed her eyes, recalling the feel of her mother's arms around her. She prayed she would never forget that feeling of love and comfort. She also prayed that Pierce would not catch up with them because of their delay in Chicago.

"Raina?" Nick watched her expression of sadness.

Raina couldn't mask the loneliness that forced her shoulders to slump. "I guess the drive has finally caught up with me. I think I'm going to turn in now." Raina began to protest when Jenny offered to assist her. "No, please stay. I'll be fine. I can take care of myself."

Nick watched as her lips tightened and knew with a certainty she was fighting back tears. "She just acts tough," he said, standing, and laid out his winning hand on the table. "I'll show Raina to the guest room."

Once upstairs with the bedroom door closed, Nick collapsed against it. "That was close." He watched her

153

walk over and sit down on the side of the bed. "You're safe here, Raina."

She looked up at him. "Sorry I put you on the spot like that, again."

Expelling a breath, Nick pushed himself off of the door. "Yes, about that. I had to call Lt. Brown. He didn't expect I'd drive straight through to Seattle without stopping." He walked over to the dresser and picked up a photo. "I hope you'll be comfortable in here."

"Can I see that picture?"

Nick carried the picture over to her.

Raina stared at an old family picture of Nick, Jenny and two older adults. "Your parents?"

"Yes."

"You look like your father, but you and Jenny have your mother's eyes."

"Yeah, we do." He stood over her, glancing down at the picture, then told her he didn't see a resemblance to his father at all.

Raina looked up at him. "One day you will see it. You know, I'll be looking in the mirror, combing my hair or putting on lipstick, and sometimes I see my mother's face staring back at me. It's kind of funny, but funny in a good way."

"I remember meeting her years ago. You're slim like I remember her and very pretty . . . but she never rolled her eyes at me or sucked her teeth at me."

She grinned. "Well, a genuine compliment from the detective. Thank you."

"You're welcome." He didn't want to leave her when she still seemed so down. "I guess I'll turn in, too. Jenny said she and Seth are taking the day off tomorrow to show you some of what makes Chicago famous. I suspect they've got something planned for her birthday, if you're interested, that is." Nick's throat tightened, hoping she was interested.

"Oh, I am, but I don't have anything appropriate to wear."

Nick looked doubtful. "You mean you didn't pick up a dress at that Wal-Mart in Ohio?"

Raina shook her head and lowered her voice. "Those people weren't nice to me in there."

"What do you mean?" Nick sat on the bed beside her. "How weren't they not nice?"

"That look." She glanced at him. His body heat sent a sizzling stir to her stomach.

"I don't follow. What kind of look?"

"The look that says, 'Hey, sister, what you doing with that white guy?' That look, and it wasn't nice. And, to make matters worse, you insisted on paying for my Wal-Mart items, even after I told you I had gotten all that money from Max," she said.

Nick assessed what she'd meant by *that look*. "Raina, do you honestly give a damn what narrow-minded people think about the two of us shopping together? Did somebody say something to you directly?"

She shook her head. "No, but I heard them snickering when I was in the dressing room. A couple sisters thought I had left, but I was still deciding which jeans to try on next, you remember?"

"Yes, because you'd already tried on six pairs and were still searching. So why didn't you tell me then what was said?"

Raina stared at him for several seconds and finally understood. Nick didn't have a clue how she felt. The store was located in a predominantly African-American area. To Raina, all her brothers and sisters were looking down their noses at her, judging her, because she was shopping with a white man . . . one who insisted on paying for her items. "They probably thought you were my old man, or, worse, my pimp. And exactly what would you have done if I had told you then?"

"Pardon my language, but I would have told them they needed to mind their own fucking business."

Raina shook her head. "Nick, you and I both know how cruel people can be, and, even if they are narrow-minded, they're still entitled to their opinions, you know."

"Yeah, I know, but if it happens again, I want you to tell me, and I don't mean tell me after the fact. You address ignorance head-on or those people, whom as you say are entitled to verbally announce their negative, biased and nasty opinions, never get it and they never learn."

Raina stared at him for several seconds, because that's exactly what she wanted to say to those girls in that store. "You're speaking like a cop," she said.

"Hey, guess what? I am one, and I'm here to protect you. You got that, lady?"

Raina tightened her lips and puffed up in a joking manner. "Oh, yes sir, officer." She was so tempted to rest her head on his shoulder as they sat side by side.

Nick finally stood up. "I'd better let you turn in." He reached down and touched her shoulder. "You're going to be okay, Suraina." He grinned when her eyes narrowed up at him.

Raina's hand came up to cover his. "Oh, yeah, thanks for introducing me using my full name. Goodnight."

The warmth of her hand on his was unexpected and memorable. Nick was reluctant to pull his hand away. "I better go before Jenny and Seth get the wrong idea again."

Raina only nodded her head and watched him leave.

After a full day of sightseeing, shopping and catching part of a baseball game, Raina didn't think she would have energy to go to a jazz club to celebrate Jenny's birthday. But she couldn't wait. She missed going out to a club and dancing. The few times she and Leon had gone to a club, he always preferred to watch people dancing.

Raina closed her eyes when a wave of sadness threatened to take the momentary calm away. She didn't think of Leon at all. Instead she saw Rachel, Mr. Coates and Mr. Antionelli. And then she saw Pierce. But the second he invaded her mind, Raina's eyes flew open. Her heart raced and her stomach tightened, almost forcing her to throw up those two Chicago-style hotdogs she'd eaten earlier. Looking at her reflection in the mirror, a piercing whistle came up from downstairs, and thankfully, the fear and nausea retreated once again. She knew Nick was calling her. He had done that while she was in the dressing room at Wal-Mart.

Raina chuckled, remembering the look Nick shot her when she asked him to teach her how to whistle. They were sitting on his deck Thursday night waiting for the hotdogs to grill. First, he outright refused, saying it wasn't ladylike, then gave up after a few instructions. But now, Raina curled her tongue and pulled her lips in, but gave up after several attempts in the mirror. She just looked ridiculous. One last touch to her hair, which she'd decided to wear out in loose waves and she hurried from the room.

They were all standing in the foyer waiting for Raina. Nick had been eating plain M&M's from a two-pound bag Raina insisted on buying at the ballpark. When he looked up and saw her coming down the stairs, Nick almost choked on the candy. He was shaken to the core as he watched her float down the stairs . . . To me? No, he corrected.

Seth whistled low and appreciatively. "Suraina, you sure dress up nice. Don't she, Nick?" Seth patted Nick soundly on his back. Still, Nick wasn't able to say anything or take his eyes off of her. She was simply gorgeous.

Jenny smiled, first at Nick and then at Raina. "What a beautiful dress. Where did you get it?"

Reaching the landing, Raina smiled and said, with a wave of her hand, "This old thang, I made it myself. I can't for the life of me remember why I packed it in my bag." And she couldn't, but did recall packing in a hurry and grabbing items from the hangers and dresser drawers. "I'm sorry I took so long," she said, her eyes flitting over to Nick. She thought he was quite handsome in denim jeans, a dark gray polo shirt, which heightened the color of his eyes, and a black sports jacket. In fact, she thought he looked downright sexy.

"Don't apologize. It was worth the wait, wasn't it, Nick?" Jenny looked at her brother as he continued to gawk at Raina.

Realizing that he was standing like a statue, with a mouth full of candy, Nick finally managed to speak. "Yes, absolutely, you look . . . great, Raina."

The foursome headed out, and Nick was glad he didn't have to drive. Looking out the windows as Seth drove the SUV, Nick was able to drink in the beauty sitting beside him on the backseat, as her perfume tantalized his nostrils.

Once inside the jazz club, Nick was immediately pulled into many pairs of waiting arms, and after an hour-long reunion, Nick finally made his way to the table where Jenny and Seth were seated. But alarm made his entire body go tense. "Where's Raina?"

Jenny pointed to the dance floor. "She's dancing. You're just traveling buddies, right?"

Nick watched Raina dancing with a tall guy, all the while telling himself that he was working. He was just looking out for his witness, and if she wanted to dance, so be it. He figured if she felt comfortable with the guy touching her casually as they danced, that was her decision.

Although she was enjoying the dance, Raina wanted to go back to the table, seeing that Nick was there. Seeing how the women flocked around him, she decided he was a lady magnet. She saw him touch them here and there, and in return those women blushed and batted their plumped-up eyelashes at him. When the dance ended, her partner escorted her back to the table. "Well, thanks again," she said pleasantly to him.

"Thank you, pretty lady. Hey, you never told me your name."

Raina's eyes slide over to Nick, who she noticed sat watching her with interest. "Oh, I didn't, I'm sorry. My name is Eloise." She grinned when Jenny and Seth repeated the name with wide eyes. She then took the empty seat next to Nick.

Nick bit his lip to keep from laughing. He knew she was sharing a joke with him. But the more Nick watched her, the more Raina tried to ignore him. Finally, he laughed for several seconds and then croaked out, "Eloise?"

Raina laughed, too. "It was either that or Hannah, another old-fashioned name."

The two of them laughed even harder at the baffled looks they received from Jenny and Seth, who were totally out of the loop of the private joke.

After making Jenny suffer through the happy birthday song, Nick pulled his sister to dance, as Seth danced with Raina.

On the dance floor, Jenny tried to talk to Nick. She'd seen several emotions cross her brother's face as he watched Raina. "Aren't you going to ask Suraina to dance?"

"I hadn't thought about it, Jenny," he said tightly. But, truthfully, he couldn't stop seeing her float down the steps in that sexy dress. Her shapely legs commanded him to look.

"Oh, yes, you have." When another slow melody began, Jenny steered him over to Raina, and took her husband's hand, leaving Nick and Raina facing each other awkwardly.

"Well, don't just stand there, Detective," Raina said, holding out her hand to him.

Nick couldn't have stopped himself if he wanted to. He fitted himself loosely within the circle of her arms. Immediately the memory of the two of them standing in his kitchen slammed into his head. He fought to control his breathing, but when she rested her head on his shoulder, Nick fought for even more control as his arms eased around her small waist, bringing her closer to his body. Nick was careful to keep his hand from touching the exposed skin of her back, as her light perfume warmed him inside and out. His fingers itched to touch her wavy hair, resting on her bare shoulders. He prayed his body wouldn't embarrass either of them before the slow melody ended. Then he prayed it wouldn't end at all.

Once again, Raina experienced the incredible feeling of being folded in a blanket of security, warmth and sensual tension. With Nick's strong arms around her, her fears were at bay. She was safe, lifted. She decided she liked Nick, and not just because he was acting as her bodyguard and protector. She liked the man she had come to know over the past few days. Her personal protector came complete with a raw masculinity that made her dormant sensual senses go haywire. That, in itself, was an oddity, because Raina kept men at a distance.

Raina never let herself get too close to men in particular. She guessed it was a self-protection mechanism to avoid getting hurt. At times, she wished she could be more like some of her friends. They were outgoing and coy and could weave their boyfriends around their little finger. But she didn't want that, either. Raina wanted what she had always wanted, always longed for . . . to be in love with a man who would love her, adore her and take her breath away. She could see that in Jenny and Seth, and they were strangers to her. She could see it in Max and Debra, and long ago, she used to see in her parents, too. She hoped to find that kind of love one day, before it was too late—like before Pierce took her life.

"The song is ending, Raina," Nick whispered in her ear through her veil of hair.

The shock of his warm breath on her ear sent a shock to her system, forcing her to lift her head quickly. "Hmm?" Lingering there, with her eyes closed, Raina inhaled his cologne and, for a split second, she wondered how his lips would feel on hers. She thought how easy, and how bold, it would be, if she for once did something reckless. Even the thought of him kissing him sent a line of fire bouncing in her chest.

"I said the song was ending," Nick repeated, absorbing the warmth of her cheek against his. A couple of inches lower, and his lips would be on hers. Abruptly, he shook the thought away and pulled himself away from her. Although he fought against touching her bare back as they danced, he couldn't prevent it from happening when he propelled her ahead of him to the table.

At the table, each seemed uncomfortable, each very much aware of the other.

"You two look great together," Jenny said, smiling at Nick. "Dancing, I mean."

Nick sent his sister a warning glance. He knew what she was thinking and she was way off-base about the situation . . . way off-base.

Forcing her attention from his profile, Raina wondered if he felt something pass between them as they danced. She could count the number of times their bodies touched over the past few days, and each time she was shaken by it. Something was happening. Something intense, and as much as she forced it away, that something, that feeling, kept returning stronger with each slight touch, each look. She was spared from dwelling on it further when the band keyed up and the leader officially opened the microphone for live karaoke. "So, who's singing tonight?" She glanced at Jenny and Seth. "Oh, come on, nobody brave enough? Nick?"

Nick was still recovering from the effects of the dance with her. "Forget it."

Raina felt the heat of his eyes searching her face. The force of it sent her heart into a somersault with awareness of him. In that moment, Raina knew she was acutely aware she was attracted to him . . . a white man.

Pulling her eyes away from Nick, she stood up, grinning at their shocked expressions.

Raina walked up to the bandleader and two backup singers, and then the band began the intro music to the song she requested. Within seconds, her voice, graceful, clear and melodious, filled the nightclub, stilling everyone and capturing their attention as she sang "How Do I Live."

For the life of her, Raina didn't know why she asked the band to play it. She wondered if she had subconsciously remembered the words and related them to her present situation. She didn't even need the prompter showing the words, she knew them by heart. She sang the song for Nick's ears only. She couldn't understand it. She didn't even know him. Yet she sang a song from her heart for the man who would be on his way in a couple of days. And still, she decided to sing it for him because she honestly didn't know how she would live without his protection, or his eyes searching her face, or live at all, for that matter.

At first Nick waited, thinking she would probably sing some silly song. But never did he expect her to sing such a song that flowed from her. Her voice touched him everywhere between his ears and his feet. And he couldn't take his eyes off of her as she sang so powerfully, so beautifully. He'd heard it before, but never had the song affected him as it did now. And there, he discovered another surprise; Raina had a beautiful voice. Everyone's attention was focused on the beautiful woman singing on the small stage.

As she masterfully hit high notes, Nick's stomach tightened as he watched her. It was then that he recognized absolute longing . . . or was it sadness? Regardless, how wonderful it felt to listen to her, to watch her, to touch her. He knew he had no right whatsoever to think of her as anything other than a witness . . . and another man's woman. When the song ended, the noise level exploded in the nightclub.

Holding her cheeks in embarrassment, Raina made her way to the table just as the bandleader stepped to the microphone. "That was beautiful—everybody give Eloise another hand."

Brushing her hair behind her ear, Nick leaned closer. "Another surprise. Tell me, how many more are you going to show me before we get to Seattle?" He lingered there, enjoying her perfume and the feel of her hair between his fingers, and on his face.

Raina shuddered when his fingers touched her ear. The warmth of his breath flitted across her skin, sending delightful shivers zigzagging throughout her body, coming to stop at the center of her. Stunned with the sudden rush, all she could do was sigh. And when he repeated his question, she experienced it all over again.

Raina was spared answering when the tall guy returned, requesting another dance with her.

As the evening moved on, Raina and Nick didn't share another dance together. But her eyes did stray to him time and again, as he easily moved to the line dance. The vision of him standing in a towel that first night floated before her eyes as she watched him twirl a woman around in his arms, his hands splayed across her bare stomach. When the woman threw her head back onto Nick's shoulder and pressed her body against him, Raina couldn't help wishing that it was her in Nick's arms. She was so distracted watching Nick and the woman that she'd forgotten about her own dance partner. Looking over "what's his name's" shoulder, she saw Nick returning to the table but was suddenly reluctant to join him.

Nick's gaze darted over the couples on the dance floor until they collided with hers. Then he watched her quickly avert her eyes.

Almost two hours later the foursome returned to the house. Both Jenny and Seth had become aware that Nick and Raina had been awfully quiet since before leaving the club. Jenny breezed into the living room and turned the stereo on. "Well, I've had a wonderful birthday and I'm so glad my brother came home for it," Jenny said, throwing her arms around Nick.

Thrusting his hands into his pockets, Nick shook his head at her slightly slurred speech. "I think you've had more than a celebratory glass of wine, Jen. What do you think, Seth?" Nick's eyes strayed to a reserved Raina. He wondered if, like him, she was uncomfortable after such intimate contact, dancing.

"I'm not complaining, the best sex ever is when they loosen up after a couple of drinks." Seth chuckled, walking across the room to help Nick make a pitcher of cocktails.

Nick cringed. "Hey, you're talking about my big sister." He passed Jenny a drink, and then one to Raina.

He couldn't look at her without wanting to hold her in his arms again.

Seth laughed. "So what gets 'em going for you, Nick, your little lemonade drinks here?"

Shit. Nick groaned inwardly, wishing he hadn't said anything at all, then settled his eyes on Raina. "I'm glad you had a good time tonight, Raina."

From the moment they entered the house, Raina felt like the room had begun to shrink slowly around her. She was hot, and the house was stifling her. Something was wrong, and it had started back at the club. She looked up, vacantly. "How do you know I did?"

Her tone told him that she was upset at him. "You didn't have a good time, Raina? What's going on with you?" he asked, walking up to her, but she sidestepped him.

"Did something happen that I'm not aware of?"

Jenny sensed something was very wrong with Raina. She recalled the look of alarm on Nick's face when he'd first come to the table and didn't see her. Picking up a remote, she turned the stereo off. "Okay, enough of this, what's going on with the two of you?" Walking up to Raina, she saw tears pool in her eyes. "What's wrong, Raina? You look scared to death, honey."

Hearing Jenny's quiet voice, a sob escaped Raina. She couldn't explain what was wrong because she didn't know herself what was wrong. She felt as if she was on the verge of screaming and didn't know why. It all started before they left the club. She'd become downright scared to death, and the nausea returned, the nausea that came each time memories resurfaced of what happened that night in the restaurant. She remembered looking around, wondering if someone was watching her, because that's exactly how she felt. The hairs on the back of her neck stood up, almost painfully. Her eyes frantically searched for Nick, but he was dancing.

"Raina, what's wrong?" Nick said, watching her with concern.

Nick's cologne engulfed her senses and she shook her head, backing away. That's when she knew what had happened. It was the smell of Pierce's cologne. She smelled it that night in the restaurant. The sweet scent covered her face when she was crouched down behind the door that night. The air rushing though the partially opened door forced the scent up her nostrils . . . only it was mixed with the acrid smell of blood, death and evil.

With Jenny holding her hand, Raina struggled through her sobs. She was compelled to express what she was feeling. "I–I smelled his cologne . . . at the club. It was sweet. I could smell it when I was crouched down on the floor—hiding, because I was . . ." In her mind, Raina watched the scene unfolding from that night. "How could I live, Nick? Who decided that?" Her eyes searched Nick's face for answers.

"Nick, what's going on?" Jenny asked, holding onto Raina tightly.

Seth, who was a paramedic, had gone into the den for his medical bag, having recognized Raina was having a panic attack.

"Raina, what happened at the club tonight?" Nick asked.

It was then Raina cried out what had been suffocating her for the past week. "He killed them . . . all three of them, and I–I . . ." She got up from the couch and pressed her back to the wall, hugging her body tightly. "Oh, God. How could I be so selfish? Nick, I left Rachel there and she died. How could I do that? Wh–who decided that I should live?" she wailed, pointing to her chest with sudden exhaustion. "Rachel had a son, and I left her there to die."

Nick was there the moment she would have collapsed to the floor. He sat her back down on the couch. "Raina, it was nobody's decision. It was your will to survive and your instincts that got you out of that restaurant. You're not responsible for those people dying that night. Do you think you are?" Nick asked quietly.

She searched his eyes. "Nick, I left her there. I couldn't even warn her, and I–I shouldn't even have gone there that night." Sobbing, Raina dropped her head onto his shoulder. "How could I do that?"

Cradling her head to his shoulder, Nick told Jenny and Seth the real reason why he was taking Raina to Seattle.

Jenny sat down beside Raina, feeling terribly sorry for what she must be feeling.

Seth immediately took Raina's blood pressure. "Raina, I think you're having a panic attack. My guess is that something triggered a memory or you saw somebody tonight who may have reminded you of the killer. What happened at the club tonight?" he asked.

In the hot, shrinking living room, Raina sat up. "I–I smelled the killer's cologne. It was very sweet. I looked for

Nick and couldn't find him. I tried to call out to him, but he was dancing. I wanted to tell him that somebody bumped into me. The man was quickly crossing over to the bar to someone waving at him. But when he bumped into me, and mumbled an apology, I saw Pierce's face from that night. I saw him turn toward me, extending out his hand to Rachel, like he was a gentleman and . . ." Raina sat up quickly as she held onto a snippet of memory. Her eyes searched Nick's, who was sitting directly in front of her on the coffee table. "Oh, my God . . . Nick, Pierce has a tattoo on his forearm above his wrist," she said, in a rushed breath, touching her own wrist.

"You remember seeing a tattoo?"

"Yes, it's weird looking. I only saw a band with squiggly letters or numbers, but I think the tattoo is quite large, maybe going up his forearm." She looked up at Nick. "He touched it after killing Mr. Coates, and that's when I saw it."

"Are you sure?"

"Yes, I'm positive. He was glad about what he'd done."

Nick was dialing Lt. Brown. The implication of a tattoo was enormous. If Raina could describe it, that narrowed the margin significantly of identifying Pierce. He got the voice mail and left a message. Nick apologized to Jenny and Seth for not telling them the truth up front.

Jenny shook her head. "The bigger picture here is that Suraina is in pain over her guilt for having survived that horrible ordeal. She blames herself for those people dying, and she questions why she was spared. Raina, is that what you're feeling?"

Wiping her eyes with the tissues Seth had given her, Raina felt relieved—finally, it was out. The room, as well as her body temperature, was no longer stifling hot. She nodded her head, yes. "I feel an enormous pressure in my chest, Jenny. It's so heavy with guilt and it's been there since that night. I've asked myself repeatedly who decided that I should be spared. I'm not special. I haven't done any miraculous things in my life . . . even Nick said that I was selfish and careless." She sent him a brief look, recalling the harsh words he'd hurled at her in the airport conference room.

Nick felt the accusatory looks Jenny and Seth shot him. His words were harsh and ruthless as they replayed themselves in his head. *Damn.* He was entrusted to protect her, and he clearly recalled beating her down without thinking. He was a cop, for Christ's sake. How could he fail to recognize a victim regressing? He took her hand in his. "I wish I could take those words back now. I am sorry I forgot you are first and foremost a victim, Raina."

When his hand tightened around hers Raina longed for him to hold her in that comforting spot within his arms again. "I'm sorry, too, Nick, and despite what I've put you through, you opened your home to me and never got angry with me for invading your space this week. But I am sorry for changing my seat, too." She turned to Jenny. "I ruined your birthday, didn't I?"

Jenny waved. "Honey, most of my birthdays are generally boring, but this one is going in the books for sure. But, aside from this tragic thing you're going through, you got Nick here and that still makes this birthday special. Suraina, you're going to be okay. In time, just go with your gut feeling, you'll see," she said confidently and passed Raina her glass.

Raina tipped her glass to Jenny's. "Nick got you a gift," Raina said and met Nick's surprise stare as she pulled a small jewelry box from her purse, then passed it to Jenny.

Jenny opened the box and lifted a gold heart charm, inscribed with her name on one side and Nick's on the other. "It's just lovely," she sighed, her eyes misting over.

Seth set his glass down and belched. "Come on, wife, time for some birthday nookie." Grinning, he turned to Nick and Raina.

Jenny giggled. "I love the charm, thank you. We'll be quiet, don't want Nicky here getting all squeamish." She then kissed them both and said goodnight.

Nick was beyond squeamish. He was embarrassed as hell, watching them run from the room like teenagers. "They're really sick. I guess I'm not turning in yet, and you may want to stay away from the second floor for a few minutes," he said to Raina.

Still embarrassed for her meltdown, Raina blurted out the first thing that popped into her head. "Seth did say it was birthday nookie. I think it might take longer."

"Speaking from experience," Nick asked, raising his eyebrows at her.

"No, more like wishful thinking," she sank back with a shake of her head, not meaning to say that. "I'm sorry about tonight, Nick."

"You have nothing to be sorry about. I should have recognized what was going on with you emotionally." Sitting on the couch beside her, both glanced toward the ceiling when a thump from upstairs penetrated the room. Nick immediately got up, turned the stereo back on and returned to the couch. "I don't even want to hear that. As a matter of fact, I want to think they're up there moving furniture," he said, dropping his head to the back of the couch, chuckling.

"Yeah, redecorating their bedroom at this hour," Raina said as she, too, rested against the couch. The music filled the room pleasantly. "Nick, am I really going to be okay?" Raina asked wearily.

He took her hand, enfolding it with his. "Don't you remember what I told you? I am here to protect you, that's my job." He caught her rolling eyes. He'd wanted to touch her face, but he just held her hand. "Hey, you have a very nice voice."

"Oh, thanks," she murmured, aware their fingers were intertwined.

Each glanced up toward the ceiling when another thump was heard. Nick shook his head and said the first thing that popped into his head. "Hey, um, how about another dance?" He needed a distraction from what was going on upstairs directly over their heads.

Nick stood up, still holding onto her hand, and loosely held her in his arms. They moved quietly with the flow of music. As he'd come to expect and welcome, her head rested on his chest, closing the distance between them.

Neither knew when it happened, but the second their bodies touched, the atmosphere in the room changed, becoming tense. Each warmed, despite the central air flowing silently around them. Each became aware of the other.

He should have controlled the situation, but Nick couldn't stop his hands from moving upward until his fingers touched her bare back—something he'd wanted to do back at the club when they danced. He blamed the alcohol for his boldness, and when she didn't protest, Nick allowed his hand to move up to her neck, where his fingers touched her skin ever so slightly.

Raina was back where she wanted to be, where she'd longed to be, in his arms. Closing her eyes, she drank in his exhilarating masculine scent. Every nerve in her body was affected when his hand touched her skin. Desire surged through her body with a speed that made her legs tremble, making her dizzy with want. Regardless of the fact that he was a stranger—a white stranger, at that—Raina wanted him as she had never wanted another man before.

Raising her head slowly, Raina let her cheek connect with his, as she glided her hands up his back. She was thrilled to feel his tense muscles under her hands, as much as she was thrilled when his solid thighs moved against hers as they danced.

Easing back, Nick gazed down into her eyes. Liquid chocolate, he thought, just seconds before he lowered his head. He kissed her eyelids, first one, then the other. When he heard her soft whimper, he took it as an invitation to do what he had anxiously wanted to do and lowered his lips to hers. Nick never thought a simple kiss could be so powerful, so stimulating, but it was, and he wanted to taste more of her.

Raina clung to him, caught up into an exhilarating mix of desire and apprehension. Simply put, he was a man she desperately wanted. She was awed by the intensity of what she was feeling for this man. *A white man! Lord, what am I doing?* Even as the question nestled itself in her mind, Raina didn't let it stop her from pressing her body into his as he continued to kiss her. She was caught up with his slow, sensuous swipes across her lips. She felt him press his body into hers and couldn't help the intake of her breath against his mouth. But when she felt his body pulsating against hers, she wanted more, even when she knew it was wrong.

Nick eased her lips apart and took pleasure in the silkiness of her tongue. He enjoyed tasting his spiked lemonade on her lips. He thought he liked it better this way and continued his exploration of her lips and the contours of her mouth as he deepened the kiss. They had long ago stopped dancing. The music and the thumps upstairs all faded into the background. All that mattered was the feel of her body pressing into his, and the blood pounding in his ears, and lower. There was no room for imagination as to the state of his body. Instinctively, lowering his hands to her backside, he pulled her even closer to him. The shock of that connection sent an erotic explosion to his senses.

It was wrong, but still Nick kissed her, caressed her . . . wanted her. He was now the one taking liberties that he knew he shouldn't. But after several more tense seconds enjoying the sweetness of kissing her, he reluctantly broke off the kiss. He rested his perspiring forehead against hers and slowly dragged his hands up from her derriere to her waist.

As seconds ticked on, neither moved or spoke. Each was thankful for the music flowing around them . . . its purpose new, masking the sounds of their breaths, audible and racing.

Finally, Nick stepped back from her, his eyes searching her face. Remorse for his weakness and actions was etched deeply upon his face.

Try as she might, Raina couldn't stop her eyes from running down his body. Openly, unabashedly she stared at him, before raising desire-filled eyes up to his. He was just a man, having a physical reaction to simple lust. *It isn't about me*, she thought. Moving away from him, Raina picked up her glass from the coffee table.

Watching her, Nick was pulled from his stone-like stance. "Raina, I need to apologize. My behavior was, to say the least, inappropriate." Remorse blanketed his face.

Raina noticed that desire had darkened his eyes to a steel gray, and his pupils were larger. "Don't apologize, I enjoyed that kiss. I think as much as I enjoyed dancing with you and being held in your arms."

Her eyes pulled at him from someplace deep, someplace held in reserve, and he ached to touch her again, but fought against it. "Yes, I enjoyed it, too. Only it shouldn't have happened. I shouldn't have let it happen." Nick needed distance from her and walked over to the stereo, picking up the remote, intent on examining it instead of her lips.

Sensing he really didn't want to admit that he, too, enjoyed the kiss, Raina knew that he was as affected by it . . . but he was sorry it had happened. He was remorseful. Why? It was just a kiss. Raina bristled. Resolving, once again that she had no room for anything remotely intimate in her life, her reflective thoughts were as effective as any cold shower. It also brought her back to her reason why she had to flee Pittsburgh in the first place.

Setting her untouched glass down on the coffee table, Raina walked over to Nick, talking at his back. "I guess I'll turn in now. Hopefully, everything is over with up there." She rubbed her hands together in an effort not to reach out and press them against his back or rest her cheek there, maybe just to inhale his masculine scent once more.

"Hope you're right," Nick said, not turning around . . . he couldn't look at her without wanting to crush her body against his. "Good night."

She didn't want to leave him feeling guilty. Didn't he believe her when she'd told him that she had enjoyed him kissing her? But that wasn't it at all. She knew he was entrusted to protect her . . . not to kiss her or light a fire in her that began that first night at his house.

Raina had never been one to go with the moment. She was cautious to a fault. It was that cautionary nature that had been her constant companion on many sleepless nights alone, wondering why she was so lonely. But tonight, she decided to go with the moment. She walked around to stand in front of him.

When Nick looked up, he saw a fire behind her eyes. At first, he thought she was about to slap him again, but she didn't. Instead, she took the remote from his hand and put in back on the stand, then turned and slowly ran her hand up his chest. She wasn't about to slap him at all.

Raina's hand eased up to the back of his neck, and there she provided just enough pressure to bring his head down to hers. With her eyes boring into his eyes, she lightly kissed his lips. His eyes reflected his turmoil. His confusion matched hers. He wanted her, but he was struggling. Then his eyes softened. When Nick exhaled the breath he'd been holding, Raina molded her body into his.

It was a tense battle until Raina raised her other hand and circled his waist, pulling him intimately closer to her. Kissing him, she became lost in the depths of his eyes.

Nick believed he was dying a slow, torturous, wonderful death. It was a simple, one-sided kiss, but his body trembled when desire hit him with a force he struggled to control. He couldn't hide how much she was affecting him again. His eyes searched hers, pleading for her to stop. She ignored him, and when he parted his lips to speak, to put a stop to her assault, she took that opportunity to slip her tongue inside his mouth. Then he was the one to sigh deeply, whimpering in surrender, as he crushed her against him, frantically kissing her to the point he thought he was perhaps too rough. His hands glided over her body, ending up in her tumble of hair, his senses overloading, because of her.

After several minutes, Nick ended his assault on her mouth, stilled his roving hands and then held Raina back at arm's length. Gulping in deep breaths, he ground out, "Raina, please, we cannot, do this—for many reasons." Even as he said it, Nick's body fired flicks of pleasure, causing his hands to grip on her shoulders. "You must know that we can't . . ." he repeated as he raked angry, guilty eyes over her, disgusted with himself for his own weakness.

Embarrassed again, now confusion was written across Raina's face. Raina struggled to come to terms with her emotions . . . she had been wrong, dead wrong. He didn't want her after all. What a fool she had been to think he really wanted her. Why had she put herself in such a position for this man? Raina's fury was mounting by the second. *He probably thinks I'm just some black girl throwing herself at him . . . like those silly white women did at the club. Well, that sure as hell won't happen again.* Raina thrust his hands from her shoulders, raking angry eyes over his face. "You're right, we can't do this, and one of those many reasons you mentioned is that you're just too chickenshit, Nick."

Nick gaped at her, not understanding why she was angry at *him*. "What?"

"You heard me," Raina fired back. "You play-acted with those airheaded bimbos at the club tonight, touching them and teasing them. But I'm here and we feel something and even if you act like it's not there—it's there. It's consuming us and I know you feel it, too. So what is it really, Nick? Are you too afraid to think beyond your job? Is that it, or did I get it right the first time, you're just too chickenshit to give into what you really want? Actually, I'm thinking you're the loser here. But then, who am I kidding to think you would want me, right?" Brushing past him, Raina snatched her purse from the coffee table and ran upstairs to the guest bedroom. Nick watched her go, and then closed his eyes. He thought she was right on most counts, but he couldn't tell her that. What was foremost in his mind was how much he wanted her. But he shouldn't and he couldn't tell her that, either. But the reason why he couldn't do that wasn't because he was chickenshit or afraid about his job like she accused, or even that she was a witness. It was simply because she was another man's woman. It was a line Nick never crossed. After polishing off the pitcher of spiked lemonade, Nick fell asleep on the couch. It took Raina several hours before she could fall asleep. But just before she did, she vowed to forget that Nick Laprelli existed as anything other than a bodyguard and babysitter. She blamed whatever misplaced feelings of longing that still clung to her on the alcohol and the stress of what happened at the club tonight.

That brazen, wanton woman downstairs wasn't her. No, that wasn't her at all.

CHAPTER 8

They left Chicago very early the next morning. The ride was tense for both, to say the least. The only conversation occurred when Nick announced he was stopping for a restroom break, to get gas, or to stretch their legs. Raina's only response was a noncommittal shrug of her shoulders.

Thanks to Jenny and Seth, they left with a cooler filled with sandwiches, fruit, snacks and bottles of cold water. Nick kept the satellite radio on a light jazz station, while Raina buried herself in a thick novel. She had put earplugs in her ears to listen to her iPod.

Four hours later, at another rest stop, Nick suggested they eat at one of the stone tables. There he decided to talk to her again, but Raina got up, took her sandwich and water bottle and moved to another table. A few hours later, at another stop, they finished their meal in silence and then Raina got up and walked over to a small pond and watched a group of ducks.

After a few minutes, Nick walked over, standing beside her. "Raina, please talk to me. Are you angry at me about what didn't happen last night? You must know why we couldn't. Don't you?" Foremost in his mind was her relationship with Chief Coleman, his commander.

Raina didn't look at him. She couldn't without recalling sheer humiliation over her behavior last night. Only her dark sunglasses concealed her red and angry eyes. "Do me a favor, don't talk to me and stay out of my space, Detective."

Nick threw up his hands. "Oh, okay. So we're back to that again? Fine, but just tell me if you're pissed because I didn't take you up on what you offered last night."

Glad for the dark tinted lenses, Raina faced him. Otherwise, she didn't think she could look into his eyes and not remember last night. "Offered you? I think you flatter yourself too much . . . I didn't offer you a thing," she spat out in indignation.

Nick smiled with a shake of his head. "Sorry, honey, but I know an offer when I get one."

Raina reflected on what he had said and wondered if that was how she appeared to him. Had she offered herself up to him like some desperate, pitiful woman whose libido went completely out of control over a dance and a kiss?

"You can believe what you want. I really don't care. You have one purpose as far as I'm concerned and . . ."

Nick cut her off before she went into a tirade. His head wasn't ready for that again. "Then why did you call me chickenshit if you weren't upset about what didn't happen last night? About what couldn't happen between us, Suraina. And you damn well know you would have thought I was taking advantage of you if I had taken what you *did* offer."

Raina forced away the feeling of longing when he called her by her full name. Her traitorous mind wouldn't stop the vision of the two of them dancing, kissing. She simply pulled her iPod from her jeans pocket, and, before putting the earbuds into her ears, she looked up at him. "I don't care what you think, so why don't you just do the job you were ordered to do. Get me to Seattle and don't talk to me, you got that?" When she stomped back to the SUV, Raina felt hot tears stinging her eyes, but refused to give in to them . . . as much as she refused to let him see how upset she really was.

Yeah, I got that.

That conversation had been several hours ago, and now Nick's anger level had risen to match hers. And it didn't help matters that his body still ached from having fallen asleep, intoxicated, on the loveseat in Jenny's living room. As a result, he'd awakened with one hell of a hang-over. It was easy for his sour mood to match hers. Pulling his baseball cap low on his forehead, he, too, kept his dark sunglasses on as he pushed the SUV further west.

As the day continued, Raina reflected on their forced road trip. Today the experience was much different from the drive from Pittsburgh to Chicago. On that part of the trip, she and Nick laughed together, listening to the comedy channel on the satellite radio. They sung old-school songs. Then there was the heated and lively debate they'd had when she told him the government needed to legalize drugs. Nick thought she was out of her mind, and told her so as they crossed state lines.

She hated to admit it, but she had actually enjoyed his company. Now she just wanted to get to Seattle . . . the sooner the better.

Nick had received her message, loud and clear. Since their last conversation, he'd decided to behave as if he was on a stakeout with an officer he didn't get along with. It was easy. He would do his job, but otherwise ignore her. But now, exhaustion was claiming his limbs. When he suggested she take over driving, Nick was surprised when she said no. And he wasn't sure, but he thought she flicked her middle finger at him. "Raina, either you drive or I'm pulling into a parking lot and sleeping for a few hours."

"I don't drive on the highway and I don't know this vehicle," she mumbled.

"What are you talking about? This SUV is a piece of cake. Trust me, you can handle it."

"I don't trust you, and I'm not driving," she said, staring out the passenger window.

Nick was back to wanting to throttle her. "Either you drive or I will pull over into that lot ahead." He pulled the SUV out of traffic, then crossed his arms, mimicking her. "It's your call."

"Fine!" Raina retorted, throwing her travel pillow and book into the backseat.

Nick got out, expecting her to do the same. But when he crossed in front of the SUV, he looked back in the window to see her climbing over into the driver's seat. He got in and showed her how to adjust the seat and mirrors. "Just stay on this road, heading west."

"I heard you the first time," Raina said after adjusting the seat, and then pulled into traffic.

Nick reclined his seat, pulled his cap over his eyes and immediately went to sleep.

A few hours later, Nick awakened and groggily read-justed his seat. He took a hefty gulp from his water bottle, which was resting in the console. Stretching, he glanced over at Raina. "You okay?" He looked out the windshield at the dark sky, then back at her. She looked tense as she stared dead ahead. "Raina, what's wrong? Where are we?"

"I–I don't know. I have no idea where we are. I stayed on that road like you said, but there was a detour, then there was a downpour for ten minutes . . . so I followed the rest of the traffic," she said through clenched teeth. Her white knuckles gripped the steering wheel.

Nick glanced back out the windshield again, then bolted upright when he saw a sign looming ahead that read KANSAS CITY. "Sweet Mary," he said, in shock. "Are you crazy? Do you know we're heading south? I told you to go west." His mind was calculating how far off track they were. "Christ, if you were lost, why the hell didn't you wake me up?"

Raina ignored him again.

"Answer me. Why didn't you wake me if you were lost, or better yet, press the damn Onstar button above your head for help?" Nick pointed to an indicator on the rearview mirror. He couldn't find any more words. He watched dumbfounded as the Kansas City sign disappeared when she drove on under it.

Raina pulled the SUV off the two-lane highway, easing safely onto the shoulder. She came to a full stop before turning to him and letting go of the tension that had been choking her for the past few hours. "You said you wanted to sleep, so I let you sleep. I don't know this SUV, so how was I to know what it had in it and what it didn't? And, I told you, you ass, that I wasn't comfortable driving on the highway, so don't you blame me for getting lost. It's your fault, not mine!"

Nick's anger had risen to match hers. "I sure as hell will blame you. Do you realize we're miles south of where we're supposed to be?" He threw up his hands. "I don't believe this shit." His patience was long gone. "Step out. I'll drive!" he thundered.

This time Raina did get out and, when he passed her at the front of the vehicle, Nick grasped her arm, pulling her up against him. With the headlights shining brightly on them, he saw fear in her eyes. "You should have awakened me. Again you made a careless and thoughtless decision, Raina," he said.

When she snatched her arm from his hand, Nick had little doubt about how furious she was and released her immediately. He got in the SUV, slamming the door shut behind him.

But Raina didn't get in the SUV. She marched up the access road at a quick pace, fury, resentment and humiliation in each step she took. At that point, she didn't care what happened to her. She thought if Pierce had been following them, then perhaps he, too, was lost. But if he wasn't, she made an easy target as she marched up the shoulder of the highway.

Nick was busy readjusting the seat and conferring with the GPS for their location and the quickest route west. When he looked up, aware that Raina hadn't gotten into the passenger seat, he saw that she was way up the road and moving onward at a fast clip. He just watched her walk for several more feet, almost disappearing from his view, then he put the vehicle into gear and drove ahead, pulling up alongside her. "Well, we are in Kansas, so where you off to, Dorothy?" he called out through the passenger-side window sarcastically.

Raina continued walking as she yelled over at him, "Go stuff your jokes and leave me alone." As angry as she was with him, she was equally angry at herself for getting lost.

Nick heard the catch in her voice, and knew she was scared and probably crying. Pulling the SUV several feet ahead, he got out and walked back toward her. When she attempted to walk past him, he captured her hand, stopping her. "Raina, I'm sorry for what I said back there. I know you're tired. Let's go get something to eat and I won't ask you to drive again."

Raina pulled her hand from his, but did walk back to the SUV after several seconds of staring down at the ground. She knew her situation. She needed his protection.

Just a couple miles further, Nick spotted a 24-hour diner and pulled into the parking lot. "Looks clean enough. You want to get something to eat here, maybe some soup or a burger?"

With her arms folded across her chest, Raina's eyes scanned the people sitting inside at the booths and tables. "Looks like you'll fit in there better than me."

Not sure what she meant, Nick's eyes scanned the customers in the diner. They were all white. His face went tight. "Raina, I don't play that race card crap. That is a public diner, obligated to serve its patrons. Now, are you going in there or not?" Then he got his answer.

Raina got out of the SUV and slammed the door shut, popping his ears with the force.

Once inside, Nick felt all pairs of eyes turn their way as he steered Raina to a booth and slid into the seat across from her. When the waitress came over, he inquired about the soup. Not at all friendly, she recited the soups, offering to bring him a bowl. When Nick asked Raina if she wanted a bowl of soup, she ignored him and continued looking beyond his shoulder to the parking lot. But Nick also noticed the waitress had ignored Raina. Glancing around, he saw the pairs of eyes had remained on them. "Forget the soup," he said.

Not meeting his eyes, Raina wanted to hear him say he'd felt the same vibes she'd felt from the other customers, and definitely from the waitress. "Why didn't you order the soup?"

"I changed my mind. Let's go," he said, sliding back out of the booth.

It was only after they were back onto the interstate that Nick spoke. "I would guess that those are some of the ignorant people we talked about before. Anyway, I need to gas up, so we'll get something to eat and stretch our legs at a fast food place." It didn't escape his notice that Raina was back to sulking. When they did stop, she barely ate her burger or fries.

As Nick drove on, each mile driven felt like ten. It was either very late or very early. He glanced at a sleeping Raina. He was frustrated as well as exhausted, and it didn't help he had no conversation to keep him awake. The music playing on the radio was making him sleepy, so Nick decided it was time to change their mode of travel, and reached up for the Onstar button.

When Raina awoke, her attention went to the road signs outside the window: Denver Airport, Next 3 Exits.

"What are you doing?"

Nick ignored her. But inside, he was fuming as much as his head was aching. Oh, just great, she's awake, he thought, preparing himself for her condescending lecture.

Raina's voice rose with her agitation. "I know you heard me. Where are you going?"

Nick wished she would close her mouth . . . her sexy, sweet mouth, that is. When an onslaught of heat washed over him, forcing him to relive their actions of last night, he quickly took the second exit for the Denver Airport. Unfortunately, he took the turn much too quickly.

Raina's breath quickened as he careened around the sharp curve, throwing her to the passenger side door. "What are you doing, you idiot?" she screeched.

As soon as Nick cleared the exit ramp, he had to slam on the brakes to avoid running into the back of a sedan waiting to merge into traffic. The passenger-side tires dipped low toward the embankment, rocking the vehicle hard and causing dirt, gravel and dust to kick up around them. When he sped up to clear the ramp, he slammed the gear into park and turned to her, paying no heed to the blaring horns of passing motorists, annoyed at him for such a dangerous move.

The jostling of the sharp turn, followed by the sudden stop, pitched Raina forward hard against the seatbelt, which snapped taut across her body. Wincing at the sharp pain in her shoulder, she looked about wildly, positive they had been in a collision. Her book, bottle of water, iPod and most of the contents from her open bag had been all thrown from her lap and landed either on the dashboard or on the floor. With fear and anger, she turned unbelieving eyes on him. "You could have killed us! Are you insane?"

"Yes, I'm insane, and probably all the other things you want to call me. Yes, lady, I'm all of that for not fighting harder against this damn assignment that I was forced into!" As he shouted, Nick pulled off his sunglasses and visually assessed that she was okay and not injured by his reckless stop. "To answer your question, or rather your demand, let's just say I'm sick of this bullshit, okay? I'm tired of driving, so we're going to take a quick flight from Denver to Seattle. That should make you very happy. The way I see it, you'll be with dear old Dad a whole lot sooner than if I continue to drive." He turned and resumed driving. "Hope I've answered your question, Ms. Wade?" When she only glared back at him with wide, frightened eyes, Nick threw the SUV into drive and sped from the embankment, once again causing gravel, dirt and rocks to slap up against the doors and windows.

Raina had no time to recover, but she did process what he had said. He was sick of her. Well, fine, because she was equally sick of him, too. She was sick of the drive and she was sick of running. But mostly, she was hurt. She had dropped her guard and allowed Nick to step on her already bruised ego. She wondered how was it possible for two men, as different as day and night, to do that to her in a matter of days. But more importantly, she wondered, why had she put herself in that position in the first place. Refusing to give into the desire to scream or throw something, Raina began collecting her things from along the dashboard and the floor.

After cleaning out the SUV and returning it to the auto rental counter inside the airport, Nick had to take long strides to catch up with Raina. When he did, he reminded her of the seriousness of the situation they were still in. Her vacant stare was expected, but the second he'd finished talking, she resumed her fast pace to the ticket counter. The desire to strangle her was uppermost in his mind, and seconds later it was followed by the desire to hold her in his arms.

At the ticket counter, they were informed the only flight to Seattle was by way of Las Vegas. The flight was scheduled to leave in forty minutes. Nick grated his teeth. To come so close, and not be able to attend the conference, was like adding salt to a wound. He presented their ID cards to the clerk and purchased two one-way tickets.

Raina walked over to the seating area and sat with her back facing him. Glancing around, she was surprised to see so many people excitedly waiting to board the flight, whereas she was miserable.

Cringing at the $700 cost of their tickets, Nick turned to look at Raina's rigid profile and thought they needed some distance, even on the short flight. "Please upgrade those seats to first class," he murmured to the ticketing clerk.

Raina's head was hurting as much as her shoulder was. Sensing the area was badly bruised, and that a hot welt was forming from the seatbelt locking up across her chest, she pulled a compact mirror from her bag to get a quick look at it. But her attention was on Nick standing several feet behind her at the ticket counter. When he turned, she noticed he walked with an air of confidence and strength on solid, slightly bowed legs. He had the type of face that made a woman wonder what he was thinking about. She had come to recognize that over the past week because she had watched him many times. The memory of the two of them kissing returned to her mind and settled there again. Yes, she was very attracted to him. Raina knew in her heart she was ready to throw caution to the wind. She would have slept with him even though she knew it was wrong.

Stepping over her outstretched legs, Nick took the seat beside her and passed her a ticket.

Dropping the compact mirror back into her bag, Raina sat looking in the opposite direction. She took the ticket he waved in front of her and jammed it into her bag.

Nick couldn't wait to get on the plane, if only just to rest for an hour. Glancing at Raina, he was desperate to talk to her. He knew she was frightened and hurt because he'd seen her panic when he stopped the SUV. "Raina."

Raina held up her hand to stop him from talking to her. In fact, she reached for her travel bag and stood up, but Nick quickly grabbed the strap, stopping her.

"Where are you walking off to now, Dorothy?" His eyes panned around, making sure no one was paying any attention to them. They weren't.

"I told you to go stuff your jokes. But if you must know, I'm going to the restroom."

Nick grabbed his bag and stood up.

"W–what are you doing?"

"I'm going with you. You told me to do my job, remember?" Nick said.

She couldn't believe him. "You're not going to the restroom with me," she hissed.

Nick spotted an airport security officer and waved the man over. After showing his ID, Nick explained he was escorting his charge. They were escorted to the private restroom for airport personnel.

Once inside the overly cold, but empty, restroom, Nick walked over to the sink, removed his cap and splashed water on his face. He then went into one of the stalls and took a long leak. When he came out and washed his hands, he saw that Raina was still standing at the sink. Ignoring the daggers her eyes shot at him, Nick checked his watch and reminded her they only had a few minutes before boarding the plane. He suggested she take care of her needs.

"I wasn't raised without parents who didn't teach me any better. I'm not using the restroom with a stranger in here with me," Raina said with arms folded across her chest.

Nick had had enough. With lightning speed, he thrust out his hands, sending water droplets flinging from them, and backed her up against the cold wall tiles, his body pressing into hers. Leaning over, he stared into her eyes. "A stranger . . . is that what I am to you, Raina? Huh? Am I still a stranger to you after you've pressed your body intimately against mine like this?" Nick said, moving his body against hers. "Am I still a stranger to you after you've put your tongue in my mouth, caressed me intimately and then got pissed off because I turned down what you offered up in the heat of the moment? Am I still a stranger for getting you all hot and bothered and not putting out your flames, sweetheart?" Nick dipped his head to hers, his lips grazing her ear as he spoke, quietly, sensuously. "But you were wrong to call me chicken-shit, because you're a hypocrite for not owning up to what really happened," Nick whispered, letting his lips dip to hers, teasingly. His body heated instantly at the memory of what did happen between them. Her rapid breathing feathered against his face and the heaviness of her breasts strained against his chest. His body was succumbing to being so close to her again and Nick was unprepared when she responded.

In total humiliation, Raina would have scratched out his eyes, had he not had both of her wrists pinned to the wall. But when his lips touched hers, sending a rush of desire to well up within her, renewing her memory of abandonment of the previous night, Raina swiftly lifted her knee to his groin. Gasping in pain, he released her immediately.

Through intense pain, Nick managed to fall against the wall. Had he not angled his body so that his back was now flat against the cold tile walls, he surely would have slumped to the floor. Trying hard to focus on her retreating back, Nick couldn't even catch his breath to call out to her. It even hurt to hold himself as he did instinctively. His groans echoed off the tile walls.

Raina walked back out of the stall to see him struggling to stand upright. His face was drained of color and his body quaked. At the sink, she tried to ignore his raspy breathing, as she went about washing her hands.

After several minutes, Nick was finally able to hunch forward. He was still having trouble uncrossing his eyes enough to focus on the crisscross check pattern of the black-and-white tile floor. Bad move. The floor tiles were suddenly dancing up at him. He knew what was coming next, and lifted himself up off the wall just in time to lean over the tall trash can and promptly throw up for several seconds. That only made him feel marginally better, but not by much of a margin. Making his way slowly to the sink, Nick brought water up to his face and rinsed out his mouth.

Moving away, Raina watched him gulp handfuls of water with shaking hands and then put his cap back on. With effort, he lifted his bag and said nothing as he walked to the door. With his hand on the knob, he waited for her to approach.

Raina walked to the door. When he hesitated opening it, her narrowed eyes clashed with his deadly, unbelievable gray ones.

Nick swallowed several times before finally being able to speak. "Don't you ever do that to me again." Forcing his mind off his pain, Nick pulled himself up to his six feet and opened the door, then followed when she exited.

They were the only passengers seated in first class. And although they were sitting on the same row, on opposite sides of the plane, each thought it wasn't far enough.

Nick cursed. The changes in air pressure caused him discomfort as the airplane climbed higher. He wished he could just lie down with an ice pack, but all the while he blamed himself for his predicament. He had purposely pushed Raina, putting the blame on her and knowing he was at fault for kissing her in the first place. *What the hell was I thinking?* Glancing up at the flight attendant, he asked if she'd had any aspirin. When she replied no to the aspirin, she offered to bring him a ginger ale. "Thanks, two please," he murmured as she hurried off to get his sodas. Nick sensed Raina was smirking at his discomfort so he turned, staring blankly out the darkened window.

Although she had ignored Nick as best she could, Raina hated what she had done to him. Closing her eyes, she wondered for the tenth time what was happening to her. It wasn't like her to be mean or spiteful. She was never hurtful. But recalling everything he had said to her in the restroom, she knew he was right. She had led him on and when he didn't reciprocate or "put out her flames," as he'd accused, she became embarrassed. That's when she got mad. He made her feel needy and wanton, feelings she couldn't remember feeling before. She even wondered if he thought her to be the type of woman who just slept around with neither control nor scruples. Certainly, that's how she felt. *No wonder he turned me down.* Guessing if she was a guy, that's exactly what she would have thought. The fact that it had been over a year since she had been in an intimate relationship didn't help her feelings of absolute dejection. Even then, she didn't feel such want. It was consuming her, making her want *this* man in particular. That had never happened before. Raina realized Nick's attentiveness to her wants and needs, made her want to be close to a man again. It made her want to be in a relationship of mutual desire and maybe . . . something that seemed beyond her grasp . . . like commitment and love.

Opening her purse, a small bottle of aspirin lay on top of her see-through plastic bag. Although she heard him ask the flight attendant for some aspirin, Raina had to wonder if he would accept them from her. She stole a sideways glance as Nick slumped in his seat. Memories of the past week flooded her mind. Despite her invading his home and his space, Nick had simply been pleasant, and even fun, to be around. He made her laugh and encouraged her to talk about herself. Recalling the few weeks she had dated Leon the Loser, he rarely, if ever, asked her anything about herself. He did, however, talk nonstop about himself. But Nick seemed genuinely interested in what she did, her childhood, and her likes and dislikes. He listened intently when she told him about her talks with Mr. Antionelli and about her concerns for Janey and Julie. But Nick also made her feel safe, and since that second night, when they stood in his kitchen, she believed him when he told her he wouldn't let anything happen to her. No one had made her feel so protected with a simple embrace or softly spoken words. *I'll protect you* . . .

Nick gulped the contents of one of the small cans of soda. When he lowered his head, he looked down to see two aspirins in Raina's outstretched hand. His eyes lifted, but did not meet hers. He looked back to the aspirin. His private ache won out over his embarrassment. He took the pills and mumbled "thanks" at her retreating back.

When the flight landed in Las Vegas, it was two-thirty in the morning. There, they learned that all flights to Seattle had been cancelled due to heavy rains there. The next flight to Seattle wasn't expected to depart until the late morning, and that was only if the rain in Seattle had slackened or stopped completely.

Nick approached Raina, who had wandered off to a bank of slot machines. He told her their options, sleep in the airport or grab a couple of rooms at a hotel. She had been steadily feeding quarters into a slot machine, and when she won $20, Nick sensed her reining in her excitement when she mumbled it was up to him. Unable to catch himself, Nick grinned watching her scooping up the quarters and stuffing them into her pockets. He realized he liked seeing her laugh, then told her they needed to hail a taxicab. After instructing the driver to take them to Caesar's, Nick couldn't help watching her taking in the passing sights. At the check-in desk, Nick was surprised to learn his reservation was still in the system for the conference. He requested two rooms with a connecting door.

When they stepped onto the elevator, they were immediately pushed back to the rear by a crowd of happy guests piling in after them. Nick groaned when the panel lit up for every floor.

Raina ended up standing in front of him, her back almost pressing into his chest. Feeling the heat coming from his body, her eyes lifted, meeting his in the closed mirrored doors.

"Well, hello, pretty lady," a well-dressed brother addressed her. Raina nodded politely.

"Are you in Vegas for a few days of fun and good times?" he asked, running a finger down her bare arm. "Are you single?" She replied she was. "Well, they say what happens here, stays here. You want to hook up as friends and maybe play some tables?" Again, he ran a finger down her arm.

Nick had heard enough. He also had enough of the stranger touching her and staring at her cleavage. "The lady has a travel buddy," Nick said, meeting the man's glare from under the brim of his baseball cap, wishing his sidearm wasn't strapped to his ankle. His face tensed when his eyes met Raina's in the elevator door again before returning back at the stranger.

"I wasn't talking to you, country boy. I was talking to the sister," the man said, annoyed.

Nick locked eyes with the man. "What part of 'she has a travel buddy' didn't you understand? Besides, this sister is my friend," he added, needing to dispel any possibility that Raina was alone. He told himself he needed to do that for the sake of protecting her, right?

Raina watched the expressions of the man in the mirrored doors. She saw unmasked resentment in his face. It was the same thing she had perceived from the women in the Wal-Mart and from those locals at the diner.

Raina chose not to comment on what had happened as they walked quietly down the hallway side by side. Stopping at her room, Nick went inside and checked it thoroughly before going to his own. When he opened the connecting door from his side and knocked on the door for her to open, he noticed her startled look. "What's wrong?"

"The zipper on my travel bag is jammed."

"I'll take a look at it." Nick walked into her room and she quickly walked over to the window, staring down at the activity on the Strip.

After clearing the zipper, Nick let his eyes trail down to her derriere, recalling the feel of her in his hands when they danced, when they kissed.

"You would think it was eight o'clock on a Saturday night instead of almost three in the morning, huh?" she said absently, fascinated by the lights along the Strip.

Nick crossed the room to stand several feet away from her and looked out the window. "Yeah, it's pretty intense here." His eyes strayed past hers. "I'm starving. I'm going to order room service. Can I order something for you?" Needing to distance himself from her, he walked over to the desk, picked up the guest services book and began scanning it.

"Whatever you get, I'll have the same," Raina said absently.

"The lady is adventurous," he said, picking up the phone and ordering club sandwiches, apple pie and garden salads. "Food is on the way." He turned to go back to his room, but her question stopped him. She asked why he'd already had a reservation at the hotel. Nick told her about the conference he was scheduled to attend that week.

"What's the conference about?" Raina asked, resting her forehead against the window.

"Law enforcement . . . I, um, needed this training and credits to make sergeant, then one day, maybe lieutenant . . . who knows." He turned to leave again.

Surprised, Raina turned around. "You're making the department a career choice?"

"It's as good as any other, isn't it?"

"You know you can still attend the conference since you're already here."

"I have orders. I can, and will, be fired for not following them."

"But we're ahead of schedule, aren't we? I can take the flight to Seattle myself." Raina certainly didn't want to be more of a burden to him than she already was.

"I have orders, Ms. Wade." Nick turned and walked to the connecting doors. "I'll let you know when the food arrives."

CHAPTER 9

Scotty was calling out for him.

His voice was a strangled, painful, gut-wrenching yell. Nick's gun was drawn as he searched the dense clump of trees. "Damn, how'd this happen?" Suddenly, he heard a shot ring out, then another. Darkness cloaked him. "Scott, where are you, man?" Nick pulled off his sunglass, only to wonder why he'd had them on in the darkness in the first place. He ran and cleared the trees and saw Scott sprawled out on the ground. "Oh, God." His lungs burned and still he was no closer to Scott's body. He couldn't save his friend.

Scanning the area, his eyes becoming accustomed to the darkness, he wondered where the shooter was. When he turned back to Scott, he was no longer on the ground. He was propped up against a tree and Pierce was standing over him. Nick saw the cigar cutter, and knew what was about to happen. He watched in horror as Pierce cut off Scott's pinky finger, his blood spurting everywhere, the red droplets splashing on the leaves and dripping loudly to the muck of ground cover. Nick turned and kept running and tripping over more dead bodies laying face down in the muck and stench of dirty water, clotted blood pools and dead leaves. Falling, he struggled to reach for his gun, which flew from his hand when he tripped over the bodies.

When he cleared debris from his face, he saw that Pierce was now standing over someone else . . . a woman. She was tied to the base of a tree. Who is she? Suddenly, he watched Pierce stepped back to shoot the woman in the head, and then saw her face. It was Suraina Wade. She was looking at him with tears pooling in her wide brown eyes. She was silently pleading for him to help her. But Pierce had already taken aim. Nick knew he couldn't reach her in time.

"Oh, Jesus. No, please God. No, no . . . not again. Not her, oh, please . . ."

"Nick . . . Nick? Wake up, Nick."

He came awake with a start . . . Raina was standing over him, touching his bare shoulder. Warmth radiated from her hand. She was alive. She wasn't hurt. His hand instantly covered hers tightly, holding it in place on his shoulder, soothing him. Suddenly, Nick was embarrassed and unable to meet her questioning eyes as he gulped in air.

Reluctantly pulling her hand away, Raina took in the fright on his face. "I knocked and when you didn't answer, I came in . . . you were having a nightmare." She watched him go to the mini-refrigerator, grab a bottle of water and quickly drain it. So quickly, that a lot of it missed his mouth and ran down his chin and onto his bare chest. Her eyes followed the water lines. Heat surrounded her face. "I . . . um, came to let you know the food arrived."

Disoriented from his nightmare, Nick looked for the food cart. "Wh–where is it?"

"I'll get your tray. It was delivered to my room." He told her she should have come to him and couldn't meet her eyes, recalling how she was in his dream, and his reaction to it. But she said it didn't matter and walked back through the connecting door without another word.

Nick watched her leave. *It did matter.* What if it was Pierce disguised as a hotel waiter, he thought. And there he was having a nightmare like a child. Some protector he was. Carrying his tray and dragging his chair to the window to look out, Nick thought she right. Las Vegas was awesome. Finishing off his meal, his eyes strayed to the connecting doors, and suddenly he recalled all the meals he and Raina had shared together the past week. It startled him that although she'd caused him intense pain, and for the most part had been a royal headache since they left Chicago, he now missed her company. He couldn't help but remember the days at his farm where they talked and laughed. Nick realized he hadn't laughed in a long time, definitely not since Scott died. He visualized Raina's laughing face . . . yes, he missed it.

Raina sat in the middle of the bed and finished her pie and salad. She had begun sketching, then her eyes strayed to the large window, looking out at the same view Nick saw. She wondered again how she had become such an awful person. That just wasn't her. She felt terrible for kneeing him like that. But he had frightened her. It was the first time she had seen him vulnerable or in pain. She remembered years ago the same look was on her brother's face, just before he fell to the ground after she had mistakenly hit him with that baseball bat. She shook the memory from her head when she heard a knock on the connecting door. "Come in."

From the doorway, Nick told her they needed to put the serving cart outside the door. He walked further into the room, noticing she hadn't eaten her sandwich. "You need to eat. Didn't you want your sandwich?"

"No, do you want it?" She remembered him telling her how he'd grown up with little food and having to go to bed hungry. She also recalled the mean words she hurled at him in the bathroom, reminding him that he hadn't had parents to teach him better. Enormous guilt burned inside her chest.

"Yeah, sure, if you don't."

"It's yours, then." Raina watched Nick carry the sandwich over to the window. "What was your nightmare about?" When he turned to her, she dropped her eyes to her sketchpad.

"It doesn't matter," he said quietly.

"It seemed troubling. You also had one in the SUV when I was driving."

"I'm sorry." He didn't want to talk about his dream with her, or with anyone for that matter. He was still processing it himself. "What are you drawing now?"

She told him it was her brother, Marcus.

"Guess you miss him a lot, huh?"

"I do. I was thinking I might go to Hawaii and see him while I'm on the West Coast. I have to apologize for something terrible I did, years ago," she said quietly as she sketched.

"I find it hard to believe that you could have done anything terrible to your own brother." Nick walked over to the bed and glanced at the sketchpad. "Nice-looking guy, looks like you."

"Yes, he does look like me." She put her pencils down and met Nick's gray eyes. "Besides teaching me to fish, my brother and my dad taught me how to play baseball. The one thing they kept telling me over and over was to stop showing off when I swung the bat. I would kind of shake my hips. Anyway, one day, Marcus was standing behind me, and I accidentally hit him down there."

Raina dropped her eyes from his. "At first I laughed because he looked so funny with his face all scrunched up, then I got scared when the color drained from his face. He cried out and fell to the ground. He stayed in pain for a long time and wouldn't let me come anywhere near him. I–I didn't mean to do that to him, but nobody believed me. I was such a brat at that age. Nick, I certainly didn't mean to cause you that kind of pain. You opened your home to me and you're taking an awful risk getting me to Seattle." She looked up when he sat down slowly on the bed, facing her. "Honestly, I'm so sorry." Raina buried her face in the sketchpad. "I'm not an awful person. I–I don't know what's happening to me," she wailed.

Nick sat watching her. He hadn't expected her to apologize to him or even talk civilly to him again. Easing the sketchpad from her hands, he said, "You're ruining the picture."

"Nick, please forgive me," she said, sniffing back tears.

"I can't forgive you, but maybe I deserved it for what I said to you in the restroom, Raina. It was unforgivable of me to push you like that and to throw our actions back in your face. I am equally to blame, and perhaps that's what I needed to keep my priorities straight."

"Are you okay?"

Nick laughed lightly. "Ah, as well as can be expected. Good thing I don't plan on making any babies anytime soon." He soon wished he hadn't said that because she dropped her face to her hands again and began crying in earnest. He reached for her hands, but she refused to move them and that made him smile. "Raina, listen, what made it more painful was the fact that I . . . well, I was remembering us dancing and kissing and when I pushed you up against that wall. I was turned on, a lot, because it was nice being close to you." Nick managed to ease her hands away from her face. "So you see I was affected by the moment, as much as you were. But I made a decision for both of us not to cross the line. I had to, Raina, for both our sakes. I think you know that." His hands were sliding up and down her arms, soothing, pulling them toward him.

He was right, and she did know that. When Raina lifted her face to his, she leaned forward slightly, as he did. Her intent was to rest her head on his shoulder, but just then Nick's cell phone, clipped to his belt, buzzed loudly. He got up from the bed and answered the call.

He turned and looked at her when her cell phone rang also, then walked out of her room and pulled the connecting door, leaving it ajar. But Nick stood on his side of the connecting door and heard her say, in a soft voice, "Hi, Max."

It had been three days since Pierce arrived in Seattle. He hated the soggy city. He was surprised the city just didn't shut down when it rained so long. He had already ruined a pair of leather shoes.

After three days lingering around the Seattle airport, he was becoming sick of the place. He'd been waiting for Raina Wade to step off one of the eighteen flights that departed Pittsburgh over the past week. Sure she should have arrived now, but there was no sign of her.

Pierce recalled seeing one young woman he thought was her. After following her out of the airport to a waiting taxi, the woman had arrived home to a husband and three children.

The delay was making him angry because he had to get back to Pittsburgh. He would have thought a young woman, running scared, would have taken the quickest route.

He had other priorities to get to and his time was running tight. He'd only briefly thought about going onto his next assignment and coming back for her, but Pierce's cautionary nature kicked in. No. He had to take care of her before he was able to move forward. She was the only link to the hit in that restaurant.

Returning to his hotel room near the airport to get another change of shoes, Pierce pulled out his laptop computer and brought up all of the information he could find on Raina Wade. Her beautiful face was already committed to his memory, but he couldn't afford to make another mistake and follow the wrong woman again.

The following morning, Nick got up early, went down to the lobby and crossed over into the conference center where the conference was being held. At the registration desk, he saw his name printed on the check-in sheet for attendees. Absently picking up a program, he shook his head and turned to walk back out of the conference room. When he glanced up, he couldn't hide his shock. Raina was leaning against the back wall. She was holding a bag and watching him. He'd thought she was still asleep and walked up to her, each step cautious. "Good morning." His eyes searched her beautiful face.

"Good morning," Raina said, lifting herself from the wall. "According to the Weather Channel, it's still raining in Seattle. So I called the airport and confirmed that our flight is delayed." Nervously, she forged ahead. "Anyway, the way I see it, you have this opportunity to attend some of those workshops you're registered for." She nodded toward the brochure in his hand, then handed him the bag she was holding. "Nick, please attend your workshops. You're already signed up, and here is your bag of freebies and goodies."

He opened the bag, peeped inside, then looked up at her. "Oh, it's a goody bag." He tested the weight of the bag. "There's a lot of stuff in this bag, Raina. Are you sure the flight is delayed?" She nodded. "Well, since I'm here, maybe I could just check out one presentation or listen to the keynote speaker. He's renowned for his advances in investigative techniques," he said.

"Well, that's good. Anyway, our flight leaves at six-thirty, so that gives you a full day of workshops." Raina pointed to a room further inside the conference center where breakfast was set up for participants. "Breakfast is already set up. The croissants are the size of footballs."

"Nice. What'll you be doing if I listen in on a work-shop or two?" Her response to his question was to reach down into his goody bag and pulled out four rolls of quarters.

"Oh, I see. Is that enough, or do you need more?" Nick thought he needed more of her.

Raina shook her head no, and dug her hand into her jeans pocket. Then she held out a thick wad of bills for him to take.

He looked at her questioningly. "Hey, no, what's that? I'm not taking money from you."

Raina surprised him by grabbing the front of his polo shirt, pulling him to her and easing her hand into the front pocket of his jeans. "Yes, you can." Then, picking up a sealed cup of coffee from the table beside her, she handed it to him. "Cream and sugar."

Nick was still reeling from her pulling him close to her and sliding her hand into his pocket. He managed to suggest they exchange cell phone numbers. "Raina, please be . . ."

"I know. Be careful and on guard at all times. You sound just like Max, and by the way, I told him we were en route to Seattle, and that you were taking detours to make sure we were not being followed. He said he expected you to make those kinds of decisions." Raina also recalled Max reminding her to stay on her best behavior and not to do anything to piss the detective off. *Too late for that,* she thought.

"Yeah, I pretty much told Lt. Brown the same thing when he called," he said, passing her cell phone back to her and then watching her turn and head toward the exit.

He watched her hips moving in a pair of snug-fitting black jeans, trying hard to remember what word she had used to describe the girl, Rachel's, backside. *Oh yeah, her trunk . . . sweet.* Noticing the black cap she had on with a law enforcement logo, he called out. "I like the cap."

Raina turned. "I'm glad. Check out your goody bag, Detective." Then she left.

Although Nick was engrossed in the conference workshops, he managed to call Raina twice. At five o'clock that evening, Raina called Nick on his cell phone to tell him all flights to Seattle had been canceled for the day. It was still raining heavily there.

Returning to his room at the end of the day, Nick was surprised that Raina was not in her room when he knocked on the connecting doors. He went in search of her, but in the elevator, a feeling of uneasiness moved over him, realizing he shouldn't have left her alone for so long.

After several minutes of craning his neck over rows of slot machines and scanning gaming tables, Nick spotted Raina amongst a sea of twenty or more of those black baseball caps.

Watching her, he was mesmerized by her antics at the table. He let his eyes trail down her body, then they widened in shock. "Whoa!"

Stacked in front of Raina were several piles of chips. She'd just placed several chips on the board, chanted something, and wiggled her fingers above the table.

Hanging back, Nick grinned when her table buddies copied her actions. But when her number hit and everyone at her table roared, Nick was no longer laughing . . . he wanted in.

Raina grinned boldly as several more winning chips were stacked in front of her by the dealer. It was then that she felt heat against her back. She knew instinctively it was Nick and glanced at him with a tentative smile on her face.

Nick nodded to several players he recognized from the conference, then looked over Raina's winnings. "Looks like you're having a good time."

Her face lit up to see him. "I am having a good time, and so are my new friends."

Nick looked down into her upturned, red face and guessed she'd had more than a few drinks. Picking up her glass, he tested the contents. "Raina, my drink?" he said, squinting at her.

Raina grabbed his arm, pulling Nick down to whisper in his ear. "Shhh, I'm Eloise." The mix of his cologne and facial stubble immediately hit her senses, forcing her to pull back.

"O-kay," Nick said slowly and finished off her drink. When he asked if she'd been to the room or eaten any-thing, she told him no.

Raina was about to place another bet when Nick cap-tured her hand, stopping her. Nick pulled off his cap and then dumped her chips in it. "Okay, high roller Eloise, time to take a break. Let's go get some dinner, I'm starving." Groans echoed from her tablemates.

"Oh, okay," she said, clearly disappointed. "Are we ordering room service again?"

"Hell, no. There are way too many excellent restaurants in Las Vegas to order room service."

Turning from the cash-in window, Raina was shocked to get back $1,200. "I–I can't believe this! Nick, I was just, you know at the table, doing my thing and, and boom! Twelve hundred dollars, just like that. This town is amazing. I'm going shopping." She laughed, fanning herself with the bills.

Nick was glad to see her laugh. "Eloise, sweetheart, you can do a whole lot of shopping at Wal-Mart with $1,200, and they have them here in Las Vegas."

"Huh? Uh-uh, no way. Besides, there's a boutique in this hotel that has the cutest dress. I just have to get it, you know what I mean?"

"No I don't know, but you have a dress. That pretty red one." *The one with the low back, where my hand touched and lingered against your silky skin.*

Raina tilted her head at him. "That's not red, it's merlot, and it needs cleaning. Look, give me an hour to go buy that dress, then run upstairs and shower, and I'll meet you right back here." Raina was excited for the first time since that night in Chicago.

He couldn't help but laugh. "Raina, is this your first time in Las Vegas?"

Raina could tell he was making fun of her. "Duh?"

Deciding that fate had made it possible for them to be there, he was going to show her the sights with a night out on the town. "All right, Eloise, I'll meet you back here in an hour." He grinned when she took off toward the boutique, calling out "cool" over her shoulder.

CHAPTER 10

At a quarter before eight, Nick was waiting down in the hotel lobby. He kept eyes trained on the bank of elevators.

Raina stepped into an empty elevator. Again, she admired the dress she had paid a chunk of her winnings on. It was a body-hugging above-the-knee black dress with a rhinestone empire waist. The rhinestone pattern criss-crossed under her breasts and ran down into the side seams of the dress. It was accompanied by a matching three-quarter-sleeved jacket. And to tie it all together, Raina brought a pair of black stilettos with rhinestone heels. She had pulled her wavy hair up into a loose pony-tail and fastened a rhinestone clip to the side. She kept her jewelry simple—just a pair of rhinestone stud earrings. Squinting at her reflection in the mirrored doors, she suddenly frowned. "Stop it. He'll think you're offering your-self up again." *But I'm not.* "Okay, yes, I'm really attracted to him . . . but there is a line and we just won't cross it. We won't, because I won't let that happen again." Feeling stronger in her resolve to ignore her attraction for Nick, Raina was full of confidence when the elevator arrived at the lobby level and she stepped out.

Nick had just taken a sip of his club soda when he spotted Raina stepping off the elevator. "Oh, wow." The words rushed from him when he finally exhaled. She was stunning and, again, had taken his breath away, but then his breath halted for another reason.

"Hello, again, sister." The brother from the elevator walked over to Raina, his tone condescending.

Oh, Lord, not him again. Raina cringed when the man made a beeline for her. She recalled the look he'd fixed on her when Nick announced they were traveling together. To be polite, she just said, "Hello."

"You out alone, or is the white boy lurking around?" He ran a finger down her forearm.

"I'm not alone," Raina said, focusing on trying not to lick her lips.

The stranger openly ogled her cleavage. "Why are you wasting your time on a white guy? They only want to sample forbidden fruit, baby. Give brothers a chance, know what I'm saying?"

Raina absorbed what he had said. "What I do isn't anybody's business, least of all yours. You're just some guy from an elevator, but you thought it was okay to put your hands on me before, and just now, you did it again. How can you do that and think it's okay?"

The man's face registered surprise at her tone. "Sorry if I offended you," he said.

"What if I were your wife, here on business? Would you want some strange man in a crowded elevator touching her like that?"

"How do you know . . ." he began.

"The tan line on your ring finger tells me you're married. So I guess you removed your ring in anticipation of having a little fun in Vegas." Raina eyed him levelly. She had used her gut instinct to get out of that restaurant with her life, so this guy didn't even come close to scaring her. It made her stronger and, because of that, she wasn't going to back down from him, or any man, for that matter, ever again. "Yeah, I'm not as naïve as you think."

"Like I said, I didn't mean to offend you."

"Well, you did. You took unwanted liberties with me, and that wasn't cool. Good night." Her curt dismissal sent the stranger off with slumped, dejected shoulders. When Raina turned from his retreating back, she took one step and was toe-to-toe with Nick. "Oh. Hi." She stumbled in surprise and stepped back, lest he smell her breath and know she'd been eating a chocolate candy bar before rushing from the room.

"Hi yourself. You okay?" He'd heard her entire conversation.

"Yes, I am." A wide smile spread across Raina's face as she nodded appreciatively at him. Nick had changed into a beautifully fitted black suit with a navy blue dress shirt and matching tie. "Hey, you look great." Actually, she thought he looked better than great. His gray eyes took on a bluish hue and his cologne sent her senses into overdrive. "Oh, Nick, you went shopping," Raina teased, pointing to his suit. "You found a Wal-Mart, didn't you?"

"Ha, ha, ha," he said sarcastically, raising his hand and tucking a stray curl behind her ear. "I didn't have a choice but to go shopping for a suit here in the hotel, Ms. Know-It-All. I had a feeling you were going to come down here all dressed up and I'd look like some country hick." He laughed at her expression. "And yes, I heard what that guy said about me. He doesn't know me to make that kind of judgment, but I take my hat off to how you handled him." His eyes covered every inch of her, appreciatively. "Suraina, you are absolutely beautiful. Come on, sweetheart, Las Vegas awaits you." Nick angled his arm for her and was warmed throughout when she looped her arm around his.

They dined on a full-course dinner at a five-star restaurant, feasting on steak, lobster, vegetables and excellent wine, all to jazz played by a quartet of musicians.

Raina was excited and decided, at least for a little while, to put her worrisome thoughts away. She wanted to enjoy the evening. When their dessert of chocolate mousse cake arrived, Nick excused himself to use the men's room. Closing her eyes, Raina had to force away the vision of Mr. Antionelli clutching the plate of chocolate cake to his chest. When she reopened them, she noticed two women in particular watched Nick as he passed by their table. In fact, she noticed the two women had watched them constantly, from the moment they were seated. Raina met their covert stare head-on and recognized the same looks she received from the women in Wal-Mart. They didn't like what they saw—a white man with a black woman. It was no different than the man in the elevator. Sipping her wine, Raina sensed she was the focus of the women's hushed, giggly chatter behind their cloth napkins. She didn't like it one bit. She would bet anything they were wondering what Nick was doing with her. Quelling the instinct to just get up and ask them what their problem was, she decided against it. When she glanced around, she spotted an interracial couple on the dance floor. She thought they looked great together.

It saddened her to know those women watched her and Nick with dislike. Because she had never dated outside of her race, Raina didn't know to expect such bigotry and aversion. In fact, it never crossed her mind how she and Nick might look to others. She now had empathy for those interracial couples who were brave enough to leave their homes. They had to encounter such ugliness on a daily basis. She could only imagine how those folks dealt with the leering looks while trying to act normally and go about their business. Seeing Nick returning, Raina experienced a quivering in her stomach in anticipation. As he approached, the two women sitting at the table called out to him. He stopped, spoke briefly, and then returned to their table. Raina smiled tentatively. She realized how handsome he was and it struck her how much she was going to miss him . . . miss his gaze that seemed to warm her all over.

"Hey, how's the chocolate cake?" Nick asked, sliding into his seat.

Raina's eyes inched up from her untouched dessert to the women. They were smirking again and she was dying to ask him something that wasn't at all her business to ask.

"What's wrong?" Nick asked, seeing a fretful look on her face. "Come on, out with it, Suraina."

Maybe it was the quiet way he said her name, or maybe her curiosity was getting the best of her; whichever it was, Raina wanted to know what was said. "Well, okay. Those two women have been giving me a very direct look all evening," She let out a breath. "Anyway, I saw you go over to their table, that's all." She sampled a forkful of chocolate cake and met his gaze.

"And you were curious as to what they said to me?" He watched her nod her head. "All right, they asked if I wanted to party, and I told them no, that I was on a date with the most beautiful woman in here tonight."

Raina looked up at him. "You said that, really?" she asked around a mouthful of cake. When he nodded, she pressed on. "If you wanted to hook up with them tonight, I can make my own way back to the hotel, since I don't think this is really a date anyway. Well, not in the traditional sense of a date." Warmed by embarrassment, Raina fanned her face with her hand.

Nick thought about what she had said. "Suraina, contrary to what you and probably women in general believe about men, white or otherwise, we don't all just jump into bed at every invitation." He tilted his head back in the direction of the two women. "First, I don't sleep around like that, and second, I do think we're on a date, in the traditional sense. It feels like one to me. I showered and got all dressed up. You don't think this feels like a date?"

"Actually, it's been so long since I've been on a real date I honestly can't answer that."

Nick smiled. "Oh, really? What about Leon the Loser, that wasn't a real date?"

"Not really." Thinking about Leon brought back the reason why she had to leave her home and her dark cloud returned. "You remember when you asked if Leon had dumped me?"

"I didn't ask. I made a statement and you corrected me . . . emphatically, as I recall."

Raina rolled her eyes and sat her fork down. "Whatever. Anyway, Leon did end our friendship. He said he wanted a relationship with more, um, let's just say, movement."

Nick nodded, savoring another bite of his dessert. "I get it. He wanted a relationship with more dancing, you mean?" He grinned at her narrowed eyes and pinched lips.

Raina became serious and quiet for several seconds before answering him. "No, Detective, Leon wanted an intimate relationship with me, and I just wanted someone to go to the movies with. You know, someone to go grab a bite to eat with on a Saturday afternoon. That's not dating, it's hanging out. There's a difference." She glanced up to find Nick studying her.

"So, it was like this . . . I got all dressed up that night and arranged to meet Leon at that restaurant. I had purposely arrived fifteen minutes late, just to make a grand entrance and to . . . well, to show Leon just what he was not going to get. You see, I had it all planned. I was going to tell him that I didn't want to hang out with him anymore. I was tired of pretending that I was into him when

I wasn't. But then Leon flipped the script. He told me *exactly* what he wanted from me and I said, 'Leon, that's so not going to happen.' He got up, dropped a $100 bill on the table and left me sitting there all dressed up in my too-tight-to-breathe-in dress and my kick-ass shoes. I looked so pitiful and . . . dumped." Raina hesitated when the scene at the restaurant flashed before her eyes. "That's when Mr. Antionelli offered to fix me a special dessert, with chocolate. He acted like it wasn't a big deal." Remembering the old man's kindness, Raina raised wistful eyes to Nick. She was at a loss as to why she felt compelled to tell him all of that. "At least, that's how Mr. Antionelli made me feel."

Nick could only imagine why she couldn't go out on dates or just hang out on a Saturday afternoon with Max Coleman. He guessed Suraina Wade was a very lonely mistress. And that, he thought, was such a waste. He thought she should be dating and not involved with a married man. Sitting his fork down, he tucked the stray curl behind her ear again. "So, is this a date or not, Ms. Wade?" he asked, his eyes searching hers, probing her soul and liking what he saw.

Relieved that he didn't push for more details, Raina grinned then she said, "Yes, Detective, I–I think this is a date because I, too, showered and got all dressed up."

Two hours later, Raina was sitting beside Nick in a roller coaster seat, slowly chugging upward. She couldn't believe it when he said he was taking her on a memorable ride . . . certainly, not what she'd thought. But when he pointed up to a roller coaster looming up two blocks away, her mouth dropped open. Now she was anxious for the thing to get going. Mainly because she needed something else to focus on besides how wonderful the left side of her body felt pressed against his right side in the tightly confined seat.

Nearing the top, Nick leaned over and asked if she was scared, but one look at her face told him she was not. He couldn't help but look at her—she was so beautiful. Sitting snugly beside her as the car rocked up the climb, he couldn't keep his eyes from straying to her breasts, also moving along with the climb. And when the wild ride started and she screamed, Nick still watched her face, mesmerized. When she grabbed for his hand, clasping it as the roller coaster sent them on a body-pitching, fast-paced ride, he couldn't think of any other place he wanted to be. Nick realized in that moment, he wanted her, more than any other women he'd ever known.

As the roller coaster slowed down before going for another sweep, Raina turned to find Nick gazing at her intently. When he leaned closer to ask if she was okay, the sudden rocking of the car threw them closer together.

In that instant, the roller coaster ride was forgotten. Raina's pulse quickened when Nick's mouth inched closer to hers. She realized he was going to kiss her and she wasn't going to stop him. In fact, she waited with anticipation for it. Much like their first kiss, it was both stirring and powerful. Within seconds, her body was pitched again, this time into an onslaught of desire. Every nerve in her body zinged alive when she felt Nick's hand caress her cheek, holding her in place as the kiss became more passionate. Her tongue sought his, as fervently and as hungrily as his did hers. They were still holding hands, only tighter now, and her hand was pressed against his upper stomach. His heavy breathing caused his taut stomach muscles to move against the back of her hand, sending a feeling of profound emotion in Raina. It stunned her so deeply she pulled back quickly, breaking off the kiss—even when she didn't want to. For several seconds, all she could do was gape at him. *What in the world is wrong with me?* But Raina already knew. She wanted him. The image was reflected in Nick's eyes.

Damn, Nick swore silently. *What the hell . . .* The roller coaster would soon come to a stop and he would have to get up. *Damn.* His body was showing the effects of kissing Raina. He took in her heavy breathing and her wide eyes gazing at him. With her red lips parted, he wanted to kiss her again. Instead, he fastened the buttons of his jacket and stood up when the roller coaster came to a full stop. As people around them chatted excitedly, Nick kept her hand encased in his. He guided Raina from the platform and escorted her to a quiet area near a concession stand. "Raina, I'm so sorry I did that. I didn't mean to. Well, actually I did, but I shouldn't have." Searching her face, he again saw that she was frightened of him. What a fraud he was, he lambasted himself. All that talk about not crossing the line and there he was, not only crossing the line, but erasing it completely with the bottom of his new shoes.

Raina was glad it was evening and that they stood in a shadowy area; otherwise, she was sure Nick would have seen the stunned expression on her face and maybe even guessed that her heart was pounding and doing all kinds of flip-flops. Even now, several minutes later, her body hummed. And it didn't help matters that he was still holding her hand, and by the guarded expression look on his face, she could only guess what he must be thinking. He was her protector and not her date . . . in the traditional sense. But Raina also guessed Nick was probably hoping that she didn't zap out on him again, like she'd done in Chicago. Pulling in a deep breath, she extracted her hand from his. "Hey, we're on a date and that happens. Forget it, everything's okay, Nick." Raina's attention flew beyond his shoulder to the concession stand. To her delight, she spotted rows of glistening red candied apples. Pointing to the apples, she said breathlessly, "Oh, Lord. I've got to have one of those." She stepped around him on shaky legs.

Had she not walked around him to the concession stand, Nick would have told her he didn't want to forget it. Truthfully, he wanted to kiss her again and again. Unbuttoning his jacket in the desert heat, he walked over to stand beside her just as she grinned and took a bite of the sugary shell of the candied apple. Raising his eyes to the darkened sky, Nick turned his back to her, refastening his jacket. "Oh, Lord," he mumbled, repeating what she'd said just moments earlier, only he added, "give me strength."

All too soon, they returned to the hotel. It was after one in the morning. Nick went into her room, checking it thoroughly to make sure no one entered while they were out. Then he walked into her bathroom to wash his hands of the sticky syrup from the additional candied apples he carried for her. "Raina, I can't believe you had to buy more of these things," he said, returning to find her rewrapping the treats in the plastic wrap they purchased at a convenience store before coming back to the hotel.

Raina laughed. "What are you talking about? It's fruit, so it's good for you, farm boy," she teased, raising her own sticky fingers and threatening to run them across his face.

"Uh-huh. What about all that sugar?" Nick said, jumping back and ducking around her.

"Oh, well, what can I say? By the way, Nick, what did that clerk say to you in that store?" she asked after washing her hands and recalling the store clerk, an elderly black woman, saying something to him that sent him into a laughing fit. She noticed his wide grin. "What did she say?" Raina quickly shook away a passionate thought watching him lick his lips, reining in his chuckles. "I mean, I saw her look at me and then you started laughing. What was that about?"

"Promise me you won't freak out," Nick said, scratching his head in embarrassment.

"Okay."

"Well, when I paid for your items, she reminded me that men don't need to use plastic wrap anymore since condoms are so readily available."

"What does that mean?" Raina looked aghast at him as he laughed. "Is that true?" she asked.

"In a pinch . . . and that's all I'm gonna say." Nick walked over to look out the window.

Processing what he'd just said, Raina looked up at his back and pictured a naked man wrapping himself in plastic wrap. That's when she started to laugh and couldn't stop as she stumbled over to stand beside him. The fact that he tried to ignore her only made Raina laugh even harder. "So, tell me, Nick, in a pinch, um, have you . . ."

"No! Now stop laughing." Nick noticed her lips were red from eating the candied apples. He ached to taste them again.

"Oh, that's so funny, my face is on fire," she said, causing him to raise the back of his hand to her flushed cheek. It was warm, but Nick didn't pull his hand away. Instead, he turned his open palm to caress her cheek.

The air in the room sizzled the moment he touched her face. Raina slowly turned her head, delighting in the mix of warmth and strength in the hand that held her face so gently. His cologne thrilled her senses and she watched a play of emotions crossing over his face. When he did nothing more, Raina took a step closer to him and placed a light kiss on his cheek, then stepped back from him. "Thanks for the date, Nick. I had a great time tonight," she said, flattening her back against the wall, facing him, watching him.

Dropping his eyes down, Nick battled with himself over what couldn't happen between them. It was wrong to want her so much, but that didn't stop his heart from hammering in his chest each time he looked at her or touched her. She was a victim who needed his protection, and she belonged to another. He just couldn't ignore any of that, he thought, watching as she stepped out of her shoes. "Those are nice shoes, too. I meant to tell you that earlier."

"Thanks. I hope they don't look too much like stripper shoes." Raina thought he was probably the only man to ever touch her soul and elicit such need in her with a kiss and realized, again, that she would miss him. "So you noticed that I have a thing for shoes, huh?"

"Yes, I've noticed, and I don't think they look like stripper shoes." Nick crossed to stand in front of her. "I had a great time tonight, also. Thanks for being my date, Eloise," he teased, raising her hand to his lips and placing a kiss on the back of her hand. When his eyes met hers, Nick was taken aback . . . her fear was visible. "Raina, you're going to be okay," he said slowly.

Raina pushed away the looming dark clouds lurking just beneath the surface of her calm exterior, threatening to return. Tomorrow, they would say goodbye and she would probably not see him again. The feeling was unsettling and just as frightening as the possibility of the killer finding her. But it was her desire to touch him again that moved her hands up the front of his chest as he stood before her. And she didn't stop there. One hand rested against his cheek, as her other hand eased around his waist, pulling his body closer to hers as her head dropped forward. Raina fought against kissing him, though the urge to do so was so overwhelming. Instead, she rested her forehead on his chest and closed her eyes. Seconds ticked by until she felt Nick lifting her chin. When she dared to open her eyes, his lips blurred as they descended upon hers in a tender kiss.

Nick never wanted to kiss a woman so badly before, despite how immoral he knew it was to do so. Still, he couldn't explain what was happening. He kissed her tenderly at first, but that soon turned into a deep kiss as their passion mounted and she held onto him tightly, molding her body into his. *She belongs to another . . . she's a victim . . . she needs you.* Abruptly, Nick pushed himself away from her. "Damn," he said, angrily raking his hand over his short hair.

Raina lifted her hand, to touch him, but he stepped back. "It's okay, Nick."

"It's not okay. I didn't mean to, ah . . . hell!" he ground out.

Raina grinned, recalling his words in the airport. "What? Get me all hot and bothered?"

Nick looked up at her, waiting. "Yeah, something like that. Listen, Raina, I . . ."

She didn't want another apology from him. She was the one to blame this time for kissing him in the first place. "Good night, Nick. I'll see you in the morning for breakfast."

Without speaking, Nick turned and walked through the connecting door, closing it behind him.

Lifting her body from the wall, Raina turned to the window, letting her eyes drop down on the Strip. She knew in time her hot and bothered flames would fizzle out; they always did. She hoped Nick didn't see her for what she really was—a woman starving for a man's touch. A man who would cherish her, maybe even love her. Wasn't she worthy of the kind of happiness everyone seemed to take for granted? Closing her eyes, Raina reflected back on her last intimate relationship. It ended over a year ago because it wasn't what she wanted. It didn't consume her and it wasn't passionate. That relationship was hanging out with someone that included intimacy. Even that she recalled was with a take-it-or-leave-it attitude. It was nothing like the ache she felt for Nick. And since her life expectancy was in jeopardy, Raina sensed she would never have what she was looking for . . . all because of a crazed killer named Pierce.

Resolving to not waste any more energy on feeling sorry for herself, Raina looked up and down the Strip. It was almost magical. Tomorrow, her life would change, again. But she would always remember Las Vegas, and she didn't want to miss any of it—least of all, by going to sleep. Her eyes lit up and danced along with the lights outside her window.

Pulling off her short jacket and tossing it on the sofa, Raina thought of a way to watch all that activity . . . why waste time going to sleep, she thought as she moved an armchair away from the area in front of the window. Next, she went to the edge of the bed and began to pull the mattress to the floor, which was not as easy as she'd originally thought. After several minutes of pulling, pushing and tugging she'd managed to get the mattress onto the floor in front of the large floor-to-ceiling window. Her plan was to watch the activity down on the Strip until sleep claimed her. It would also give her something else to concentrate on other than Nick's kisses.

After tossing his jacket and tie onto the bed, Nick grabbed a bottle of water from the mini-refrigerator. Sipping the water, he looked out the window. Unlike Raina, he didn't really see the activity lighting up the Strip. The thoughts circling in his head raged and battled with the powerful yearning he had for the woman in the next room. He wanted her with a desperation that he blamed on simple lust for a beautiful, sexy woman. That had to be all it was. After all, he was a man with a healthy sexual appetite, although that appetite had gone unfulfilled since the death of his friend. It even seemed too much of an effort for him to call on a female friend for a date, traditional or otherwise. "Damn," he whispered in frustration and gulped half the bottle of water. Hearing a thump next door, his head jerked suddenly, stilling him instantly; then he heard it again. It came from Raina's room, and immediately Pierce came to mind.

Releasing the strap on his ankle holster, adrenaline sharpening his senses, Nick quietly inched to the connecting door. Listening at the door, he heard another thumping sound and prepared himself as he silently entered the room in a defensive stance. His eyes rapidly scanned the room, finally settling on Raina, pushing a table into a corner. "Raina, what's wrong?" he asked in a rushed voice. His eyes took in the state of the room, the mattress on the floor, her panting and sweaty brow. "What happened?"

Startled that Nick had rushed in, Raina looked up to see his gun drawn. "It's okay. I just pulled the mattress to the floor," she said as if it was an everyday occurrence to pull a queen-size mattress to the floor. Then she went about fixing the sheets on it as she told him about wanting to watch the sights. "Can you help me move the mattress closer to this window?" she asked.

"Sure." With the task complete, Nick stood up. His eyes widened in shock as Raina stood up, as well. "What's that?" Nick blinked into view a large, red and purple bruise that stretched from Raina's right shoulder. "Raina, wh–who did this to you?" he asked, his eyes tracing every detail of the bruise.

At first, Raina didn't know what he was talking about, but when he lightly touched her shoulder, she knew he was referring to the bruise. "Oh, this—well, this is from that harebrained stop you made en route to the Denver airport. It looks worse than it feels." She tried to lighten the moment, seeing his shock as he remembered his actions when he stopped the SUV so quickly. "You should have seen the lady in the dressing room at that boutique. Lord, when I came out to look at my dress in the tri-fold mirror . . . well, she all but gave me the hotline number for victims of domestic abuse. Yeah, right . . . like I would let some idiot hurt me that way." Raina let out a laugh as she rambled on. "And she even said that her ex-husband was an ex-bounty hunter, and that he was available to beat up whoever did this to me for a fee, if I wanted," she said, hitching her thumb at the bruised area.

Nick could only stare at her, his mouth open. *Yes, my reckless, harebrained stop. That's exactly what it was.* He now understood why she didn't take off her jacket all evening, despite the Las Vegas heat, as they walked along the Strip following the roller coaster ride. He recalled offering to carry it for her when he saw her fanning her face. Then there was the one dance they shared in the restaurant. He recalled her wincing, as if in pain, when he stood behind her chair with his hands on her shoulders, encouraging her get up and dance with him . . . despite the two women still ogling them. "Why didn't you tell me?" Nick said, now standing just inches in front of her. His fingers gently touched the bruise. It was the only imperfection in her otherwise flawless caramel skin. And he had caused it.

Raina stepped back from his touch, putting a stop to the erotic visions that suddenly filled her head when his fingers touched the top of her breast. She wanted to forget about how the bruise happened because it also reminded her of the incident in the airport restroom. "And say what, Nick? Turn into the little princess you initially thought I was? Well, forget it, because I have." Her tone was curt as she walked past him, but Nick captured her hand, stopping her.

"Why didn't you tell me you were hurt when I stopped the SUV like that?"

Raina blew out a breath. "Look, it only hurt on the plane, Nick. So when I gave you two aspirin for your pain that I caused, I took two aspirin for the pain you caused. Come on, let it go." She patted his arm in a gesture that said as much. But she was stunned when he raised remorseful eyes up from her chest up to her face. "Nick?"

He felt tremendous guilt over hurting her, although he had done so unintentionally. "I'm no better than the idiots I'm forced to lock up every day. My actions were unforgivable and I'm sorry. I shouldn't have gotten so angry at you because I was forced to take this assignment, or because I was miserable about the argument we had the night before. None of that was your fault. But I wanted to make love to you that night, and I even blamed you for making me feel that." Nick shook his head sadly. Seeing evidence of her pain was more than he could take. "I'm so sorry."

Raina's heart broke hearing the total dejection in his voice. But she knew he would have been upset had he seen the bruise earlier. That's why she purposely bought the dress that she did; it came with the short jacket, when she really wanted the dress that had thin spaghetti straps. When she tried the dress on, the bruising was visible. "Nick . . ." Raina paused, searching for words. "Look, I pushed you when we left Chicago. I took my anger out on you. I'll own up to that because I didn't mean to. But the further we drove away from Pittsburgh, the further away I was getting from my life there . . . my home, my work, my friends and Janey. I'm heartsick that I'm not there for her right now . . . and then you made me drive." Raina blew out another breath and laughed. "Nick, I never drive on the freeway. I'm directionally challenged.

Really, I get lost all the time, and those stupid road signs just made it worse for me. So there I was, staring straight ahead, scared to death, and I couldn't tell you. I didn't want to wake you up because I knew you were exhausted. Then you had that nightmare, and that scared me, too, because you seemed so tortured. So, I took my anger and frustration out on you, and in all honesty, it wasn't about what was offered at your sister's house. So there, I take ownership of that, too—of what I started at Jenny's. I was furious at you for taking me away from everything I was leaving behind in Pittsburgh . . . all because you get to go back there to your life and I cannot." Standing before him, Raina took his hand in hers, encouraging him to draw his eyes up to hers and away from the bruised area. She was surprised when he rushed into her arms, but she was astonished how easy it was for her to envelop him within her arms and comfort him. At that moment, nothing else mattered but holding him, soothing him.

"Oh, sweetheart, I'm so sorry for everything," Nick mumbled, holding onto her tightly and burying his face in the hollow of her neck. "I should have been more sensitive to what you were going through and not about the assignment. Honestly, it wasn't about that, either," he said, resting his forehead against hers. "As we got closer to the West Coast, I selfishly became more and more irritated about missing the damn conference."

Raina pulled back to look at him. "But you're here, now." She nodded toward the window. "Nick, you can stay and not miss the rest of the conference. I'll get to Seattle just fine."

Nick shook his head as emotions clogged his throat. "It's not just that, Raina." He swallowed, meeting her eyes. "Scott Morgan and I were supposed to be attending the conference together. We were going to take the sergeant's exam together. I can't tell you how guilty I feel for being here." He pulled her close to him again and buried his face in the well of her shoulder and neck again. Then Nick gently, tenderly kissed the entire area of the bruise. "I'm so sorry for hurting you, Raina," he mumbled against her skin, now damp from his tears.

Raina's hand went up to cradle his head. Although her heart broke for his pain, the pleasure that shot through her from the feather-light kisses sent a heated path zigzagging to the core of her being. She let her head fall back as Nick trailed kisses down to the bottom of the bruise. Try as she might, Raina couldn't stop the flow of desire surging through her. It was heaven. The breath she held finally rushed from her lungs when his lips came up to kiss her cheek. She turned her head slowly, enjoying the warmth and stubble of his face. Pressing her cheek to his lips, she inhaled the lingering scent of his aftershave seconds before hungrily capturing his seeking lips. Several minutes passed and still, they stood there kissing, passionately, rooted to the spot near the window. There, Nick and Raina started down a path of no return. No more watching the other walk away unfulfilled and unsatisfied; no more longing, craving and yearning to touch and be touched by the other. This was it, this was now and there was no turning back.

This is wrong. The rational part of Nick's conscience was taking a back seat to what his body wanted. And what he desperately wanted was Raina Wade. He yearned for the woman who was branding him with her touch. Her chocolate eyes showed him glimpses of hope that life would get better, and that his grief wouldn't always consume him. Her eyes warmed him from the inside out and her laughter tickled and awakened something unfamiliar in him. Her kisses made everything he knew to be wrong fade away and disappear. Nick's wandering hands were given permission to explore the contours of her body as she pressed into him, and soon his hands found the back zipper of her dress. He eased the short sleeves down her shoulders with care, kissing a path as the dress slid down and away from her body. Then stepping back from her, Nick let his eyes take in her absolute beauty as she stood before him, unwavering, in black lace undergarments. Swallowing almost painfully, Nick raised his eyes to find her watching him. "You didn't buy that at that Wal-Mart, did you, Raina?"

Releasing another breath, she laughed. "Ha, ha, ha. You like it, Detective?" Her eyes searched his before pivoting around, giving him a view of the back before turning back around.

"I like everything about you, Suraina Wade," Nick said, closing the distance between them. Effortlessly, he lifted her up in his arms and carried her over to the wall nearest the window, then sat her down on her feet.

Raina watched Nick turned out the lights on the nightstands. Next, he fully opened the drapes, casting the room in a kaleidoscope of colorful lights spilling up from the Strip. "What are you doing?" She smiled when he returned to her, allowing her eyes to run over him. It was pure and simple—she wanted the man. And despite all the reasons why it was wrong, she still wanted him with a need that was foreign to her.

"This way you get to see the sights out there without anybody seeing the sights up here," Nick said, returning to her and tracing the outline of her breasts with his hands. Then he unhooked the front of her bra, letting it, too, slide down her arms and to the floor. His gray eyes took in the perfection of her full breasts, and then he dipped his head to sample them, cautiously, tenderly, and yet passionately.

Instinctively she cradled his head. "Nick," she gasped, savoring his mouth feasting on her, eliciting responses that also sounded so foreign to her ears. Feeling unabashed and needy, Raina couldn't fully comprehend the depths of what she was feeling for this man—this white man. To want him was almost unthinkable and unreal, not at all like the prudish person she knew herself to be, but did she want him to make passionate love to her? She most certainly did. And despite knowing she would probably not see him after tomorrow, Raina knew with a certainty that he made an impact on her life, however long or short that may be. She would never, ever forget him. How could she? He made her feel something powerful and beautiful inside, something amazing that made her want that which had always escaped her: absolute desire and true happiness. And it wasn't the lovemaking that would soon occur that would settle into the recesses of her mind to comfort her later. Rather, it was already realizing how much she was going to miss his presence in her life. As her body burned from his caresses, Raina wasted no more time pondering what conflicting feelings she was really feeling.

"Nick, I'm warning you. Don't you get me all hot and bothered and even think about leaving me hanging. I don't think I can let you walk out of here tonight." And she wouldn't just let him walk out, either. Not when the line had been crossed again, and definitely not when her dress lay on the floor. Raina truly was offering herself to him and would freely admit it.

"Don't worry, sweetheart, I'm not going anywhere. I'm right where I want to be," Nick whispered. His eyes widened in surprise when Raina grabbed the front of his shirt and quickly unbuttoned it. But when she dropped hungry kisses to his bare chest, Nick thought his knees would buckle from the lightning bolts running rampant through his chest and beyond. He brought her lips up to his and proceeded to drop a wayward line of kisses straight down her body, where he removed the last of her lacy garments along the way, reaching the center of her. He touched and tasted every inch of her. When at last he ended with a reversed path, Nick lifted a writhing Raina up in his arms, carrying her over to the mattress . . . down on the floor, in front of the large window.

Raina felt him moving away from her and glanced up to see Nick undressing. She was captivated when he stood at the foot of the mattress totally naked. He was all male, one totally sexy package. It was then that Raina covered her mouth, hiding an embarrassed grin, followed by a giggle. "Hey, Nick, um, have you heard what they say about black men? You know the size thing?" She took no shame in openly staring at the perfection of his maleness.

"Ah, no," he said, watching her covering her giggling for several seconds before moving forward and joining her on the mattress. His intense gray eyes bored into hers, sobering her instantly. "What do you say, Suraina Wade?" Nick kissed her, easing her back down. "I only care about what you think, and what you feel, and what you want."

"Oh, well in that case, I think I can now say that it's not just black men anymore." Abruptly, Raina backed away from him. "Oh, wait . . . do you have, you know protection—or do we have to use something else, 'cause this is a pinch?" Her eyes flew over his left shoulder to the desk where the items she'd picked up at the convenience store were scattered, including the box of plastic wrap.

Following the direction she was looking, Nick let out a laugh. "We're good. Besides, don't you know cops really do protect and serve?" He grinned when her mouth dropped open.

Grinning, Raina threw her arms around his neck, pulling him to her when Nick opened his hand, showing her the small foil packet. "And they're always prepared. Good timing, Detective. You want to handle that, like now." The sight of his naked body, as well as his hands running up and down her thighs, was pushing her over the edge, sending her desire level up several notches. Raina recalled the first night at his house, when she voyeuristically stared at his sleeping body. Even then, she wondered how it would feel to run her fingers through the spiraled hair on his chest and stomach and now she took the time to do just that, delighted when he groaned deeply in response to her touch.

Nick needed no more encouragement than that. Within seconds, he'd brought their bodies together in one agonizingly slow move. Each trembled in anticipation as their moans echoed in each other's ears. Nick became totally in tune to Raina and the rhythm of her body . . . her movements acted as a beacon for him. He wanted to possess her. He wanted to please her. He delighted in the sounds she made when he touched her body. Her whimpers and sighs of pleasure were a passionate sonnet whispered in Nick's ears. The result was as effective as her touch, sending ripples of gratification to his nerve endings as he pushed her to the threshold of release more than once.

Raina was on the verge of tears from the extreme balance of pleasure and desire. Her body moved with a will of its own. Her thoughts were incoherent and jumbled . . . that is, thinking about anything except the two of them. She couldn't get enough of him, and soon gave up trying to act as though she and Nick were just having a one-night stand. She sensed it was so much more than that—at least for her it was. This white man who was making love to her was touching a part of her that she had always held back from her past lovers, too afraid and far too cautious to let other lovers go the distance to her inner self. And yet, in a short period of time, Nick had managed to elicit mind-numbing releases from her, shattering her to the point that she lost herself, clinging onto him and crying out his name, savoring the force of his thrusts and the heat of his kisses when she did.

It was in that moment, Nick watched the beautiful Raina Wade fall apart beneath him. He couldn't remember seeing anything so wonderful, or so powerful. Watching her touched him on a deep level, somehow comforting him with familiarity. But then he realized he had seen it before. The first night Raina stood in his kitchen, wearing a simple pale green pajama set. He kissed her open mouth and realized tears spilled from her open eyes. It was a splendid moment as he kissed them away, a moment Nick would remember for the rest of his life. When he felt her moving beneath him again, it was then he who raced along the wave as rockets fired sparks of pleasure from his brain and throughout his body. It took him several long seconds to realize Raina was riding the wave with him. Lifting her tightly against him, soon it was she who was pushing him to the edge of sanity. Nick cried out her name, and his release was so forceful that it left him trembling with aftershocks. In that moment, Nick wanted to claim her for himself—only he couldn't.

Afterwards, Raina and Nick held each other close. They shared kiss after kiss for several blissful moments. They touched, they smiled, and when they drifted off to sleep, still entangled in each other's arms, each thought of the impact of having crossed the line.

Three hours later, Raina watched Nick sleep. Like her, he lay on his side, facing her with the sheet covering his midsection. Her body still hummed from their second round of lovemaking. She felt totally female, and for a little while, totally complete and satisfied. Extending her hand, she traced the tattoo on his upper arm, recalling he'd told her it represented his father's family name, a symbol of some sort. Her hand shook when Pierce's tattooed forearm flashed behind her eyes. Shaking the invasive vision and accompanying nausea away, Raina noticed that in the light spilling into the room from the wide window there was very little difference in their skin tones. His bare arm appeared lighter, with a bluish hue from the outside light, and her hand appeared only slightly darker against his arm. Raina realized this was the first time she had thought about their difference in terms of skin color. Letting her eyes trail down the length of his body, she realized it wasn't that she hadn't seen it before—it was just that it didn't matter before. It still didn't matter, she thought. Aside from him being white, she really didn't see a difference between him and any other man having two arms, two legs, ten toes and ten fingers. Finally raising her eyes from her perusal of his body to his handsome face, Raina gasped, finding almost translucent gray eyes gazing back at her. Nick whispered that she wasn't fair.

"I'm not fair about what?"

"You, checking me out like that. It's kinda rude, you know." His eyes searched her face.

Raina laid her hand on his chest. "What you mean is, I beat you to it, right?"

"That's exactly what I meant," Nick said, his hand coming up to cover hers.

"So you didn't get enough of checking me out a couple hours ago?"

"No," he said honestly and gathered her against him.

Raina smiled when he reached under the pillow, pulling out another foil packet.

Nick had set his watch to awaken him just before dawn. He kissed the bruised area of her shoulder as she slept soundly. "You're so beautiful, Suraina. I'll miss you more than I have a right to, and I'll never forget you," he whispered, kissing her sleeping lips.

After a few minutes, Raina awakened to find Nick watching her. "What are you doing awake?" she said, snuggling against him.

"I wanted to show you something pretty awesome," he whispered.

Raina giggled. "I think you already did. Several times, as a matter of fact."

"No, sweetheart, I wanted to show you this." Nick turned Raina around in his arms, spooning her so that she was facing the large window. There, in a burst of yellow and orange and lavender, the sun was creeping up over the mountains in the distance.

Taken aback, she was at a loss for words to describe the sight and gave up trying. "Nick?"

"Um-hum," he murmured against her hair.

"I'll always remember this . . . will you make love to me again?" she asked quietly, watching the colorful hues creep up further.

Nick smiled. "It'll be my pleasure," he said, angling their bodies so that each could watch the spectacular sight outside the window. Soon, Nick and Raina were once again spiraling to a place of pure bliss where, for brief moments, only they existed . . . without uncertainties or barriers or differences.

By midafternoon, Nick and Raina were sitting in the back of a taxi heading to her father's house in Seattle. The rain had all but disappeared, leaving the city basking in a warm summer sun. Raina's hand was tightly encased in Nick's, but she was struggling to keep her trembling in check as the taxi pushed on, closer to her father's house. Filled with trepidation, she stole a quick glance at Nick. There was so much she had wanted to say to him. Unfortunately, by the time they'd finally awakened, showered and went out to breakfast, time slipped by all too quickly. Still, she wanted to tell him how much the previous night and the previous week had meant to her and how much she would miss him—prepping to say just that, her breath halted when the driver came off the expressway. Time was still slipping by, quickly.

Closing his eyes, Nick felt her trembling beside him. Fresh memories of how she had trembled in his arms shook him. He asked the driver to pull over for a few minutes. Then Nick opened the door and got out. Still holding Raina's hand, he encouraged her to walk with him.

Raina followed him to a large tree, and watched him remove his sunglasses. "Nick, what are you doing?" She had already guessed he was beating himself up for crossing the line, the line each of them had now crossed. She searched his face, settling on his gray eyes, committing them to memory to console her for the weeks, months and years to come. That is, if she lived that long.

"I wanted to tell you that last night wasn't just about the sex. I don't want you to think that's all it was for me." His eyes searched hers for understanding. "I also wanted to say that I wouldn't have changed anything that's happened between us, Suraina." Nick pulled her into his arms, kissed her deeply and held her tightly against him. He'd wanted to tell her that a night of making love to her was like nothing he had ever experienced before, and that he never felt such closeness with any other woman like that. But Nick didn't say any of that; he had no right to say it. Instead, he whispered in her ear, "But it was great sex, wasn't it?"

The warmth of Nick's breath warmed her ear, and Raina held onto him tightly before pulling back and gazing up into his eyes. Speaking seemed an effort, so she just nodded in agreement. In truth, Raina sensed she would never feel that wonderful and whole ever again. Tracing his eyebrows with her fingertips, she said, "So you wouldn't change a thing, huh? Does that mean you're no longer mad at me for taking your favorite fishing rod and catching the bigger fish?" When he laughed, Raina threw her arms around his neck. "No guilt and no regrets. But I'll miss you, Nick, and I'm sorry for being a pain in the butt before."

For a few minutes longer, they stood embracing under the tree. Each wanted to say more, but didn't. Finally they walked back to the waiting taxi, holding hands.

Hearing her father's voice on the other side of the door seconds before it opened, Raina quickly stepped to the right, leaving Nick to stand there, staring up at her father.

At six feet, one inch tall and 250 pounds, Michael Wade was an imposing man. That is, until he smiled. The smile that spread across his face, meeting the intense eyes of one of his best trainees, who also caused him much grief, was a genuine smile. "Nick," he said.

"Sir," Nick croaked. He didn't know if he had lost his voice from guilt after spending the night with this man's only daughter, or the fact that he indeed missed the man whom he considered a friend and mentor. "It's good to see you, sir," he finally said, extending his hand.

"How about Michael?" he said, grasping Nick's hand and pulling him into an embrace of genuine affection. After several seconds of backslapping and grins, Nick reached out, grasping Raina's hand, and pulled her in front of him. But then, Nick went weak for an instant when Raina jumped into his comforting arms, throwing her arms around his neck and burying her head into his chest, something Nick would guess she had done many times. Putting his sunglasses on, Nick squeezed his eyes shut. He couldn't help recalling how tightly they held onto each other earlier when they showered together that morning. He groaned inwardly.

Engulfed in his big arms, Michael's heart broke, realizing what his girl had witnessed. "Everything's going to be all right, you believe that," he said, setting her down to her feet.

Nick adjusted the baseball cap on his head. It was time for him to leave, and he didn't want to. "I, um . . . guess I should take off now. I have the taxi waiting," he said, indicating the taxi idling behind him in the large circular driveway.

"What?" Both Raina and her father turned to him, surprised.

Michael moved Raina aside. "Nicholas, you weren't just going to drop my girl off and then leave, were you?" Michael listened as Nick explained, saying that Suraina was probably tired and that he didn't want to intrude. He knew Raina never used her full first name and wondered how Nick came to use it so freely. "That's bull, Nick," he said. "You can at least stay and have an early dinner. My driver can get you to the airport in twenty minutes."

Raina held her breath, hoping he would stay, if only for an hour longer.

There was no room for argument. Nick spread his hands in surrender. "Guess who's coming to dinner?" he said, then bounded down the steps to pay the taxi driver, but not before joining Michael and Raina, laughing heartily at the irony of what he had said.

Once inside the mansion-style house, Michael escorted them into the living room. There, Nick saw a young male, whom he recognized from Raina's sketches. Next, they were in for another surprise when they were introduced to Michael's girlfriend. A petite, pretty woman named Ellie . . . short for Eloise. Raina and Nick exploded into laughter for several seconds, sobering only when they realized the trio was staring at them oddly. But Raina put everyone at ease by explaining that was the name they came up with as her travel name, for security reasons.

The light dinner of seafood and salads and vegetables was excellent. Nick listened intently as Raina explained the work she had been doing with the mentoring program and all she had done with Janey, who was her first mentoring student. But Nick also covertly watched her. Flashbacks of the past week and last night unfolded like falling eight-by-ten photos. He was going to miss her. When Raina talked about Pierce's capture, it was as if it was a sure thing in her mind, causing Michael and Nick to share a look, as each knew, unless something drastic occurred, a swift capture was unlikely. After dinner, Michael pulled Nick away to talk in his den, leaving Raina, her brother and Ellie talking in the living room. A short while later Raina went to fetch Nick, wanting to show him around the property before he left for the airport.

Using one of the spare cars, Raina drove to the edge of the property, to a secluded cliff overlooking the Pacific coast. The sun would soon begin its descent, blanketing everything a brilliant orange. Nick and Raina sat in the car, watching boats bobbing in the colorful water.

Nick pulled Raina into his arms. "I've got to leave you. I don't want to, you know."

"Yes, I know," she said, kissing him, surprised when desire flickered anew. Pulling back, she said, "I've got to tell you, I can't believe how my body responds to you. It's like I can't control it."

Nick caressed her cheek, before trailing his hand down, cupping her breasts through her short blouse. On impulse, he nuzzled her cleavage, freeing her from the confining bra as he lifted her from the driver's seat and onto his lap. "I know exactly how you feel," he said huskily, capturing her lips.

Raina pulled away from him, slid back into the driver's seat and started the car.

Nick pulled his cap lower on his head, wishing he hadn't fanned a fire that couldn't be squelched. He said nothing as she drove away from the cliff. Expecting them to return to the house so he could get his bag, he was surprised when she stopped the car after driving for only a few minutes to a cabin. Nick frowned when she got out of the car and came around to the passenger door. She was waiting for him to get out, and when he didn't, she opened the door and pulled on his arm. He followed

Raina as she walked over to the cabin, unlocking the door. "Raina, sweetheart, what are you doing?" he asked.

Standing on the raised stone step, Raina stood eye to eye with Nick and kissed him deeply. When she pulled back, she said, "I'm going to give you a proper send-off, Detective."

Nick's hands eased around her waist, allowing her to pull him inside the cabin. But he held her away from him. "Suraina, remember what I said about us cops being prepared to serve and protect? Well, I'm fresh out of my reserve supply." His heart thudded in anticipation when her arms eased around his neck. "But, we can make do," he said in a rush, glancing around in a comical fashion. "Where's the plastic wrap?"

Laughing and pushing him back, Raina waved a plastic package before his wide eyes. "I rummaged through my brother's travel bag while he was on the telephone lining up a date."

Nick plucked it from her fingers. "Oh, that was very sneaky of you, but very good detective work, Eloise." He laughed at her squeal, and together they fell onto the bed.

CHAPTER 11

It had been three weeks since Raina arrived at her father's house. She sat in her room, working via the new laptop computer her father bought for her. He insisted she use it, as well as the new cell phone, fearing that hers could be traced to her new home. Rereading the latest email update from her boss, Mimi, about a collection of lamps for the soon-to-be-launched line of home décor, Raina struggled to come to terms with her new life. It wasn't working.

Try as she might, Raina couldn't get excited about the new line. In fact, she hadn't been excited about anything since Nick left three weeks ago. Glancing across the room to the window, another wave of loneliness swept over her. It always did when she thought about her home, and about him. She only had to close her eyes to see his face. She missed him, and she ached for his touch again. A knock on her bedroom door interrupted her thoughts. "Come on in, Dad," she called out.

Michael Wade was more than happy to have his daughter with him. He could only imagine how she must be feeling, but there was no way he would allow her to stay in Pittsburgh where a professional killer was looking for her. "Hi, honey," he said, bringing in a vase of yellow roses. "These are for you, from Ellie."

"That was nice of her. I have to call and thank her," she said, accepting the vase and setting it on her dresser, then turning back to him.

"Why don't you come downstairs and thank her in person?" Michael had expected Raina to have adjusted to her new living arrangements by now, but she hadn't. Since the first night she arrived, he noticed she had become depressed, lost weight, and rarely left her room.

"I'm working, Dad, but I'll call her later," Raina said, sitting back at her desk.

Michael sat down beside her. "Raina, you can leave this house anytime you want. I have security here for you. Ellie told me you still haven't shopped for clothes, so how about a shopping spree on me?" His comical flipping of his eyebrows didn't make her smile.

"I have tons of clothes, Dad, and I'm hoping that I'll be able to go back home soon . . . that is, as soon as the police catch Pierce." Raina turned back to her laptop, already knowing what her father was going to say. He always did whenever she mentioned the police capturing Pierce, or her return to Pittsburgh. To Raina, it was a sure thing. To her father, it wasn't.

"That might take some time, Raina. I have told you this before." He covered her hand, forcing her to stop typing and face him. "But the police will catch him eventually. Honey, is there something more going on with you, other than that killer, I mean?"

"No," she said.

"I know you miss back home, and your girlfriends and Janey, too, but was there a boyfriend that's got you so out of sorts? Raina, talk to me. Tell me if there is anything I can help you with," Michael pleaded, desperate to help her.

Raina sniffed. "Dad, you know I didn't have a boyfriend. I'm just still so upset about . . . well, why did I have to be the one to run away and hide?"

"And live, Raina. You're alive because you got out of that restaurant." Michael smiled suddenly. "You know, I never told you how proud of you I was for rigging up that contraption that night. Baby, that took guts. You stayed there and did that on the chance that man would come out into the alley, which he did. You get those brains from me, you know." He smiled.

She raised skeptical eyes at him. "Right, so I guess Uncle Max told you about that?"

"No. Nicholas told me. He also showed me the crime scene photos." Michael hadn't pressed Raina for details because Nick filled him in on what happened at the restaurant.

Her eyes inched up to his. "What else did he tell you?"

"He told me that I have a very smart, courageous and beautiful daughter with a mean streak, and that you reminded him of me," Michael said and chuckled.

Raina rolled her eyes heavenward. "Right. I'll bet you put him on the spot, and grilled him about our trip out here."

"I didn't grill him. I'm actually glad he was assigned to bring you here. He's a fine detective. I'll tell you this, as a rookie cop, he was a royal pain. He questioned my authority at every decision I made, especially if it wasn't what he wanted. One day I came right out and told him if he kept pressing my buttons, I was going to lock him up."

Raina wasn't aware that she was smiling. "Why . . . what did he do?"

"He got mad at me because I wouldn't let him go on a stakeout with a female recruit. But then, every male officer wanted that detail. When I said no, he went behind my back and changed the duty roster, putting himself on the detail anyway. When I found out, I locked his ass in a cell for his full eight-hour shift," her father said with a grin on his face. "Only I forgot about it and remembered about twelve hours later. Then he stopped talking to me, and filed a complaint to my superiors. Raina, I know you think it was mean of me to lock him up, but it wasn't. I showed him who was in authority. Nicholas had no role model or other male figure showing him otherwise, but he later learned how to respect those who were in authority."

"Yes, he told me his parents were alcoholics and his teenage sister raised him."

Michael's face registered surprise. "Although I haven't seen him in a few years, I do keep tabs on how he's doing, mostly through his lieutenant."

Raina had been holding onto every word her father said, and wanted to hear more.

Michael walked over to the dresser, smelling the roses. "Nick told me something else."

"Wh–What else did he tell you?" She watched her father pull a yellow rose from the vase and break off the stem.

"He thanked me for being a father figure and mentor to him. He said he appreciated me for encouraging him and even kicking his butt on general principle. He also said I had you to thank for that. It means a lot to know that I mattered to Nick." Michael turned and saw her gloomy face. "Baby, what is it?"

"Nothing, Daddy, but I'm glad Nick told you that," Raina said. "I know firsthand the importance of being a mentor, Dad. But it's equally important to know the support, encouragement and trust you give to those kids or young adults comes from the heart and hopefully leads to them making positive, healthy choices in their lives."

Michael listened with pride swelling in his heart. He also noticed her face brighten as she spoke about the mentoring program and what it meant to her. "Raina, I purposely haven't pressed you about your ordeal, but trust that I will not let anything happen to you." Michael kissed her forehead. "I have to run along now, I've kept Ellie waiting."

Raina waited for him to leave and recalled the conversation she and Nick had upon arriving in Chicago. She was glad Nick talked to her father, thanking him.

Nick sat in his kitchen, waiting for his dinner to heat up in the oven. He'd had a long day at work, and his current sour mood was the result. Earlier in the day, he'd received a loud reprimand from Lt. Brown about missing an important meeting. Then the robbery suspect he'd been questioning got up in his face because Nick had failed to secure his wrist restraints. Nothing seemed to be going right lately. At work, his mood was angry and irritated. The littlest thing could set him off. At home he was just plain miserable.

After removing the casserole from the oven and then pouring himself a glass of lemonade, he welcomed the memory of Raina Wade, specifically the night they stood in his kitchen. And now that he knew how sweet her kisses were and how wonderful her body felt against his, beneath his, above his . . . he craved more, but more than that, he missed her company. How could a woman create such a void in his life after only a week, he wondered?

As Nick sat eating, his eyes strayed to the unfinished backsplash above the sink, until Reed let out a bark. Turning, Nick glanced up to see his friend and sergeant, Dennis, standing on the other side of the screen to the French doors. "Hey, Dennis, what the hell brought you all the way out here?" Nick immediately noticed Dennis's weary face. "You want some chicken casserole?"

"As long as you didn't make it." He sent Nick a doubtful look and pulled out a stool.

"No, I didn't, but it's pretty good," Nick said, preparing a plate of food and passing it to Dennis. Nick already guessed what brought Dennis there. "I'm fired, right?"

"No. I just stopped out to check on you." Dennis took a forkful of the casserole and, liking it, dug in for more, then looked up at Nick. "So, talk to me. What's going on with you?"

Nick lifted his shoulders and said, "I'm fine. Busy, and getting those five new cases yesterday didn't help."

Dennis knew Nick was anything but fine. He was one surly sourpuss. This was worse than he was after Scott Morgan was killed. Dennis noticed the change in Nick's attitude and demeanor after he returned from Seattle after babysitting Raina Wade for that week. He thought Nick's mood was somehow related to that trip, or what may have happened during it. "Nick, what happened when you escorted Ms. Wade out to her father?"

Nick almost choked on his food. "What? Nothing. I escorted her there, period."

"All that time together? You're a healthy, single guy, and Ms. Wade was one hot number. I still can see her in that dress, you know, that night in the station. You saw her, right?"

"Dennis, I was there, remember?" Nick didn't want to talk about Raina.

"Oh, right. Man, when she hit you, wow . . . it was like a shot had been fired off in there. I mean, cops were ducking for cover." Although Dennis laughed, he watched Nick closely. He was waiting for his friend's fuse to blow. "I'll tell you this, if she were my honey, and had popped me like that, well, I just gotta tell you, I'd probably get so turned on, I'd just throw her up on the desk and BAM! Go for it, you know what I'm saying? She looked the type, all hot and wild," Dennis laughed, shoveling another forkful of food into his mouth.

Nick gulped his drink. Sometimes Dennis was a sonofabitch, he thought. "Well, Dennis, I think Ms.

Wade would probably have popped you, too, if you had tried a move like that," Nick said slowly.

"Why would she slap me? I got a lot in common with her . . . for one thing, we're both black. I could have put my suave moves on her," he said, laughing harder and smacking his hand on the counter. "But I know what you're saying, though." Dennis raised his eyebrows. "I'm sure she's used to getting it good from Chief Coleman. I'll bet he's got suave moves, too."

Nick guessed Raina wouldn't give Dennis the time of day. Besides, he was old enough to be her father, and the man was married with kids. With anger building to the boiling point, Nick pinched the bridge of his nose. Max Coleman was married, with kids, and yet that didn't stop Raina from having an affair with the man, or from loving him. Frowning, Nick recalled the e-mail he received a few days ago from Coleman, advising everyone he was going out to the West Coast on business. *Business, my ass.* Nick fumed inwardly. He knew the man had gone to see Raina. After gulping down the rest of his lemonade, Nick slammed the glass down, wondering if Raina had taken her lover, Coleman, to that same cabin for *a proper send-off.* He recalled her words, just before pulling him into that very cabin.

Dennis saw the train wreck approaching, fast. He got up and opened the French doors, encouraging Reed to go outside, and closing them when he did. He went to the refrigerator for a beer and removed his sidearm, setting it on top of the refrigerator. He could see Nick's face was tight. "So yeah, man, I just keep thinking about that body of hers, and all that sweetness, and that booty. Can't you just imagine that bouncing on your . . ."

It all happened so fast, but Nick couldn't explain how it was the right side of his face was pressed down onto the cool granite island top, or how his right arm ended up behind his back, pressed painfully between his shoulder blades. "What the . . . ? Have you lost your damn mind? Dennis, get the fuck off me," he huffed and groaned as Dennis hitched his arm up further.

"Oh, no, good buddy, you'll hit me." Dennis chuckled, pressing his 200-plus pounds into Nick's side, keeping him still.

Gnashing his teeth, Nick hissed. "No–no, I won't hit you. I'm gonna kill you!" He grounded out, thinking his friend had truly lost his mind. Still, he couldn't move.

"Why did you swing at me, Nick?" Dennis asked. He had already added up two-plus-two, and Nick's reaction reinforced his suspicions. Dennis pressed his elbow harder into Nick's side, causing him to grunt louder. "Why did you get so angry about what I said about Raina Wade?"

After a few more painful jabs and pulls on his arm, Nick realized what Dennis was doing, and went slack. "O-kay, okay . . . because she's sweet. She's a good person."

"Okay, sweet and good. What else to make you swing at me?" Dennis pressed again.

"And, I got close to her . . . we got close, real close."

"Um-hum. Real close, and what? " Dennis hitched up Nick's arm again.

"I miss her a lot, okay," he said, slumping against the kitchen island when Dennis let go.

"Why was that so hard to say? You got close to her. You miss her a lot. What else, Nick? You telling me you got a thing for her, or was it about getting it on with a black girl?" Dennis watched as Nick tested his arm.

"Screw you, Dennis. It had nothing to do with her race, or mine," Nick said.

"So you feel a little something for her?"

Closing his eyes, it hit him suddenly. He did feel something for Raina Wade. "Yeah."

"What about Max Coleman? What if he finds out that you got up close and personal with her on your road trip? You were on the clock, Nick. He'll assume you screwed up another case . . . a case that he is personally involved with." Dennis's voice rose with agitation, realizing the situation was worse then he had originally guessed.

"I wasn't thinking about any of that." Nick couldn't think straight. He kept seeing Raina and Max Coleman in the cabin, as they had been that day—having a mind-blowing quickie.

"Nick, you've got to tell Lt. Brown," Dennis said.

"And tell him what? That I've fucked up this case by sleeping with the witness?"

"Yeah, that would do. But, Nick you slept with a *traumatized* witness. I was there that night she came to the station, scared to death and shaking like a leaf. She was fragile then, and I know a week with you didn't change that. I was there when she gave a statement and puked her guts when she saw the drawing of Pierce. She was a victim, dammit! What were you thinking?" Dennis moved menacingly to Nick, scowling. "Did you hurt that girl?"

Nick's jaw dropped. "What? No, it was consensual, and what we both wanted."

"You had better be straight with me or I'll break that arm."

"I didn't hurt her. It was a night in Vegas, and we connected and . . ."

"What?" Dennis stared at Nick with large, bulging eyes. His mouth dropped open in disbelief. "Hold the phone . . . did you say Vegas . . . Las Vegas?" He watched Nick nodding. Dennis blew out a breath. "Sit down and start talking, and don't leave anything out."

"Look, Den, I'll tell you everything, but this is off the record, understand?"

Dennis shook his head sadly. "Yeah, just as long as you understand this. We just got word that a hit went down in Chicago, right about the time you and Ms. Wade were there. Identical to Pierce's M.O. A small-time drug dealer with a pissy reputation was knocked off at a nightclub, and on karaoke night, at that. It was full house, and our boy was able to blend in, do the deed and fade out, and nobody saw or heard a thing."

Nick paled visibly, recalling Raina's panic attack over smelling someone's cologne at the nightclub . . . on karaoke night. "Oh, my God."

Pierce was sitting at his laptop computer editing his collage of victims. The pictures he took on his digital camera were later uploaded onto the computer. He thought it was an impressive sight to see a person going about their regular routines of their despicable lives one minute, and the next they were gone. Snapping his fingers, he whispered, "Just like that." With a click of the mouse, he switched screens to bring up the motor vehicle identification picture of Raina Wade. It infuriated him that he hadn't been able to locate her. For a month, he had been looking, and so far nothing. It appeared as if she dropped off the face of the earth, but he didn't think so.

Pierce was a patient man, if nothing else. In two weeks he would be going to Vancouver to finish up an assignment and then he would get back on track to find the elusive Raina Wade in Seattle. When Pierce switched back to his collage, he moved the mouse to drag the pictures around, placing them exactly where he wanted them to go. After several minutes of clicking and dragging photos, his eyes focused on the picture of the man he had followed to the back room of a nightclub in Chicago. Recalling how the man begged and pleaded for his life when he realized what was happening was Pierce's moment of joy. Gently he touched the newest tattoo above his wrist. Anyone who might see it would only see a series of ribbons with calligraphy script inside, although each ribbon served a purpose. Turning his attention back to his computer monitor, Pierce dragged the picture of the dead man across the screen to place it next to his "before picture." In that picture, the man sat at a table with his cronies, laughing, drinking and listening to karaoke.

Pierce's hand froze. His dark eyes studied the picture closely. Only he wasn't looking at the man at all. His eyes inched up to the pretty girl singing on stage. "No, it can't be," he said as he clicked the mouse pointer, enlarging the picture several times. Pierce stared, transfixed, into the face of the pretty girl standing up on the small stage. "No, that can't be her, not in Chicago." Switching screens again, he brought up the motor vehicle picture of Raina Wade, committed it to memory again, then went back to the picture at the nightclub and made it even larger. "It's her . . . holy Christ." Pierce sat back, his heart pounding as perspiration dotted his forehead. Slamming his eyes shut, he recalled the events that led up to that hit.

He had been at the club for an hour, talking to a brunette who couldn't stop blinking her eyes. He'd even thought about killing her, just to stop those damn blinking eyes. When the bandleader announced the microphone was open for karaoke, he thought the timing was perfect, and took that opportunity to call his mark on his cell phone. He'd previously set up a ruse that he wanted to score a large quantity of drugs. After leaving the bar, he followed the man into the back area where the restrooms were located. "That took ten minutes." It always did when he did his work in a public area. He then returned, having to cross the dining tables en route to the bar. The brunette was still there, blinking and waving for him. It was then he bumped into the pretty girl . . . the one who sang earlier. Mumbling an apology, he recalled touching her elbow, turning back briefly in her direction to make sure she was okay . . . Pierce's eyes flew open. "It was her." The woman he'd been searching for somehow ended up in the same nightclub. He even remembered her singing, and the long applause that followed. If only the blinking brunette hadn't distracted him, he would have been more attentive to what was going on in the nightclub.

His mind raced. Two separate hits. Two separate cities—what kind of coincidence was that? Only briefly did he think she was aware of who he was, or what he did for a living.

But there was still a possibility she had recognized him when he bumped into her. But he didn't think so. She seemed more focused on watching the dancers. Nonetheless, he couldn't help wonder why she was there. Or had she just happened to be in Chicago on a stop-off to her original destination . . . Seattle. He smiled sardonically, thinking he could kill two birds with one stone. After all, Seattle wasn't all that far from Vancouver.

Raina stood in the sunroom of her father's house, putting the finishing touches on a painting. It was a special painting. It was the lake on Nick's property. Stepping back from the easel, she smiled, welcoming the warmth of her memories.

"It's beautiful," a voice called out from behind her.

Raina whirled around, hearing her uncle, and flew into his arms. "Uncle Max!"

"And look who I've brought with me?"

Peeping around Max, Raina's face lit up to see that Debra, Max's wife, stood behind him. "Debra, I'm so glad to see you." The two women embraced tightly, but Debra's trained therapist's eyes flew over Raina appraisingly. "You've dropped a couple of pounds," she said.

Arm in arm, the two walked to the sofa and sat down. "I didn't even realize I had lost weight until I put on a pair of jeans," Raina said.

Debra sensed more was going on with Raina than she was letting anybody know. She glanced at the painting. "That is just a beautiful lake, Raina. Where is it?"

"It's on Det. Laprelli's property. I—I was walking and came upon the most amazing lake. I'd sketched it while I was there and just decided to paint it a few days ago." Raina absently recalled her father telling her just that morning that Max was coming out for a little R&R, but she couldn't help wondering what had happened back in Pittsburgh. *Had Pierce been apprehended? How was Nick doing?* "So, Uncle Max, tell me why you're really here?"

"What are you talking about? I came to see my niece."

"And maybe your brother, too?" Raina pursed her lips in frustration at Max. Their last argument sent her running from Max and Debra's house. That had been three months before that night when she showed up at the police station. "You know, Uncle Max, maybe now would be a good time to let go of all that old stuff between you and Daddy. I mean, really, who cares that he didn't want his younger brother to join the police force?"

Standing, Raina walked up to him, removed her sketchpad from his hand and flipped it closed. Several pages behind the sketch of the lake was a drawing she'd sketched of Nick. Dropping the pad back onto the table she recalled what Nick had said in Vegas. "Wasn't the PPD as good as any other place to start a career? Besides, it really is old news about the two of you having a falling-out when you joined the force. I mean, for crying out loud, you two just need to get over all that old crap before it's too late and one of you dies. Then neither of you will have a chance to move on." At first, Raina wasn't aware that her voice had taken on an angry, controlled edge as she spoke, or that she had spoken so vehemently. When she stopped talking, and the words resounded in her head, she quickly turned around, an apology on her lips for her uncle. But to her further shock, her father stood in the doorway, his raised eyebrows telling her he had heard her. "Dad, I—" Her eyes then flew to Max, then to Debra. "That's not what I really meant to say. Well, at least not like it sounded."

Michael and Max shared a look of concern about Raina, even as each drew meaning from the truth of her words. Michael clasped his brother's hand and shared a hug. "She's right, Max, we're old men now and I guess it is time we need to get over that old crap."

Cringing, Raina was ashamed at what she had said. "Dad, Uncle Max, I–I'm sorry for what I said before. I just got scared and wondered . . . oh, I don't know, if they have been any changes I needed to know about, that's all," she said, fishing for information.

Max decided not to tell Raina about the hit in Chicago. "No, dear, there have not been any new developments on the case," he said, then followed Michael out of the room.

So Nick must be okay, then.

As soon as they left, Debra turned to Raina. "Okay, they're gone, now tell me what's really wrong . . . and don't tell me it's nothing. You look clinically depressed, Raina. You've lost weight, and after hearing that impassioned bashing of your father and uncle . . . well, that just tells me you're also edgy and angry. Professionally speaking, honey, all of that tells me a whole lot."

"And, why wouldn't I be clinically depressed and edgy? Debra, have you forgotten that I was forced to pack up and leave my home in the span of a day? But hey, I guess that can make one just a little bit angry, too." She plucked a tissue from a box sitting on the table and walked over to the painting again.

"Yes, I suppose you're right." Debra went for another approach. "I really do like that painting, Raina. I want to be sitting right there on those rocks, with the sun on my legs and feet."

Glad Debra dropped the subject of her mental health, Raina brightened. "I know what you mean, and those rocks were slippery, too. If it wasn't for Nick, um, Det. Laprelli, I would have fallen and sprained my ankle."

"Really?"

"Uh-huh."

"He's nice and kind of sexy, too, isn't he?"

Facing the painting, Raina mumbled, "Uh-huh," then turned to Debra. "What?"

"Nothing. Oh, I forgot to tell you what happened last week. I went to a cookout. It was the annual thing the community puts on for the officers in the district. Max couldn't go, so I went and took Kira and Troy." Debra walked over to a full tea-serving cart that was set up with a steaming pot of tea. "May I?"

Coming out of her reverie of that day at the lake, Raina offered to fix Debra's cup of tea.

Debra waved her away. "Anyway, that Nick Laprelli sat at the table with us. He had his dog with him," she said absently, admiring the china pattern of the tea set.

"Reed," Raina said, remembered hugging the dog tightly before leaving Nick's house.

"Oh, right, that is what he said his dog's name was." Debra tested her tea and smiled. "Can you believe, now those kids want a dog? It didn't help matters that Nick went on and on about the joys of having a dog, and how Reed was going to be a daddy because some dog down the road was having puppies soon."

"Mitzy," Raina said, absently.

"So we've been invited out to his farm. The kids are still settling in with us, poor little things. I just want them to have some normalcy in their lives. I told Nick about them, and he told me that going out to his grandparents' farm when he was young was a lifeline . . . helped him deal with having alcoholic parents." Debra's eyes lifted to Raina, noticing she had her complete attention.

"Anyhoo, like I said, he is such a nice guy." Debra sipped her tea.

"Yes. How was the rest of cookout?" Raina stared blankly into space.

Debra giggled. "Well, later, when the cookout was winding down and more officers were coming off duty, girl, it was a spectacle, when Nick and this other officer poured vodka into the big jug of lemonade. Half an hour later, we were all doing wacky line dances." Debra's giggles had turned her face red. "I can still dance like nobody's business."

Raina grinned. "Well, with Nick's spiked lemonade, I can only imagine."

Debra watched her above the gold leaf rim of the delicate tea cup. "You miss him."

"Hum," Raina mumbled, then looked up quickly, coming out of her trance. "What?"

"You miss him," Debra repeated.

"Debra, wh–what are you asking me?"

"It wasn't a question, honey. It was a statement based on observation and conversation. You. Miss. Him," she enunciated and sat her cup down. "Admit it."

"Okay, I guess I do. He–he made me feel safe. You know how terrified I was."

"You don't feel safe here, in your father's home?"

Keeping a tight rein on her emotions was making Raina's throat sore. "I–I guess I do."

"But Nick Laprelli made you feel safer? How so?"

"Debra, why are we even talking about him?" Raina asked.

"Because I get the feeling that he is, perhaps, what you're missing most. Maybe it's just the safety of his arms. But, whatever it is, it is making you sick, mentally and physically."

Raina dropped down beside Debra on the couch. Her eyes closed, holding fresh tears behind her lids. "He did make me feel safe at a time when I was anything but that. I was always on the lookout for Pierce." She was absolutely not going to tell Debra how she really felt about Nick, because she was still dealing with her misplaced feelings. Besides, she wouldn't do anything that would jeopardize his job.

Debra stood up, seeing the determined set of Raina's mouth . . . meaning she was through talking. "I'll just say this, Raina. He's a very nice, single guy, and so what if he's white, if that was a concern." Debra waved her hand when she saw Raina about to protest. "I had better get downstairs to see what Troy and Kira are getting into. But one more question, okay?"

Raina braced herself. "Okay."

"What are you going to do with the painting?"

Raina glanced back at the painting, becoming lost in it again. When she turned back to answer Debra, the room was empty.

Debra had already walked out of the sunroom.

Two weeks later, Nick was working at his desk when he was summoned to Lt. Brown's office. Inside the office,

BERNICE LAYTON

Nick was surprised to see Max Coleman and Dennis Walker in attendance. Nick's eyes flew to Dennis, wondering if his friend had broken his confidence.

Luckily, Nick was called to the meeting to provide statistical data on several cases the department was primed to solve. Lyle Brown raked critical eyes over Nick, noticing his rumpled appearance. "Laprelli, why do you look like you haven't slept in days?"

Nick shook his head. "Don't know, sir. I've been sleeping like a baby," he lied.

"You don't look like it."

"Sir, I am in plain clothes," Nick said, smoothing down the front of his wrinkled denim shirt with his hands. "Guess I should've pressed the shirt."

Lyle's eyes narrowed. "There you go again with that smart mouth. You know what happened the last time, don't you, or would you like another babysitting assignment? Because I've got a mother of three, and she needs an escort down to Florida, with her kids—all under the age of five." His blue eyes twinkled when Nick very quickly shook his head. "I didn't think so," Lyle added.

Picking up on the conversation, Max said, "I take offense at that, Lyle. I'm glad Nick got Suraina safely to Seattle." Max sent Nick a tilt of his chin.

Suraina. Nick could hear his own voice hoarsely calling out her name as their bodies thrashed together passionately. He was saved from responding when Lt. Brown began the meeting, detailing how the department was given additional resources to clear up several key cases. Hearing Raina's name and knowing that Max

Coleman had been with her two weeks ago was more than Nick could stand. He desperately wanted to know how she was doing. Her cell phone and email address were no longer valid. He'd thought about taking a chance and calling her father's house on the pretense of following up on the case, but he'd been sent on a mandatory training assignment immediately upon returning to the station from Seattle. Then he was told he was officially off the part of the case involving Raina Wade. None of that helped, though. He thought about her every day, and with each passing day, he missed her even more.

"Laprelli!"

Lyle Brown's bellow intrusively pulled Nick from his thoughts. Looking up, he saw several eyes zoning in on him. *Ah, shit.* Recoiling, he could only exhale slowly, very slowly.

Almost another two weeks had passed when Nick arrived home one evening to find a package sitting on his front porch. Noticing a Seattle post office box, he hurried to unwrap it.

Nick's eyes took in the full 18- by 22-inch cherry wood-framed painting of the creek. It was an extremely accurate painting of the creek in the full bloom of summer, as it looked now. Smiling, he said, "The *Andy Griffith Show* Pond, as Raina called it." Studying the picture, Nick saw that Raina had painted him in it. He was sitting on the jagged rock, with his favorite brown fishing rod dangling from his hand. But when his eyes traveled further up the painting, beyond the trees, barely visible in the blue sky and puffy white clouds, was the smiling face of Scott Morgan. Nick sat the painting on the chair, stepping back from it quickly. Pain pricked his unblinking eyes . . . he could not take his eyes off the painting. Only hearing Reed noisily burying his nose into the brown paper wrapping, did Nick pull his eyes away from the painting. "Yeah, I know exactly how you feel, Reed."

Raina decided it was time to start living again. First thing, she forced herself to stop dwelling on the painting of the creek. She had to get rid of it because her thoughts remained on Nick with it there. So she framed it herself and then mailed it off to him. She hoped that would put him out of her mind, stop her from missing him so much.

The next thing on her agenda was to go to the fabric warehouses to check fabrics. Over the past two months, she and Mimi exchanged e-mails extensively concerning the home décor catalogue, which would soon be launched. Raina missed being at work where everything was happening for the anticipated launch of the catalogue.

Raina also went shopping for more clothes, and although she still worried about Pierce, she resolved not to be a prisoner any longer. She was cautious when she went out, even with the ever-present security guard assigned to accompany her whenever she did. That she didn't like, and when she confronted her father about it, he told her either the guard stayed put, or she did. Only then, did Raina back down and accept the presence of the friendly, protective guard. One of her favorite spots on her father's property was the area overlooking the Pacific coast. She had spent many days there reading or just sitting in the sun, or sending encrypted e-mails to Janey.

On this day, that is where she sat. With her eyes closed, she remembered the day she and Nick sat in the car watching passing boats. That is, before he pulled her onto his lap . . .

CHAPTER 12

When Nick arrived at Max Coleman's house for a scheduled meeting, he was immediately pulled into the family room by the kids, Troy and Kira. They were excited to show him information they'd gathered about caring for a puppy. Ten minutes later, that's where Debra found him. Watching from the doorway, Debra took in the sadness in his eyes. *The same as Raina's,* she thought, then escorted him to the living-room where the meeting was being held.

Nick wondered why Mrs. Coleman asked if he was okay as she showed him to the living room. *How could I be?* he thought. He was in the home of his commander, who had a little something on the side . . . a little something he was now intimately familiar with. *Hell, no, I'm not okay.* He felt guilty because he liked Mrs. Coleman, and couldn't for the life of him understand how her husband could cheat on her. But then he realized he was no better. He was a cop who violated protocol by taking a witness to bed, and now he couldn't get her out of his system.

Passing Nick a packet of documents, Max began the meeting by announcing the priority of the investigation concerning the hit man, Pierce. Then he announced the PPD would soon be releasing the sketch of Pierce. "I've explained the ramifications of releasing the sketch to Ms. Wade, but she was adamant we should go ahead and do it anyway."

Nick's mind screamed, *No!* It was a bad idea to release the picture. "Why would she risk her life like that? It would be suicide." Nick wasn't aware he'd spoken out loud. Lt. Brown responded.

"Look, Nick, we all realize how personal this case is to you. And, like you, we all want Pierce to pay for what he did to Scott, as well as to your friend, Antionelli, but Ms. Wade is willing to help."

Max rubbed his head. "What can I say, except to say that she is a stubborn woman? She knows the risks, all of them, and she also suggests releasing the drawing of the tattoo, as well."

Nick's stomach tightened. "What is she thinking?" Nick reined himself in when he caught Dennis tensing. "I mean, there are other ways of tricking Pierce out of hiding."

Max shook his head. "Yes, I agree. But I saw her, and she doesn't look good. She has lost weight, she's depressed, and, well, she's just not in a good place right now, emotionally." Max wasn't about to tell the assembled group just how emotionally fragile his niece was. "She needs as much closure on this thing as all of us do on Scott Morgan. Now I suspect that once the picture and tattoo hit the airwaves, the media will run with it and we're going to get every lunatic out there calling in, if only to get their fifteen minutes of fame, or . . ." Max paused. "Or perhaps it is for the six-figure reward that will be offered for Pierce."

Nick was still trying to wrap his mind around Raina's health and mental state. He pictured her face . . . sad and scared, softly crying. He wished he could hold her in his arms.

"Her father has pulled in a favor from his connections at NSA for assistance, and already we got a partial lead on someone who may have spotted Pierce scoping out the nightclub where he popped a small-time drug dealer in a toilet stall. It is believed he had been there at least a couple of days." Max turned to Nick. "But that was at least a day before you and Raina arrived there. I'm glad you didn't go to that nightclub," Max said, taking a seat. "I hate to think what would've happened if Pierce had spotted her anywhere in Chicago. Because if he's the one who broke into her condo, he knows exactly what she looks like."

Nick exchanged a look with Dennis. He knew Dennis had to be thinking the same thing he was . . . he was withholding key information. If Raina's panic attack was a direct result of Pierce actually bumping into her, than she was right on target and now had another identifier on Pierce. His cologne was sickly sweet, but distinctive. She later told Nick that she could probably recreate it using some fragrance sticks and essential oils. To tell his superiors what happened in Chicago meant the end of his career. But not to meant jeopardizing Raina's life even more. He couldn't bear the thought of anything happening to her because he didn't disclose what he knew. He had to tell them, and stood up to do so. "There's something I . . ."

Just then, Debra came into the room, stopping beside Nick and announcing that lunch was all ready. "Oh, since you're up, Nick, can you give me a hand with the trays?"

Startled, Nick turned to her, distracted by her interruption. "Huh?"

"Go on, Nick, we're already covered the basics, but what were you going to say before Debra came in?" Max sent Debra a raised eyebrow, which was met by a wink from her.

"Oh, it was nothing." Nick turned quickly to catch up with Debra.

In the kitchen, Debra and Nick chatted about work schedules, the puppies Mitzy would be delivering soon and the upcoming visit out to Nick's place. With Nick's help, Debra had finished loading the serving trays and glanced up to see Max coming into the kitchen.

"So, Nick, is next weekend okay to bring the kids out to your farm?" Debra asked.

"Sure. I'm off next weekend. Come on out around lunchtime." Nick watched Max walk over to kiss his wife on the cheek. The desire to throttle his commander settled over him, something he truly wanted to do at that moment.

"Hey, I'm off next weekend, too, so I'm looking forward to seeing your place." Max sent Nick a sly wink before saying, out of Debra's earshot, "In the daylight, this time."

Sonofabitch. Nick snarled inwardly as he picked up a tray and followed Debra out.

Pierce had taken a chance on completing another assignment when he wasn't able to focus. Since seeing the picture of Raina Wade in Chicago, she filled his thoughts. He couldn't understand what the problem was—she simply had to be eliminated. He unexpectedly had to return to Pittsburgh, interrupting his search for her in Seattle.

Why the hell couldn't he find her? Pierce soon got his answer the second his fingers stopped their rapid movement across his keyboard.

After doing a more thorough Internet search on Raina Wade, he had come up with a family relation, Michael Wade. Pierce sat back in his chair, fixing a startled glare at his computer monitor. "I don't believe this," he said.

Timing was of the essence while he was in Vancouver. He had run out of time there and had to leave in order to catch a flight back to Pittsburgh by late the next afternoon.

Pierce had been in his office working on his laptop when a light tap sounded on his office door. He engaged a screen saver and looked up. Counting to five, he slowed his breathing, as he forced himself from the mindset of a killer to that of RJ Mortison, attorney at law. He smiled up at his secretary. "Carol, how are you doing?"

Carol had been RJ Mortison's personal secretary for five years. To Carol, RJ was not only the absolute best boss ever, he was also an excellent, high-profile criminal attorney. Truth be told, RJ was an excellent attorney. He had had an excellent teacher: his father was a renowned criminologist-turned-attorney who had later been appointed to the bench. Carol also thought RJ was positively the finest looking man, but he had no interest in her as a woman at all. From what she had seen, on occasion, his preference was for leggy brunettes with brains, mostly attorneys like himself. In the five years since she had been his secretary, Carol could say she knew nothing of RJ's personal life. He was just what he presented himself to be—a successful, sought-after criminal attorney who traveled a lot.

Carol hated to admit, even to herself, but there were times when she thought the other side of RJ was probably someone she wouldn't want to know, or even trust, for that matter. Then there were the times she thought he looked almost deadly.

Making her way into RJ's large office, Carol was excited to hear about his latest business trip where he had provided legal support and assistance to needy people, pro bono. She took delight in hearing about the outside work RJ did to help those people in need. He always rebuffed praise and he did his own paperwork. "Hi, RJ, welcome back. Do you have a few moments to spare?"

"For you, always, Carol," RJ said, watching her limp toward his desk. RJ always felt a twinge of renewed anger remembering how Carol almost died in a car accident a few years ago. The drunken driver who rammed into her compact car was a local businessman with a string of DWI/DUI offenses. He had only served six weeks in an alcohol detox facility in lieu of jail time.

RJ watched Carol take a seat, adjusting her long skirt over the leg brace she had been forced to wear since that accident. He thought she was a great secretary. She didn't press him with endless questions about his cases, and although she was very pretty, he never thought about her in a sexual way.

Smiling pleasantly, he remembered his encounter with that businessman at a private gym. It was there RJ had gotten retribution for the damage poor Carol had suffered. RJ waited until the pompous man had gone into the steam room, and with his gun silencer in place, RJ emptied several rounds from his gun into both of the man's legs. Then he carefully lifted the bloody legs to the sitting ledge so that the man didn't bleed out. In RJ's mind, it was simply a case of cause and effect. He didn't want the man to die; instead, he wanted him to live . . . without legs. RJ smiled each time he thought about how his perfectly aimed bullets turned the man's legs into bits and pieces of bone and flesh.

"You look awfully happy," Carol said, watching a smile spread across his handsome face.

"Carol, I'm just glad to see you. It looks like you're getting around a little bit easier." It had been three years, and her gait had not changed. Rounding his desk, RJ opened her hand and placed a small rectangular box containing a pair of diamond stud earrings in her hand.

Raina awakened from another dream, disoriented. Her breath coming out in gasps, she tried to wrap her

CROSSING THE LINE

brain around the fuzzy things she kept dreaming about, only nothing made any sense. Climbing out of bed, she experienced another wave of homesickness. She wanted to go home. Although her suite in her father's house was quite comfortable, with a separate sitting area, it still was not her home.

Today was Janey's birthday and the members of the church were hosting a roller-skating party for her and another girl in the mentoring program. Over the past two months, Raina and Janey had texted and e-mailed each other on a weekly basis. Raina was more than delighted to get the positive reports from Mrs. Wilson, the coordinator of the program, on Janey's accomplishments, as well as a report on Julie's new job as an office clerk.

It was Saturday again and Raina had absolutely nothing to do. Raina had grown to hate the weekends since being in Seattle, because they stretched out way too long. During the week she had work to occupy her mind. At the bedroom window, she gazed down onto the manicured lawns and recalled the last normal Saturday she had in Pittsburgh—the Saturday before her world fell apart.

She'd gone shopping with her girlfriends Andrea and Kia. It was then she came up with the plan on how to break things off with Leon the Loser in style. On that Saturday they had gone shopping for the perfect dress, and next she picked up the shoes. Afterwards the trio went out for dinner and a movie. It was a perfect Saturday.

As always, whenever she thought about the shoes, it brought on another vivid memory of Rachel, causing that painful ache in her head and chest to return. Raina realized how much her life had changed since that terrible night . . . all because she wanted to show Leon the Loser a thing or two. *I was so careless.* Nick was right to accuse her of the same thing.

Gloom was becoming her constant friend, and she felt as if she were dying inside.

"Raina?" Michael stood in the opened doorway of her bedroom.

Raina spun around. "Dad, you scared me," she said breathlessly.

Michael remained in the doorway. He hated seeing his daughter like this. But he had another pressing matter to discuss with his secretive daughter. "Raina, I want to talk to you."

Raina knew her father was probably at his wit's end. He had done everything to make her comfortable and secure. And today, especially, she didn't look forward to yet another discussion about how safe she was. He would only reiterate how no one would dare come into his home. To Raina, that was part of the problem . . . it was his home, and she felt like a houseguest who had long ago worn out her welcome. Raina walked over to Michael with a half smile plastered on her face. "Dad, can we not talk about how safe I am here, please?" She patted his forearm.

"All right. Can you come down to the study?"

"Oh, okay. Give me a few minutes to get dressed and I'll be right down." She guessed he had bought her another piece of jewelry. Of course she would again pretend to be thrilled to receive it.

Michael was sitting at his desk working on his computer when Raina came downstairs twenty minutes later. He smiled when she walked up behind him, throwing her arms around his wide shoulders and kissing him soundly on the cheek. Such a familiar thing for her to do, he thought lovingly. "Baby, I love you with all my heart, you know that, don't you?" he asked.

Raina sensed something was wrong. She wasn't about to get another piece of jewelry. "Of course I know that. Dad, what's wrong?"

"I want to ask you a question, Raina. It's kind of personal, because I don't like what I've been thinking this morning," he said, watching her nodding and wringing her hands, another familiar thing she did when she was nervous. "What happened en route to Seattle?"

Her heart rate slowed. Had she been holding her breath that long? "What do you mean?"

Michael tapped a few keys on his keyboard and angled the wide, flat screen monitor for her to see. "You know I have a full security system in place here at the house. I also have the exterior grounds of the property monitored, Raina."

Unsure what he was talking about, Raina glanced at the monitor. All she saw was the cliff overlooking the water, then turned to him questioningly. "Dad, wh–what is it?"

Tapping another key, Michael watched Raina as she saw what played out on the screen.

It was a playback of her driving up to the cabin, then getting out of the car and rounding the hood to the passenger side. She was laughing, as she pulled Nick's arm to get out of the car. Next, she watched as she stood on the step, kissing Nick, molding her body into his and, finally, pulling him into the cabin. She thought they looked happy. Raina didn't want to see anymore. Besides, she had relived that day many times over. Aware that her father was watching her—waiting for her to explain the video—she got annoyed. But then, she had another thought. Explain what? And that's when she got angry. Turning from the computer monitor, she met her father eye to eye. "Yes, and . . ." She noticed his eyes were now condemning and furious.

"Don't get flip with me, young lady. You explain that," he said, thrusting his finger at the monitor as his voice rose, "because what I'm thinking at this very second isn't pretty. Mostly, I'm thinking how fast I can get back to Pittsburgh and kill Nicholas Laprelli!" he ground out, pushing his chair back and standing.

Raina shook her head. "Now why would you do that? Because you saw us go into that cabin?" A chilling thought came to her mind then. "Please tell me you don't have the inside of that cabin under surveillance, too."

"No, I don't, thank God. But this tape starts out with you driving up to the cliff and . . . sitting on his lap in that car. Of what I've seen, you've been . . ." Michael shook his head, unable to say anything more.

Never in a million years would Raina have thought she and Nick were being videoed. Knowing that her father had seen what happened when she sat on Nick's lap in the car—him kissing her, then opening her blouse, caressing her, sent heat up to her face, turning it red with anger and embarrassment. Raina knew all too well that one word from her father could end Nick's career. She wouldn't let him do that. She stood up, strength lifting her spine and returned her father's stern glare. "Dad, listen, I'm a grown woman and who I . . ." Hesitating, searching for a softer approach, Raina gave up. "You know, for real, Dad, it's like this. Who I chose to be with, intimately, really is none of your business. I'm a grown woman."

Michael pinned her with his eyes for several seconds, trying to calm his rising blood pressure. Yes, his baby girl was no longer that. At any moment, he expected her to stamp her feet, and that actually made him just want to hold her in his arms. "Raina, as a detective, Nicholas was entrusted to get you here to me safely, not to . . . to take advantage of you. I hope you know the difference."

"Of course I know the difference, and what you saw on that tape is . . ." Raina stopped.

"Is you and Nick Laprelli about to—engage in an inappropriate activity," Michael finished. "It's painfully obvious to me that the two of you did a little more on your trip here than just share a long ride." His eyes glowed painfully at his choice of words. So much that he angrily snatched up the remote and pressed play. Unable to watch it again, he turned away from the screen. This time, the tape showed Raina and Nick leaving the cabin some forty minutes later. They walked arm in arm to the car, then stood locked in an embrace, kissing passionately before getting back into the car. "Well, so much for you showing him the property, daughter."

"Dad . . ." she began with a quiet warning tone, but her eyes blazed at him.

Michael exploded, then. "Don't you Dad me, dammit! When did it start? Tell me!"

Raina recoiled at his fury. "Dad, please listen. Nick and I got close, that's all, and we're both adults . . . consenting adults, over twenty-one."

"I was worried about you, Raina. I had been at my wit's end waiting for you to arrive. The only consolation I had was in knowing that it was Nicholas who was bringing you here to me. I trusted him. How could you let him do this?" Michael spat out angrily.

"What are you talking about? I didn't let him do anything. We made the decision to . . ." Regrouping, Raina walked over to the sofa when he sat. "Dad, we got close, that's all it was."

"Close, huh, and what about Las Vegas?" He turned to her, waiting for her to deny what he'd also found out that morning; they had spent a night in Las Vegas. "Is that where the two of you first got . . ." Michael pursed his lips, his eyes dancing along the ceiling, before rounding back to hers. "Oh, how did you put it . . . where you two got close?" He threw her words mockingly down at her upturned face.

She didn't answer right away. But as she met his tight face with her own, Raina made a decision, now as mad as he was. "You know what, I'm not going to justify what

Nick and I did, or when it first happened. Like I said, we're both adults and really, Dad, it's none of your business to know anything about whom I chose to sleep with!" There, she said it. Only she wished she could retract her words when his eyes filled with pain. "Daddy . . ." she said softly.

"I'll have him fired for what he's done!" Michael roared, ignoring her rolling eyes. "And believe me, Raina, my decision has nothing to do with you *sleeping* with him, either." He sneered. "Do you think his sleeping with a pretty girl is news? The Nick Laprelli I knew was a skirt-chaser, and now he's added my daughter to the list of skirts he's lifted!" Michael rubbed a hand over his salt and pepper hair. "But don't you worry about it because I won't have him fired for his indiscretion with you. Nooo, I'll have him fired for his obvious insubordination . . . for not following the direct orders of his commanders, dammit!"

Raina fired back, sarcasm dripping from her words. "Oh, please. Give me a break, Dad! You mean your brother, your friends and the rest of your buddies on the police force? Well, I'm sure you don't want that to get out, do you? I mean, come on, Dad, how many daughters of ex-police captains get 24/7 police security across the country—while, I might add, being given $5,000 cash for expenditures. All the while, that very detective was forced to shift his other cases to the side. All because your cronies, um, sorry, I mean, your buddies, thought those cases were far less important than escorting Raina Wade to her father. Some cases, I might add, were due in court while he was babysitting me here! Hmm . . ." Raina mimicked him by pursing her lips and rolling her eyes heavenward. "Nooo, I don't think many daughters of ex-police captains get that, do you? Oh, and don't even get me started on the whole nepotism factor you were granted to get me here to Seattle in the first place, and tucked away into the safety of your security-laden palace!" Raina finished her rant by glaring back at him, her arms across her heaving chest. She all but patted her feet, waiting for his comeback.

Michael sat down. "I'll deal with any assistance I may have been granted by the PPD. I just don't believe you could be so irresponsible, and all for what, Raina, a one-night stand?" Suddenly, a thought shot through Michael's head, forcing him to bolt up from his chair again. "Or did it start earlier, while you stayed at his house?" He couldn't even wrap his brain around that; she was his little girl, after all. "Oh, good Lord, you didn't even know him."

"No, Dad, it didn't start then. It wasn't like that, so stop making it all about Nick. I was a willing partici-pant." Raina went from being angry to being scared about what her father could do to ruin Nick. Still, she could also see that he was hurt by her words. She crossed over to him, but he moved away from her. "Daddy?"

"How involved were you with him, Raina?"

Raina stood strong. She was not going to justify sleeping with Nick to anyone, least of all to her own pig-headed father. "Dad, I'm a woman. I have feelings and desire and . . ."

Michael held up his hand, stopping her from going on. "He told me how I was important to him, that I was his mentor, surely as you were yourself. You know the importance of honesty and trust. So, forgive me for being mad at him for enjoying himself with my traumatized daughter. Don't you dare defend him to me with your misplaced feelings and desires!" With nostrils flaring, Michael continued his outburst. "I understand you're grown and all, but he's a cop, for Christ's sake. He had a job to do and he compromised both it and your safety. Did the two of you forget there was a sadistic killer out there searching for you to end your life?" This time when she rolled her eyes, he turned her chin back to face him. "Obviously you did, because Nicholas thought it was okay to run a line on you. I thought you were smarter than that, Raina," he said, dropping his hand and stepping back.

"What? Run a line? Oh, come on, Dad, give me a break. I'm not stupid. We had an encounter." Raina said the words, but in her heart, she felt it was more than just an encounter she'd shared with Nick. "It's over and I'm asking you not to do anything to jeopardize his career. Nick has chosen a career path that you put him on in the first place. Dad, I wanted him."

"Sure you did, as much as he wanted you, right?" Michael said, doubtful. "Why don't I think it was just a case of him running his line on a pretty black woman? And don't look at me like that, because some white men do that," he said, ignoring her shocked expression.

Raina flopped down on the couch. She was stunned that he would say such a thing to her. "You're no different than those narrow-minded bigots who looked at me and Nick with unmasked hostility. Dad, you and Mom didn't raise me to see skin color as a barrier to the person. Where is this coming from?"

Michael sat beside her and took her hand in his. "You're right. Your mother and I raised our children to see people for what they were, but baby, some white men just want to see, well, they just want to . . ." At a loss for words, he looked to her. "Do I have to spell it out, Raina?"

"To do a black girl is what you're trying to say, but I don't believe that. It certainly wasn't how it was between us." She watched his eyes close. "Dad, I got to know him."

"How, Raina? You were a victim, fresh from witnessing a horrific crime, and he knew that. Under those circumstances you were not capable of being rational or even thinking coherently. In my book, he took advantage of you in your fragile state of mind." Michael stood up, resolved. "And his commanders will see it that way also. Trust me, they will."

Noticing the downward set of his mouth, Raina was standing firm. "I'm asking you . . . no, I'm warning you, don't you do anything to get Nick fired, Dad. I get that you're upset because you think he just slept with your daughter on a whim, but you're wrong. He didn't take advantage of me. And even after he blew me off, more than once, I still wanted him." Unable to say more, Raina patted his arm and turned to leave.

Michael watched her as she talked. He could only ask her a question that came to mind when she stepped away. "Are you in love with Nicholas?" His eyes widened.

Raina hadn't reached the door yet, but her father's words stopped her in her tracks. It was a thought so unreal she couldn't wrap her brain around the possibility. "Only a fool falls in love over the course of a week, Dad."

CHAPTER 13

Debra and Max arrived at Nick's house with Troy and Kira on a sunny Saturday afternoon. Everyone was excited not only to see the farm, but to go to visit Nick's neighbors to see Mitzy's recently born puppies.

Nick was more than happy to have company. The walls of his house were closing in around him and he'd grown exceptionally bored the past few weeks. He was delighted when Debra called to reschedule the visit, which had been cancelled twice—first, because Troy had a stomach virus and again because of Max's work schedule.

Nick watched Debra walk over to the sink and run her hand across the backsplash of the finished tile work. An image of Raina flashed before him.

"I have iced tea, soda and beer," he said just as Max came in from the deck, asking to use his cell phone charger. Nick pointed to the counter. "Just unplug mine there on the counter, it should be charged." A few hours later, Nick walked inside the kitchen from the deck, when his cell phone rang and grabbed it up from the counter. "Hello?"

"Hel–Hello?"

Nick's hand shook at hearing Raina's voice. It covered him like warm water, soothing him, surrounding him, comforting him. Shaken, he could barely speak. "Raina?"

"Nick?" Raina asked.

"Yes, it's me. I–I accidentally picked up Chief Coleman's cell phone. How are you, Raina?" Nick leaned against the counter, but kept his eyes focused out on the deck.

"Oh, I'm okay. I–I thought for a minute I'd dialed your number by mistake."

"It doesn't have to be a mistake. You can call me anytime. Why haven't you?"

"You haven't called me," she said, then listened to him saying he didn't want to bother her, then asked if she was okay.

"I'm okay." Longing forced Raina's shoulders to slump forward and she unknowingly raised her fingers to her lips, stifling a soft sigh that escaped her.

"Are you really okay, sweetheart?" Nick whispered, sensing she was anything but okay.

"Nick, I have to tell you something." She told him that her father found out about them being in the cabin. "I'm sorry Nick, but when he cornered me with the tape and, well, you remember how I was when I, um . . ."

"When you manhandled me," Nick said, finding it odd that he was smiling, despite what she'd told him. He was talking to her, and that was all that mattered. He could deal with everything else.

"Yeah, I was pretty bad, wasn't I?"

"No, you weren't. You were wonderful," he said, quietly. There was so much he wanted to say . . . so much he couldn't. He just held the small phone tighter, as he stood rooted to the kitchen floor. "Hey, I love the painting and,

Raina . . ." At that moment, Nick saw Max standing out on the deck. The older man was about to come inside the kitchen. "It was nothing. I'd better give Max Coleman his phone," Nick said.

"That's okay, Nick. I'll call him later. Bye." As much as she hated to, Raina quickly ended the call, fearing she would say more, knowing she shouldn't.

Nick sat the phone back onto the counter. When he looked out to the deck again, he watched Max walk over and put his arms around Debra. Nick swallowed the painful lump of loneliness that hit him full force. It occurred to him that before he had met Raina Wade, he never knew what heartache felt like.

Every time RJ Mortison had to go to the police station, he always picked up useful bits of information. On this particular day, he sat in an interrogation office waiting for his client to be escorted in from the holding cell. RJ had become a familiar sight at the police stations in and around the city. He knew many officers and civilian staff by name. He made it his business to know their names. It proved useful as he conducted his other profession—where he was known only as Pierce. In that profession he was judge, jury, prosecutor and hangman. It was in that profession where he received the most reward. It was this other profession he held onto tightly, so as not to let it cross over into his daily life as the high-priced attorney RJ Mortison.

Today, a particularly chatty officer had given him a juicy tidbit that shocked RJ. "Word is the chief's got himself a little hottie on the side, but he's got her in hiding . . . witnessed that hit a while back."

Replaying the conversation over in his head, RJ had to wonder if the chief's girlfriend and Raina Wade were one and the same. The irony of the situation was more than plausible, he thought, glancing up when spied Nick Laprelli.

RJ bristled watching the detective saunter further into the small room. Standing, RJ stood and briefly shook hands with Nick. He sensed the detective didn't like him. But then why would he; after all, he'd ended the life of his former partner. "Hello, Detective, I guess you know I'm waiting to interview Mr. Anderson. He's been arrested on a DWI/DUI charge."

"Well, if you get him off, then you're worth every penny Anderson will have to fork over to you. But he failed the field sobriety test. In fact, he reeked of booze when I pulled his naked ass up off that prostitute," Nick said, biting his lip. He didn't care for RJ Mortison.

RJ resumed his seat. "Say, I heard there was another hit that occurred a few weeks back." RJ needed to get as much information as possible before he moved further in his plan to eliminate Raina Wade. He couldn't take a chance on doing anything if she was in the company of Chief Coleman or his associates. Now, seeing a shadow crossing the detective's face confirmed to RJ that Nick Laprelli was probably one of those associates. "I know you're unable to tell me anything, but is there any truth to a possible witness?"

"Sorry, RJ, but you know we can't disclose anything, especially to high-priced lawyers such as yourself," Nick said, grinning at the fake wounded expression he got from RJ.

"I was just thinking some misguided gentleman may need my legal expertise, that's all."

"Misguided? Are you kidding me, RJ? A professional killer is not misguided. He's a wacko nutcase, walking into a waiting grave." Nick walked to the doorway to leave.

"Yes, I guess you're right, Detective," RJ said, pretending to be focused on writing on his legal pad, but Nick's next words caused his right hand to shake.

"Besides, who is to say our killer isn't parading around under another profession, like a doctor or high-priced lawyer—you just never know about people, right?"

RJ noticed that when the detective left the room, he was grinning.

No sooner had Nick returned to his desk to attack a mountain of new reports then he was summoned into Lt. Brown's office. To his surprise, it was not a barking order. But the minute Nick entered Lt. Brown's office, he was immediately on guard. Lt. Brown, Dennis and Chief Coleman were in attendance, and none of them looked happy.

Lt. Brown wasted no time in getting down to why he had summoned Nick into his office. "Have a seat and start talking, Detective." Accusing blue eyes bored into steel gray ones again.

Nick was at a loss. He noticed Chief Coleman looked serious "Sir?"

Lyle came right to the point. "Why don't you tell us all about your trip to Las Vegas?"

"Yes, we're all waiting to hear about a second detour you took, Detective. You care to explain how that happened?" Max said.

After clearing his throat, Nick explained the particulars of having Raina drive and getting lost, then the flight from Denver to Seattle, via Las Vegas. "So with Seattle rained out, we had no choice but to stay in Vegas until the weather cleared. That's documented in my report."

Lyle lifted a file from his desk, extending it to Nick. "You've got a couple of certificates in there, the pretty ones with impressive seals and everything. So, let me be the first to say two things to you, Detective Laprelli. First, congratulations, and second, you're suspended effective immediately, until your entire trip out west is investigated and your time is accounted for. I should also tell you there will be an Internal Affairs investigation . . . that comes from a higher office than mine. So I suggest you start tracking backwards to account for the time you were on the clock, and I mean down to the last minute until you returned to this station."

All Nick heard was *you're suspended.* He expected to be angry, but he wasn't. He simply nodded his head, thinking, *Okay, suspension. I can handle that. I can finish the other kitchen wall now, or maybe start on the upstairs . . .*

"What were you thinking, Nick?" Lyle asked sharply.

"Sir, I assure you, Ms. Wade was in no danger."

"Well, I happen to know those workshops were closed to non-law enforcement personnel. Was she safely tucked away while you attended all those workshops?" Lyle pointed to the folder.

"She, ah . . ." Nick glanced at Coleman. "She was playing the tables, gambling, sir."

"I know what playing the tables means," Lyle said tightly. "Are you're telling me our witness was out in the public, possibly exposed to a killer. Is that a fair statement, Laprelli?"

Nick sat back slightly and pictured Raina with all those winning chips at the gaming table. She was laughing and free of worry or fear. "Yes, that's a fair statement, but I kept her safe and out of public view as much as possible," Nick said, seeing the narrowing gaze of Lt. Brown. "It being her first time in Vegas . . . she, um insisted . . ." Nick spread his hands. "Other than cuffing her to the table in her room, what was I supposed to do?"

Lyle stood up quickly, pushing his chair back against the wall with a thud. "You were supposed to do your damn job, smartass! You were supposed to guard and protect our witness. Your charge, and now the reason for your suspension! Now, before I kick your butt from my office and out of this station, do you have anything else to tell me—tell us—about your wayward trip out west?" Lyle thrust his long arms toward the window.

Nick thought, yes, he had compromised her safety. He should have been more committed to guarding her, and not slept with her.

"Detective, did something else happen?" Max Coleman finally spoke from the side.

Nick looked to Dennis for help, but only received raised eyebrows in return. "Yes sir. Something else happened." Nick bit his lips and waited until Lt. Brown resumed his seat. Then he watched Max Coleman move to stand closer to Lt. Brown's desk.

"When Ms. Wade and I stopped in Chicago, it was my sister's birthday. There was a celebration at a local nightclub. It was live karaoke night." Nick dared a glance at his superiors.

Lt. Brown shrugged. "Okay, live karaoke. Not a big deal. Or was it, Detective?" Even to his own eyes, it was disconcerting to see his best detective under investigation by I.A.

"Yes, sir. It ended up being a big deal when, Raina, ah, Ms. Wade . . . well, she had a panic attack at my sister's house. It was a total meltdown, sir."

"What are you talking about, Nick?" Max was on full alert. Every muscle in his body tensed, vividly recalling Raina looking haunted and thin when he saw her in Seattle.

Gone was the friendliness Nick felt from Max, when he and his family visited Nick's farm. "Sir, I'm sorry I didn't mention this before." Nick was at a loss how to tell this man that his girlfriend had had such an emotional crisis. "Chief, maybe we can talk in private."

"I'm still waiting for you to explain 'total meltdown,' Detective." Max sensed the Raina he saw a few weeks ago could very well have been the result of a total meltdown.

Without further hesitation, Nick told them what occurred at Jenny's house. "Ms. Wade later told us she had encountered someone at the club, and the man's cologne was similar to Pierce's." Hearing it back in his own ears, Nick's remorse went deep. Again, he regretted having left her alone to dance. If he hadn't, she would never have come apart like she did. But he knew from that night at the club, that he needed distance from Raina, and what he was feeling for her.

Nick couldn't compromise the investigation any further. He couldn't say that he thought Raina Wade was the most beautiful and fascinating woman he had ever known. "We did everything to make her feel comfortable and feel safe, and that's when she remembered the tattoo. I called Lt. Brown immediately upon hearing that," Nick said.

Lyle had been flipping pages on a notepad, then looked up sharply. "Wait a minute—that was around the eighteenth of June when you called me." Lyle handed the notepad to Max before dropping down into his seat, affixing unbelieving eyes on Nick. "Karaoke night," he murmured. "That was the night of the hit at that night-club in Chicago."

"Jesus Christ! I–I don't fucking believe this!" Max thundered, looking up sharply from the notepad. "Are you aware that the guy who bumped into her in that club was almost certainly Pierce himself?" he shouted, his face contorting.

Max grabbed Nick up by the collar and shoved him up against the door frame, knocking over two chairs in the process. He seemed totally unconcerned that both Dennis and Lyle were trying to restrain him from choking Nick to death. "You idiot, do you realize that you all but delivered Raina into the hands of that man? I ought to kill you myself. Her father and I trusted you to get her to Seattle, and all you cared about was that damned conference and not about her safety." Max was breathing fire as he stared in Nick's face.

"I'm sorry. I . . ." Nick said, out of breath as he held Max away from him.

Max flung his hands from Nick's shirt collar as he pushed back from him. "Shut the hell up!" Max thundered, stomping over to the window before turning back to face Nick. "I went on Lyle's word that you were the man for the job. All this time, you never said how you'd put my niece's life in jeopardy. That's not only unforgivable, Detective, but I'm personally charging you with insubordination and recklessly jeopardizing this case and the witness, you understand me?"

Niece. Nick heard nothing else past the word *niece.* He was flabbergasted, gazing into the now-familiar looking brown eyes. *Niece.* "Ms. Wade is your ni–niece?"

"That's exactly what I said. Michael Wade is my step-brother, and we were extending professional courtesy in getting Raina to Seattle. The idea was to keep that quiet to prevent personnel from thinking Raina was getting special treatment, which, in fact, she was."

"I didn't know she was your niece, sir," Nick said blankly. It appeared that even Dennis was surprised by that information.

"Does it matter to you anyway?" Max said through pinched lips.

Intense relief is what Nick felt. Raina wasn't Coleman's girlfriend, like he'd thought all this time. But he also felt like crap for thinking unkindly about her for being in that kind of relationship in the first place. He should have known better. "I guess it shouldn't." But it did matter to him. It mattered a lot. When Lyle told him to begin his report, Nick left the office. But walking to his desk he was still processing that Raina was Max's niece. He began recalling the two times he'd seen them together. True, he'd never actually seen them act like lovers, and their conversations, now in retrospect, didn't seem like lovers talking, at all . . . still, he wondered why Raina never told him. But then he realized why she hadn't . . . because she had been instructed not to disclose their true relationship, especially to him. *If I'd only known.* Then what? He was still in no position to do anything. Nick had spent countless hours beating himself up for having slept with her, and always came away feeling guilty for crossing the line, and taking another man's woman to bed.

Nick reflected back on the time he spent with Raina. He wished he had known she was Coleman's niece, and not his lover.

Raina couldn't take it any longer. The condemning look on her father's face each time he looked at her was more than she could bear. She couldn't understand what upset him more—that fact that she wasn't his precious baby girl anymore, or that his grown-up daughter had slept with the big bad, detective—that is, a white detective.

Whichever it was, his chilly reception and his non-communicative grunts whenever she tried to talk to him were heartrending, making her more depressed than ever.

The straw that broke the camel's back had happened three days earlier, when she joined Ellie for lunch at the tennis club where she and Michael were members. Her father had gone out of town on business for a week. He wasn't due to return for two more days. She and Ellie were going to have lunch at the tennis club, after she played a match. Raina headed up to the dining area after changing clothes. There she found Ellie and her father. Hoping he was in a better mood, Raina bounded to their table, smiling, having caught them sharing a brief kiss, but her smile all but disappeared when Michael looked up, seeing her. He didn't look happy.

"Welcome back, Dad," Raina said, running her hand across his shoulders and sliding into her chair, adjacent to his.

"What are you doing here, Raina?" Michael was indeed surprised to see Raina. Since their argument a few weeks ago, he'd tried to avoid her. Not because he didn't love his daughter, but because he felt such betrayal from both her and Nick. While he was away, his thoughts constantly remained on his daughter. Unfortunately, the betrayal he felt went deep.

"Michael?" Ellie whispered, surprised at how he was speaking to Raina.

"I asked what you're doing here, Raina?" he said tightly.

"Well, Dad, I'm having the king crab salad. That's what I'm doing here," she snapped, her tone matching his.

"I suggest you watch that tone with me, young lady," Michael said.

Noticing other members picking up on the tension coming from their table, Ellie suggested Michael lower his voice, then explained she had invited Raina to lunch. Ellie turned a sympathetic smile to Raina. "Raina, you're having the crab salad? I think I'll have that, also." She rested a hand on Michael's forearm. "Michael, are you having your usual, the steak tips?"

"No, I'm not staying," he said, meeting Raina's gaze dead-on. Lifting his napkin from his lap, Michael was prepared to leave, but Raina stopped him.

"No, Dad, you stay. You know something, I'm sorry you don't even want to be in the same room, let alone share a meal, with me." Raina's throat burned with constriction. "I'm sorry that you hate me so much, but I'm not going to hate myself because of what I did, or who I did it with." With more conviction in her voice, Raina pushed her chair back. "Since you have a problem with me, you need to either deal with it like an adult, or you need to release me from the imprisonment in your home. That way you don't have to run away each time you see me. I'm sick of this!" Raina waved her hand at his scowling face.

Michael captured her waving hand, which Raina snatched away and stood up. "Don't you talk to me like that again, Suraina, or I'll . . ." His words died out because his heart was breaking, watching tears slide down her cheeks.

"You'll do what, Dad? You'll lock me in my room? Forget it, you're already done that."

Ellie was at her side, encouraging her to sit down, but sent Michael a pleading look.

"Ellie, if Raina wants to leave, then let her. Raina's told me she's grown. She has adult feelings and she is capable of making her own decisions," he said, grabbing up his water goblet.

Raina stormed from the dining room, retrieved her bag from the concierge and had the driver, Jefferson, take her back to her father's house.

By eight-thirty that evening, having slipped away from the house, Raina was on a bus headed to Los Angeles. She'd purchased a one-way ticket, which she had planned on changing when the bus stopped in Sacramento. There, she would purchase another ticket . . . to Las Vegas.

Raina had a plan. Okay, so a psycho killer was after her. Well, so far he hadn't found her. But, if things worked out the way she hoped, she would soon have a sense of peace in her life—in spite of the fact that her heart was breaking into pieces again. First, she had to say goodbye to Nick, and then to her father earlier at the club.

In the hours since leaving the tennis clubhouse dining room in total embarrassment, Raina called her friend, Andrea, back in Pittsburgh to wire her some money. As previously arranged, Mimi deposited Raina's paycheck into an account only Andrea had access to.

Raina called Andrea on the non-traceable, prepaid cell phone she purchased in the bus terminal. She knew Andrea would be more than happy to assist in what she believed was a mystery in the making. But after Raina explained the favor she needed, she sensed her friend wavering. Only after Raina fully explained what she wanted Andrea to do did she get her friend's enthusiastic agreement.

Sitting in the darkened interior of the partially full Greyhound bus, Raina hoped Andrea, who was such a mystery buff, came through for her . . . she had to, Raina's plan depended on it.

But what about her own mystery, she wondered, recalling how she'd had Jefferson drop her off at the house and telling him she wouldn't be going back out. Then she went to work. Raina created a digital photo ID on her computer so she could travel under an assumed name. She knew she would need an ID to get the money Andrea was wiring to her at the Greyhound terminal. Knowing the wire transfer would take a couple of hours to process, Raina devised a plan to get away from the house without being spotted by the guard or housekeeper.

Raina spent two hours applying a jet black hair rinse to her brown hair and then donned a black wig. Next, with the use of eyeliner pencils and makeup, Raina created a very Asian look. She didn't even recognize herself in the mirror when she had finished.

Armed with Michael's password to the monitoring system, Raina was able to reset the alarm and lights at the back of the house and the grounds. The lights had been set to go off at 6:50 that night, then come back on at seven o'clock sharp.

When Ellie called the house to check on her, she told Raina that Michael had to go into his office and wouldn't be home until after seven that night.

Perfect. By the time her father got home, Raina would be long gone. Ellie also told her that Michael was beside himself for his behavior. Hearing that, Raina opened up and told Ellie what she and Michael had argued about. To Raina's surprise, Ellie had laughed. "Oh, is that all? Well, who in the world cares? My second husband was as white as baking flour, and I didn't care what anybody thought about it because I was happy. Well, that is, up until he went to prison for embezzlement of his company's funds, but that's another story I'll have to tell you about later."

She would miss Ellie a lot and knew she was going to be worried about her, but it couldn't be helped, Raina thought, staring blankly out at the darkened horizon whizzing by. The bus driver had announced a while ago that they were already in Oregon.

Raina had taken every precaution regarding her safety. If Pierce was looking for her, then she was not going to make it easy for him to find her. Because she planned on hiding in plain sight . . . right under his elegant, pointed nose. And that was something she knew she could do, because not only did she know what he looked like, but Raina also remembered something else about the hit man. As his name implied, Pierce had an intense and most painful effect on those unfortunate people he crossed paths with.

Raina was almost positive she knew who he really was, but would have to rely on Andrea to come through for her and help her get the evidence she needed.

To say that Andrea was nervous was an understatement. For someone who had read more mystery books than she could count, she simply couldn't explain what made her so anxious standing there. It was just a police station.

At first, Andrea couldn't pry any information out of the secretive Raina, but then her friend finally broke down and told Andrea that she and her father argued about the trip and it involved the detective. *I wonder what could have happened between them? Certainly not what just ran through my mind.* Andrea knew Raina to be way too uptight and prudish to do something like sleep with a white dude . . . no way, not conservative Raina. But standing there and watching the detective pound on his keyboard, Andrea had to wonder just what did happen. Or maybe it was just what Raina said, she argued with her father.

Nick had just completed his report when he caught movement and glanced up to see a pretty young woman fidgeting just outside the unit. "Miss, can I help you?" Nick said, getting up and walking over to the railing that separated the detective's unit from the waiting area.

Oh, my God . . . what a cutie pie! Okay, this answers a lot of questions . . . some I hadn't even thought of yet, Andrea thought, sending an impish grin up at the detective, then reminding herself to get to why she'd come there in the first place. *The favor.* Andrea needed only to find a binder containing current/active investigations. The next part involved a little acting on her part. "Oh, um, yes. I hope you can help me. Well, actually, it's about my friend . . . you see, she's in deep, deep trouble . . . with, um, her boyfriend."

Nick decided to begin the paperwork on the case. He would write up the initial report and then turn it over to one of the other detectives. "Okay, well, come on back to my desk and I'll get some preliminary information from you so we can help your friend."

"Oh, okay, sure," Andrea said, following him to his desk. She was so busy checking out his rear that she collided into his back when he stopped and indicated for her to take the seat beside his desk.

Andrea spent five minutes giving a story of a fictitious girlfriend with a verbally abusive boyfriend. She answered all of the detective's questions, except providing a name and address. She sensed his genuine concern and her convoluted story began to waver. Tilting her head sideways, her eyes inched past him and onto the binder she was looking for. It was right on his desk. *I only need to snatch the one-page report on that Pierce guy . . . but how?* Andrea's mind was jumping to come up with a way to get the detective away from his desk.

Forcing her eyes to mist over, she let her shoulders slump forward.

"Miss, can I get you something? Water?" Nick asked, noticing the woman's agitation.

"Actually, hot tea would be better. I-I see there's a vending machine over there." Andrea pointed a shaking finger at the reception area and then quickly dug into her purse, pulling out several coins and dropping them into Nick's hand.

"All right, hot tea it is. I'll be right back." Nick walked to the vending machine, fairly certain that the young lady was talking about herself . . . she was the victim. There was no girlfriend . . . he'd seen it all before. He decided to get her a cup of hot tea from the clerk's office instead of from the vending machine. Once she relaxed, she would talk.

There were only two other detectives working in the unit and both were engaged in telephone conversations. With her heart thumping wildly, Andrea stretched her arm over across Nick's desk and flipped open the binder. Her search was slowed because the individual reports were encased in plastic sleeves, and she was keeping constant check on all three detectives. Angling sideways, she continued flipping until she spotted the computerized drawing of the killer known as Pierce. It was there, just as Raina had described, by the date of the crime. It was then that Andrea's fright became real. The drawing put into perspective just how much trouble her real girlfriend was in. "Oh, Raina," she whispered, forcing her eyes away from the face of the handsome killer to quickly skim over the report, detailing several execution-style murders he was reportedly connected to. When she tried to snatch the plastic sleeve from the binder, it wouldn't give. *No.* To make matters worse, Andrea glanced over again to see the detective pouring hot water into a cup. Not looking back, she gave the plastic sleeve another tug, harder this time, and it came out freely. She quickly stuffed it into her purse. All the while her eyes darted back and forth among the three detectives. Within seconds Andrea had slipped back out of the unit, walking quickly to the garage, as Raina had instructed her. The second she cleared the police station and rounded the first corner, she plastered her perspiring back against the nearest wall, fearing she would collapse if she didn't. And it didn't help her already jumpy nerves when two police cars whizzed by with sirens blaring. Sure they were coming for her, Andrea took off running over to the next street, where she had parked her car.

"Aw, damn," Nick mumbled, returning to his desk and finding the woman gone. Absently sipping the hot tea, he hoped she would return. His eyes dropped to the binder of active reports, but he paid no attention to the two pages sticking out from the bottom. Flipping the binder open to the report connecting Pierce to Scott Morgan's murder, Nick read it again, but he knew it by heart. His anger renewed, as did the smiling face of Raina Wade in his memory.

Nick was too distracted by his memories of Raina to connect the young woman he'd just seen to the haphazard reports. Knowing his suspension would begin when he submitted his report, he lifted the document to the printer and carried it into Lt. Brown's office. Nick wondered why he was so ready to condemn Raina for being involved with a married man. In retrospect, he thought she spoke more passionately about her work with the mentoring program and the kids than she did about Max Coleman.

CHAPTER 14

"Damn . . . Raina's missing!"

Nick's running thoughts came to a screeching halt the second he entered Lt. Brown's office and heard Max Coleman's expletive fill the room. Holding the cell phone tightly, Max dropped in a chair. "That was Michael. Raina's missing," he said in a heavy voice.

Nick heard the words again and, for several seconds, was unable to move. But he was full of questions. "Missing? How could that happen? Michael has security. What happened?"

Furious, Max looked up. "I don't owe you an explanation concerning Raina, do I?"

Desperate and scared, and trying hard not to show it, Nick's fear hit another level. "Sir, I—I'm concerned about her welfare, and her . . . Ms. Wade's safety."

"Well, that does us a hell of a lot good now, doesn't it, Laprelli? On your watch, you put her life in jeopardy."

Lyle was on his office phone trying to get as much information on Raina's disappearance as he could. So far, there was none.

Nick hung on every word Lt. Brown said to the caller. He sensed the situation was bleak. As soon as he hung up the phone, Nick pounced on him with questions. "When was she last seen? Where was she last seen, and more importantly, was Pierce spotted anywhere in or around Michael's property?" As he spoke, Nick was praying hard that Pierce hadn't located Raina. He wanted answers, but all he was getting was impatient looks from his superiors.

Dennis thought this was the worst possible thing that could have happened. He, too, silently prayed that Pierce hadn't found Raina. He felt Nick's frustration. One thing for sure, he could see that Nick was about to lose it, and Chief Coleman, oblivious to Nick's pain, looked ready to choke him if he asked one more question. "Nick, I'll take that report and you can leave. Your suspension is in effect." Dennis held out his hand for Nick's ID badge and service weapon.

"I would like to assist in the investigation to find Ms. Wade. I don't need a badge. I can do that on my own time," Nick said, tensing when Max Coleman got up and began pacing.

With his worry about his niece reaching its limit, Max took it out on Nick. "Detective, I hold you person-ally responsible for Raina being out there. You had better pray that she's just being stubborn and angry after arguing with her father. But I promise you this, if it's any-thing more than that, you will never carry a police shield again. I just pray that Pierce didn't find her."

Lyle hung up the phone. "Max, what did Michael say?"

"That he and Raina had a bad argument today, and when he got home . . ." Max paused.

What? Nick mouthed, silently.

"The security system had been turned off, disabled," Max said.

"The back area, th–that area overlooks the cliffs, doesn't it?" Nick asked weakly.

Max closed his eyes briefly, reining in his fear. "There's no evidence to suggest she, um . . . went that way," Max mumbled, his blood pressure rising with his fright.

Nick couldn't take it anymore. Easing from the room, he all but ran down to the interior parking garage. There, leaning against the steel column, he forced the painful tears not to come. His dream that first night in Las Vegas replayed swiftly in his head. Pierce found her. He must have traced her to Seattle after all. Max Coleman was right to blame him, he thought. It was his fault if Pierce found Raina.

Only then, did his guilt give way to hot, angry tears.

Raina jolted awake when the bus rocked to a stop and the doors opened with a loud hiss. Lifting her bag from under her body, she pulled out a bottle of water and took several sips as she squinted out the window.

Immediately her mind was transported to her road trip with Nick. She only had to close her eyes to remember his tender kisses or the sheer masculinity of his passionate sighs in her ears.

Forcing the vision away, Raina dug into her backpack for her compact mirror and flipped it open . . . only to gawk at her reflection. While sleeping in her disguise as a biracial Asian woman, her face had been replaced by that of a raccoon! Her makeup had smeared to black circles around her eyes, made worse now by a sprinkle of fresh tears on her eyelashes. Thankfully, no one seemed to notice, or maybe they were just too polite to mention the state of her face. Pulling out her makeup bag, she quickly went to work, reapplying her makeup while the passengers were getting off the bus.

Within two hours, and with the use of her new ID, Raina was on a commuter flight, headed to Las Vegas. She had no idea how long she would stay there. It was just a familiar starting point as she moved further east. Memories assailed her in abundance, and she wished Nick was there with her. Since that couldn't happen, Raina decided she would do the next best thing when she cleared through the airport in Las Vegas and hailed a taxi.

Just one hour later, under the brilliance of a scorching August afternoon, Raina looked up at the clear blue sky after removing her wide-brimmed hat. Heaven seemed close enough to touch. Tucking her backpack closer to her body and testing the seat restraint, she rested her head against the back of the seat of the roller coaster as it chugged slowly up the tracks.

She couldn't help but remember sitting in that same seat just a few short months ago. Then, for several heart-stopping minutes, she did something she hadn't done in months—she laughed out loud and screamed joyously along with the other thrill-seeking riders.

All too soon the roller coaster ride ended and Raina found herself walking along the Las Vegas Strip, eating a candied apple, but even that didn't taste the same to her.

With exhaustion seeping into her bones, Raina was becoming a walking zombie. She boarded a trolley to an area described as old Las Vegas and checked into a non-descript, definitely not elegant hotel. Once inside her room, Raina dropped into a chair and looked around.

There was no Strip to look down upon, because her room faced a pool that needed cleaning. The room was functional, from the varnished headboard, dresser and table, to the scratchy but clean guest towels.

After showering and removing her makeup and wig, Raina glanced out the window. "Okay, so it's not Caesar's, and Nick isn't in the next room, ready to protect me . . . but I'm still alive." The way Raina saw it, if Pierce was truly looking for her, he would have found her by now. Basically, she didn't think Pierce had any idea where she was. But, fortunately for Raina, she knew exactly where she would start looking for him. *Pittsburgh*.

After testing the chair she had pushed under the door knob, Raina dropped to the bed, exhausted, and promptly fell asleep.

CHAPTER 15

Nick had tossed and turned each night since Raina disappeared. His one thought, his only thought was of her. Where could she be? He felt so utterly helpless and had no one to call, no one to give him information on the investigation into her disappearance, and that, too, was his fault.

A departmental e-mail had been issued advising of his suspension and depriving him of police powers until further notice. The e-mail warned that any personnel caught sharing information concerning any cases with him would also face suspension or termination.

Nick sat at the kitchen island waiting for a pot of coffee to finish brewing. His mouth was drawn downward. Suspension was a bitch. He only had his thoughts and his dog to console him, but even Reed was keeping a safe distance from his sullen master.

But Nick was more than sullen. He was scared. He knew firsthand what Pierce was capable of, and with each passing day, Raina's trail was getting colder. Initially, he figured since he was on suspension, he could do whatever the hell he wanted to do. That's when he went out to look for her. On a hunch, he guessed if she was okay, she may make her way back to Pittsburgh. But quietly scouring the downtown streets undercover and showing her picture around, all he got was negative head nods, shrugged shoulders of indifference, and offers to buy drugs. He'd even staked out the back lot of her condo building for two nights, but for nothing. He'd also checked out new police reports that had been filed and their status, hoping for tidbits of information. That is, until his police access code had been terminated on the third day of suspension. He was now truly cut off from any inside information. But Dennis did promise to let him know if anything developed regarding Pierce, and information regarding the killer would, by definition, concern Raina. Where could she be?

A tap at the French doors drew his attention away from the coffeepot. Nick glanced up to see Debra Coleman at his door. "Mrs. Coleman?" he said, opening the screen door.

"Please call me Debra," she said, noticing his worried expression—identical to Max's.

"Okay. Please come in, Debra." Nick stepped aside for her to enter. "I just finished a pot of coffee, can I get you a cup?" Nick asked, trying to hide his surprise at her visit.

"Yes, thank you," Debra said, walking into the large kitchen. "I guess you're wondering why I'm here, right?"

"Well, yeah. I mean, you're more than welcome. But, um, yeah, I am wondering." Nick watched as a smile split her beautiful cocoa face, lighting up her eyes.

"Relax, Nick. I like you, but not like that. Besides, I'm here to give you information on the woman who I think you do like—like that," she emphasized.

Nick almost choked on the hot coffee caught up in his windpipe. "Excuse me?"

"My step-niece, Raina," Debra said confidently.

Nick rounded the island. "What is it? Is she all right?" he asked, dread filling him.

"No one's heard from her. But I heard Max and Lyle talking last night at the house and found out that Pierce did another hit, down in Washington D.C. The poor man didn't die right away. He had an emergency panic bracelet on because of some medical issue. Anyway, as soon as the cleaning crew arrived to clean his office, they called the paramedics. He was still alive. It's hush-hush, but the man gave the police a description that seemed to match that killer, Pierce."

"That doesn't mean anything," Nick murmured quietly, wondering how it was that Debra knew he had feelings for Raina—something he was only just coming to terms with.

Debra covered his hand with hers. "Nick, that murder was five days ago, in D.C. There is no way that Pierce could have gotten to Raina then. Five days ago, she was in Seattle arguing with her father, remember?" She watched when it dawned on him what she had said.

"You're right. Oh, God." Nick paced again, then came back to her. "Then where is she and why did she leave Michael's house?"

"Look, I feel terrible for eavesdropping, but I heard that Raina and Michael had a really bad argument a few weeks ago. Michael had been brewing and stewing about it ever since. He told Max that his anger got the best of him following that argument, and he all but ignored Raina and didn't talk to her." Debra shook her head sadly. "Poor Raina, she didn't even have her father to turn to, and now she's probably out there all alone and terrified." Debra stepped down from the stool and walked into Nick's office, encouraging him to follow her. Inside the office, she pointed to the painting and then turned back to him. "When I first saw that painting, you were not in it, Nick. It was still wet because Raina had just finished painting it the day Max and I arrived in Seattle. She was very despondent, Nick. I'm a therapist and I assessed her as clinically depressed. Now, when I was here last, you told me a friend painted it . . . is Raina that friend, Nick?"

"Yes," Nick said, crossing his arms across his aching chest.

"You love her, don't you?"

"Yes," he said quietly, finally admitting aloud his feelings for Raina.

Debra patted his arm. "Oh, Nick, I'm so glad. You two will be magic together, and I couldn't think of a nicer guy for her."

Staring at the picture and recollecting the day he and Raina fished at the creek, Nick let out a half sob, half laugh. "We were magic. It was magical just getting to know her. She's smart and beautiful and honest, and I found myself either wanting to strangle her or just hold her in my arms." Lifting darkened eyes to Debra's grinning face, he added, "Definitely strangling her in the beginning, though. But we're back to square one—where is she?"

Debra nodded. "I know you think Max is a tough guy and you'd be right, but when it comes to family, he hurts badly. Nick, he is hurting just as deeply as you are right now."

"I know, Debra, and I appreciate you coming out here and telling me what you did. I've been so desperate to get information, but nobody can disclose anything to me."

"I know, and if I hear anything else, I'll call you." She patted his arm caringly. "I wanted you to hear this good news firsthand. I've got to run." With Nick trailing behind her, Debra breezed back through the kitchen and out the screened door.

Nick's heart lifted measurably watching Debra pick up a peach from the basket on the deck, then wave back at him. Hope. That's what Nick felt now, but he was still worried about Raina. He knew Pierce's history. The sadistic killer didn't leave witnesses. None.

RJ sat in his office at his computer. He was once again creating a collage of his latest kill. He was also angry. After all of his research, and rechecking every detail before the hit was carried out, there had been a glitch to what should have gone smoothly.

His victim, a D.C. attorney, was supposed to be working in his office, alone, at eight that night. But RJ found him having a meeting with a client, so he had to wait. And that presented him with another problem—

he wasn't in disguise. In his haste to get the deed over with so he could fly back out to Seattle, he'd decided to forgo wearing a disguise. Critical mistake. The same mistake he had made the night of the hit in that Italian restaurant.

RJ swiveled around to the large window behind his desk. He hated mistakes. Mistakes meant flaws to the plan. He couldn't afford to make mistakes, but in a matter of months, he'd made two grave ones. First, he hadn't checked out that Italian restaurant as he should have, as he normally would have. Had he done that, there would be no witness for him to frantically search for. His second mistake occurred in Washington, D.C. While listening to a police scanner as he drove back to Dulles Airport, RJ learned the attorney he went to execute did not die immediately. In his haste to flee the man's office, he hadn't checked for a pulse when he pulled out his digital camera and captured what he thought was a dead man with a profusely bleeding hand. RJ's focus was off. In his plan to right so many wrongs, so many injustices, he'd never left a witness to his deeds. Those witnesses he'd had to eliminate were merely unfortunate mishaps, and he never left anything hanging.

Raina Wade was still hanging, and that was unacceptable. Knowing he had another kill planned for next week, RJ was altering his course because finding and eliminating Max Coleman's girlfriend had now become his primary goal. He wondered why the PPD hadn't yet released the drawing it was reported they had. RJ now wondered if that was just a fabrication or if the drawing was not at all similar to his likeness. The fact that Raina Wade was still in hiding was most likely because she saw everything he'd done that night in the restaurant, and he wasn't in disguise . . . she had escaped into the alley. Yes, she was a serious threat.

Thinking about the woman's face, RJ absently rubbed at his forearm. His most recent tattoo was painful. His hand shook terribly when he did it, but he didn't care. It meant he could still feel something human . . . proof positive that he was still a human being, notwithstanding the fact that he took people's lives in his quest to right the wrongs, the injustices, that his own father allowed to happen, had even assisted in making happen. RJ shook his father's grim face from his head. RJ hated the fact that someone had been witness to his secret undertaking. Raina Wade had judged him, assessed him as probably being demented to do such unthinkable things. "I'm not crazy. I'm of a sound, rational mind." Even as RJ whispered the words to himself, he had to wonder why it didn't sicken him to see and smell death. At times, it pleased him immensely to plan a strategy that would kill some deserving criminal. But after all of his careful research and planning, someone had seen him and could possibly identify him as RJ Mortison. That someone had to be eliminated. Part of the problem was that RJ couldn't get close to Chief Coleman . . . few could because of his security personnel.

Hearing his secretary, Carol, tapping lightly before coming into his office, RJ swiveled back around to his computer and cleared the screen just as Carol limped over to stand on the other side of his desk. He flashed a handsome smile as he calculated a time frame to clear up this critical mistake—he had to find the only witness who continued to elude him, Raina Wade.

Raina was awakened by the sound of a motor revving up. Opening her eyes, she gazed up at the blue, summer sky, peeking through the gaping hole in the roof. Instinctively, she pulled the sleeping bag closer around her aching body. Had it really been four days since she'd slept in a bed at that dank motel off the expressway over by her condo? She frowned at the reminder of that place.

Standing, she stretched the kinks from her body and again heard the motor revving. Creeping to the back of the barn door, Raina pressed her face to it to look out through a crack in the door frame. All she saw was another beautiful summer day. Glancing to the left, she wondered if today would be the day Nick would come out onto the deck. So far, he hadn't.

Just thinking about him caused her empty stomach to knot painfully. Raina turned and walked over to a box in the corner and dropped her eyes down to her limited food supply. It consisted of three peaches, a small jar of peanut butter, a jar of grape jelly, one half pack of crackers, one candy bar and one bottle of water. It was all disappearing fast.

It had been four days since she'd sneaked into the old barn on Nick's property. She knew that soon she would have to risk going back inside the house for more food from his pantry. She would have done that yesterday, but Nick hadn't left the house at all.

Picking up a peach and rubbing it on her jeans, Raina reflected on how she'd come to return to Nick's house. Not the house, really, but to the abandoned barn where old farm equipment was housed. Stealing a peek at the grotesque-looking machinery, Raina shivered. She would swear that she'd seen this very equipment in a horror film.

When she arrived in Pittsburgh, her decision was as clear as that day was. Pierce had taken her freedom and sense of well-being for far too long. It was time to take it back.

After leaving Las Vegas, Raina headed east. She traveled back the same way she came, first by plane to Chicago, then by train, then bus, and finally by taxi. When she first arrived in Pittsburgh, she sneaked into the back entrance of her condo, but, to her dismay, a large police sticker was strategically placed over her front and back doors. If either door was opened, the tape would be broken, thereby alerting the police of an intruder. But Raina hadn't broken it. With the use of a plastic knife and her fingernails, she had meticulously managed to lift a large section of the tape, allowing her to enter her condo with her key. She also knew that because the area of town she lived in was not a crime-ridden area, patrol officers were not a frequent sight—and rarely would one bother to get out of his car to check on a door seal in a building where a concierge was on duty round the clock.

Once inside her condo, Raina collapsed against the door and sank to the floor. It took her several hours to acclimate herself to the once-familiar, once-safe, surroundings. In the few months since she had been forced away from her condo and what she thought was a normal life, Raina no longer felt safe or even connected to a place she'd made her home for five years. It was dark outside, but Raina didn't dare turn on any lights. Crossing to the mantle above the fireplace, she lit a single votive candle.

When the flickering light wavered and crept up the brick wall above the fireplace, Raina's eyes inched up to the painting of Mr. Antionelli. Try as she might, she couldn't contain the overwhelming sense of grief and loss that cloaked her. For several hours she sat on the couch, reflecting on everything that had happened to her since that terrible night. "Oh, Mr. Antionelli," she whispered. "That man will pay for what he did."

Raina stayed inside her condo for two days, not daring to venture out, even for food. She was forced to eat canned soup and dried cereal. That is, when she forced herself to eat. The few times she turned the TV on, it was for company, but she kept it muted. Her bathroom trips were quick and limited so as not to alert her neighbors. The night of her second day in her condo, the telephone rang. Raina stared at the answering machine, but no one left a message. She thought it was an odd thing to happen, because no one knew she was there. Then it happened again and again. Still, no messages were left, but she was positive someone was on the line . . . their breathing was labored. Who is it, she wondered?

Pierce . . . just thinking about encountering the man accelerated her heart rate. Raina didn't have time to think anything through—like where she would go or what she would do. She only sensed she needed to leave the condo, and fast. After quickly painting on her makeup as the part-Asian woman and donning her jet black wig, she stuffed a change of clothes into her backpack and left her condo the same way she entered—in the middle of the night. Heaving a bag of trash and her dirty clothes into the dumpster on the first level, she felt like a criminal when she took the same running path she'd taken that first night with Nick . . . luckily for the hour, there were few cars whizzing down the highway she had to cross. She'd even gone to the same motel where Nick hotwired and stole a car for them. She frowned at a Chevy parked on the lot and shrugged her shoulders—Raina didn't know the first thing about hotwiring a car. She'd popped a stick of gum in her mouth, assumed a haughty attitude and checked into that dingy motel for the night. Once there, she fought hard to ignore the lecherous looks she got from the foul-smelling desk clerk.

Remembering that day, Raina bit into the sweet peach and recalled how scared she was. She'd put on her best acting skills and met the foul-smelling clerk's eyes dead-on.

"You want a single for yourself, Missy?" he asked, sucking at his yellowed teeth.

Raina got past her revulsion quickly and replied in what she believed was a home-girl slang. "Ah, naw—I'm not alone so, um, we need a double. My old man's out back taking a leak, so I'll check us in," she'd said, grinning as she noisily cracked the gum between her teeth. "Sorry, but he couldn't hold his pee no longer, you know how that is, right?"

"Yeah, I do. Well, sign in, and that'll be forty each night y'all stayin'."

Raina turned her back, dug her hand into her pocket and pulled out eighty dollars. "All right, two nights, and I sure hope it's clean, you know what I mean?" She signed the register with the first thing that popped into her mind . . . Eloise and Jimmy Jones.

The clerk had licked his lips. "So y'all gonna be worried about how clean the room is or how comfortable the bed is?" he'd asked, smiling and showing more yellowed teeth.

"Whatever. My old man just wants a bed, you know what I'm sayin', and make it a room on the end, 'cause we like our privacy, you know what I'm talkin' 'bout."

"Yeah, I do, and tell your old man to do his peein' in the toilet in the room, and not on them bushes out back no more."

"Huh? Oh, yeah, sure I'll tell him, but, ah, he really had to go and all," she said, snatching the key from his thick fingers, and all but ran from the motel office to the room on the end. Once safely locked inside, Raina called her friend Andrea and told her when and where to meet her.

As previously planned, Andrea would be bringing Raina that report, and more money.

Raina had decided not to tell Andrea where she was staying. If she had been wrong, and Pierce was on her heels, she didn't want anyone else to get hurt.

She didn't even wait for Andrea to completely come off the exit ramp leading to the motel. Raina hid in the thick undergrowth near the exit ramp. When she spotted Andrea's compact, as it noisily yielded to a stop, she rapped on the passenger side window.

Andrea gasped at the sudden appearance of a face pressed against her passenger-side window. In shock, she didn't even drive off, as one would normally do.

"Raina, is that you, girl?"

"Yes it's me, Andrea. Open the door," Raina whispered, looking around.

All Andrea could do for several seconds after opening the door was gawk at Raina, her mouth hanging open. That is, until several cars honked their horns for her to clear the ramp. Andrea drove silently for several feet before pulling the compact into a parking lot of a small coffee shop, as Raina instructed. When she turned the car off, she turned to Raina and, before she could say anything, Andrea burst into tears and pulled Raina into her arms, crushing her. "Oh, Raina, girl, I'm so glad you made it back here. I've been a mess of nerves waiting to hear from you since you left Las Vegas. Why didn't you call me back? What happened? And, really . . . honey, what is with that face and that hair?" Andrea held onto Raina tightly and didn't even try to hide her shock over her friend's appearance.

Raina eased out of the tight grip of Andrea's arms. "I'm okay, and I couldn't call you because those three stupid prepaid cell phones I brought in Seattle stopped working in Chicago and I didn't want to chance calling you until I got here."

"Oh, Raina, girl, I'm just so glad that psycho killer didn't find you. But then, how would he recognize you?" Andrea ran her eyes over her friend. Her eyes widened as she took in Raina's thin appearance as well. "My God, are you really okay, Raina?" she asked slowly, tears springing to her eyes.

"Oh, Andrea . . ." It took Raina several minutes before she was able compose herself, because on some level she never believed she would ever make it back to Pittsburgh. "I'm so tired, but I have to be here, because you couldn't get that information I needed from the police station. I mean, what you sent to me wasn't exactly what I needed. But I need your help again, okay?" Raina spent the next hour explaining to Andrea exactly what she needed her to do.

Raina stayed at that shabby motel for three days. On the fourth day, she realized she was no longer safe there. The clerk called the room far too many times than she was comfortable with. Each time, he'd said, he was just checking to see if "everythin' was okey dokey with the lovebirds." And each time the telephone rang, Raina would stuff a candy bar or chips into her mouth before answering the phone in what she thought was a deep, masculine voice. "We cool, man, we gonna stay another night, so, ah, I'll send my lady up to the office to pay, cool?" Raina sensed the clerk was suspicious of *them*.

That afternoon, Raina packed up her stuff and flagged down a taxi near the sub shop on the corner. Next, she headed to the outskirts of Pittsburgh.

By the time the taxi dropped her off in the center of the town where Nick lived, Raina was exhausted. She hadn't realized how far Nick lived from town. That is, until she checked his address in the farmer's address book she'd picked up in the general store and had to hike the back trail to his farm. She had to cross over two neighboring farms, which consisted of several acres. And it was with supreme control that she didn't scream to high heaven when several quacking ducks crossed her path as she walked around a small pond. She did, however, hold her breath when she came upon two wandering cows looking as lost and as weary as she was. But two hours into her hike, Raina almost fainted when she saw the edge of Nick's property off a lone trail. By then, it was another kind of fear that settled in her. What did she expect of him? Surely, she didn't expect him to be sitting there waiting for her. Perhaps he had moved on with his life, forgetting all about her.

She'd sat on a tree stump on that trail, catching her breath, when the prepaid cell phone Andrea brought her buzzed in her pocket. Raina was glad for the extra minutes to rest on that tree stump. "Andrea, what happened? Did you find out anything?"

Raina had indeed sent Andrea on a mission—go to the police station, pretending to be worried about a friend. She was only to speak to Det. Laprelli, and look for a book on the back of Nick's desk, marked *Current/Active Investigations*. Raina remembered it was there that first night she'd spotted his cell phone charger. It would have information she needed to locate Pierce. As a teenager, while waiting for her father, Raina used to flip through those investigation binders, wondering if some of the pictures of wanted criminals were people she encountered daily . . . like the guy in the back of the cleaners, or the new janitor in her school, etc. That is, until her father forbade her from doing it again.

But that was four days ago, and she honestly didn't know how long she could hold out.

Hearing the revving motor again snapped Raina from her reverie. She stole another peek out the crack in the door, just in time to see Nick hop on his motorcycle. He was too far away for her to see him well, but closing her eyes, she shrugged off a wave of heartache.

Dejected, Raina sat down on a wooden box and ate another peach, which she smeared with peanut butter. She wondered, how had she gotten to such a place in her life? She was living like a homeless person. She vowed if she survived to never again look at homeless people as down-and-out unfortunate souls who were probably criminals, or addicted to alcohol or drugs, or had psychiatric issues. How many, she wondered, were like her, running for their lives and living in fear because they didn't have a choice.

Since it appeared that Nick had gone off to work, Raina left the barn. Circling from behind the barn, she came out on the back end of the clump of trees. She followed an unused path she'd discovered and walked down to the creek, a ritual she'd done every day since her arrival.

With the day already warming up, promising to be a scorching August morning, the creek was a beautiful sight to behold. Kicking off her tennis shoes, Raina walked along the edge of the creek, loving the feel of the cool water circling her ankles. Thinking how nice it would be to take a leisurely swim, Raina stripped down to her underwear and waded out into the water.

Time drifted by as she floated on her back, letting the water flow over her body, warmed even more by the sun peeking through the trees above her. She listened as the birds sang out their melodies to her. Suddenly, Raina's skin pricked . . . she was gripped by an overwhelming feeling of being watched. She silently dipped under the water and then, seconds later, brought only her head up and glanced around the clearing. A cautious smile lifted the corners of her lips at what she saw.

Standing on the large jagged rock, staring back at her, was Reed. He was holding one of her tennis shoes in his mouth. He jumped down from the rock, pacing as she stepped out of the water. But Raina watched him backing up. He was tense, unsure of her, and let out a low growl.

"Reed, it's me," she said pulling on her shirt and jeans and standing several feet away from him. After a few seconds, he dropped her tennis shoe and nuzzled her neck when she bent to retrieve it. When Raina sat down on the rock, the dog laid his head in her lap, and once he was comfortable with her again, Raina ran her hand down his back. "You missed me, huh?" Smiling, she thought if he could talk, he would have said yes. Instead, he just kept his head in her lap.

Raina didn't realize she'd been crying, until Reed lapped at the tears that had fallen to the back of her hand. "I'm so tired, Reed," she said, tenderly stroking his golden coat. For the next hour, she talked nonstop, telling Reed everything she'd been through, beginning with the argument with her father. "And that motel clerk gave me the creeps, you know." Settling her gaze on the dog again, she said, "Just ignore me, Reed, I'm losing my mind bit by bit. I'll be headed to the loony bin if I survive this craziness I'm caught up in."

Suddenly, Nick's piercing whistle shattered the stillness as he signaled for Reed. The dog began to trot home, but he stopped . . . he was waiting for Raina to follow him.

"I can't." She smiled when the dog turned at Nick's second whistle, and then looked back at her again.

"Go home, Reed." Still he waited for her to follow. Raina walked over and nudged him to go up the trail. "Go on," she whispered, taking a quick look though the trees.

When the dog finally left, she sighed. *Alone again.* Closing her eyes, Raina realized she'd never really been that alone in her life. Hating the feeling of being by herself, she found she had taken delight in talking to the dog. It was comforting, reminding Raina how much she missed talking about anything. Raina already missed the small comfort she had received from Reed when he lapped at her tears as he patiently listened to her babble.

Nick stood on the deck waiting for Reed to come running from the direction of the Loemans' farm. He was just about to whistle again when he spotted him coming through the trees. When the dog didn't move to come any further, Nick whistled again and watched Reed pace along the edge of the trees, but made no move to come further.

"Now what's he up to?" Sensing something was up, Nick walked off the deck, intent on meeting Reed halfway. When he stopped and patted his leg, calling out, "Come on," Reed let out a yelp and went back through the trees. Nick was on alert now.

Nick's first instinct was to reach for his service weapon, but he didn't have it, and his backup weapon was back at the house. Shaking off the feeling of apprehension, he headed toward the trees. Knowing the area, he guessed that someone unfamiliar to Reed was probably fishing at the creek, or perhaps kids were skinny-dipping again. In no immediate hurry, Nick continued along the trail. His thoughts drifted back to the day he and Raina had gone fishing. She'd surprised him by knowing how to fish. Since Scott died, Nick had found it hard to come out to the creek. Until Raina Wade walked into his life, Nick realized he had to search hard for reasons just to get out of bed each day. But she made him laugh again and enjoy sharing a meal, going on a traditional date, discovering pleasure in her arms . . . and now, he just wanted her to be safe . . . and maybe want to go on another date, or let him hold her in his arms again.

Almost clearing the path, he could see Reed standing at the edge of the clearing about one hundred feet ahead. Nick walked past Reed, at a loss to what had gotten his dog in such a state, and then he stopped dead in his tracks.

"Raina." Her name rushed from his lips in a shocked whisper.

Hearing her name, Raina opened her eyes. Her heart flipped and flopped and dropped back into its cavity seeing Nick just a few feet in front of her. She thought he looked better than any double cheeseburger or hot, steamy bath—both of which she desperately wanted.

Coming slowly to her feet, Raina rubbed her hands down the front of her dirt-smudged jeans. Nick stood just twenty feet from her, and everything around her disappeared . . . that is, except for him. When she opened her mouth to speak, no words came forth.

Nick moved in closer, slowly. Was she a vision? He had wished so desperately to see her that she appeared before him? He didn't recall moving his feet and legs, but he was slowly closing the distance between them. Taking in her every detail, his eyes moved from her face down to her shirt outlining her wet bra, to her well-worn tennis shoes. "Raina . . ." He caressed her cheek, as if he was testing the realness of the moment. But when she molded her cheek into his hand, as she had done many times that night in Las Vegas, all Nick could do was pull her into his arms, crushing her to him. Hope gave way to relief. Raina was alive, and she was here.

Safe. The word circled inside Raina's head as she held tightly onto Nick. Raina felt safe for the first time since she left his arms in Seattle.

No words were spoken as each held onto each other . . . each fearful of letting go. But Nick's hands moved up Raina's arms and down again. She was much thinner than she was a few months ago. He pulled back to look into her eyes. Memories flooded his heart and a feeling of contentment centered in him. "Oh, thank God, Raina," he whispered against her lips.

Raina was overjoyed. This was the only man who'd ever made her feel so complete and safe, just holding her in his arms. The combination of relief, exhaustion and Nick's fingers touching her face, made all her worries disappear. Searching his familiar gray eyes, she pleaded silently. *Don't let me go.* When she finally spoke, it was in a voice as desolate, and as tired as she felt. "Nick, please don't turn me away," she said, dropping her head to his chest.

Nick's hands cupped her cheeks, lifting her face to him. "I could never turn you away, never," was all he could say before his lips descended on hers at the exact moment Raina inched her lips up to meet his. Being careful of her frailty, Nick held her within the circle of his arms. He knew she had suffered because of him.

It was a kiss of lovers long ago parted. It was a kiss of sadness, regret and longing. It was a kiss that stole their breath away, and still, each was fearful of letting the other go.

Raina ran her hands up his back, pressing her cheek against his. "You have no idea how much I've missed you," she said.

Nick chuckled against her neck, before returning to her lips once again. "Oh, I have an idea," he said, staring at her oddly. "You know what? I just had an urge for something."

"Me . . . maybe?" Raina said, not wanting to put any label on what he meant.

"Definitely that, but I was thinking more of a peanut butter and jelly sandwich." Nick grinned as he kissed her again. "Are you the one who stole my last jar of peanut butter and jelly?" But the second the words were spoken, he was no longer grinning. Pulling back, Nick studied her, his mind racing. He'd last made a sandwich on Monday, and when he went searching for those items yesterday they were nowhere to be found—today was Friday. "How long have you been here?" he asked hesitantly. "Raina, please tell me you haven't been out here as long as I'm thinking." His hands dropped to her shoulders when she lowered her head. "Sweetheart . . . no! Have you been here since Monday?"

Raina couldn't bear the look on Nick's face. She imagined she looked just like the picture he'd formed in his mind of her . . . so much for his preconceived princess. Suddenly angry, she stepped back from him. "Do you really want to hear all that I've been through to end up here, bathing in your Andy Griffith creek for four days?" Snatching her hand back from his, she turned her back to him, unable to look at him any longer.

Nick ran a hand down his shocked face. Horrified, his voice was harsh. "Oh, Jesus! Why didn't you call me, or come to the house? I've been right here, Raina. I've been worried sick about you, praying that Pierce hadn't found you." Although the barn couldn't really be seen from the creek, Nick looked that way and then looked back at her. "I can't tell you how many times I've looked out this way, and never, never did I think you would be here. How could I be so stupid? Raina, look at me, please."

When she did turn back to face him, heartache was etched into her features. "I—I didn't know what to do, Nick. I wanted to come to you, but I was afraid to."

"You were never afraid of me before, or are you back to me being a stranger again?"

She had to tell him why she didn't come to him, and it was the most unselfish thing she thought she had ever done. "I didn't come to you because I didn't know if Pierce was following me." Raina shook her head sadly. "I—I just couldn't bear that, Nick. If it wasn't for that tattletale, Reed," she pointed to the dog standing nearby, watching them, "I don't think I would have come because of that very reason."

In an instant, Nick pulled her into his arms. "Forget Pierce, he's the furthest thing from my mind right now. Let's get you to the house. And, Raina . . ." He stopped, turning her to face him. "I want to know everything about the argument you and Michael had. Then I want to know everything that's happened since you left his house, okay?"

"Okay, Detective."

By early afternoon, Nick and Raina were still sitting in his kitchen talking.

As hard as it was not to bang his fist on the table with fury, Nick sat back, listening, but his emotions ran hot with guilt. He wished he'd never left her in Seattle. "I can't believe you went back to Vegas, Raina," he said finally.

Nick ran a hand over the heavy braid lying between her shoulder blades, recalling when he'd first seen her hair that way . . . the morning he'd first showed up at her condo. He was angry then, too, he reflected. "I've missed you, Raina. I don't think I've slept since you were reported missing." Nick stood up, suddenly. "Oh, shit! I–I need to be making some calls," he said, dropping her hand and grabbing the cordless phone up from the counter.

"No!" Raina jumped up and took the phone from him, setting it back down.

"No? What do you mean, no? We need to call your father . . . oh, yeah, and dear old Uncle Max to let him know that his niece is here."

Raina held up her hand. "That was his idea and Lt. Brown's."

"But you knew what I was thinking, and you could've told me, like in Las Vegas. Especially in Vegas, Raina," he said, making his meaning clear.

"I wanted to tell you, but when Max called me that night he reminded me to keep mum on our relationship."

"Okay, I can understand why they didn't want me to know. Why don't you want me to call your father or better yet, have you call him?" Nick watched a series of emotions cross her face.

Raina wasn't ready to tell Nick of her plan to get Pierce on her own. But she would have to rely on Nick to provide her with information she needed to find Pierce. "I'm just not ready yet. Please give me some time. For now, could I please take a hot bath?" Just the thought of sinking her body into a steamy tub of water gave her goose bumps, or perhaps it was her running her hand across his shoulders, bringing him closer to her.

Pushing the vision of her nude body stepping from a steamy bath from his head, Nick lifted her up in his arms and carried her upstairs to the second-floor bathroom.

Nick didn't stray far while Raina languished in the tub. He sat on the floor in the hallway across from the bathroom, replaying everything she'd told him following the argument with her father. It distressed him tremendously to know that Raina traveled alone and stayed in cheap motels, at times too afraid to fall asleep. But most of all, it saddened him deeply to know that she had slept for four nights in the old barn. When they walked to the barn to get her backpack, Nick recoiled to see how she was forced to live since arriving on Monday. She'd slept in a sleeping bag atop old crates she had stacked up on the stone floor. With its broken timber, gaping holes in the ceiling, spiders and rusted farm equipment, the place still freaked him out—just as it did when he was a teenager. To know that Raina stayed in that desolate and dark place for four days with little food while he slept in a warm bed, with a full belly, tore him apart inside.

Hearing Raina call his name softly, Nick got up, wiped his eyes and opened the bathroom door. She was still soaking in bubbles up to her chin. It made him smile. "Where did the bubbles come from? I don't keep any bubble bath in here, it's not manly."

"I packed essential items in my backpack before I ran from the condo," she said in a sleepy voice, watching him sit down on the bathroom floor beside the century-old bathtub.

"So when did bubble bath become an essential item?" He liked the scent. It reminded him of those sugary apples she bought in Las Vegas.

"When you miss something a lot, it becomes essential, Nick," she said, thinking of him.

He caressed her damp cheek. "I've missed you, Suraina Wade."

Sensing his seriousness, emotion settled in Raina's chest. "Can you do me a favor?"

"Anything you want, sweetheart, just ask me."

"Can you undo my braid and wash my hair?" She'd actually dreamed of him doing that.

That's not exactly what he thought she would ask, but then this was Raina Wade, full of surprises and totally capturing his heart Nick thought as he went about undoing her braid. "So let me guess, you have some fancy-smelling shampoo in here, too?" Nick asked, grinning when her hand broke through a layer of foamy bubbles and picked up a small bottle containing pink liquid from the soap holder. Bending his head, Nick kissed her wet shoulder, which was peeping up from the water. He thought her shampoo smelled as good as her bath water tasted on his lips.

CHAPTER 16

Raina stood in the guest bedroom combing out her hair. She was nervous to be alone with Nick again. She had longed for him since the day he left her in Seattle, yet there she was in his home with him, and she was full of uncertainty.

Nick was in the same mindframe—he, too, was unsure of their situation. His instinct was to go to her, gather her up in his arms and never let her go, but he didn't. He didn't want to push her, considering all she'd been through. Closing his eyes, he recalled what she told him about the argument with her father. Nick assured Raina that being intimate with her had nothing to do with him wanting to be with a black woman, as her father had implied. He told her he only saw her as beautiful. Then he told her that she was not the first black woman he had been with. To which Raina teasingly sang out that he had jungle fever, making both of them laugh.

Accepting his feelings for Raina had put a different spin on her predicament. He vowed never to let her go again. He loved her, and he wanted her to know it. In fact, he wanted to shout it out loud. It was with that determination to tell her how he felt that Nick rushed from his room.

He'd only taken three steps in the direction of the guest room when he looked up just as Raina stepped out into the hallway. Laughing self-consciously, he asked how she was feeling after her extremely hot bath, all the while shaking his hand. Each laughed when he'd yelped after sticking his hand down into her bath water. He thought it was scalding.

"It was wonderful," she said, rolling her eyes when he pretended to examine his hand.

"I don't know, Raina. I bet I've got third degree burns," he said, lifting his eyes to hers.

Raina's resolve melted under the intensity of his gray eyes. She ran into his arms at the exact moment he ran into hers. The kiss they shared was powerful, each shaken by it.

This is where she wanted to be, needed to be. She was no longer nervous. It felt so right to be there with Nick, and nothing else mattered, not Pierce, her father, or her plan. Nothing outside that farmhouse mattered at that moment. Easing back, breaking off the kiss, her eyes traced his face, followed by her hands. With sudden clarity, Raina realized his was the face she wanted to look upon for all of her days to come. It wasn't a white face . . . it was just the face attached to the man she'd fallen in love with. That realization was deep. And if he could never return the feeling, she still wanted to tell him. "Nick, do you think it's possible to fall in love after knowing a person for only one week?"

Nick's shoulders fell with relief. *How could she know what I was thinking?* "Raina, it is not only possible, it's happened to me."

"W–what do you mean?"

Nick folded her hands within his. "I mean, it's possible because it has happened to me . . . with you, Raina. When I returned home, I realized how much I missed you. I tried putting what happened between us out of my mind, because I knew I couldn't have you . . . remember, I thought you were my commander's hot and sexy babe, and that meant you were off-limits. At first I thought, crossing the line would hurt us both, but then I received something in the mail that told me differently."

"Oh, right, the painting."

"No, it wasn't the painting. Jenny sent me the taped recording of you singing at the club that night. And I've listened to it many times and I know in my heart that you sang it for me."

"I did sing it for you, Nick. It was that night that I realized not only that was I was attracted to you, but that I was going to miss you, and I don't mean the 24/7 police protection. I mean miss you as a person—as a man who I got to know, although briefly." Raina sniffed. "That song was from my heart, Nick because I knew that I was going to miss you. If I were to sing it now, it would be because I love you," she whispered.

Nick cradled her cheek with his hand. "I love you, too, Raina, with all my heart. It hit me like a ton of bricks when I came to terms with how I felt about you, but I couldn't have you."

Without further hesitation, the months of lonely separation faded away and Nick lifted Raina in his arms. Carrying her to his bedroom, they wasted little time undressing each other, and for several strained seconds, could do nothing more than drink in the beauty of the other standing at the end of the bed. She whispered his name.

"Forget it, Raina, I'm not running downstairs for the plastic wrap. We're good." He struggled not to laugh, but finally gave up when she burst out laughing. Yes, he reflected, she made laughing easy again.

Sobering, Raina's eyes reacquainted themselves with him. The sight of his body warmed and excited her. Taking his hand in hers, she encouraged him to sit on the bed beside her. "That's not what I was about to say, but I'm glad you're still ready to serve and protect."

Patiently, Nick sat beside her and ran a hand down her forearm, loving the feel of her satiny smooth skin. He sensed she was uncomfortable with their newfound feelings. "It's okay, honey," he murmured, dropping feather-like kisses along her neck, stopping at her ear. He felt her shiver and turned her face to him. "I love you, Raina, and we can take all the time in the world. I'll always be here. I'm just happy that you're here, safe . . . and with me. Tell me what's on your mind."

Searching his eyes, she said, "Nick, I don't want you to suffer any more grief. If Pierce finds me, you know he'll kill me and you'll grieve again." There, it was out. She'd spoken aloud the drawback to him loving her and of her being there with him.

Hearing her condemning herself at a killer's hand filled him with rage. "Raina, I'm not going to have you living in fear any longer. I never want you living like you have been these past few months, and definitely not like you've been living since you left your father's house. I'll either see Pierce dead or locked up for the rest of his miserable life if he comes within an inch of you," he whispered passionately against her lips, loving her more for her concern about his welfare.

Seeing the determination in his eyes, Raina threw her arms around his neck. "But how? Nick, you know Pierce is like an unseen phantom." Raina closed her eyes, mellowing from his kisses. "No one can find him, right?"

"Don't worry about that. I've got tons of information. I'll find him." He pulled back and caressed her cheek, but still saw worry etched into her features. "Raina, remember that night down in the kitchen? Well, something did happen. I did feel some kind of connection pass between us. It was strong and unfamiliar, and I couldn't explain it to myself or even understand what the hell had happened, but I was as affected by that almost-kiss as you were."

Raina was already winding her hands around his neck when she whispered against his lips, "I knew it!" She was thrilled to hear him admit what she had not only felt, but accused him of months ago. All other thoughts flew from her head when his hands caressed her breasts, running his thumbs over the sensitive peaks. Within seconds Raina was ready to surrender to his touch, her body demanding he give her more.

Nick removed the last of her undergarments, taking his time in doing so. The last time they were together they were rushed, and it was sad for both of them. This time would be different because they loved each other.

His hands knowingly covered her, applying just the right amount of pressure. And when he kissed everywhere his hands touched, her trembling filled his soul on a level deeper then he'd ever felt before. When at last, Nick lifted Raina further back on the bed and kissed her passionately, he vowed he would never let anyone hurt her again.

RJ sat in the interrogation room of the police station on the pretense of reviewing a report. It was not an unusual sight. Last week, he'd even eaten his lunch there. Earlier today he'd followed Chief Coleman and his security officer from the courthouse and back to the police station.

It had taken him a week to get a confirmed schedule. He even took into account such things as today's meeting at the courthouse. He knew that within the half hour Coleman would be heading home to his wife and two adopted children. Watching Coleman go into Lt. Brown's office, RJ hoped today would be the day Coleman would pay a visit to his girlfriend, Raina Wade. Earlier, he had planted a small listening device under the desk in Lt. Brown's office. RJ also heard that strong leads had developed in the case involving that restaurant hit, and that the PPD would soon be holding a press conference. Hearing that, RJ's stomach lurched and for several seconds he didn't even breathe. RJ learned that the suspect was more than a person of interest, and capture was expected soon. But RJ knew police tactics, and guessed that was something they probably came up with to alleviate concerns in the community. That's what RJ thought until a patrol officer told him a tattoo had been connected to the suspect.

Remembering the conversation, RJ's hand trembled when he instinctively touched the area of his recent tattoo. How did they know? He'd spent hours perfecting the art of tattoo drawing. His ribbons of numbers, tattooed on his arm, represented so much to him . . . no one knew about it. Only he knew that by looking into a mirror, the numbers would become readable. But somehow Raina Wade saw it.

When Max Coleman crossed the lobby and entered Lt. Brown's office, RJ activated a tiny transmitter enclosed in his left hand and, within seconds, he was listening to Coleman talking on the telephone to someone who would soon arrive from the West Coast.

Drumming his blunt, manicured fingers against the desk, RJ summed up two facts. First, Raina Wade was possibly returning to Pittsburgh, and second, her return was connected to the release of the picture of the tattoo . . . his tattoo.

RJ wondered how things had become so bad. He'd left a witness who just happened to be the girlfriend of a police chief. It was this unfinished business that was now preventing him from continuing his mission. *Two days.* That's what RJ heard Max Coleman say. In the meantime, he would keep tailing Coleman.

Raina awakened just after midnight. Looking over at a sleeping Nick, her heart swelled with a welcome feeling of love. She ran a finger down his cheek to his lips. How many times had she seen his face behind her eyes? How many times had she wished to be in his arms again and to lose herself totally to passion unlike any other?

Feeling stronger about returning to Pittsburgh, Raina would fight to get her life back. She also felt wonderful— a stark comparison to the past three months. But that thought also brought her back to the reason why she did return to Pittsburgh. Besides confronting Nick about her feelings, Raina returned to find the killer, Pierce.

Raina needed Nick to find Pierce. She felt terrible for asking Nick about Pierce as he was about to make love to her, but his file was that important key she needed. Raina remembered the first day he'd come to her condo, he brought with him a thick file containing her report. And while he sat in her office later that morning, he'd been flipping thought it. She recalled asking him if all of those papers in the file were about the hit at Antionelli's, but Nick told her it wasn't, saying that it was his personal file. Raina needed to see that file. Armed with information that, more than likely, only she was aware of, she was confident she could find him. *And do what?* "Take back my life from the likes of that horrible man," she whispered.

Easing from under the weight of Nick's arm, Raina slipped from the bed, put her nightclothes back on, and crept from the room. Reed greeted her in the hallway, yawning audibly. Raina reached down and closed the dog's mouth. "Shh," she whispered, stealing a glance back inside the bedroom, then hurrying down the steps with Reed at her heels.

Going to the kitchen first, she gave Reed a doggie snack then spooned leftover fruit salad into a bowl for herself. Balancing her bowl and a glass of milk, Raina made her way to Nick's office. There, she settled in to search for the file on Pierce. Unfortunately, in Andrea's haste, or rather, her fright, she ended up yanking out another report on a homicide linked to Pierce. It didn't contain the information Raina needed. To her surprise, the file sat at the back of Nick's desk. Only briefly did Raina wonder if he'd been reviewing the file, and if he had, why? Had something else happened, like another homicide since she left Pittsburgh?

Swallowing away the urge to gag when she saw the drawing of the man's profile, Raina saw it was exactly as she'd remembered that night at the police station. It was embedded in her memory. Forcing revulsion away, she quickly flipped through the papers, capturing bits of information such as locations of hits and identification of the victims. The graphic descriptions of the crime scenes and the accompanying pictures disgusted her, but she did write down information she thought pertinent on a scrap piece of paper. So far, she had the names of six victims reportedly killed by Pierce. Seeing Reed come to the doorway, his ears pricked up, Raina guessed Nick was awake and would come downstairs any minute.

Nick awakened to find Raina gone. He wasn't worried because the alarm was set and Reed was quiet. He pulled on his pajamas and went downstairs. He found Raina sitting in his office drinking a glass of milk. "Hi, baby." He walked over to her, easing his arms around her body, and saw that she was holding his academy graduation picture . . . the one with her father in it. "Raina, the Michael Wade I remember has a soft heart . . . he can't stay angry long, just like his baby girl," Nick said.

"Nick, he was so mad at me. I–I just don't know what I did that was so wrong?" She gazed down to the picture in her hand, glad for remembering it was there when she tucked the file back under the stack of papers. "We're adults. How could he say such terrible things about us?" Raina sniffed real tears, painful tears.

"Raina, you're his only daughter, and you were intimate with me, a white guy," Nick said, scrunching up his face, trying to make her grin. She only rolled her eyes at him.

"Nick, if you had a daughter, would you be upset if she came home with a black guy?"

Nick thought for a second. "I would want her to be happy, and if the black guy made her happy, then I'm okay. But if the black guy mistreated her, well, then that's a whole different story, because then the black guy would be a dead guy." He took her hands in his. "I don't think it was about me being a white guy that got your father upset. I screwed up, Raina. I had a job to do, and I put your safety in jeopardy. He had every right to be upset with me. But if he's upset about the fact that we're together as lovers, then I'll deal with him man-to-man. He can't change how we feel." Nick cringed when she mentioned the power her father still has within the PPD. He fought against telling her of his suspension. "If that happens, so be it. Raina, I don't live paycheck to paycheck. I don't have a lot of expenses. This house and my truck are paid for, and if you'll remember from setting up my banking stuff, I'm okay financially. By the way, I really like that online banking stuff," Nick said, raising her to her feet. "I want for nothing, except you. What do you want, Raina?" he asked.

Raina hugged him. "I want you, but I don't want you to get in any trouble because of my father. Can you imagine how I would feel if that happened to you?"

Yeah, he had an idea. "Nothing would be your fault, because I alone made the decision that took us to Las Vegas. I have no regrets, and if I had to do it again, I wouldn't change a thing."

"I wouldn't change a thing, either."

"Really? Nothing at all?" Nick mumbled, kissing her.

"Okay, I would change how I reacted to you turning down my *offer* at Jenny's." Her eyes caressed his face. "I'm so sorry for that incident in the airport restroom."

"Oh, well, I would change that." Nick hugged her to him, again. "Let's go back to bed."

"Yeah, let's do that," she murmured, peeping back at the file. She still needed one good look at it.

The following day Michael Wade sat across from his stepbrother, Max in the backseat of the limousine.

"Thanks for picking me up from the airport, Max. You know I appreciate it."

"Mike, stop thanking me. I know you're worried sick about Raina, and, like I told you on the phone, I don't think Pierce got to her. I think she's hiding because you pissed her off. Hell, man, she stopped speaking to me for several weeks over an argument. You know she has a temper. Now, why don't you tell me what you two really argued about, because I don't believe it was just about her mouthing off to you. I think it's more, so what happened?"

Michael stared vacantly out the window as the limo pulled away from the curb at the airport. "Max, I messed up with Raina and lost my temper. What the hell was wrong with me? I mean, how could I be so blind to what she was feeling for him? Hell, I saw it when she first arrived at the house," he said, shaking his head sadly.

Max's eyes widened, totally lost. "Him? Who? What are you talking about, Mike?

Michael faced his brother. "You mean you don't know about them?"

"Them . . . who? Look, don't you go loco on me, brother. What are you talking about?"

Michael dropped his head back on the seat cushion. "Raina and Nick Laprelli became lovers while they were in Las Vegas . . . and they had a farewell tryst in my cabin before he left."

"What?" If he could, Max would have punched out the darkened window of the limo.

"You heard me, but I think it's more," Michael said, folding his hands in his lap.

358

Max closed his eyes, processing what he'd just heard. He could see Nick's face tight with agitation when he announced that Raina agreed to the release of the tattoo she remembered on Pierce's forearm. *"What is she thinking, that's suicide."* He recalled Nick's stark fear and impassioned statement. "Damn. I–I didn't know. I had no idea, none at all." Max ran a hand down his face when a thought struck him. "Wait, did he take advantage . . ."

"No, I don't think so. She told me it was what both of them wanted," Michael said through clenched teeth.

Max was furious. "That's a bunch of bull crap! Laprelli was on the clock and on assignment, dammit! He wasn't supposed to be screwing . . ." Max looked up apologetically at his brother. "I'm sorry, Mike, but you know what I mean."

"Yes, and I agree with you. That's why I told Lyle about Nick attending the conference."

"Well, that makes me feel only marginally better about suspending his ass. Here I was thinking I was perhaps a bit extreme. Then Debra's been harping on me about being fair and forgiving and all of that shit." Max grunted, slicing his hand over his short hair.

"But back to the issue at hand, Max. Where's my baby girl?"

Max heard the raw desperation and dread in his brother's voice. "I don't know, but let's go to a source and get some damn answers." Max hit the intercom button and barked orders to his driver to take the expressway, heading away from the city.

The day had turned out to be extremely warm, so Nick and Raina decided to take a swim at the creek. Lying side by side on a blanket, they stared up at the sky visible through the tall trees overhead.

Nick turned on his side, facing her, his face troubled. "Raina, we need to call your father and uncle. Honey, they're as worried about you as I was. Let's call them." He picked up his cell phone lying on the blanket above their heads.

"No," Raina said, content to stare up at the blue sky. "I thought about being here like this, and for a while longer, I just want to keep that anger away. I'll call Debra in a couple of days."

"It's not fair to put them through this any longer. They're thinking you've met a terrible fate at Pierce's hands, and I'm caught in the middle because I *want* to tell them you're here. But first thing tomorrow morning, if you don't call Debra, I will." Nick sat up and asked if she was hungry. She said she was.

"That's a good thing," he said, rubbing her thin arms. "Give me a week and I'll fatten you up on tons of farm foods and lots and lots of loving."

In the kitchen, Nick pulled items from the refrigerator to prepare lunch, while Raina went upstairs to change. When the front doorbell rang, he frowned. Everyone who visited him always came up to the back deck . . . except for that night when . . .

Nick opened the door to the two tall, similar-looking men, both of whom he had called commander, both of whom stared back at him as if ready to pounce on him. "Sirs?"

The brothers walked into Nick's house, but it was Michael who spoke first. "Don't you sir me, you sono-fabitch!" Michael roared from across the living room, pointing his index finger. It shook, as did the single-pane windows of the old farmhouse.

Nick's intense gray eyes narrowed. "Okay then, Michael," he said. "You came all the way out here for something. I'm pretty sure it wasn't to see me."

Michael stepped over to Nick, thrusting his finger at his chest. "Don't get flip with me. I can't believe what you did with my daughter, Laprelli," he snarled in fury.

Nick wasn't going to stand there and justify his intimate relationship with Raina. He didn't care who her father or uncle was. "What did I do to you, Michael?"

"You betrayed my trust, that's what you did. At this point, I wouldn't trust you to babysit a goldfish if I had one," he mumbled, turning away from Nick, disheartened.

"I'm really sorry to hear that, and I'm sorry you feel that way about me now."

"Nicholas, I don't give a damn about you right now." Michael's anger was unmasked in the booming timbre of his voice. "I want to know where my daughter is!"

Nick pictured Raina under the questioning interrogation of her father. "I care about her too, Michael. I care enough that I wouldn't have turned my back on her when she was hurting and needed me the most, but that's exactly what you did!" Nick fired back.

"Oh, of course you wouldn't, would you? Nooo, you didn't do that at all, you just took her to your bed, you snot-nosed bastard. She was just another skirt for you to claim, regardless how much *she* was hurting."

Nick looked to Max but found no consolation there whatsoever. "That's not how it was, and I didn't hurt her, Michael. I know you're thinking that, but I care for her, and I . . ."

Michael cut him off. "If Pierce has hurt my daughter, trust me, you will pay dearly."

"Michael . . ." Nick could feel the man's pain as much as he remembered his own . . . right up until the instant he walked through the trees and spotted Raina sitting on that rock. He had to tell her father that she was safe and there, with him. "Michael, listen to me . . ."

"No, you shut the hell up! I hold you personally responsible for Raina leaving the security of my home, where I was protecting her."

Nick snorted. "Oh, I don't believe you. Just how were you protecting her, Michael? By ignoring her and not talking to her, or by blaming her for sleeping with me? You're such a hypocrite, man! Don't you dare come into my home and throw your screwup in my face. You know damn well you're the one to blame for her leaving your so-called security." The words were out of his mouth before he could take them back, but he tried anyway. Nick ran a hand down his face. An apology had already formed in his head. "Michael . . ."

Michael turned on his heels. He knew what Nick had said was true, but damn if he would admit that to the man who he felt had compromised his only daughter.

Seeing the situation becoming explosive, Max reached out to touch his brother's arm. He, too, believed Nick spoke the truth. Michael had admitted to him that he'd turned his back on Raina. "Laprelli, how is it that you know what was going on with Raina?"

"She told me," Nick said, then explained about answering Coleman's cell phone by mistake. "She told me then about the argument with her father, and she sounded just awful."

Oddly, Max's cell phone rang just as Nick wondered what Raina was doing upstairs. He was sure she was listening. But his attention went to Max, grasping Michael's shoulder.

Max was talking to Debra. "Mike, it's Debra. She said that Raina just called her about five minutes ago, and she's fine—she's safe."

Michael visibly went slack with relief, and braced himself up against the entryway wall. "Oh, thank God. Wh–where is she?"

Nick listened as Max explained that Debra said the call came from a Sacramento area code and that Raina stated she just needed to get away. Seconds later, Max closed his cell phone.

"Raina's okay?" Nick asked, now positive Raina had heard the exchange from upstairs.

"Nick, as far as I'm concerned, the case involving Raina is none of your business. Nothing at the PPD is your business. You failed on an assignment by compromising the witness's safety, as well as your own. Your suspension, without pay, will remain in effect until the Internal Affairs investigation is complete, are we clear on that?"

Nick had been so preoccupied with worry for Raina that he'd forgotten about the Internal Affairs investigation or his suspension. "Yes, sir." He didn't miss the disappointment aimed at him from Michael's eyes. He was forced to look away. Nick had never been suspended before, and could now recall the many times Michael Wade had stressed to him about integrity on the job. And yet he had failed in the eyes of his commanders—both of them. He didn't feel that way in his heart. Instead, he was comforted in knowing that Raina loved him and that she was safe. He was only vaguely aware when the men left the house.

It wasn't until the limo pulled out of the driveway that Nick finally walked over to the door. He watched the limo drive out of view and closed the door. He wondered if Raina had heard everything, or just bits and pieces. Turning around, he was pulled up short . . . Raina stood on the bottom step landing, anger etched into her features. He knew then that she had indeed heard everything.

Raina heard it all, every terrible thing her father had said to Nick—all that he had accused him of doing, of being. He'd called Nick awful names. At first, she couldn't believe the irony of her father and uncle showing up at Nick's house, because she'd thought about calling her father, using her pre-paid cell phone, when she'd first went upstairs. But she'd decided to call and check in on Janey and Julie first. But to her dismay, when she came out into the top floor hallway to go into the guest bedroom, she'd immediately heard not only her father's loud accusations hurled at Nick, but her uncle's as well.

"Why didn't you tell me, Nick?"

Nick tried to downplay the situation. "Hey, I didn't call them and I didn't know they were stopping by for a visit." He went to her, but Raina stormed past him and into the living room.

"You know what I'm talking about. Why didn't you tell me that you'd been suspended and that you were under investigation? I know what all that means, Nick."

Following her into the living room he said, "I get that you're angry because I didn't tell you, what else do you want me to say?"

Raina threw up her arms, exasperated, and flopped down on the couch. "I want you to be angry, it's my fault you were suspended." Raina pushed Nick away when he reached for her.

"I'm not angry, and I don't blame you for anything. This is a work issue."

"You told me how important it was for you to work since Scott died and . . ." Raina stopped suddenly. "Wait a minute. How long have you been on suspension?" When he mumbled that it hadn't been that long, Raina stood up quickly. "How long, Nick?" Raina glared at him, waiting.

"A week," he said.

Even after all of the threats she hurled at her father, he did what he said he would do. He got Nick suspended. "I begged my father not to do anything to get you fired and he did it anyway. How could he be so unfeeling and so mad at me? I—I just don't understand why he would want to ruin your career like this." Raina searched his face for answers.

Nick felt extremely responsible for the rift between Raina and her father. "He isn't mad at you. I had a job to do and I screwed up. He had every right to report me. He's angry because he thinks I took advantage of his baby girl. Only you and I know that isn't true. Listen, I understand where Michael's coming from, but Raina, I'm not mad at him or you . . . maybe at myself. I told him I care for you, but I wanted to tell him that I love you."

"Oh, I'm so glad you didn't tell him how you feel. It's too soon. Besides, he still carries a weapon and so does Max. They would have shot you right here in your living room."

"Oh, yeah. You're right." Nick tried to make light of the situation. "Please call your father. He's very hurt and he's still worried."

"I don't want to, not now. Can't you understand that he used his power and pulled strings to get you suspended? He didn't give my threats a second thought," Raina retorted.

"Honey, he wasn't thinking about your threats. His focus was on me compromising your safety, and rightly so. I would've done the same thing if I were in his position." Tugging her hand until she sat back down beside him, Nick pulled her into his arms. "He loves you and he's worried about you. Forget about how I fit into the picture and call him."

Raina pulled back, her eyes blazing. "I'll call him when I'm ready . . . and I'm not ready."

Nick was unfazed. "What about Max? He's worried about you, too."

"And I called Debra." Seeing that he wasn't letting the matter drop, Raina went for another tactic. "Nick, I've missed you and here we are spending all this time talking about my father and uncle." Her hands traced his eyebrows. "So tell me, besides putting up that beautiful backsplash in the kitchen, what've you been up to?" Raina smiled when his face relaxed, giving in to her. She watched his eyes darkening, seconds before kissing her.

And once her lips met his, Nick forgot everything else.

Earlier in the day, RJ discovered the chief's assistant had commissioned a limo to go to the airport. Finding that odd, RJ followed the limo from police headquarters to the airport. He didn't recognize the passenger who got into the limo. Following the limo at a discreet distance, RJ was more than surprised when it pulled up to a farmhouse on the outskirts of town. Parking his alternate vehicle, the sedan, on the far end of the property, he couldn't help but wonder why Max Coleman would be coming out to the farmland.

From his cloistered position, RJ wondered if Raina Wade could possibly be hiding in that farmhouse. Though he thought it was a foolish thing to do, it was still a possibility. Fifteen minutes after the limo pulled up at the farmhouse, the two tall men were leaving. Each looked solemn as they hurried to the waiting limo. Just as RJ was about to pull the binoculars away from his face, his sharp eyes zoomed in on another man standing just inside the open door. He pulled into focus Nick Laprelli. RJ didn't think anything unusual about that, he just chuckled. He hadn't pictured the detective for a farm boy. He had no time to dwell on Laprelli, and headed back to his sedan and once again followed the limo at a discreet distance.

As he drove, the familiarity of the man with Chief Coleman nagged at him, but he couldn't place him. He did, however, speculate about that call he'd overheard Coleman having in Lt. Brown's office. RJ just remembered running back to that office to retrieve that planted listening device seconds after Max Coleman walked out.

"What the hell did you just say?" Lyle Brown barked, flopping back in his chair and fixing a glare on Sgt. Dennis Walker, who was sitting across from him, looking as calm as usual.

Dennis hated breaking a confidence, but after reading the Internal Affairs report, concluding with the recommendation that Nick be terminated, he just had to speak up. "Lyle, it's true. Nick is in love with Raina Wade."

Lyle blew out a breath. "Well, this changes the picture. So why the hell didn't you tell me this in the first place? I certainly didn't like thinking that one of my best detectives had lost his priorities. Nick being in love with our witness tells me he wasn't losing his ability to do his job . . . he just wasn't thinking with his other head."

Dennis chuckled. "Yeah, I know."

"Any more details on her whereabouts yet?" Lyle listened as Dennis explained visiting Nick a couple of times and having to be careful. "Why were you cautious, something happen?"

"Let's just say that since I put Nick up close and personal with his kitchen island, his dog isn't too happy with me. I had to keep giving him doggie snacks to keep him from growling at me." Dennis handed the report to Lyle. "So what'll we do about that report?"

Lyle tapped the report. "I'll handle Internal Affairs. Officer Walker, get Nick in here."

Dennis grinned at being called "officer."

"Oh, you're busting me to low rank, huh?"

"It could happen, Dennis." But Lyle understood what Dennis meant.

Grinning, Dennis dialed Nick's cell phone. "But Lyle, you know, you and I did speculate on something like this happening. We said things could heat up on their trip to Seattle."

Lyle sat back. Yeah, they had called it. But he also realized in the eleven years he'd known Nick, this was the first time he'd heard of him being in love.

Raina lay back on the sofa listening to Nick on the phone. Her face bore the signs of a woman in love. What had started out as cuddling up and catching up on the sofa had ended with her and Nick making love. Lunch was all but forgotten. She watched him pulling on his T-shirt and stepping into his jeans. "Hey, what are you doing?"

Nick walked sat on the edge of the sofa. "Have I told you that I love you lately?"

Raina was happy. She was content and at peace in the knowledge that he did love her. This was the kind of loving relationship she had been searching for. Emotion tugged at her heart as she ran her hand up his arm. "Yes, five minutes ago, but keep on telling me," she said quietly.

"I will, for a lifetime."

A lifetime? She wondered what he meant, but didn't ask him. "You're going out?"

"Yes." His eyes met hers. "The, um, I.A. report is in."

Her worry resurfaced. "What do you think it says?"

"I don't know, and I really don't care," Nick said, leaning in to kiss her.

Raina pushed herself to sit upright. "Yes, you do. In Las Vegas, you told me you were making the department your career."

"What else do you remember about Las Vegas?" Nick wanted to drop the subject. He got up and walked over to a basket sitting on the end table.

"I remember everything, Nick," she said.

"Good," he said and presented her with two candied apples. Raina's squeal tickled his ears and he laughed, watching her unscramble herself from the blanket covering her nudity. Nick's heart was overflowing. This was the woman he loved. His woman, and she had his heart.

"Where did you get them?" she asked, accepting the treats in both hands, not really listening when Nick mentioned a neighbor selling produce at the farmer's market. "So that's where you went early this morning."

"Um-hum," he mumbled, taking a bite of the apple she offered him. "I've really got to go to the station to sign that report." He hated the thought of leaving her. "You set the alarm like I showed you, and don't open the door for anyone, okay?" He licked her sticky fingers.

Raina sensed the seriousness in his tone. "I won't open the door. I'll probably take a long bath. My back still aches."

His eyes shadowed. Her back ached from having slept on the makeshift bed in the barn. Caressing her cheek, Nick said, "I'll massage your back as soon I return." Then he gathered her against him, kissing her red, sticky lips.

"We sort of sound like a couple, don't we?" Raina said with an uncertain frown.

"We are a couple, Raina, and I'm committed to this relationship with you." He noticed her frown. "Okay, out with it."

"It's about the couple thing, Nick. Not everybody will be as comfortable with us as we are with ourselves. I can deal with the looks we got on the road. But here I'm not so sure."

"Raina, you ever think that maybe you're the one uncomfortable with our race difference, so much so, that you care about those narrow-minded people, or what they might say about us?" Nick sat back against the couch, waiting for her to answer.

"This is new for me, Nick. I'm comfortable with us, really, I am. But, I honestly think I might feel uncomfortable knowing that people are talking about me, about us . . . like that. Like they would be judging me and thinking that I've turned my back on black men."

"I don't think that. Being with me, if that's what you want, doesn't mean giving up on black men. We're in love. And I don't give a damn what people say, forget them. They don't know what's in our hearts. I know it doesn't compare, but I had to deal with ignorant people growing up, having alcoholic parents who only thought about themselves. Jenny and I felt the scorn of people looking down on us and expecting us to be like our parents. I could either fight everybody who said something crappy to me or I could ignore them. I chose to ignore them because I couldn't change their opinions. You and I are what we are and I'm happy with us. Question is . . . are you happy with me and do you love me enough that you can look past those narrow-minded people?" Nick held his breath, praying she truly wanted him.

Raina absorbed everything Nick said. She thought back over her life the past few months and realized she was miserable without him. Despite the fact that a killer wanted her dead, at that very moment she was happy. She saw no shame in that, or in loving Nick. She had long ago stopped seeing him as a white man. A smile spread across her face as she inched closer to him. "You're right. We are who we are, and we do love each other. I want you. I don't care about those narrow-minded people or what they might say." She pulled back again, her lips tight. "Oh, but just let them say something to me directly, then it's on and they'll be going down. You may chose to ignore and not fight, well, guess what . . . I'll be fighting back . . . for us."

Nick laughed at the face she made, along with the small fist. "Oh, you think you're tough again, huh?"

Feeling stronger in their newfound commitment, Raina said, "I know I am tough, Nick. I'm walking proof of how tough I really am. I made it out of that restaurant on my hands and knees, went all the way to Seattle and came all the way back here to you, so yeah, I *am* tough."

Finally, she was alone. The second Nick left the house, Raina flew into his office to search through the documents in the file. After spending an hour doing that, she turned on Nick's computer and searched the Internet. Then she pulled out her prepaid cell phone and called Andrea at work.

"Girl, it's about time you called me back. Are you at another safe location?" Andrea said.

Hearing Andrea speaking in code, Raina grinned at her mystery-buff friend. "Yes, I am, but did you find what I asked you to look for?" On a hunch, Raina asked

Andrea to dig up a hospital record of James Mortison. If what she was thinking panned out to be true, then she alone would know Pierce's true identity. "Andrea?"

"Wait a minute," Andrea whispered. "I work in the hospital's admissions office, not the medical records department. It's not easy getting medical records anymore with all this confidentiality and privacy of records. I couldn't find much on James Mortison, just the death certificate. The man did himself in five years ago, and he was loaded with money, girl. Is that stupid or what?"

Sensing Andrea was getting flustered, Raina said, "Andrea, calm down and tell me how he died and who is listed as the next of kin. That's all I need."

More paper flipping. "Hum . . . oh, wait, here it is. Cause of death was suicide by cyanide capsules. Oh, that's so gross . . . girl, his dumb ass stuffed a bunch of capsules down his throat. That was stupid, 'cause cyanide is dangerous stuff. He only needed one capsule, not a bunch of them. That stuff bloats the body up and turns the insides to jelly mush. Um, um, um." More flipping. "Oh, I found it. The old man's son is . . . Reginald James Mortison. Hum, he sounds rich, too, doesn't he, Raina? Hey, what do you need this information for, anyway? It's not connected to . . . you-know-who and you-know-what, is it?" Andrea whispered, referring to the killer, Pierce.

Raina's eyes widened. "RJ Mortison," she mumbled absently. "Is there anything else that stands out in those records?"

"Not really. He had a physical a month earlier and everything checked out. He was in excellent health, so it's kind of weird that he would off himself. Girl, I tell you, people with money are just as loony as the rest of us, but it's creepy, isn't it?" Andrea waited for Raina to respond and, when she didn't, she prompted again, whispering, "Raina?"

"Yeah, real creepy. Thanks, Andrea. I–I'll call you back." Raina hung up the phone.

Turning back to the computer, Raina went straight to the Internet search engines and brought up photos from the newspaper about James Mortison. By all accounts, the man was a well-respected attorney. He was just about to be appointed a judge. But that's not what pulled Raina's interest to one particular photo. It was a photo of the funeral that drew a frown from her.

She moved the mouse pointer over the throng of mourners until she came to the deceased next of kin— his son. Raina read the article, and the caption. 'RJ Mortison announced he would be taking over his father's law practice.'

Rapidly clicking the mouse on the son's picture, she enlarged it until she could clearly see the man's handsome face. Raina's hand halted when bile rose up from her stomach, burning the back of her throat.

"Oh-my-God." Raina gawked. What she had only guessed was, in fact, true. RJ Mortison was the killer known as Pierce. She remembered the day she had first seen him.

It was five years ago. Raina had been assisting a clothing designer with a layout of his new men's store downtown. The designer's made-to-order suits could set a buyer back thousands of dollars. RJ was a customer who'd come to pick up a previously tailored suit for his father's funeral. Raina remembered the suit because it had been hanging on the back wall. She'd even hung up a shirt and coordinating tie, hoping the customer liked the selection and would consider purchasing the entire ensemble. She was hoping for a commission, if he did.

Standing behind a display shelf while setting up dress shirts and ties, he couldn't see her, and truthfully, she didn't want to see grief on such a handsome face. She'd even wondered if he was a model. His chiseled features could grace any magazine cover and she'd probably buy it.

Raina's hand flew to her stomach when the candied apple threatened to resurface. Without a doubt in her mind, Pierce, was RJ Mortison—attorney at law. She knew she was sitting on information that was explosive. Only now was she thankful for allowing her mind to open up that day a couple of weeks ago as she sat overlooking the cliff. It was then she finally saw what she'd been subconsciously fighting against.

At Mimi's request, Raina had been sketching a man's suit. It was only after she'd finished the drawing did she realize what she had drawn on the pad—from her mind's eye. She had thrown the sketchpad to the ground, and had become chilled to the bone. Recovering somewhat, she retrieved the sketchpad from the ground and at that moment realized that for months, she'd been fighting against the glimpses and flashbacks of that terrible night. Each time she thought about it, the killer's face would loom up like a grotesque helium balloon with a seductive smile. But that day on the cliff with the security guard, Jefferson, nearby, Raina felt safe enough to open her mind and see it all . . . relive it all, again. Only that day, she saw more.

When she'd picked up the sketchpad, Raina saw she had drawn the actual suit that RJ picked up that day from the designer . . . and she drew *him* wearing it, including the coordinating shirt and tie she'd picked out. *The suit.* And when he walked past the display shelf where she stood, his cologne, also an original, carried only by the clothing designer, wrinkled her nose. The scent was too overpowering with its fruity presence.

Sitting back in Nick's chair, Raina closed her eyes and placed herself back in the nightclub in Chicago. She recalled the man bumping into her. He was a solid mass of muscle. Moving past her fear, Raina inhaled deeply and inched her eyes up to the stranger. Her eyes flew open. It *was* him in Chicago . . . and five years later, RJ Mortison still wore the signature cologne. "Oh, no." Suddenly chilled, Raina prayed Nick returned home soon.

Nick. Her hands covering her mouth, she mumbled. "Oh-my-God." The enormity of the situation was ever-mounting. Quickly returning her attention back to the computer screen, Raina's fingers flew over the keyboard as she began an Internet search for RJ Mortison. Her eyes quickly skimmed over articles connected to the affluent attorney. Then she stumbled on something that frightened her even more. "Oh, dear God." An article was praising the attorney's legal maneuver for clearing a prominent political figure of a DWI/DUI charge when a toxicology report went missing from the evidence room at the local police station. The accompanying photo showed a barely smiling RJ standing on the steps of the police station—the same police station where Nick was at that very moment. But it wasn't the picture that stunned Raina. It was that Nick's former partner was reportedly killed by the hit man, Pierce. RJ Mortison had killed Nick's partner.

Fear crept into Raina, making her cold and still. "Oh, Lord. RJ is probably in and out of that station all the time, and no one knows he's the killer . . . of one of their own." The suspect the PPD had been looking for had been under their noses the whole time.

Raina's hand trembled and her body shivered as her mind processed the information. She had to call somebody. She ran to the living room and snatched up her cell phone to call Andrea, but the call was dropped twice. "Cheap cell phone," she muttered, setting the cellphone on the arm of the couch. When she called out for Reed, the dog appeared around a corner, and to her relief he immediately came to her, rubbing his head against her open palm, as if sensing her fright. "Oh, Reed, this is just so horrible," Raina whispered, easing down on the couch.

Nick sat at his desk in the police station. He was reviewing his report, recounting the time when he escorted Raina to Seattle. Since he'd already submitted a detailed report, he couldn't understand why Lt. Brown wanted it again. But, rereading the report, he cringed. He'd taken a traumatized victim/witness on a roller coaster ride, for Christ's sake. Yes, he needed to be terminated and believed that was the appropriate action for I.A. to take. It was no longer important. Since Scott's death he'd spent far too many hours there, working— trying to forget, all the while grieving. Opening his desk drawer, he brought out a picture. He and Scott, along with Scott's two sons, were leaving a baseball game. Only now could he look at the picture and recall the happy day without feeling that painful stab in his chest. *When did that happen?*

He recalled something Raina had told him in his kitchen: "And you can't explain it, but one day you wake up and find it doesn't hurt so much."

It didn't hurt so much anymore. Setting the picture on the desk, Nick's eyes lifted when the conference room door across the hallway opened. Michael Wade and Max Coleman, along with Lt. Brown and Dennis, were in the room. He could clearly see that Michael and Max still wore lines of worry on their faces. As a cop, he'd seen that look of worry and fear on the faces of many family members of victims, missing or otherwise. He had to tell them where Raina was.

Nick grabbed up the report from his desk and the cold cup of coffee he'd been drinking, but in his haste he almost collided with RJ Mortison. "Whoa," he said, looking up, and pushed RJ back out of the way, thus preventing the coffee spilling onto the attorney.

So focused on the two men in the conference room, RJ didn't see the detective cross in front of him. He raised guilty eyes up to Nick as he tried to play it off. "Trying to ruin my suit, Detective?" RJ said, brushing at his sleeve.

Laughing, Nick patted RJ soundly on his shoulder, then frowned when the man's cologne wafted up his nostrils. "Sorry about that." Nick leaned in closer. "RJ, your cologne is a bit strong today. You got a hot date?" Nick asked, but his attention returned back to the conference room briefly. "Yeah, um, maybe you should try another brand," Nick mumbled absently.

RJ turned in the direction Nick was so focused on. "Say, Det. Laprelli, who is that gentleman beside Chief Coleman. Is he law enforcement?" he asked in a conversational tone. Nick glanced back at Michael. "That's Michael Wade. He used to be law enforcement."

"Is that so?" RJ began to perspire. "Oh, yes, Michael . . . Wade, he used to be, the um, captain, right?" RJ felt lightheaded.

"Right," Nick said, dismissing RJ. He quickly crossed the lobby when he saw the men gathering up papers from the conference room table, preparing to leave.

RJ quickly headed to the parking garage. His mind swirled. Michael Wade. Raina Wade. The possibility of a connection between the two was too great to be a coincidence.

Walking to his Mercedes, RJ's mind connected pieces of information, like Max Coleman's phone conversation confirming the travel plans of someone coming in from

Seattle—where he had laid in wait for Raina Wade to show up.

Once in his car, RJ stared, unseeing, out of the windshield. He was deep in thought. "Now, why would the man leave Seattle?" But RJ had figured it out in an instant. "Because she's not there any longer . . . she's here." He grinned at the simplicity of the situation. "Very clever, Ms. Wade—you doubled back to Pittsburgh."

RJ drove from the parking garage to head back to his office. But while stopped in traffic behind a limousine, he reached another conclusion. "And . . . she's safely tucked away—on a farm on the outskirts of town, and she has police protection in the form of Nick Laprelli." RJ had found out earlier that day that Nick was on suspension, which he now would bet was a ruse to keep round-the-clock security on the PPD's witness . . . Raina Wade.

"But, if Laprelli is at the police station now, that would mean she's probably all alone at that farmhouse." RJ quickly veered out of traffic, made a U-turn and headed to the expressway.

CHAPTER 17

Nick stood at the doorway of the conference room. "Michael, may I speak to you?"

Wearily, Michael said, "I think we've said all we had to say earlier, Nicholas."

Max watched Nick, reflecting on the conversation he'd had earlier with Lyle Brown and Dennis Walker. He, too, could now see what he couldn't see before, not even when Debra told him before he left Nick's house today . . . that Raina and Nick were in love. Even now, he could see Nick struggling with himself. "Come on in, Nick." Max ignored his brother's scowl.

"I have nothing more to say on that earlier subject, Max. As far as I'm concerned, it's closed for discussion." Michael didn't want the entire PPD to know of his daughter's indiscretion.

"Where is she?" Max asked quietly, knowingly.

"She's at my house," Nick said, looking from Max to Michael.

Michael pushed back from the table. "What?"

For the next few minutes, Nick told them everything that had happened since finding Raina at the creek. "I begged her to call you, Michael, but she refused. But I told her if she didn't call by tomorrow morning, than I would. Only you showed up at my house today."

"She was there?" Michael's earlier words replayed themselves back in his head.

"Yes, and she heard you—heard us—arguing. She called Debra from upstairs. She must have purchased a prepaid cell phone out west. When you left, I turned to find her at the bottom of the stairs. I wanted to tell you, both of you." He looked at the brothers. "But she's fine. She's upset about your argument with her, Michael. But, listen, I wanted to tell you something else this morning, only I didn't think it was the right time."

Michael swallowed the constriction in his throat with the knowledge that Raina had heard his harsh words. "I don't want to hear anymore. You've said and done enough, Nicholas."

Lt. Brown spoke up. "Laprelli, what else did you want to say?"

Resting his hands flat on the table, Nick met Michael's hard glare. "I'm in love with Raina, Michael. All that stuff you said this morning wasn't about me as I am now. Maybe when I first joined the force, yeah, I was a hothead, but I never screwed around like you implied."

"Right, and my baby was different, is that it, Nick?" Michael fired back.

"Your *baby* is a grown woman, Michael, and she loves me as much as I love her. And I don't want to lose her, but at the same time, I'm hurting for both of you. But I will protect her with my life . . . even if that means protecting her from your biased and misplaced anger." There, he'd said it, and it felt good. Nick stood up, sliding his report across the table to Lt. Brown.

Nick walked to the door and then turned to address the brothers. "You gentlemen are more than welcome at my house, anytime. I happen to be heading back there now, and I'm gonna pick up an extra-large pizza for dinner, maybe two." His message was an invitation he hoped they took. Then he grinned when Dennis gave him a nod.

Lt. Brown was proud of Nick for standing his ground for the woman he loved. "So, Det. Laprelli, you know you may be out of a job, are you aware of that?"

Nick let out a half sigh, half laugh. "Actually, Lt. Brown, I really don't care."

Lyle pursed his lips. "Just so I'm clear, are you sure about that, Detective Smartass?"

Nick grinned. "Oh, I'm very sure." With that he left the conference room.

She'd only meant to sit on the couch to wait for Andrea to call her back, but after taking taken two ibuprofen tablets for her back pain, Raina fell fast asleep. Jolting awake, she snatched her cell phone up from the couch where it had fallen from her hand, and saw that she'd missed Andrea's call. Still exhausted, and somewhat unsettled from her revelations about RJ, not to mention spending the early afternoon in Nick's arms, Raina had plenty of reasons to be disoriented. Dropping her head to the back of the couch, she looked in the direction of the kitchen and saw Reed pacing at the French doors. She quickly got up to go let him out.

Cooing at the dog, she stepped around him to unset the alarm panel near the kitchen door, then laughed when Reed rushed past her legs out onto the deck and took off down the path.

The kitchen clock chimed three-thirty in the afternoon. *What was taking Nick so long?* She was going to tell him the second he arrived home who Pierce really was. She could only imagine his reaction upon hearing that the killer was someone the PPD trusted and allowed in their circle. And after reading some of RJ Mortison's accomplishments, she knew the entire state would question how a diabolical, sadistic killer could masquerade amongst the PPD.

Another thing she found troubling during her Internet search of the father, James Mortison, was although he was about to become a judge, he represented a lot of powerful people in his practice. Raina didn't dwell on those clients before, but knowing that Reed would take a few minutes, she decided to go back to Nick's computer for one more look.

RJ was camouflaged into the thickest clump of trees near the dilapidated barn. His small, but powerful, binoculars had been scanning the kitchen area of the lone farm house for almost thirty minutes. Suddenly, his breath halted when he stared into Raina Wade's face. She'd opened French doors and stood watching the dog run off.

He thought she was very pretty and absently wondered if Nick Laprelli had been able to remain professional with her in such confines as a cozy farmhouse. RJ doubted it. His eyes scanned past her face to the interior of the house. He watched her turn around, disappearing into a room off a wide hallway. It appeared she was all alone, and time was of the essence.

It was not his intent to deliberately hurt anyone. Only those whom he deemed a liability had to be eliminated, and, unfortunately, Raina Wade had become that. She was a threat to him and his freedom. Freedom he needed to perform what he considered a cleansing of the blight on society—those criminals who were allowed to do their illegal deeds without recourse or punishment. *No.* RJ couldn't let a liability such as a witness get in the way of what had to be done. Had his father been the decent, upstanding and respectable man he pretended to be, then RJ wouldn't have been put in the position of having to kill so many at all.

He only had this one opportunity to take care of her, once and for all, then he could get back to doing what he had to do. He had a growing list of criminals to eliminate. Walking back to his car where it was parked behind the barn, RJ cursed the daylight. He preferred to do his deeds under the cover of darkness. But if he waited much longer, he risked the chance of Laprelli returning and then he, too, would have to be eliminated. RJ hoped the detective was still at the police station, but in the event he did return, he needed to be prepared. He opened the trunk of his Mercedes. Suddenly sensing movement behind him, RJ turned around slowly. His dark eyes hooded and zeroed in on yet another problem he needed to deal with, first and foremost.

"Oh, Lord." Raina mumbled quietly as she blinked at the computer screen. Her searched revealed that James Mortison had been dubbed the "go-to" guy for white-collar criminals. His opponents had been quoted to say, "Mortison could get anybody off . . . if the money was decent."

Raina decided to take a closer look at the criminals who James Mortison did get off with non-guilty verdicts. When she cross-referenced them, her mouth dropped open. Many of those same names showed up again on another list. Pierce's hit list. "Oh, no." With her skin suddenly prickling, Raina frowned, only now realizing Reed how not come back yet.

Stepping out on the deck, she didn't see the dog and let out the only whistle she could . . . a soft but audible one. After several more whistle attempts, she gave up and just called out for him. "Reed!" Still, he didn't come running back as she had expected.

Raina noticed the stillness of the late afternoon. The sun had already disappeared and storm clouds were forming, promising a late-afternoon storm. "Reed, time to come in," she called out. Seeing she had no other choice, Raina trotted down the steps to search for the dog.

She continued to call out as she walked in the direction of the clump of trees leading to the creek. She'd bet he was most likely chasing a squirrel or cooling himself on the rocks, both of which Nick said he tended to do on these hot days. When she walked through the trees, along the worn trail, Raina became aware of how dark it was becoming, and only then did apprehension creep over her, slowing her footsteps. Slowing her pace, her eyes strayed to the trees flanking her. Only now did they seem to take on the shape of tall, ghostly figures with tentacles for limbs. "Girl . . . stop being stupid, they're just trees. I'm not scared because I've lived out here." Chiding herself was not calming her caginess, or the feeling that she was being watched. Darting her eyes right and left, she squinted through the last line of trees as she reached the clearing. She spotted Reed on the other side of the large jutting rock. "Reed?" The dog appeared to be stretched out behind the large rock, and all she could see was his hind legs. Inching closer, she wondered if he really did catch a squirrel . . . and she hoped not because she liked the furry little animals. But then, she wondered if he was hurt, because he lay absolutely still. "Reed?" she called out again, softly this time.

Raina had almost reached the area where the dog lay when something soft and foul-smelling covered her face. There was no time to react, because she couldn't.

Dazed, she sank to the carpet of grass beneath her, just as one of the ghostly tree figures loomed over her, watching.

Nick hated being away from Raina for so long, but he was going to tell her what he'd told her father and uncle. Searching his desk drawer for a menu to a pizzeria, a pair of men's shoes came into view. Glancing up, he couldn't help the grin spreading across his face. He recalled that that was exactly how Raina appeared at his desk that night back in June.

Why couldn't he see it before, Michael wondered? He recalled asking Raina if she had fallen in love with Nick and her response had been, "Only a fool falls in love over the course of a week." Yes, he could see it now. "You do love her, don't you, Nick?" Michael asked, dropping down into the empty chair next to Nick's desk.

"Yes, I do." Having found the menu he'd been looking for, Nick picked up the phone on the desk. "You still like extra-extra cheese on your pizza, Michael?" He grinned when Michael nodded. Nick added, "That's how Raina likes it, too."

"Make that second pizza with mushrooms and pepperoni," Max said, coming up behind Nick and putting a hand on his shoulder.

The second he unlocked his front door, Nick was filled with unease. The alarm wasn't set, and Reed didn't come running to him. Calling out for Raina, he didn't get a response. He walked back to the darkened kitchen, Michael and Max following close behind.

"Nick, what's wrong?" Max asked as they gaped at the open French doors.

Nick ran out onto the deck and called out for Raina. Returning back inside the kitchen, he lifted frightened eyes. Without a word, each man took off to different areas of the house to search for Raina.

Nick went to his den and noticed the computer was on. He couldn't imagine what Raina had been working on and lifted two printed sheets from the paper tray with shaking hands. He looked up to see Max come into the room with his gun drawn.

"What's that you're holding?" Max asked, nodding at the papers in Nick's hand.

"I don't know, Raina must have been working on the computer." He sat the papers down and went to Michael. "We'll find her, Michael." No sooner had the words left Nick's mouth, than the worst of all their fears came to their minds. Pierce had found Raina.

Max was on his cell phone calling in reinforcements. "Let's check the immediate area."

"Oh, God . . . I shouldn't have left her," Nick ground out when Michael handed him the cordless phone, telling him to start calling his neighbors and to think like a cop.

Within a span of some thirty minutes, Nick's house and surrounding property filled up with police and neighbors. A teenager named Connor had been one of those neighbors Nick called. He came bounding up the steps and into the kitchen carrying Reed in his arms.

Nick ran to him on shaky legs. The dog was alive, but lethargic. He rubbed Reed's coat as Connor explained finding Reed at the creek. Connor then left to rejoin the search party.

"I don't feel any lumps or anything broken. Reed wouldn't have left Raina. What could have happened?" Nick said, dread filling him.

Max rubbed at the dog's chin and picked up a distinct chemical odor. "Somebody used chloroform on the dog, Nick." His eyes flew to Nick's, then to Michael. His announcement suggesting that what happened to the dog revealed what undoubtedly happened to Raina.

Max walked over to his brother. "We're going to find her, Mike. Raina is as stubborn and pigheaded as you are, and she's got survival skills. She used them before and she'll use them again." Max's eyes dropped to the papers on the island. He recalled Nick carrying them when they walked out of his den. "What's with this stuff here on Mortison?"

Nick dismissed the papers. "I don't know about that stuff. Look, we're wasting time just standing around here." Nick's face bore the look of every fearful emotion he felt.

"I–I think I might know the answer." A female voice murmured from the doorway.

Nick stared at the young woman. He immediately recognized her from her visit to the police station, concerned for her girlfriend. He crossed the kitchen, stopping inches before her.

Andrea had been in a near panic after trying, unsuccessfully, to reach Raina since earlier that afternoon. After reading about James Mortison, she, too, had come to the same conclusion that Raina probably did . . . RJ Mortison was most likely connected to his father's death. Now, with several law enforcement officials looking back at her, Andrea realized her friend was in far more trouble than she had originally guessed after their phone conversation. "Raina's not here, is she?"

Nick's mind was tumbling over Andrea's visit to the police station and connecting that visit to what she had said when she first came there. "What does your visit to the station have to do with Raina . . . and a missing report from that blue binder?" He had discovered the theft the day after her visit, but only just now connected it to the frightened woman now standing in his kitchen.

Andrea saw his fear and heartache—he loved Raina. Letting her eyes roam the men surrounding her, Andrea blurted out everything she'd told Raina on the phone about James and RJ Mortison.

Nick and Max shared a look. "Mortison . . . Mortison? Wait a minute, as in RJ?"

Andrea rushed on. "Okay, so it's like this. Raina remembered something about the hit in the restaurant. She'd been having flashbacks for months and that's why she came back here."

Nick didn't get the connection. "I saw him at the station," he said absently.

"Yeah, he's been in and out of there a lot lately . . . too much for my comfort level," Dennis said, walking into the kitchen. He was followed by Debra, who went directly to Max.

Nick was still wondering why Raina was looking up information on RJ Mortison.

The sound of barking dogs could be heard coming up on the deck. Hound dogs. Nick turned just as another neighboring farmer came through the door. "Thanks for helping out, Lucas. Anything out there by the creek on the northern end?"

The tall, thin man was winded from handling his dogs. "Well, there're some fresh tracks out by the barn, in the back. Looks like men's shoes. Sissy shoes with wide heels and pointy toes. The dogs tracked the scent to the trees, but it stops there. But ain't nobody out there now. But somebody's been up there 'cause I found these, too." Lucas pulled items from his pocket.

Nick stared down at a black leather glove and a wad of cloth. Dread had turned into a stabbing pain in his chest. The faint odor of chloroform could be smelled. He was only vaguely aware of Dennis getting a plastic bag from the cupboard. It was a well-known fact that Pierce often used chloroform on his victims. "Pierce has her. Dennis, can we get a team to go up there?"

"Already on it," Dennis said, running out the door to his unmarked sedan.

Raina sat upright in the wooden chair. Her hands were bound behind her back. She was so nauseous, she thought she would throw up—that is, if she could. She couldn't because her mouth was gagged as well. All she could do was groan in misery.

Her throat felt thick and tight and her head was pounding. Testing her eyes, she slowly pried open her heavy eyelids. Her eyes slid from side to side slowly, so as not to make her more nauseous. Dropping her eyes downward, she saw that her legs were taped above her knees with tight duct tape.

Raina refused to give into the despair she felt. It wouldn't do any good, she thought with a part of her brain that wasn't too affected by whatever was used to knock her out. She tried to clear her throat and swallow, but the cloth in her mouth prevented her from doing so. Groaning again, she slumped back against the wooden chair.

"I can remove that if you'd like, Ms. Wade," RJ said in a quiet voice.

Raina's eyes peered into a darkened area of the room. Suddenly, a dark-suited man appeared some twenty feet in front of her. She tried to lift her heavy lids to his face, but it was still too much of an effort, so she dropped her head forward. But then she felt a warm hand sliding under her chin, and finally the gag was removed from her mouth and she was able to take a deep breath. Slowly at first, then she gulped more air into her lungs. Not good. That made her lightheaded and more nauseous.

"Is that better?"

She knew who was talking to her. She recognized his cologne. "Yes . . . better," she mumbled through a dry, parched mouth, aware that he'd walked behind her chair. Her fuzzy vision saw his dusty black shoes trailing along the floor. For a split second, Raina thought he was going to strangle her with the gag he'd removed from her mouth.

Raina squinted scratchy and blurred eyes as she tried to concentrate. Her thoughts suddenly strayed to Nick's intense gray eyes. She prayed. *Nick, I'm sorry for leaving out. Please help me . . . find me before it's too late.* She didn't hear the footsteps any longer and wondered if he was going to take his time killing her. *Time . . . I need time.*

She knew he was still standing very close behind her chair. Clearing her throat several times, trying to get past the thickness of her tongue, she croaked out, "Water, please."

RJ stared down at the brown ringlets of her hair and removed a small twig. He again wondered how he'd let things get so out of control. His task should have been done and over with back out at that farmhouse. Unfortunately, things had taken a turn for the worse when she took him by surprise and came looking for the dog almost at the same time RJ was heading to the farmhouse.

RJ had circled the trees to come up behind her when she'd come out to the clearing. Then he heard a bunch of kids cutting through the lowest edge of the creek, drinking beer, about half a mile downstream. He had to improvise or risk being seen by the teens, or by Raina Wade herself. RJ had been forced to use the same chloroform-soaked cloth he'd used on the dog.

Coming up behind her, he'd rendered her unconscious almost immediately. He'd quickly gathered her up and carried her to his car, where he'd placed her in the trunk and drove off. Only now did he realize he'd removed his chloroform glove, dropping it and the cloth on the ground, before climbing into his car and driving off. He wasn't overly concerned about those items he left behind, but it just proved how unfocused he'd become. RJ was never that careless, and blamed his lack of attentiveness on the need to flee or risk discovery by the kids.

"Yes, Ms. Wade, you may have some water."

Raina heard his steps scrape the cement floor and watched as his shoes came from behind her chair. Next, she heard water running in a faucet. *A faucet . . . I am in a basement. Whose basement, and where? Not in Nick's house.* She squinted into the darkness as he walked back toward her. *Buy some time.* "I–I know who you are . . . you can turn up the light." Raina knew she was taking a chance, but then that's all she had . . . a chance to buy some time, keep her wits about her and hope that Nick was looking for her. She prayed that he would find her in time.

RJ stopped. "Yes, I believe you've seen me before, Ms. Wade."

"You mean I saw what you did in that restaurant, don't you?" It was an effort for Raina to talk, let alone keep her fuzzy thoughts straight. Her throat constricted when memories of that night flashed in her head, assaulting her calm exterior.

"Yes, and I'm truly sorry that you saw that. It must have been a horrible sight," RJ said, walking across the concrete floor to flip on a light switch and then returning back to her.

Raina inhaled deeply, staring into his dark eyes, which seemed almost black to her. It really was him. He was no longer the grotesque sight she'd forced herself into believing that he was. No. He was just as she remembered him—just as she'd seen him in her dreams—handsome, fashionably dressed, with his cologne swirling around her. "It was a horrible sight. How could you do that?" Raina asked, pinching her lips together and shrinking back at the flash of tightness on his face.

RJ watched her, holding the glass of cold water to her lips. He smiled when she pulled her lips in, then turned her head away from the glass. "Ms. Wade, if I were going to poison you, then you'd be dead already." After a few seconds, he watched her gulp down the water, then extracted a cloth handkerchief from his inner breast pocket and dabbed the water droplets from her lips and chin.

"You killed Rachel, the woman with Mr. Coates," she said.

"Ah, yes. She was in the wrong place at the wrong time. Bill Coates was supposed to be dining alone. He always did on Monday and Tuesday nights."

Raina frowned up at him. "How could you just kill those innocent people?" Raina sniffed back tears, thankful that her thoughts were staying straight, at least for the moment.

"Ms. Wade, those innocent people were disposed of for a reason."

"Because they saw your face? Well, I've seen your face and your stupid tattoo."

RJ smiled. "So we know why we're here, then?"

A sigh escaped her. "Well, unless you plan to shoot me with a silencer, a gun going off will be very loud down here." Raina's eyes glanced around before looking up at him. "It's a basement in some large building, an industrial basement, right?"

RJ smiled again. "Very good, Ms. Wade. Hmm, so shooting you is out of the question without a silencer. On to plan B, I guess," he said in a deceptively quiet voice.

"And if you stabbed me to death, you'll have to clean up a lot of blood." Her eyes took in his tailored suit. "I'm sure you don't want to get your suit all messy. You'd have to explain that to your cleaner's."

RJ tapped his chin. "Hmm, you're right again. I happen to like this suit, too."

With sheer determination and the need to buy more time, Raina continued to play the morbid game with her tormentor. She prayed that Nick had arrived home and was looking for her.

She knew he would think the worst, that Pierce had found her, and unfortunately he'd be right this time. If only if she hadn't left the house. Through the cobwebs of her befuddled mind, Raina suddenly remembered why she'd left the house in the first place. "Reed! Oh, my God. What happened to Reed?" She shot angry, hateful eyes into his almost black ones.

"Who?" RJ asked as he slid a wooden chair over, sitting down just four feet before her.

"The dog! His name is Reed. Please tell me you didn't kill that sweet dog?"

"I didn't." RJ lifted his jacket sleeve and glanced at his watch. "Reed should be waking up as we speak, Ms. Wade." The relieved look on her face didn't escape his notice. Oddly, RJ wished he'd been allowed to have a dog. As a child he'd wanted a puppy, but his father detested the smell of animals and his mother stayed in a drug-induced coma.

"Well, I'm glad you were not so cruel as to harm a poor animal," she huffed.

RJ smiled again. "You mean as opposed to killing people, correct?"

Raina sensed he was not in a hurry to kill her and couldn't explain why he wasn't. She wondered how far she could push him as she watched him unbutton his jacket, getting more comfortable. "You know, I guess I should tell you that I know who you are, shouldn't I?"

RJ sat back and crossed his long legs. "Well, I guess I shouldn't be surprised that Det. Laprelli has shared lots of information with you."

"He didn't tell me." Raina decided to play as much cat and mouse with him as she could stand. "Nope, it wasn't him." She shook her head, then wished she hadn't when a wave of dizziness hit her again, making her eyes cross and uncross uncontrollably.

RJ grinned at the cartoonish face she made with her eyes crossing. "Really? So Laprelli didn't share information about me between the sheets, Ms. Wade?"

"Oh, that's funny," she said sarcastically, baiting him. "Come up with another guess. A better one this time, why don't you."

"Ah, but you didn't say I was wrong about you and Laprelli between the sheets."

Raina relaxed back against the wooden chair. "That's really my business, but you're not wrong, if you must know. We happen to be in love."

Surprise registered on his face. "Hmm, I'm surprised Nick would get involved with . . ."

Raina finished for him, "With what, a black woman, you mean?"

"No, that's not what I was going to say. I was going to say to get involved with anyone. He's still grieving and sort of on a path of self-destruction."

"And of course you would know that because you're the reason he's grieving. So tell me, what did Scott Morgan do that put him on your radar? Did he see your face, too?"

RJ ran a hand under his chin, studying her. She's buying time, he thought. But knowing their whereabouts were unknown, he was in no rush to end her life. He decided to participate in the Q&A with her. "I didn't *want* to kill Det. Morgan. I do regret having to do that, as I do have compassion, Ms. Wade. However, Det. Morgan had been sent documents and a video email that, well . . . yes, it would have identified me. I couldn't let that happen."

"What does that mean?" Raina frowned, not really sure she wanted to know the answer.

"Just before I was set to, um, eliminate someone, you know, kill a really bad guy, I had eliminated the man's partner in crime. The man guessed, correctly, of course, that he was next. When I showed up, the man told me he had made certain I would be apprehended."

"So he found out you were coming after him, that's good."

"It wasn't good. He'd had a video feed going from his office to a remote location. It was recording while I was there. He refused to tell me where the remote feed was going. However, by process of . . ." RJ paused, leaning forward slightly. "Shall we say, elimination of his digits, beginning with his thumbs, I was able to get that location. He'd sent a video email to his friend's boat. Unfortunately, that friend was Det. Morgan, and by the time I arrived there, he was already reviewing the video. He'd put two and two together and when he reached up for his cell phone, he found me . . . and the barrel of my gun." Watching her recoil, RJ added, "I had no choice, Ms. Wade, you must understand that. But I was swift, he felt nothing."

Revulsion was now making her nauseous again. "No, I don't understand that, but why don't you call me by my first name. I'm sure you know it, and I'll call you by yours." Raina's hope was beginning to wane. Listening to him talk about taking lives in so matter-of-fact a way, she was positive he was truly a sadistic and diabolical killer.

"Okay, Raina," RJ smiled, murmuring as he inched closer, gazing into her brown eyes.

She mimicked him by inching her face as close to his as her as her restraints allowed. "Okay, RJ," she whispered. With an intense feeling of satisfaction, Raina watched the shock register on his handsome face. She smiled across at him as a deadly stare replaced his smile.

For several long seconds, it was a stare-off; neither looked away from the other.

Not giving him an opportunity to recover, Raina pressed on. "You seemed surprised that I know your name? Well, yeah, I guess you would be, right? I mean, come on, Pierce does have a kind of scary quality to it, though. You know what I'm saying? It's like it could be a killer's name. But now RJ Mortison, it sounds so professional, like a lawyer, you know what I mean?"

RJ's teeth were clamped shut, and he worked his jaw muscles into a frenzy.

"And you know something else, RJ?" Raina watched him struggling not to come unglued.

At that point, RJ was still in shock. He was incapable of responding, but perspiration covered his forehead and upper lip. He merely lifted his shoulders, wondering how she'd found out who he really was.

"Well, although your style is different from your father's, I'd have to say that you, too, have that screwed-up idea of how to balance out the injustices of our legal system."

RJ stood up so quickly that the wooden chair flew out from under him. He kicked it away in absolute anger and frustration. How could she know of his struggles? He paced before her, feeling perspiration begin to collect under his dress shirt. "You know nothing of what you're talking about, Raina. I think you've been listening to Laprelli's bedroom chatter a bit too long."

"No, that's not true. You see, RJ, no one but me knows who you really are. Think about it . . . if the police department knew who you really were, we wouldn't be here in this basement. You've killed one of their own. It is a basement, isn't it? I hear water above me and it smells damp down here. Yeah, I think we're somewhere underground, near a sewer system, I'll bet." Raina was forcing him to think many things all at once, but she didn't miss his eyes glancing upwards and knew she was right.

RJ had stopped his pacing. "Tell me, how is it that you know about me, Raina?"

Fear was riding the edge of Raina's sanity as she watched him. But that same fear pushed her forward as she pressed for more time. Specifically, the time she needed to continue to work at the duct tape binding that held her hands together behind her back. "Okay, but since you're in no obvious hurry to kill me, or as you might say, eliminate me, why don't you give me another glass of water. But you'll have to answer something for me, first."

RJ watched as a slight smile curved her lips. He thought she had a lot of nerve and went to refill the glass of water. Returning, he held the glass to her lips. "Okay, what is it?" he asked, watching her sip the water before answering.

"Well, I was wondering how you think I did at karaoke night. You remember, that night in Chicago when you bumped into me?"

RJ was rarely, if ever, shocked, but he thought this little powerhouse had just shocked him speechless.

Nick's large kitchen had become command central. The grounds of his property had been thoroughly searched. The hound dogs had picked up on a scent that went nowhere except the creek. The leather glove had been sent to the forensics lab downtown with a rush from Chief Coleman himself, but even Nick knew that was a four- or five-hour process to recover anything.

It was after eight at night, and Nick stood in the doorway of his kitchen. He was overwhelmed by the number of people who were there for Raina, but they were also there for him. Their strength gave him more hope than he would've had if he had been alone. He feared that Raina would meet the same fate as Scott . . . just as it was in his dream in Las Vegas.

He wondered how could he have searched his whole life for the kind of love he shared with Raina, and yet have it snatched away so suddenly? He'd promised to protect her, and now he just prayed that she wasn't hurt or someplace cold and alone. If only he hadn't left her . . . guilt settled onto his slumped shoulders.

Michael saw the look of worry and love on Nick's face. He, too, prayed that she was alive and once again using her skills to stay that way. He walked over to where Nick stood and patted the younger man's shoulder. "Raina's a smart girl, Nicholas . . . she'll come back to us."

Nodding in agreement, Nick fought back the dread and dismay he really felt.

Debra, Andrea and several neighbors had been keeping everyone full of coffee and food. But even Debra's emotions were getting the best of her, so she slipped out of the kitchen and into Nick's office where Kira and Troy were nursing Reed. When she sat at the desk, her hand brushed the wireless mouse, inadvertently disengaging the screen saver. She began reading what came up on the screen, and hit the print key. Several minutes later, Debra rushed into the kitchen. "Hey, I think I found something."

Max was at her side glancing at the papers she held out to him. Then he walked over to the counter where the other papers where put aside. "Nick, come take a look at this."

Suddenly Nick and Max's eyes fell to the papers. Was it possible the information they were seeking had been right under their noses the whole time? Spreading the papers out on the center island, side by side, they studied them, one by one.

Nick looked up as Lt. Lyle Brown came into the kitchen. "Was RJ still at the station when you left, Lieutenant?"

"RJ Mortison? No, he left earlier. Why? What does he have to do with anything?"

Absently, Nick watched Kira, who'd come into the kitchen and was now drying her hands on a paper towel at the sink. He watched her pull a bottle of lotion from her small purse and smell the contents, obviously liking the scent. He vaguely heard her say she was going to rub some on Reed's back to cover up "that awful smell," referring to the chloroform residue.

The connection drew Nick's dark eyebrows together. "Today, I told RJ he needed to lighten up his cologne . . . his spicy, sweet cologne." Nick's breath came out choppy as he met the questioning eyes of everyone staring at him. "What is the one thing Raina has consistently said about Pierce?"

Max knew what Nick was thinking. "That his cologne was sweet-smelling, to the point it made her sick. She also told me that first night that she would recognize that cologne, and that it may be a custom blend by some designer she knew."

Lt. Brown was rapidly processing what he was hearing. "Nick, what did you say caused Raina's melt-down in Chicago?"

Nick recounted her fright. It was triggered when she smelled the cologne of the man who bumped into her at the nightclub.

"We all know when RJ is in the station because his cologne lingers in the air long after he's gone. Does anybody know if RJ has a tattoo?" Lyle watched Nick shrug his shoulders. "Well, dammit, give me something more compelling to go on than the man's cologne if you want me to issue an arrest warrant for this guy. I for one would hate to see RJ turn and sue the hell out of the PPD for something so flimsy, and, I might add, circumstantial."

Nick returned his attention to the papers again. "It's him, Lt. Brown. RJ Mortison is Pierce." He grabbed up the papers in his fist. "It's right here. Raina found the link, and I believe she found out the reason why he kills."

"Explain that, Detective," Lt. Brown said.

"Look, it's all here. Raina pulled up a list of some fifteen people that James Mortison got off. These fifteen people had cases dropped to lesser charges or thrown out altogether. In some cases, the evidence disappeared. But, had these things not happened, these fifteen *criminals* would have been convicted and serving time." Nick ran a hand through his hair in frustration. "Okay, look . . . here are the names of the people believed to have been killed by Pierce. So far it's ten. And these ten people were charged with crimes, but they got off, or were found not guilty by some technicality. Don't you see what RJ is doing? He's going after the people his father got off, one by one."

"Well, damn," Lt. Brown said loudly.

Nick pressed on. "I know, it sounds crazy and straight out of some movie, but look, Raina found this out by searching the web and reading a file that I have on Pierce's killings. Then she used my secondary password and searched the arrest records of these ten people, who were reportedly killed by Pierce." As Nick said the names of the ten people, he laid out the arrest record, then the corresponding court case outcome. "All got off, and now all are dead. Why the hell didn't we see this?"

"It all seems to fit, and I'll bet anything RJ probably got a lot of his information down at the station, from cops," Dennis said, and explained about reprimanding a patrol officer a few weeks ago when he overheard him talking to RJ about an investigation. "Yeah, I heard him making reference to something about the chief's hot little girlfriend being under 24/7 protection." Dennis looked uncomfortable when Debra's eyes rounded on him, as did Max Coleman's.

"What?" Both Debra and Max thundered at Dennis before looking at each other.

"I have no hot little girlfriend, Sergeant. What are you talking about?" Max said.

Lyle eased Max away from Dennis and explained that it had gotten out around the station that he'd had a hot little hooker girlfriend, concluding the rumor stemmed from what happened the night Raina came in. "Max, you're the one who said you didn't want your true relationship with Ms. Wade to get out. So, cops come up with their own interpretations," Lyle said, glancing at Nick. "Even Nick thought that up until the day we suspended him. Remember, he didn't know she was your niece, either."

Max just rolled his eyes and would have laughed if the situation wasn't so serious.

"Still, that doesn't explain how Pierce, or possibly RJ, found Raina all the way out here at Nick's place. The farmland isn't exactly local or littered with city folks, you know," Max said.

Nick answered in a shallow voice. "It's simple. He had to follow me home."

"You said you've been home and Raina's only been here a few days, Nick, so who else came out here in the past day or so?" Debra's soft-spoken voice drew the men's attention.

"We did . . . Max and me," Michael said after processing all he'd heard.

"You're right. Damn!" Max ground out. "I just figured it out. If RJ thought Raina was my girlfriend . . . Well, whatever, if he thought that, he had to have been following me and today he would have followed me from the airport to here. Then back to the station, because he arrived there minutes after Michael and I did."

"It's RJ. I'm positive it is," Nick said, his voice pleading. "Chief . . ."

Max didn't need to hear more. Within seconds, he'd barked out orders to get an arrest warrant for RJ Mortison and search and seizure warrants on his home and his legal office.

Nick closed his eyes. He sadly thought the dream he had in Las Vegas was coming true. He eased away from all the activity in the kitchen and went up to his bedroom. There, his eyes flew to the monitoring system. "Shit! Why didn't I look at this earlier?"

It was still in record mode. He rewound the tape back to after he'd left the house earlier. After a few minutes, Nick watched as Raina opened the French doors, and he saw Reed fly past her legs. He pressed fast forward, letting his eyes scan the area of the trees. He saw nothing until a short time later, when Raina came to the door again and went out onto the back deck. He smiled sadly watching her twist her lips, trying to whistle and failing. Even with the volume up, he could barely hear her.

Intense pain, unlike anything he'd ever known, filled his chest watching Raina walk off the deck, calling out to Reed. He slowed the playback and set his attention to the area of the barn. Unsure of what he was seeing, Nick watched the slow play and spotted movement . . . and the back end of a black car. After rewinding and playing it in a slower mode, he zoomed in on the area. He saw the movement again, this time in more detail. It appeared to be a man in a dark suit opening a trunk, then disappearing into the thickness of the trees.

A few minutes later, Nick watched the man bending over the trunk and closing it, and although he wasn't quite sure, Nick thought it was a body. "RJ, you piece of crap, you're dead."

Nick opened his closet and retrieved his back-up weapon, a 9mm automatic pistol. In his gut, he believed that Raina was still alive. But he felt her fear and her coldness from that fear. But he also believed what her father had told him earlier. Raina would use her smarts, or rather her smart mouth, to buy some time . . . knowing he would come looking for her.

Nick needed to find Raina on his own. He left the house by the front door. Stuffed in his pocket was one of the sheets of paper Raina had printed out. He'd discovered that Raina had also used his secondary password to get access to RJ Mortison's motor vehicle record, which showed his home address.

Nick drove away from the farm with one thought . . . he would find her.

Raina watched RJ pacing. She also noticed him rubbing at his forearm, the area of his strange tattoo. "You know, I thought your tattoo seemed out of character for someone who . . ." She shrugged her shoulders when he stopped pacing in front of her.

"Who what? You haven't been short on words thus far, Raina."

"Oh, right." Raina nodded. "You mean for someone who's about to be eliminated, huh?"

"For lack of a better word, that'll do." RJ's eyes flitted over her. He knew she was scared, but was acting tougher than any of those people he'd had to kill so far. She'd yet to cry hysterically, like he'd expected. He was curiously fascinated by the workings of her mind, and he admired her tenacity.

Raina chuckled lightly. "Hey, you're crazy if you think I'll go down without a fight, or at least without getting answers to questions I've wondered about. You'd probably do the same thing if you were in my position, wouldn't you, RJ?"

Regaining his composure, RJ picked up the chair he'd previously kicked away and sat in front of her again. "Raina, I'll give you credit for that. What's your question?"

Watching him, she shook her head. "Uh-um, you didn't answer my first question."

"I thought you sounded great and you have a very beautiful voice. I actually remember bumping into you." After studying her face in the picture on his computer collage, then transporting himself mentally back to that night in Chicago, RJ did remember her.

"You touched my elbow when you apologized to me. How could you be so considerate and polite after having just killed some idiot drug dealer?" Raina recalled finding that information when she looked through Nick's file. It stunned her to know that it was Pierce himself who'd bumped into her just minutes after killing a man. Her breakdown hadn't been triggered by some random stranger with the same cologne, after all. "I guess you thought he deserved to be killed like that."

RJ rested his hands on his crossed legs, watching her. "He was more than just an idiot drug dealer, Raina. He was a killer himself, and he sold bad drugs to bad people. That's a terrible combination. By eliminating him and his bad drugs, I did a good deed. And, by the way, drugs don't flush down a toilet as easily as they portray it on television." RJ grinned.

Raina nodded. "You only killed off a bunch of sewer rats. I guess that's how it is to take a life. You can't feel, so it's no big deal to you." He asked her how she would look at it.

"I wouldn't have killed him. I would have believed in our judicial system and let them deal out the appropriate punishment for him. We're not judge and jury, RJ."

"He was a small-time dealer, Raina, and, since the age of sixteen, he'd been selling drugs and getting away with it. Every bleeding heart refused to charge him as an adult, so he felt he was untouchable, and he had been. Our judicial system is a joke. They would have slapped him on the wrist and given him one year, and our legal system would have suspended three to six months. He would have been back out on the streets in another three, doing the same thing. My way was better and more cost-effective."

"And what about the other dealers? You can't kill all of them." She watched him rub his forearm again. Raina shook her head. "You know, I remembered you rubbed at your tattoo at the restaurant. What does it mean?"

"It represents retribution and justice," RJ answered, not at all surprised she knew of it.

"You know, I figured it was something like that. I can see how you'd need a constant reminder of your deeds."

"Really?" She was unnerving him, throwing him off, and he didn't like it.

"Well, sure. I mean, your father got all those guilty criminals off without so much as a slap on the wrist, you know, like that drug dealer would have gotten. So you're resetting the balance, aren't you RJ? You're doing the opposite of what he did. You're righting his wrongs, aren't you? I'll bet the only difference is that no one is paying you cash to do it."

RJ inhaled a deep breath, then released it slowly. "My father was an idiot and a murderer himself. After keeping my mother in a chemically induced coma after she'd suffered a head trauma in an accident, I silently watched as he accepted bribe after bribe, filling his fat pockets with hush money. Money he didn't even need. When I was a teenager, he forced me to follow in his footsteps. It was expected that I'd become an attorney. I had no control over my life, no aspect of it." RJ spread his hands briefly. "So I did. I became what he used to be . . . a respected attorney. Only he had a beautiful and loving wife, who he decided to murder because he thought his colleagues took pity on him. He used his legal powers to make that happen, with the court's blessing. But unlike him, Raina, I don't accept bribes and if someone's guilty, trust me, my dear . . . they don't get off. If anything, I assist as they dig themselves deeper into a hole and walk away with clean hands."

"So one by one, you're trying to balance out the number of criminals your father got off. RJ, your deep-seated anger stems from the child in you who lost his mother at a young age. That's traumatic. As a mentor, I've listened to more kids than I can count talk about that same sense of loss. They had no one in their corner, no one to guide them past that anger and rage they felt." Raina watched a shadow cross over his handsome face. She knew, he knew she was right. "I feel so sorry for you. Yes, your father was an idiot, but you didn't have to follow in his footsteps . . . not this way, RJ. How many people have you killed, so far?"

RJ had been holding his breath, listening to her truthful words. "It doesn't matter."

"Oh, right, because you have to now count those unfortunate witnesses, too. But I think you do know. Those ribbon tattoos on your wrist contain numbers, an obscure script of case documents. Anybody looking at them would think they're some kind of calligraphy script within the ribbons . . . that is, until they look at them reversed." Raina believed she was talking to a lost cause. RJ was too far gone, and he was a lost cause. "That's how I saw them that night in the restaurant. I looked out into the mirror hanging on the wall when you extended your hand to Rachel. You know, maybe it's a good thing that your father died. Can you imagine all the criminals and crooks he would have gotten off? Then you'd have ribbon tattoos up both arms. That's disgusting." Raina cringed and made a face as if she'd tasted something sour.

RJ couldn't answer. He was remembering his father's gurgling and choking on the water when he forced him to ingest those cyanide capsules. All the while his father was cursing him, saying that he would surely see him in

414

CHAPTER 18

Nick couldn't say what was pushing him as he drove his F-250 pickup truck, but he'd made it downtown in record time to an address Raina had penciled in under RJ's vehicle registration information. It was a tax assessment for a condo RJ owned. The area had been in the process of major renovation. For three blocks, warehouses had been renovated into shopping complexes and many were still in the process of being renovated into lofts.

Turning off the lights to the pickup one block up from the address, Nick's eyes ran along the lofts at the end of the block. Everything was dark, and a chill ran through him when he thought of what could happen to Raina in such a dark and isolated place. But, unlike his dream, he planned to reach her in time, and, if he didn't, he would just kill RJ himself.

With his gun drawn, he inched up the back alley, scanning the buildings. As he drew closer to the last building, Nick spotted a black Mercedes. *RJ's Mercedes.* Splaying his hand across the hood, it was cold to the touch. It was almost 10:15 at night and, according to the time on the video, the black car pulled away from the barn around 4:30 pm.

The significance of the cold car told Nick that RJ most likely had not gone back out after he'd arrived home. His eyes took in every inch of the back of the building. Darkness from top to bottom greeted him and, straining his ears, he only heard the scurrying of rats, a cat screeching and a dog intermittently barking. He patted his jacket just to make sure his six-inch flashlight and crowbar were still securely fastened to his belt. Next, he proceeded to climb up a metal rail and hoisted himself up to the fire escape. Stopping at the first two floors, he shined the ultra-bright flashlight in the large windows and only saw empty, unfinished lofts. Large plastic sheets waved and flapped loudly as a cross-breeze moved around them.

Climbing higher, he reached the top floor. Nick looked into a window. Not seeing any movement, he pulled out his flashlight and peered inside again. Nothing except another large area, but on closer inspection, he noticed there were no plastic sheets. He could see across the large room to what looked like a lived-in section of the loft. With the elbow of his jacket, Nick busted in the windowpane and, within seconds, he managed to slither inside the loft.

Raina's plan was backfiring. She'd wanted to see RJ come unglued just enough to throw him off and keep him talking as she loosened the tape. Instead, she believed she was watching him turn into the evil monster he really was. Gone was his soft, seductive voice and smiling face. In its place was a face that was twisted, hunched over, and just twenty inches from hers.

"Answer me. What do you mean that you picked out my shirt and tie?"

"Get out of my face, RJ," Raina snarled, angry that, although he was close, he wasn't close enough for her to strike.

Easing back, RJ ran a hand down her cheek. The hand was now cold and hard. "I could have killed you long ago, but I didn't, Raina."

Raina snatched her face away from his hand. "So should I be less afraid now? Why should I tell you anything else? You'll only kill me anyway," Raina fired back and fought back frightened tears, but she was scared to death and the duct tape wasn't coming apart as she had expected. She was as scared as she was the night she stood in the alley behind the restaurant, knowing he was just inside the door. "I hope it took forever to get all of that ash and cigarette butts from your suit and your shiny hair," Raina huffed.

Laughter bubbled up quickly inside of RJ. The emotion was foreign to him. Rarely did he laugh, let alone to the point his stomach was in knots. "You're right! That did take some time, as did the detailing of the car," he said, leaning forward. "Yes, your little stunt did cost me a bit of pocket change." Chuckling, he kissed her forehead and stood up.

Raina cringed in disgust when his cold, wet lips left her forehead damp. "I sure hope you don't use those cold lips on women. It's as big a turnoff as your cologne, RJ."

RJ laughed again. "Raina, I do like you, ah, but sweetheart, what must be done . . . simply must be done. But I like to tidy things up, so before I do what . . . well, you and I both know what I must do, will you tell me how you came to pick out my shirt and tie. I got a lot of comments on them."

When he stood up, Raina lifted her bounded legs and kicked as hard as she could to his groin area, only she missed and ended up kicking his thigh. "Okay, so it's going to be like that," RJ said with extreme patience. He reached into his jacket pocket.

"No! W–wait a minute, I–I thought you weren't going to shoot me. You lied to me, RJ." Panic gripped Raina into a trembling spasm. "Besides, a shot will reverberate off these walls."

"There you go again," RJ said, extracting a gun from his pocket.

Raina gasped, horrified. "You'll get caught, I guarantee you that, and you'll burn in hell, but you'll be in good company . . . right down there with your father."

RJ removed his hand from his pocket, showing her a silencer, just seconds before twisting it onto the barrel of his gun. "Yes, you're right. He even told me that himself."

"Okay, okay . . ." Raina rushed on. "I–I'll tell you how I know about the shirt and tie." She watched as a crooked smile tugged at the corner of his mouth.

RJ dropped his hand with the gun to his side and transferred his weight from one foot to the other, waiting her out. "Anytime you're ready to tell me, Ms. Wade."

"Ms. Wade? I–I thought you were going to call me Raina, remember?"

"I changed my mind. It makes killing you less personal, you know what I mean?" RJ said, mimicking her and then grinning at the sarcastic curl of her quivering lips.

"Oh, the sadistic killer has jokes, only that wasn't funny." *Don't cry. Don't let him make you cry . . . stay strong, baby. I'm coming for you. I love you and I'll protect you with my life.* Raina wondered where those thoughts were coming from. She closed her eyes and wondered if this was what a scared person thought about when faced with imminent death. She pictured Nick's face the day they had fished at the creek. It was that day when she first felt something tremendous for him. Although he was just a stranger then, she felt it. Her father's words came to her just then. *"Are you in love with Nicholas?"* Raina wanted to shout out what she couldn't then and now wished she had. "Yes, yes, yes, I love him, Dad . . . I love him." Her throat tightened knowing not only was Nick going to be hurt by her death, but so was her father, who would for-ever remember their last argument.

"Are you napping in the midst of your impending death, Ms. Wade? I must be slipping."

Raina opened her eyes with a sad shake of her head. But in doing so, her eyes trailed slightly to a dark corner, just to the right. Was there movement there, or was she just seeing things? "Oh, um, the suit . . . a few years ago, I helped a clothing designer set up his new store down-town. That was the day you came in to pick up the suit you wore to your father's funeral. I coordinated a shirt and tie with it. You told the designer that he'd made an excellent choice."

"I remember that. He was such a suck-up, and he took all the credit. That's too bad. Thank you for tying off that loose end, Ms. Wade." RJ lifted the gun to Raina's forehead.

"Watch your suit, RJ. Brain matter is probably messy, but then you would know that, right?" Raina closed her eyes tightly shut.

She heard a single shot.

Raina thought it odd that she didn't feel pain as she'd expected. *Am I paralyzed?* Squinting, she opened just one eye, barely. What she saw shocked her. RJ stood before her with a contorted face. Then her eyes flew to the gun that dropped from his profusely bleeding hand. It hit the concrete floor with a loud clack. Lifting wide eyes to him, Raina's brain barely registered that if RJ had put a silencer on the barrel of his gun, where did the sound of a shot come from? Bright red blood dripped to the floor from RJ's stump of a right hand. There weren't even any fingers left. Raina suddenly remembered seeing all those crime scene photos of Pierce's victims—all with missing fingers. Her first thought was that it was poetic justice, and she forced back a giggle as she looked at his hand; her second thought was, what's going on?

RJ's amazed eyes slowly shifted from Raina's as he stumbled around in the direction of the stairs. He stared into intense gray eyes . . . eyes deadlier than his own, coming closer to him.

For a split second, Nick quickly assessed that Raina appeared unharmed and returned his attention back to RJ, nodding toward RJ's bloody stump. "That was for putting your hands on Raina. The next one will be for Scott Morgan . . . so come on, RJ, you bitch." Nick pulled the trigger again when RJ lurched for him. The bullet struck RJ heavily in the chest, and Nick watched as he tumbled to the floor.

"Nick," Raina whispered his name, unaware of the swarm of police breaking the glass and crashing in the basement windows and clamoring down the stairs.

"I'm right here, Suraina." Within seconds Nick was kneeling before her and removing the tape from her legs, then from her hands as his own hands trembled with relief.

Fear, as well as relief, had turned Raina into a sobbing mess. "Oh, Nick, I'm so sorry. I left the house even after you told me not to."

Nick was so relieved that he'd reached her in time that he couldn't speak. All he could do was drop his head to her lap. No words came when she lifted his head and wiped his tears away.

"Can you stand up, sweetheart?" Nick asked, alternately rubbing at her legs and wrists.

"Um-hum, I've been flexing them to keep the blood flowing." At the mention of blood, Raina's eyes dropped to RJ's lifeless body. The blood pooling around his dead body looked as black as street tar. Raina thought it was fitting for someone with a black heart. She also thought it was ironic that he lay dead on a dusty concrete floor, his tailored suit all bloody and dirty.

"I'm so glad I found you. I love you so much, Raina," he said, kissing her gently before helping her to stand and enfolding her in his strong arms.

"I love you, too, Nick." Closing her eyes, so many words circled in her head, and Raina threw her arms around his neck, hugging him tightly. Intense love is what she felt. This is what she'd been searching her whole life for. Then, opening her eyes, another word came. "Dad?"

Nick reluctantly released his hold on her, but stayed close, watching Michael crush his daughter to him. He smiled watching the older man drop kisses to her face, all the while examining her for signs of trauma, followed by Max, who did the same thing.

Nick turned when his emotions threatened to overtake him. He sent up a silent prayer, thankful for the path that guided him to find Raina in that basement. He'd been just about to leave the top floor loft when he moved aside a strange-looking screen panel beyond the living room area. It captured his attention, because it looked so out of place . . . it looked antique and was covered with pictures of a beautiful older woman. Behind the screen Nick found RJ's collage of pictures of dead people with severed fingers. When he drew closer to the wall, he spotted one picture that made him shiver. It was of a table full of young males in a nightclub and Raina was in the background . . . up on the small stage getting ready to sing—to him.

Now, the many *what ifs* came. What if he'd never walked over to that old screen panel with the pictures of who Nick would guess was RJ's mother. If he hadn't walked over to inspect it further, he wouldn't have heard mumbled voices coming up the pipes from the three floors below. And, what if he hadn't found his way down to the correct section of the basement? In such a large building, Nick could have easily ended up on the other side and, had that happened, he would've been too late to save Raina. Nick truly believed it was Scott calling out to him from that area, because when he reached the first floor, he'd found a door there ajar. Pulling it open and creeping down the steps, it led him down to the basement just seconds before RJ had prepared to end her life.

EPILOGUE

In the three months since the night that left RJ Mortison dead, Nick and Raina established a normalcy to their lives, with one difference . . . one beyond their racial difference. They were madly in love, and they let everybody know it.

Nick had been reinstated to the PPD and would soon take the sergeant's exam. Raina had returned to work full-time and moved back into her condo, because it was closer to work and to the newly formed chapter of the church's mentoring program. Raina was delighted when Janey and Julie volunteered to be part of the junior mentors program. Thanks to the grant that she wrote, funding was received. She would soon write another grant where police officers would serve as mentors. Nick had already signed up to be a mentor to Scott Morgan's sons.

After a period of adjustment, Raina managed to put everything that happened with RJ behind her. Following Debra's suggestion, she settled into a support group to deal with her ordeal, which she thought of less and less. Nick's love and support made that possible.

Thanksgiving dinner at Max and Debra's house was a wonderful, joyful spectacle. Raina was surrounded by her father and Ellie and her mother and stepfather. Her brother, Marcus, came, as did his girlfriend. Andrea and her new boyfriend, who just happened to be an author of mystery books, also came.

A month later, at Christmas dinner with everyone in attendance again, Nick asked Raina to marry him. With all of the hoots and shouts, Nick barely heard her squeals. "Yes, yes, yes." Nick decided to court Raina. His goal was to take her on as many dates as she needed to feel comfortable with him. Saturday was their "date day" to hang out and go to the movies.

Raina could say she'd found her soul mate in Nick. Their relationship was exactly what she'd been searching for—the type of love that made her feel whole and complete. She embraced their racial difference because it made them special as they mapped out the course of their lives together. She no longer looked to see if people resented seeing them together. Raina was taking what Nick told her to heart, and she didn't care what others thought about them. Nick told her he never saw the looks anyway.

Raina and Nick agreed to not try and change the world to accept them as a couple. Instead, they decided to embrace their diversity with love and hope, because they were happy.

The following summer, Raina and Nick were married out at the creek. They were surrounded by an abundance of colorful flowers, sunlight and glistening water. Everyone who knew them attended their wedding, wishing them well. When Nick watched Raina being escorted by Michael and Max, coming through the clump of trees on a bed of pink rose petals, to where he stood near the jagged rock, he'd never experienced such a feeling of love for a woman in his life. Their reception was held in the very large, newly built gazebo, which stood in the spot where the old dilapidated barn used to be.

Within a week of the wedding, the couple traveled to Italy, where they were surrounded by the family of Mica Antionelli. His daughter, Maria, and his widow sold the restaurant in Pittsburgh and returned to their village, where they hosted a dinner for the honeymooners and sixty relatives.

With their emotions barely in check, Raina and Nick were placed at the head of the table. It would have been Mica's place. There was the picture Raina had painted of Mr. Antionelli hanging on the wall.

Each noticed the picture was slightly different from the one Raina kept for herself, which now hung in the living room at the farmhouse.

In this picture, Raina had painted the old man happily smiling as he picked his peas.

THE END

ABOUT THE AUTHOR

Born and raised in Baltimore, Maryland, Bernice Layton works full-time and is an avid reader of novels, mostly romantic suspense. She is a member of Romance Writers of America and happily resides with her husband. She is the mother of one daughter, NaTiki, who inspires her to keep writing with this phrase in mind, "all things are possible with love and friendship, and the endless possibilities of past, future, and present encounters."

This is Bernice's second published novel for Genesis Press, Inc. Her debut novel, *Promises Made*, was released in 2008. She plans to write several more books. You can visit her at *www.bernicelaytonauthor.com*, *www.myspace .com/booksbyb*, or email her at *booksbyb@yahoo.com*.

2010 Mass Market Titles

January

Show Me The Sun
Miriam Shumba
ISBN: 978-158571-405-6
$6.99

Promises of Forever
Celya Bowers
ISBN: 978-1-58571-380-6
$6.99

February

Love Out Of Order
Nicole Green
ISBN: 978-1-58571-381-3
$6.99

Unclear and Present Danger
Michele Cameron
ISBN: 978-158571-408-7
$6.99

March

Stolen Jewels
Michele Sudler
ISBN: 978-158571-409-4
$6.99

Not Quite Right
Tammy Williams
ISBN: 978-158571-410-0
$6.99

April

Oak Bluffs
Joan Early
ISBN: 978-1-58571-379-0
$6.99

Crossing The Line
Bernice Layton
ISBN: 978-158571-412-4
$6.99

How To Kill Your Husband
Keith Walker
ISBN: 978-158571-421-6
$6.99

May

The Business of Love
Cheris F. Hodges
ISBN: 978-158571-373-8
$6.99

Wayward Dreams
Gail McFarland
ISBN: 978-158571-422-3
$6.99

June

The Doctor's Wife
Mildred Riley
ISBN: 978-158571-424-7
$6.99

Mixed Reality
Chamein Canton
ISBN: 978-158571-423-0
$6.99

2010 Mass Market Titles (continued)

July

Blue Interlude
Keisha Mennefee
ISBN: 978-158571-378-3
$6.99

Always You
Crystal Hubbard
ISBN: 978-158571-371-4
$6.99

Unbeweavable
Katrina Spencer
ISBN: 978-158571-426-1
$6.99

August

Small Sensations
Crystal V. Rhodes
ISBN: 978-158571-376-9
$6.99

Let's Get It On
Dyanne Davis
ISBN: 978-158571-416-2
$6.99

September

Unconditional
A.C. Arthur
ISBN: 978-158571-413-1
$6.99

Swan
Africa Fine
ISBN: 978-158571-377-6
$6.99$6.99

October

Friends in Need
Joan Early
ISBN:978-1-58571-428-5
$6.99

Against the Wind
Gwynne Forster
ISBN:978-158571-429-2
$6.99

That Which Has Horns
Miriam Shumba
ISBN:978-1-58571-430-8
$6.99

November

A Good Dude
Keith Walker
ISBN:978-1-58571-431-5
$6.99

Reye's Gold
Ruthie Robinson
ISBN:978-1-58571-432-2
$6.99

December

Still Waters...
Crystal V. Rhodes
ISBN:978-1-58571-433-9
$6.99

Burn
Crystal Hubbard
ISBN: 978-1-58571-406-3
$6.99

Other Genesis Press, Inc. Titles

2 Good	Celya Bowers	$6.99
A Dangerous Deception	J.M. Jeffries	$8.95
A Dangerous Love	J.M. Jeffries	$8.95
A Dangerous Obsession	J.M. Jeffries	$8.95
A Drummer's Beat to Mend	Kei Swanson	$9.95
A Happy Life	Charlotte Harris	$9.95
A Heart's Awakening	Veronica Parker	$9.95
A Lark on the Wing	Phyliss Hamilton	$9.95
A Love of Her Own	Cheris F. Hodges	$9.95
A Love to Cherish	Beverly Clark	$8.95
A Place Like Home	Alicia Wiggins	$6.99
A Risk of Rain	Dar Tomlinson	$8.95
A Taste of Temptation	Reneé Alexis	$9.95
A Twist of Fate	Beverly Clark	$8.95
A Voice Behind Thunder	Carrie Elizabeth Greene	$6.99
A Will to Love	Angie Daniels	$9.95
Acquisitions	Kimberley White	$8.95
Across	Carol Payne	$12.95
After the Vows	Leslie Esdaile	$10.95
(Summer Anthology)	T.T. Henderson	
	Jacqueline Thomas	
Again, My Love	Kayla Perrin	$10.95
Against the Wind	Gwynne Forster	$8.95
All I Ask	Barbara Keaton	$8.95
All I'll Ever Need	Mildred Riley	$6.99
Always You	Crystal Hubbard	$6.99
Ambrosia	T.T. Henderson	$8.95
An Unfinished Love Affair	Barbara Keaton	$8.95
And Then Came You	Dorothy Elizabeth Love	$8.95
Angel's Paradise	Janice Angelique	$9.95
Another Memory	Pamela Ridley	$6.99
Anything But Love	Celya Bowers	$6.99
At Last	Lisa G. Riley	$8.95
Best Foot Forward	Michele Sudler	$6.99
Best of Friends	Natalie Dunbar	$8.95
Best of Luck Elsewhere	Trisha Haddad	$6.99
Beyond the Rapture	Beverly Clark	$9.95
Blame It on Paradise	Crystal Hubbard	$6.99
Blaze	Barbara Keaton	$9.95
Blindsided	Tammy Williams	$6.99
Bliss, Inc.	Chamein Canton	$6.99
Blood Lust	J.M.Jeffries	$9.95

Other Genesis Press, Inc. Titles (continued)

Other Genesis Press, Inc. Titles (continued)

Eve's Prescription	Edwina Martin Arnold	$8.95
Everlastin' Love	Gay G. Gunn	$8.95
Everlasting Moments	Dorothy Elizabeth Love	$8.95
Everything and More	Sinclair Lebeau	$8.95
Everything But Love	Natalie Dunbar	$8.95
Falling	Natalie Dunbar	$9.95
Fate	Pamela Leigh Starr	$8.95
Finding Isabella	A.J. Garrotto	$8.95
Fireflies	Joan Early	$6.99
Fixin' Tyrone	Keith Walker	$6.99
Forbidden Quest	Dar Tomlinson	$10.95
Forever Love	Wanda Y. Thomas	$8.95
From the Ashes	Kathleen Suzanne	$8.95
	Jeanne Sumerix	
Frost On My Window	Angela Weaver	$6.99
Gentle Yearning	Rochelle Alers	$10.95
Glory of Love	Sinclair LeBeau	$10.95
Go Gentle Into That	Malcom Boyd	$12.95
Good Night		
Goldengroove	Mary Beth Craft	$16.95
Groove, Bang, and Jive	Steve Cannon	$8.99
Hand in Glove	Andrea Jackson	$9.95
Hard to Love	Kimberley White	$9.95
Hart & Soul	Angie Daniels	$8.95
Heart of the Phoenix	A.C. Arthur	$9.95
Heartbeat	Stephanie Bedwell-Grime	$8.95
Hearts Remember	M. Loui Quezada	$8.95
Hidden Memories	Robin Allen	$10.95
Higher Ground	Leah Latimer	$19.95
Hitler, the War, and the Pope	Ronald Rychiak	$26.95
How to Write a Romance	Kathryn Falk	$18.95
I Married a Reclining Chair	Lisa M. Fuhs	$8.95
I'll Be Your Shelter	Giselle Carmichael	$8.95
I'll Paint a Sun	A.J. Garrotto	$9.95
Icie	Pamela Leigh Starr	$8.95
If I Were Your Woman	LaConnie Taylor-Jones	$6.99
Illusions	Pamela Leigh Starr	$8.95
Indigo After Dark Vol. I	Nia Dixon/Angelique	$10.95
Indigo After Dark Vol. II	Dolores Bundy/	$10.95
	Cole Riley	
Indigo After Dark Vol. III	Montana Blue/	$10.95
	Coco Morena	

Other Genesis Press, Inc. Titles (continued)

Other Genesis Press, Inc. Titles (continued)

Naked Soul	Gwynne Forster	$8.95
Never Say Never	Michele Cameron	$6.99
Next to Last Chance	Louisa Dixon	$24.95
No Apologies	Seressia Glass	$8.95
No Commitment Required	Seressia Glass	$8.95
No Regrets	Mildred E. Riley	$8.95
Not His Type	Chamein Canton	$6.99
Nowhere to Run	Gay G. Gunn	$10.95
O Bed! O Breakfast!	Rob Kuehnle	$14.95
Object of His Desire	A.C. Arthur	$8.95
Office Policy	A.C. Arthur	$9.95
Once in a Blue Moon	Dorianne Cole	$9.95
One Day at a Time	Bella McFarland	$8.95
One of These Days	Michele Sudler	$9.95
Outside Chance	Louisa Dixon	$24.95
Passion	T.T. Henderson	$10.95
Passion's Blood	Cherif Fortin	$22.95
Passion's Furies	AlTonya Washington	$6.99
Passion's Journey	Wanda Y. Thomas	$8.95
Past Promises	Jahmel West	$8.95
Path of Fire	T.T. Henderson	$8.95
Path of Thorns	Annetta P. Lee	$9.95
Peace Be Still	Colette Haywood	$12.95
Picture Perfect	Reon Carter	$8.95
Playing for Keeps	Stephanie Salinas	$8.95
Pride & Joi	Gay G. Gunn	$8.95
Promises Made	Bernice Layton	$6.99
Promises to Keep	Alicia Wiggins	$8.95
Quiet Storm	Donna Hill	$10.95
Reckless Surrender	Rochelle Alers	$6.95
Red Polka Dot in a World Full of Plaid	Varian Johnson	$12.95
Red Sky	Renee Alexis	$6.99
Reluctant Captive	Joyce Jackson	$8.95
Rendezvous With Fate	Jeanne Sumerix	$8.95
Revelations	Cheris F. Hodges	$8.95
Rivers of the Soul	Leslie Esdaile	$8.95
Rocky Mountain Romance	Kathleen Suzanne	$8.95
Rooms of the Heart	Donna Hill	$8.95
Rough on Rats and Tough on Cats	Chris Parker	$12.95
Save Me	Africa Fine	$6.99

Other Genesis Press, Inc. Titles (continued)

Other Genesis Press, Inc. Titles (continued)